THE SERPENT'S SEED

A NOVEL

DAVID MARING

This is a work of fiction. All characters, names, incidents, organizations, and dialogue in this novel are either the products of the author's imaginations or are used fictitiously.

Copyright © 2012 David Maring
All rights reserved.
ISBN: 1478138734
ISBN 13: 9781478138730

ACKNOWLEDGMENTS

To Judy whose constructive criticism took my manuscript to a new level.

To my children, Lorie, David, and Robert who encouraged me to finish writing this novel.

To Waldo whose comments were very helpful.

To my friends Gayle Britt, Bill Craine, Elise Crosby, and Jeannie Johnson, who spent many hours reviewing the manuscript.

To my fellow writer, Libby Bernardin, who made several suggestions to improve the story.

PROLOGUE

The fallen angel, given the name Serpent by man, looked at the earth spinning on its axis. How many eons had elapsed since he had corrupted God's plan by sowing his seed within the Maker's creation.

The Serpent looked forward to the events described in Revelation, when he would return and exercise dominion over the Earth.

God, bound as with a chain by the irrevocable spirit of free will given to the creatures below, watched from the heavens.

I

Timbuktu had once been a center of learning that boasted a library rivaled only by those that existed in Alexandria and Rome during ancient times. While political upheaval had contributed to its downfall, the changing climate provided Timbuktu's death knell. Nothing remained in the city now except thousands of struggling poor with no place to go.

In the underground basement of this library on a hot windy day, Professor William Weston discovered the map, his goal at last accomplished, after years of tedious work. No longer was it necessary to suffer eyestrain looking through dusty materials in obscure places. The city of *Enoch* was now within his grasp.

Rachael Goldstein's knowledge of ancient languages allowed her to interpret the document for the professor under the light of a candle held by the old custodian. When she finished translating, this man took a fistful of American dollars and turned his back as they departed with the document. With the ancient map in hand, the pair traveled to their tents on the outskirts of Timbuktu where their servant, Imnah, waited with tubs of hot water to remove the day's accumulation of dirt and sweat.

After several shampoos, the sand was finally out of Rachael's hair. The task completed, she reached in her trunk and pulled out the only outfit she brought to this backwater besides baggy pants and work shirts. Tonight they would celebrate their last day in this God-forsaken land. Professor Weston had promised to open the wine Imnah recently purchased at the marketplace.

When Bill Weston stepped out of the tent that evening, he saw that Imnah had placed the folding dinner table near a blazing fire. Strange how the desert, so hot during the day, always freezes at night as the temperature plummets. Shivering, he stepped closer to the warmth of the fire. A moment later, the servant brought him a goblet of wine. As the liquid flowed down his throat, it produced a warm sensation, which brought relief from the cold.

Emerging from her tent, Rachael saw the professor standing in the distance. Pausing a moment, she observed him. She had learned little from this man about his personal life during their time together. He was always so deeply engrossed in his project that if one did not know better, it might be said he was obsessed by it. She had discovered from other sources that her employer was forty and divorced. Apparently, his wife had left him for another man. Rachael thought, maybe that was why he buried himself in the pursuit of biblical archaeology and doesn't seem to have an interest in the opposite sex, or perhaps his wife left him because of it. He was a handsome man but probably a little too old for her. Nevertheless, this job had so isolated her socially, perhaps if he would show a little interest she might reciprocate.

Bill saw her coming toward the fire. How beautiful she looked in the black skirt and light blue blouse, so much better than in those loose-fitting work clothes. This was the first time he really noticed her as a woman. Perhaps it was the wine or maybe just the loneliness he felt.

"The food is almost ready," he said, as Imnah poured Rachael a glass of wine.

At the table, they indulged in the prepared goat meat and rice. As they devoured the food, she noticed how the light from the fire, dancing in the background, caused his blue eyes to sparkle. Her tongue loosened by the wine, Rachael talked about her past.

Rachael's family immigrated to Israel when she was only three. Her father, Dr. Benjamin Rabon, fled Yemen only one-step ahead of the death squads bent on killing the Jews and seizing their property. It had been emotionally devastating to her father, whose ancestors had been in Yemen since they fled the sacking of Jerusalem by the Romans centuries before.

Rachael's interest in archaeology had begun at an early age. She was encouraged by her father, who was the department head of middle-eastern studies at Hebrew University. As the only girl with three older brothers, she had always been doted upon. The death of her mother when she was nine left Rachael living a sheltered life under her father's watchful eye until she entered the university. There she fell in love with a student whose family emigrated from America. Her family approved of the marriage, provided she postpone the wedding until after graduation. A year later when her fiancé, Jerome, received his six months mobilization orders as a member of the Israel Self-Defense Force, they decided to ignore the wishes of family. The day after their wedding, Jerome reported for active duty. A week later, he was dead, killed by a device exploding beneath his personnel carrier. Mourning his death, she buried herself in schoolwork until graduation.

Rachael's present position as the professor's assistant required her to accompany him through the barren lands of the Middle East and North Africa. The job not only entailed personal hardship but also the dangers that were always present in this political explosive environment. Americans and Jews weren't the most popular people in this part of the world.

That evening she learned only the bare-bone details about her employer's personal life. She wondered why he wouldn't loosen up and show a more compassionate side. Perhaps her desire to scratch the surface and see what lay beneath attracted her to this introvert.

Rachael heard the professor announce it was time to turn in for the evening. Their plane was leaving at noon the next day. As they stood up from the table, he leaned over and kissed her on the lips, then turned and walked in the direction of his tent.

Bill was in turmoil. Why did I kiss her? Perhaps the wine clouded my judgment. He didn't want to get close to Rachael or any other woman. He still hurt inside when he thought of Mary Belle. She had been his sweetheart in college. They married the summer before he entered graduate school. At Harvard, a student from a wealthy New England family caught her attention. Buried up to his eyeballs in pursuing an advanced degree, he didn't realize she was having an affair until the day she moved out.

2

After loading the luggage in the jeep, Imnah drove Bill and Rachael through the crowded bazaar toward the small airport without incident. The servant had been so helpful during their stay. Bill knew he would miss him as he watched the man glide the vehicle with ease through the traffic mingled with people and livestock. He felt fortunate Imnah wandered into their camp the day after the person recommended as a guide by the local authorities died in an accident.

On the way to the airport, Imnah, a man who had only spoken before in a local dialect, asked in broken English if he could join the expedition to Enoch. This man was more than the illiterate peasant he had pretended to be, Bill thought. *Did he eavesdrop on my conversations with Rachael?* Suspicions aroused, Bill remained noncommittal about the request.

Their twin-engine plane was several hours late arriving at the dirt landing strip that passed as an airport. The plane finally lifted off to Cairo where they would take connecting flights, Bill to the States, while Rachael would travel to Jerusalem. Later, she would join him for the meeting with Walter Henley, an antiquity dealer in New York City.

The possibility of obtaining funds from the university to finance an expedition to find the city of *Enoch* was nil, so Bill went outside his familiar academic circles. An acquaintance had placed him in contact with Henley. His appointment to meet with him in a few weeks could not have come at a more opportune time. The discovery of the map should enhance his chances of getting the necessary funds approved for an expedition.

***

Henley met with the investors in the backroom of his antiquity store to discuss the request for funding from various individuals. He formed this group ten years ago. It proved to be profitable to all concerned and provided a cover for his other activities. Many times skirting the law, the group used Henley's store and business connections to fence artifacts from around the world.

"So what's the situation on this biblical archaeologist?" asked Raymond Jones, a multimillionaire from Chicago.

"I'm meeting with him next week," Henley answered.

"How much is he asking us to contribute to his project?" Raymond inquired, intent on pursuing the issue.

"The last conversation I had with him, he indicated five hundred thousand."

"Is anyone else going to share in the cost of this expedition?" asked Ron Moses, a banker from San Francisco.

"I don't think our Bible scholar can find anyone who will offer him financial support for what many will see as a hare-brained fantasy."

"Why are we interested?" asked Sam Mendel, seated at the far end of the table.

"I have a person working with this scholar who keeps me informed. I can tell you Professor Weston's extensive research has finally paid off. He has it."

"Has what?" asked Raymond.

"The map."

"What map?" asked Robert Osborne, an antique dealer from New Orleans.

"A map that shows the exact location of the City of Enoch. The first city on earth that was built by man."

"If he locates it, what does he expect to find?" asked Mendel.

"I don't know what items of value might be there. It's a gamble, but since we'll only chip in a hundred thousand apiece, it's a sum we can all easily afford to lose. So, do I have your commitment?"

The men nodded in agreement.

***

Rachael had solitude at last on the long flight to New York. She had just spent two weeks with her family and visited Jerome's grave. They begged her to stay longer, but she wanted to be at the meeting. If the funds were not forthcoming, she would be out of a job. There weren't many positions for her line of expertise outside of teaching. Her mind wondered back to the hours spent over the last year translating ancient texts. She had enjoyed the challenge and the professor had become dependent on her expertise. She greatly admired the man professionally. Although he had only limited knowledge in the area of dead languages, he was an impressive biblical scholar.

Bill was waiting for Rachael at the coffee shop next door to his hotel. The Acropolis was a new architectural marvel located near the site where the twin towers once stood. He looked down at his watch. Rachael should be here soon. Otherwise, he would have to go to the meeting without her. He was surprised how much he had missed her, the short time they were apart. Perhaps it was because they were constant companions since he hired her; deep down inside, he knew it was more.

"Sorry I'm running late," Rachael said, as she approached his table carrying a wet umbrella. "Didn't think I'd ever get a taxi this morning. With the weather so bad, I guess everyone is trying to catch a cab."

"You look like you got drenched from the blowing rain. Sit down and have a cup of hot coffee. It'll shake off the chill of this air conditioning."

"Do we have time?"

"Yes. Henley's place is only four blocks away. I arranged with the hotel for transportation when the weather turned nasty."

On the way over, Bill noticed the stylish outfit Rachael was wearing. Damp from the rain, it clung to her body as she sat across from him in the hotel limousine. The skirt rose slightly above her knees, revealing a pair of lovely legs hidden from his view for the past two years by her work pants.

After they entered the shop, an employee directed them down a corridor. In the back was a spacious room dominated by a large conference table. Their prospective financier, a short round man with a deep brown complexion, dressed in an expensive suit, sat at the far end smoking a cigar. Rising from his chair, the man crossed the room to greet them. In contrast to his clothes, he had on cheap cologne that reeked. The scent reached them while he was still several feet away.

"Good morning, Dr. Weston," Henley said, grabbing Bill's hand in a firm handshake.

Then turning to Rachael, he introduced himself while his eyes stripped her. She did not like this man. He had an aura of evil about him.

When they took their seat, Henley wasted no time in getting to the heart of the matter.

"You want five hundred thousand dollars of my investors' money to fund an expedition. Tell me why I should give it to you."

"Since this is the first time we've met, I'd like to tell you in detail about my research, but I don't know how much time you'll allow me to present my information."

"You have one hour to get my interest. I can tell you the investors gave me complete authority to make a decision. So give it your best shot."

Bill had been up most of the night preparing. He swallowed hard.

"The Bible recounts God's creation of Adam and Eve that has been recognized by the three great religions of the world: Judaism, Christianity and Islam. According to biblical accounts, their firstborn, Cain, killed his brother, Abel. Afterwards, he fled to the Land of Nod where he took a wife. The firstborn of this relationship was named Enoch. In honor of this child, Cain built the first city in recorded history and named it after his son. That is all the scriptures contain. Other ancient text tell us more. My assistant and I have traveled throughout the Middle East and to Africa studying old manuscripts, clay tablets, and tracing down local legends. Not only have we found the *Land of Nod*, but we also know where the site of *Enoch* is located. If successful, our expedition will unlock the history of man's early ancestors. It will allow us to fill in the blank pages of the origins of all civilizations that followed."

Then Bill focused on where he thought the investors' interest might lie.

"According to an ancient legend, the first accumulation of wealth by man was in Enoch. The story speaks of gold and diamonds in large quantities buried by a catastrophe."

"What kind of catastrophe?"

"It's unclear. It could have been an earthquake or maybe a volcanic explosion. Perhaps it was man-made. Whatever happened, *Enoch* disappeared from history. The people were killed or dispersed by the calamity."

"Then the riches must still be there," Henley said.

"I'm afraid we won't know the answer until we dig."

Henley tried to appear attentive, although he already was aware of this information and more. He knew he would approve the funds and had known it for a long time.

"Rachael, are you going on the expedition?"

"Yes, Mr. Henley, I'll be assisting Dr. Weston."

"In that case I'll approve the funds," he said, with a smile that showed the gold fillings in his teeth.

"Professor, if you'll send me a detailed account of your expected expenses, I'll have my accountant go over them and work out a method of periodic payments to your bank account as those needs arise."

"I can assure you the money will be carefully spent."

Chuckling, Henley said, "I have no doubt that my accountant will make sure of that. Now, let me walk you to the door."

At the front, Henley handed a white envelope to Bill.

"Just a little advance to cover your initial expenses."

Opening it, Bill saw a cashier's check for fifty thousand dollars.

"This means we can get started."

"Don't forget, my lawyer is preparing the terms of the contract that we discussed over the phone last week. He will be forwarding the documents to you. We will expect fifty percent of any gems, gold, and artifacts that you are entitled to after the Iranian government gets its share,"

As they were walking out of the door, Henley leaned over and whispered in Rachael's ear.

"We need to get together next week for dinner if you're still in town. I'd love to talk ancient languages with you. It's always been a subject of great interest to me."

Somewhat stunned, Rachael was at a loss for words. She did her best to give him a pleasant smile and without answering, stepped onto the street.

"I heard Henley," Bill said when they were in the limousine.

"I don't have a good feeling about that man."

"Are you going to have dinner with him next week?"

"Not unless you order me to. Of course, I don't want to jeopardize our funding."

"Once we get this check deposited, I can afford to send you back to Israel to finish our research before the expedition. That way you won't have to make excuses to avoid Henley."

A smile came over Rachael's face. "That would be a relief."

On the way back to the hotel she said, "I need to talk to you about someone I recently met in Jerusalem, who might be interested in helping us on our project." She told him about Irad Lamech from New York, a graduate student at Hebrew University in Jerusalem, whom Rachael's brothers had introduced her too. The two had quickly discovered common interest–dead languages. Rachael knew Irad was attracted to her in more than a professional way; the physical attraction was not mutual.

3

Rachael was in Jerusalem only a few days before she convinced Irad to obtain a leave of absence from the university to assume a position with the expedition. Impressed with his knowledge of the ancient world from their previous conversations, she believed he would be a great help in making the dig a success.

The professor had sent her back to track down a lead obtained earlier. An artifact that could be important to their research might be available in a small village lying in a place known as the Wilderness of Judaea.

Because of numerous military roadblocks, it took a full day to reach the outskirts of the village. One officer encouraged Irad and Rachael to turn back because of fundamentalist Muslim attacks in the nearby countryside. It was dark by the time they arrived. Knowing that nothing could be accomplished that evening, they set up a tent on a hill near the village and settled in for the night. The next morning they were up before sunrise. Sitting near the campfire Irad built, Rachael decided it was time to give him more details. She reached into her backpack and pulled out a sketch of the map found in Timbuktu.

"Irad," she said, "the professor has given me permission to show this to you."

Rachael moved closer to him so they could both view the sketch. She observed Irad as he studied it. He was taller than most men. She had to look up to see his face and couldn't help but notice how incredibly attractive he was. Why was he still unattached, she wondered. *Maybe he was like the professor, putting all of his energy into a career.* Of course, to an outsider she might also appear that way, but she knew better. There was more to life than the study of dead languages.

Irad continued to study the map as Rachael talked about the professor's project. She described what they had uncovered concerning the location of the *Land of Nod*, and explained that the first step in the process was to locate the *Garden of Eden*.

"Eden lay north of where four great rivers converged at the Persian Gulf, miles inland in ancient times from where it is located today," she said. "Two of the rivers are well known, the Tigris and the Euphrates, but the location of the others referred to in the Bible as the Pishon and the Gihon have been lost in antiquity. The professor believes ancient documents and new photographs from space, when examined together, provide crucial information about their location."

Pulling a geographic map from her backpack, she unfolded it and spread the document on the ground.

"You see the river Gihon flowed through western Iran and is today is called Karun. Experts have been on the wrong track trying to locate the Gihon. For a long time they believed it was the Nile because it flowed out of the land of Cush, which was Ethiopia. The professor is convinced that the Gihon is the Karun because the Kassites, descendants of Cain, dwelt along its banks and called the land Kush. You can see why scholars were confused."

"What about the other missing river?"

"The Pishon, according to the Bible, flows around the land of Havilah, which the professor feels certain is part of present day Saudi Arabia and Kuwait. Satellite pictures have recently confirmed his theory. They show a concealed riverbed beneath the sands. This river, now dried up because of climatic changes, once originated in the Hijaz Mountains near the city of Medina and flowed into the Persian Gulf where the other three joined it."

"So the Land of Nod lay east of Eden," Irad said, "and within its boundaries, Cain built Enoch. If the map is authentic, it confirms the professor's theories."

The next morning when they entered the village, Irad and Rachael were dressed in clothing that blended well with that worn by the people of the region. Making their way to a mud hut on the outskirts of a cluster of similarly built homes, Rachael knocked on the old wooden door that bore the address they were seeking. A young boy answered.

"We have come to see Shimar," she said in the local dialect that she learned from her father. "Tell him Oreb has sent us."

Oreb, a friend of Bill's father, knew Shimar through family contacts.

The boy disappeared for a moment. When he returned, they were invited in, and led to a room at the back of the hut. Inside on the dirt floor lay an old man on a cot.

"Ismal," he said, directing his comments to the young boy who had answered the door, "get tea for our guests."

Motioning for them to have a seat on a rug beside the cot, he sat up just as the boy brought in a wooden platter. On it were three cups of steaming hot tea with ginger.

"Oreb sent you?" he asked.

"Yes," Rachael said.

"What do you want?"

"We understand you have an old staff that came from Enoch."

"Well, what if I do?" asked the old man before launching into a coughing episode, which eased when he drank some tea.

"We would like to buy it."

The old man thought for a moment. I promised my ancestors never to part with this item, possessed by my family for many generations. My grandson, Ismal, and I are the last of the family line. I don't have long to live. What good is the staff to me anyway? It is cursed. Maybe this instrument of the devil brought on the calamity that has almost wiped out my family line.

Looking at Ismal standing in the corner, he knew the boy was penniless. A few gold coins would keep his grandson from starving when he was gone.

"How much are you willing to pay?"

"We need to see it first."

"Get it, Ismal."

When the boy returned, Irad and Rachael examined the staff. It was eight feet long, most unusual for a staff to have such height. That, with its large circumference, made it extremely heavy. The wood was of an unknown origin. Attached to the top was a golden knob. The figure of a serpent was engraved on the staff, and there was a map carved into its wood.

"How much do you want?"

As was the custom, the old man asked for more than he thought the buyer was willing to pay. Rachael was surprised at the demand. It was less than she had expected. Not wanting to offend him, she haggled until the price was lower. She paid in gold coins from a bag she carried hidden on her person.

"Can you give me the history of this staff?" Rachael asked.

"It belonged to the *Nephilim* at one time. My ancestor took it from the descendants of Cain at the battle of Enoch in the ancient days, and it has been in our family's possession since that time."

How strange for the man to use the term, *Nephilim*, Rachael thought. Her mind raced back to Old Testament class. They were mentioned in Genesis, which said the sons of God mated with the daughters of men and produced these giants.

"I always thought that was nothing but a myth," she said to Irad in Hebrew.

The old man began to have another coughing spasm that even the hot tea did not seem to alleviate.

"Perhaps you could come back tomorrow," the young boy said.

"Yes. I'll be feeling better then," the old man said. "Come and see me tomorrow, and I will tell you the legend of the *Serpent*."

"We'll be back to hear your story," Irad said.

Rachael was glad to be back at the campsite. She would be even happier to return to Jerusalem where she knew the staff could be safely stored. If word got out about the staff or the gold coins, their lives would be forfeited in this sinkhole.

Irad was kind enough to offer to protect the item that evening, but Rachael didn't want it out of her sight. The excitement of the day and the discomfort of the staff under her blanket kept her from sleeping most of the night. Irad seemed concerned. She saw him sit up several times in his cot during the night and gaze at her. Just before daybreak, she finally dozed off to sleep.

The sound of vehicles passing on the road near the tent awakened Rachael. She stepped out of the tent just in time to see an Israeli military convoy pass by driving toward the village where the old man lived. Looking around, she realized that Irad wasn't there. For the next hour, she worried that something might have happened. Then she heard him call out to her.

She turned and saw him coming down a sand dune a few yards away.

"Where have you been?" she asked when he reached the tent.

Holding up two canteens he said, "When I got up this morning, I noticed a hole in our water bag so I went into the village to replenish our supply."

Rachael looked at the canvas bag attached to the side of the jeep and saw it was empty.

"It must have sprung a leak on the rough terrain getting here," she said.

Handing her one of the canteens, Irad went over and added more wood to the fire so he could cook breakfast. Later that morning they examined the staff together.

"The inscription is unlike any of the dead languages I've studied," Irad said. "Perhaps the infrared light at the university could enhance the marking."

"I don't recognize it either. Maybe my father or one of his colleagues might have a clue to its origin."

That afternoon the jeep's short wheelbase allowed it to travel along an old rocky path, which Irad had discovered that morning. The path took them around to the far side of the village and ended a few hundred yards from the old man's mud hut where a disturbance was taking place.

"I think it best if I go down alone," Irad said.

A few minutes later, he returned.

"We've got to get out of here. Shimar and Ismal have been killed, and the villagers are blaming it on the Jews."

"A military patrol passed our tent this morning going toward the village," Rachael said.

Later that day, they stopped for a military roadblock. The officer in charge was the same one who had warned them not to go into the area.

While a private checked their identity cards, the officer said, "I see you have finished your business down there."

"Were your troops in the village this morning?" Rachael asked.

"One of our units was there. Seems an old man and a boy were brutally murdered. Strange."

"What do you mean?" Rachael asked.

"The man had his tongue cut out and the seal of a serpent branded upon his forehead.

"And the boy?"

"Strangled."

4

The meeting with the assassin was short and to the point. "Imnah will be arriving in New York this weekend for a meeting with me on Monday. I do not expect him to make that meeting. Is that understood?"

"Yes," said the assassin, who didn't anticipate any problem eliminating the *drone*. After all, he was trained in the art of killing. In his profession there was no room for error. A mistake could not only cost him a place in the hierarchy but also threatened his life.

When the assassin left, the man sat down at the table in his conference room and lit a cigar, then reached over and picked up the letter he received that morning by special dispatch. He slowly read the contents for the second time that day. The secrets of the ages, lost even to us, are about to be uncovered. It's good one of our own is now on the inside. That meant the *drone*, Imnah, was no longer needed. He had served his purpose and now could be eliminated. It was important to remove *The Society's* footprints.

That same weekend, Bill was in New York City to see a colleague. Although Bill's area was biblical studies, his friend, Sam Rison, was known as the authority on the *Nephilim* and in fact had written several articles on them. That is why, when the call came from Rachael about the staff, he contacted Sam immediately.

Anxious to meet with Sam, he stepped outside the airport that Saturday to catch a taxi. Was that Imnah getting into a cab across the street? He started to yell, but before a sound had time to leave his lips, the door on the cab closed, and the vehicle sped off. I must have been mistaken, he thought. After all, what would Imnah be doing in New York?

Sam lived in a small apartment downtown. It was all the space he needed after his wife died.

"Please be patient with me, Bill, if I seem somewhat long-winded. I haven't had many visitors since my retirement. Some of what I am going to say is old news. Perhaps I can sprinkle it with enough new information to keep this from being a wasted trip."

"I've never had a conversation with you that didn't give me new insight."

"The term *Nephilim* is often used interchangeably with the term *giant*. The term literally means the fallen ones or those who came down. Other biblical terms used to describe them are *Rephaim* and *Serpent*. It would be intriguing to ascertain the origin of these creatures. The first mention of them is in *Genesis*. Suddenly, there appears a passage–the sons of God came down and, finding the daughters of men attractive, had intercourse with them. According to the scriptures, children born of those relationships were not only giants but also heroes of the ancient world. Many theories have been espoused over the years on the meaning of those passages. One is that angels sent by God cohabitated with the women on earth. Another is that they were fallen angels. According to the most recent interpretation by theologians, they are the descendants of Seth who called themselves the *Children of the Lord*. As you know from the seminar materials I sent, my research leads me to believe the various theories are all off the mark."

"I've read your articles and your theory certainly makes more sense than the others. Tell me more about your idea that the *Land of Nod* was inhabited by people who were large in stature."

"When Cain took a wife, legends outside the Holy Scriptures describe the offspring of Cain as larger than Seth's descendants. The passage in the Bible, which talks about the Sons of God coming down, is in my opinion simply a geographic matter. I believe the Land of Nod, lying east of Eden, was situated on a higher elevation. Perhaps in the Zagros Mountain chain. I have theorized that they came down from the mountains and mated with the inhabitants of the Babylonian Plains who were of normal size and perhaps Seth's descendants. Of course, those scholars that believe the flood of Noah's time covered the whole earth think the *Nephilim* drowned with everyone else. I don't prescribe to that logic because the flood is only a local catastrophe limited to the plains of Babylonia. Besides, there are numerous references to them in the Bible after the flood."

"I agree. Logic supports a limited flood. So, the descendents of Cain, which would include the *Nephilim*, may still exist today among us."

"Like I told you earlier, the Bible says exactly that. After the flood, they are mentioned in Genesis, Numbers, Joshua and Samuel. However, my favorite source on that point is the passage contained in Deuteronomy where it describes various *Nephilim*, including King OG, whose iron bed was thirteen and a half feet long and six feet wide."

"Their existence after the flood only strengthens your argument that it was a local catastrophe," Bill said. "Let me give you some information that lends even more support to your theory."

Bill told him about the staff Rachael purchased and the information she learned from its former owner.

"That's interesting, and if true, it goes a long way toward proving my theory."

Bill reached into his briefcase and withdrew sketches of Cain's staff.

***

It was Sunday morning when the assassin entered the lobby of the hotel. Avoiding the personnel at the desk, he went straight to the elevator and rode to the fourth floor. Locating Imnah's room, he put his ear to the door. Hearing no sound, he inserted a master key into the lock. Opening the door slowly, he peered inside. The sound of the shower running in the bathroom told him that his quarry was there. When the drone emerged, the assassin wrapped one arm firmly around the drone's neck and with his hand pulled the neck back until he heard it snap. Letting the limp body drop to the floor, he rummaged through the room to give it the appearance of a robbery and then quickly departed. Another assignment successfully completed for *The Society*.

It was the second homicide scene Detective Thomas O'Conner had viewed that Monday, and it wasn't even noon yet. Just back from a two-week vacation, he found a stack of paperwork waiting on his desk, and now it didn't seem like he was going to get a chance to look at it.

"What do we have here, officer?" he asked upon entering the hotel room.

"It looks like a robbery, detective," said the young man in his crisp new uniform. "I believe the man's neck is broken."

"Any identification?"

"Not a thing. The wallet is missing. His clothing and luggage have absolutely no trace of anything that would give us a clue who this victim was or where he came from."

"What about the hotel registration?"

"It was personally made by a corporation, but surprisingly the payment was in cash."

"Well the corporation should be easy to trace from the address on the registration book."

***

On Tuesday morning, Dr. Benjamin Rabon was with his daughter in his study examining the staff. The inscription resembled the ancient writing he was familiar with in southern Yemen, the ancestral home of his people. But it was not close enough to those ancient writings for him to decipher.

"We need to contact John Elesbaan and arrange a time to meet with him," Dr. Rabon said. "He's an expert in this area.

"I want Professor Weston involved when we meet with John," Rachael said.

"In the meantime, Dr. Rabon said, "we can take the staff to the university and examine it under the infrared equipment to get a better view of the marking. Let's go over there this afternoon."

***

Tuesday morning on the way to catch a plane back to Charleston, Bill picked up a newspaper from the coffee shop. Later, seated comfortably in first class, he read the headlines. Finished, he began to browse the smaller articles to see if anything there might be of interest. His eye caught a story on a murder at a hotel in Manhattan. The article described the deceased and commented that he had no identification on him. The story had a small photograph of such poor a quality that it was barely visible. The police requested anyone who knew the victim to contact Detective Thomas O'Connor of the New York City Police Department. Could it be Imnah, wondered Bill as he stared at the picture. No, of course not, was his immediate thought. But it wouldn't hurt to make a call.

Thomas had never been to Charleston before. The view as he flew over the Carolina coastline was beautiful. From reading a book on the plane, he knew this city had been established in 1670 and had the most-preserved historic district on the east coast. As the plane circled, he saw the gleaming white structures of the Citadel, a famous military college founded in 1842. He planned to spend an extra day and take a tour.

When Thomas had first spoken to Dr. Weston, he thought it was just another caller with useless information. However, his interest was piqued when, in response to the photo faxed him, the professor replied with an affirmative identification. Thomas knew it might lead to a suspect in the murder. He wanted to meet with the professor in person. He learned from years of experience that the best way to evaluate a witness or suspect was eye contact. The time of the landing was perfect for the luncheon scheduled at noon.

The restaurant was on a side street near the Four Corners of The Law. It was named that because the federal, state, county, and municipal government buildings were erected on its four corners. When he entered, the waiter led him to a secluded area in the back of the restaurant.

Bill saw the detective enter the room. His soft voice on the phone had projected an image that could easily mislead one into thinking the person on the other end of the line was somewhat effeminate. Nothing could be further from the truth, Bill thought as the man approached. Although the detective looked to be in his early forties, Bill could tell by Thomas' physical appearance that he must spend time keeping his six-foot frame in superb shape.

"Thomas O'Conner, I presume," Bill said, as he rose from the table to greet the detective. "I hope you had a good flight."

"It was a pleasant trip down. I've always wanted to visit your fair city, though not under these circumstances. Let's talk business later. I don't want to spoil the delicious meal I'm sure this restaurant has to offer."

An hour later, pushing the empty plate to the side, Thomas said, "Tell me everything you know about this man called Imnah."

"Like I said on the telephone, there's little information I can give you. The first week we were in Timbuktu, the person hired through the local authority was killed in an automobile accident, or so an official informed us. The next day this small man, Imnah, showed up at our campsite right after breakfast. He indicated he was experienced as a guide and servant. So I hired him. He was handy to have around."

"What was his full name?"

"You know, he never said. Moreover, since he was paid in cash, I never had a reason to ask. Imnah didn't talk about himself. Now that I look back, it was somewhat strange the way he took care of our needs without ever letting us know anything about himself. It was almost like he was a mindless automaton."

"Is there anything else that drew your attention?"

"Yes."

"What's that?"

"The day we left Timbuktu, he asked if he could join our expedition. And that was the first time he spoke English. It aroused my suspicion."

"Expedition?"

"A project involving an archaeological dig in Iran."

"Who's your assistant?"

"Rachael Goldstein. She's in Israel now. She couldn't add anything to what I've just told you."

"I have to ask you this. Why were you in New York, and where were you the morning of the murder?

5

John Elesbaan was giving a series of lectures. The first one was at the Brookings Institute of History in New York City. Arrangements had been made for Rachael, her father and Irad to attend the seminar and have John join them for dinner afterwards. Bill, who also planned to attend, asked his father to come, knowing the seminar would be interesting, and his dad would have an opportunity to enjoy a stimulating discussion afterwards.

When the group met at the seminar that afternoon, Rachael was surprised at how handsome Bill's father looked for a man his age. So that's where her boss got his good looks.

"Good afternoon, Dr. Weston," Rachael said, as they approached. Both men answered the greeting. Laughing, Bill's father said, "With so many doctors in this group, I think it's best if we just call one another by our first name. I'm Henry."

"So nice to meet you. Let me introduce the people in my party. I'm Rachael; this is my father, Dr. Benjamin Rabon, and our friend, Irad Lamech."

"Please just call me Ben."

Bill couldn't help but notice what a big man Irad was, and his sculptured features were striking. He wondered about the relationship between Irad and Rachael. A professional one or was it more?

The Brookings auditorium was filled to capacity. They had just taken their reserved seats when the President of the Institute introduced the speaker for the evening. He ended the introduction by reminding the audience that tonight's lecture on the historical Jewish connection between Arabia and Ethiopia was the first of three lectures by Dr. Elesbaan addressing that part of the world.

Ben, who was sitting next to Henry, leaned over and whispered, "He has a lot of depth in his subject matter. Several years ago, when he was an undergraduate, I had him as a student in a special summer course on dead languages. Since then he has become one of the world's foremost authorities."

"Let me start this lecture by stating that new discoveries on the ground and from the air are changing our views on the ancient history of this region," Dr. Elesbaan said. "One of the questions you may be asking yourselves is what does Arabia and Ethiopia have in common. To answer that question we must consider the demographics of the area. First, let's look at what a recent study reveals about the early inhabitants of Ethiopia. Originally settled by the descendants of Cush, who was Noah's grandson, they were later joined by the offspring of Moses and Zipporah. At a much later date, *Menelik* founded the City of Axum and became the first King of Ethiopia. This ruler was born of a sexual union between the Queen of Sheba and King Solomon. It is important to note that the land of Sheba lay not in Ethiopia, as we once thought, but in Yemen at the bottom of the Arabian Peninsula.

Menelik, as a young man, went to visit his father in Israel, where he remained for several years, and, in fact, received his education at the temple in Jerusalem. When he left Israel, King Solomon ordered that a male member of every prominent family in Israel accompany his son back to Sheba. A few years later some of these Jews went with *Menelik* to Ethiopia and helped build the City of Axum where they remained, intermarrying with the local population. This empire later expanded its borders not only into Yemen but also into the Sudan, which, in ancient times, was known as Nubia.

Because of their skin color, the earliest inhabitants of Ethiopia were called Reds. They were historical connected to Adam, who was made by God from the red earth of the Zagros Mountains in Iran. These Ethiopians were a finely featured Semitic people, in sharp contrast to the races of central and southern Africa. Even today archaeological digs in Sudan show that where these groups lived in the same locale, the Ethiopians created a high level of civilization with homes of stone, while the Nilotic peoples, who were always filtering into the area, had thatched huts.

"Now let's turn to Arabia. Although it did not have a parallel development, it does share some of the same Jewish bloodlines, starting with the sons of Ham, later strengthened by Ismal, a child of Abraham, and by the migration of Dan's descendants.

Located on the bottom of the Arabian Peninsula, the area we today call Yemen had such a large Jewish population that over the centuries they dominated the political and cultural life of the land and eventually put a king on the throne of Sheba, who incidentally was later defeated by the Christian king of Ethiopia."

Rachael felt a general uneasiness halfway through the lecture as though someone was watching her. Looking up, she saw Henley seated in the balcony. He gave her a smile and then turned his attention back to Dr. Elesbaan.

When she arrived last night, there was a message waiting for her at the hotel desk. It was from Henley, who welcomed her back to New York and asked that she call him. Although hesitant to do so, she decided it was best not to snub the expedition's benefactor. He had been pleasant enough on the phone, asking her to join him for dinner that evening. She begged off saying that she had an exhausting day and a commitment early the next morning for breakfast. He had accepted her excuses without comment but said he would keep in touch and hoped the preparations for the expedition were going well. How did he know she was in New York? Maybe the professor told him.

Detective Thomas O'Conner purchased a ticket for the seminar when he learned Bill would be there. He wanted to talk with him further about the murder investigation. Since the meeting in Charleston, he had made a thorough investigation into the man's background and felt certain he was not involved in the killing of the man known as Imnah. Confident of that, he was ready to disclose what he had learned. He hoped the man could help put the puzzle together or at least enlighten him.

The lecture Thomas dreaded as boring was surprisingly interesting. He spotted Bill early in the program sitting with a group of people who were obviously academic types. Particularly the female, who must be the assistant. She was attractive, probably in her mid-twenties, no more than five-feet-four inches, with a well-shaped body that didn't have an ounce of excess fat on it. He used his years of work experience to analyze her. By the end of the lecture, he thought he had her pegged. Even from a distance, she gave off vibes that would make the average person think she was confident in herself and cool as a cucumber. He didn't believe it.

As they were about to leave the lobby to catch a limousine to the restaurant, Bill heard someone call his name. Even before turning around, he recognized the voice as belonging to the detective.

"What are you doing here? I didn't realize that one of New York's finest would have an interest in such a mundane topic."

"It is always good to broaden one's horizon. How long are you going to be in New York?"

"I'm flying out tomorrow afternoon."

"I hoped we might get together while you're here. There are matters involving my investigation that I'd like to discuss."

"How's your schedule tomorrow morning, Thomas? Maybe we could get together at my hotel coffee shop."

Thomas pulled out the pocket calendar from the inside of his coat.

"What about ten?"

"That works for me," Bill said.

The detective turned to depart.

"Before you leave, please let me introduce you to my group."

Rachael observed the detective with some interest. The professor had said how impressed he was with the man. Apparently they hit it off well in Charleston. It was exciting to be around someone who dealt in the dark world of murder. When introduced, their eyes met. *What was going on in his head?* Was he trying to read her thoughts? Maybe he was just thinking like a detective, analyzing everyone he met.

La Bohemia was one of Bill's favorite restaurants in the city. He pulled strings to get reservations and a private dining room where everyone could feel comfortable discussing the topic that brought them to New York. When they entered, a band in the ballroom upstairs was playing for guests who wanted to liven up their night with dancing after dinner. The maitre d' at the entrance led them to a secluded room off a narrow hallway, seating them at an oblong table that had a view of a garden outside. A short time later, John Elesbaan joined them.

"I can speak for all of us in saying that your lecture was most informative," Henry said. "There's been so much new information coming out lately that I feel the very concept of ancient history, as we understood it, is about to change."

"That's right," John said. "The changes are mind-boggling as we dig into new sites. Then there are the photographs from space that have aided in the study of the ancient world. For instance, the ancient caravan trails from Sheba cannot be seen with the naked eye or from aircraft in our atmosphere. But from space they are very clear. Moreover, the DNA and facial reconstruction by computers now reveal where certain groups came from and their physical appearance. It's all so fascinating."

"I have a question," Bill said. "If Sheba was in Yemen, doesn't that change the whole idea that the Ark of the Covenant was taken to Ethiopia?"

"Perhaps it was taken to Yemen instead," Henry interjected.

After a brief discussion, joined in by the rest of the group, it seemed to Henry that John was not only being evasive but kept trying to change the subject from the Ark. Interesting, he thought.

John pulled from his coat pocket the sketches Bill sent of Cain's staff.

"In all my time studying the writings of the ancient world, this is the most interesting item I've seen. I wish I could tell you of my success in deciphering it, but I can't. It has similarities to the writings of the Sumerian civilization and to the recent discoveries in Yemen. But unfortunately, not enough to translate. I know it's a giant leap, but I'm willing to stake my reputation on what I am about to say. Colleagues, this may represent the original written language of man on which all later languages were based. If my theory is correct, it would turn the academic community upside down. Instead of languages developing gradually and separately throughout the earth, it may be that all evolved from one written language somewhere in Iran or the Babylonian Plains or even in Yemen."

When the discussion concluded, everyone in the party left, except Bill and Rachael, who along with Irad, decided to take this opportunity to listen to the band playing in the ballroom. After a couple of drinks, Irad asked Rachael to dance. Watching from their table that was located on the edge of the dance floor, Bill began to feel a tinge of – could it be jealousy? The moment was interrupted by the sound of a familiar voice from behind his chair.

"Professor."

He turned, and there was a set of shining gold-filled teeth smiling at him.

"Mr. Henley, come have a seat. I'm with Rachael and a friend of hers. They're on the floor right now."

"Yes, I saw them when I came in."

"We're in New York to attend a seminar."

"Yes, I know. I was there but didn't get a chance to speak before you left. The e-mail you sent a few days ago indicated you were leaving for Iran after Labor Day."

"Yes. That's still the plan. Rachael and I are going with the advance party. My father and Dr. Rabon have agreed to join us later. We're trying to get John Elesbaan to come, but because of commitments, he may not be able to get out by Labor Day."

"Hello, Mr. Henley," Rachael said, as she and Irad approached the table.

"Just call me Walter," he said rising from the table to greet her.

Just then, the band struck up a slow dance tune.

"I believe you promised me this dance," Bill said, as he reached out and took her hand.

"Thought I'd save you from dancing with Henley, he whispered in her ear.

On the dance floor, he slipped his arm around her small waist and pulled her close to him.

"I hope you didn't want to dance with our benefactor."

"What do you think?" she asked, smiling at him.

"I think you'd rather be with me than with Henley."

"It's more than that."

"I don't know what you mean by that statement, and I'm afraid to ask."

"Ask, Professor," she said, the alcohol having loosened her emotions.

"Just call me Bill, tonight."

Suddenly, Bill saw a look of concern in Rachael's eyes. There was a tap on his shoulder before he could ask Rachael what was wrong.

"You can't have all the dances with this beautiful woman," Henley said.

Before Bill could respond, Henley had Rachael in his arms, and they were dancing across the ballroom floor.

6

Bill was waiting in the coffee shop when Thomas arrived.

"I'm glad we were able to meet this morning. I could use your help on some aspects of my investigation."

"I'll help in any way I can, Thomas."

"The autopsy performed on Imnah showed a faint imprint on the back of his neck." Thomas handed Bill a sketch of it.

Bill studied the sketch.

"It's a serpent. A symbol used over the years by people in numerous civilizations. Regardless of its use, the serpent has always been viewed by righteous people as a symbol of evil."

"I've contacted the police in Timbuktu about the circumstances of your first servant's accident. The investigating officer was intrigued by the fact that the single car accident was not severe enough for the man to have ended up with a broken neck. And he noted in his report that the man had a faint imprint of a serpent on the back of his neck. Now that can't just be a coincidence."

Bill felt a chill go down his spine.

"I agree. It's too strange to be a coincidence. But Thomas I can't think of anything at the moment to add to my previous statement."

"What about a cult?"

"Let me check with my father. He's written several articles over the years on various cults and has many contacts in the academic community in that area. Perhaps he could be of some help."

"Thanks."

"Were you able to track down the corporation who paid for Imnah's room?"

"No, unfortunately it was a dead end. No such company exists."

"That means the murder must have been prearranged," Bill said.

"I was intrigued by what Dr. Elesbaan said last night at the seminar about tracing geographically the origin of a person by DNA. I've requested it on the body. It may not be helpful, but my investigation is currently at a dead-end. Maybe it will provide me with a lead."

A drone watched as the two men left the shop. Seated at a table close enough to overhear the conversation, he knew his master would be interested in the discussion.

***

Comfortably seated on the plane, Bill reached into his briefcase and retrieved the unfinished copy of a manuscript tracing the history of the Yemenis people. Dr. Rabon had given Rachael and him each a copy of it last night, asking them to review it.

"*Yemen at an early stage in the development of civilization was an important center of trade on two major routes; one was ocean-trading commerce between Africa and India and the other a land route that ran up the coast of the Arabian Peninsula. In ancient times, several city-states developed. One of these was the Kingdom of Sheba with its capital at Marib. The people, called Sabaeans, built a dam upstream from their capital. The dam was one of the wonders of the ancient world. It provided water for irrigation and made the desert bloom. This added to the wealth of the country, which was already flourishing from its control of the ancient trade routes and the sale of its locally produced frankincense and myrrh.*

Recent excavations have discovered writings from the earliest period of Sabean's history speaking of giants who were in the land when a people calling themselves The Children of the Lord arrived. The Giants, who used the Serpent as their symbol, were called the evil ones by the new immigrants. One tablet found in an ancient ruin used an alphabet that might be the original Semite alphabet from which all the other alphabets are derived. We haven't ascertained which group it came from."

Bill's eyelids grew heavy. The next thing he knew, the cockpit announced the plane was landing in Charleston.

***

The Leader opened a box of expensive cigars recently received from Cuba. Leaning back in his large high-back custom chair, he smelled the aroma of the cigar leaf. The conference table before him contained several files received that morning from the Noba. He delayed reviewing them. Instead, he enjoyed the moment, rolling the leaf of the tobacco plant around in his mouth. A few minutes later, he reached down and opened the file on top. Everything was in code. Except for the elite of The Society, it appeared to be gibberish.

"*William Weston…Born Abbeville, South Carolina… Mother died…Aneurysm of the brain when he was ten…*

Father married her sister the next year...Child rebelled... Enlisted in Marine Corp against his father's wishes before finishing High School ...Basic training at Parris Island... Reached rank of sergeant...Special unit in Panama... Awarded medal for valor under fire...Had religious experience...Reconciled with father... attended Furman University...Married...Harvard Post Graduate...Biblical History of the Middle East...Divorced...Joined Marine Reserve Officer's Program...Commissioned Second Lieutenant...Assigned to Intelligence because of ability to speak and translate Arabic, Kurshish, Farsi and several African dialects...Still in Reserves...Presently holds rank of Captain...Currently Department Head of Archaeology at Charleston University...Granted one-year sabbatical to pursue archeological dig in Iran.

The Leader's phone rang. It was Henley. He wanted permission to continue surveillance on the detective. They spoke in a language that the modern world would not recognize. He gave Henley authority to use The Society's resources. The Noba would keep close tabs on the detective's investigation. If he got too close, the man would be eliminated. Hopefully, that would not be necessary. The death of a police officer always brought unwanted attention. When the conversation was over, a receptionist brought in his lunch.

Henley believes he's important now that he has been promoted to the second circle, the Leader thought.

But he is a *Lonsho*. A person with contaminated blood in the eighth degree. Still he has been useful to The Society, and he does carry within him the gene. Unfortunately, as a *Lonsho*, he cannot be inducted into the first circle and therefore will never be eligible to sit on the *Council of Twelve*.

Lunch over, it was time to read another file. The next one on the stack was Dr. Henry Weston. Quite an impressive academic background, the Leader thought, while looking at the contents.

Speaks…Arabic…Hebrew…Several local eastern dialects…Served…Green Beret…Vietnam…Desert Storm…Retired…Rank of Colonel…Written books… Civilizations of Persia…the Babylonian Empire…Middle Eastern Cults… Presently, a professor in biblical studies at Furman University."

The receptionist interrupted his reading to inform him the three o'clock appointment was waiting.

***

Rachael heard a knock on her door. Looking through the peephole, she saw her expected companion for the evening. This was Rachael's last night in New York and she intended to let her hair down. Tomorrow she had a flight to Israel where she would be under the suffocating protective wing of her family.

In the cab on the way to the Midtown Club, Irad said, "Walter Henley called me today and asked about dinner. I explained we were going dancing at the club and then out to dinner later. I asked him to join us. I hope you don't mind."

"No, I would've done the same. We can't forget that without his help there would be no expedition." Inside she was agitated. First, the professor had decided to leave today, and now her evening with Irad was spoiled.

Henley was at the club waiting. He had read the file on Rachael before having a drone deliver it to the Leader. Rachael's family was orthodox and belonged to one of the most puritanical sects. They held their women to a high standard expecting them to keep their virginity until marriage. Yes, it was right there in the file. Rachael was a virgin when she married at twenty. The Jewish tradition of hanging the bloody sheets from the window of the bedroom to prove it was followed. The report also indicated her social life became non-existent after her husband's death. That was probably why her academic record was so spotless. What a prize she would be for the right devil who caught her in a moment of weakness, and that could easily be arranged.

The club was packed when Rachael and Irad arrived. He saw Henley at a table on the left side of the dance floor and led Rachael through the crowd toward it.

"Good evening, Mr. Henley. I'm so glad you could join us," Rachael said.

"Now remember, I want you to call me Walter. After all, I'm only twenty-two years older than you," he said laughing.

How would he know my age, Rachael wondered, as she gave him a smile.

The Long Island tea the bartender kept pouring affected Rachael. She could feel her brain starting to squeeze. What was in this drink anyway? It certainly went down smooth and didn't taste like it had much alcohol. Feeling a little dizzy, she asked Irad to take her from the club to dinner. She hadn't eaten since breakfast. Then everything went black.

Where am I? It was like a dream, lying on a king size bed while Irad pulled her clothes off. And there was Henley standing at the foot of the bed watching with an evil grin. The room was so hot, perspiration was running off her naked body. Henley was on the bed now. His hand was caressing her. She wanted to get away, but her body wouldn't move. She tried to cry out, but no sound came.

"Please somebody help me," she finally managed to scream.

"You're going to be all right," a man in a white jacket said.

Opening her eyes, she looked around. She was in a hospital and there was a doctor smiling at her. A man standing in the corner said, "You're just dehydrated from all the alcohol." It was John Elesbaan. When the medical doctor left the room, she sat up in the bed.

"John, what am I doing here?"

"The doctor said you've got a severe case of dehydration."

"I feel really sick. I'm so embarrassed."

"On my way into the club, I saw Irad bringing you out. You looked ill, so I suggested that we bring you to the emergency room."

"Where is Irad?"

"He's downstairs getting coffee.

7

Rachael had to stay in the hospital for a few days while they ran tests. The doctor questioned whether the drinking caused her condition. He suspected something more sinister.

With time on her hands, Rachael picked up a copy of her father's manuscript.

"For centuries, the Queen of Sheba's kingdom has mistakenly been placed in the land of Ethiopia. This confusion was in part because of the Ethiopian legend that their line of kings descended from a union between their Queen and King Solomon of Israel. Archaeological excavations in Axum last year, at a site designated as the burial place of the Queen of Sheba, uncovered an interesting inscription

that I was able to decipher using my knowledge of the ancient Sabean language."

"Here lies the tomb of the Queen of Sheba, mother of our great King Menelik, son of Solomon, who brought the bones of his mother out of Arabia, so upon the king's death his body might be placed beside the great queen and, before judgment day be transported to Jerusalem and placed in Solomon's tomb, so when the trumpet of the Lord sounded from the heavens, the three could rise together to face the Almighty One."

It was her father's opinion this inscription would clear up the historical confusion. Rachael continued to read.

"It is becoming more obvious, as we dig deeper into this region's past, that the Kingdom of Sheba brought civilization to Ethiopia when it established the city of Axum and then extended its dominion over the surrounding countryside. A few generations later, the Kings of Ethiopia conquered their former homeland. Such things over the centuries confused historians, and they mistakenly put Sheba geographically in the land of its former colony.

The Queen of Sheba came from a land rich in commerce, agriculture and religion. The ruling class worshipped the sun until the queen converted to Judaism when visiting Solomon in Jerusalem around 900 B. C. The Old Testament tells how the queen heard about the

Wisdom of Solomon and his divine protection from the heavens. She traveled to Jerusalem to test this wise man with questions and to find out more about his God.

Coming from a land that had grown wealthy from trade, she brought a large quantity of gold, precious gems, frankincense, and myrrh. It was the largest gift the king ever received. When she arrived, Solomon was impressed with the riches. If we believe Ethiopian legend, he was even more impressed with her beauty and tried to seduce her. She resisted at first because she was a virgin queen and her people were puritanical in their belief and monogamous in their relationships. According to legend, she left Jerusalem both pregnant and the wife of Solomon. Her obvious condition would have cost her the throne if she had not returned to Sheba as his queen."

***

"Bill, this is John Elesbaan," said the voice on the other end of the line.

"It's good to hear from you."

"I wanted to discuss a few things. Are you busy right now?"

"Just a moment, please."

He stuck his head out of the door, and told the young intern, Megan, he didn't want to be disturbed.

"Have you heard Rachael is in the hospital?"

"No, what's wrong?"

"She checked in last night. They thought at first it was dehydration aggravated by drinking. Now they're running further tests. There might be foul play involved."

"What do you mean?"

"They suspect something was put in her drink at the club. She's going to be in the hospital for a couple of days."

"I assume from what you said, she's no longer in danger."

"Not now. I went by to see her this morning and she was sitting up reading."

"I'm glad she's all right.

"I'm still working on joining you in Iran. I'd like to be part of the expedition."

"We wish you could be directly involved if there is any way you can arrange it."

"Bill, we just had a person from Mississippi last week who requested a grant from an academic committee I serve on. He's trying to get funds for a computer project he's developing. He claims it will decode dead languages."

"Did he get the grant?"

"The committee turned him down. Although he might be on to something, he doesn't have a college education, and you know how snobbish the academic community can be sometimes. This man really knows his stuff, degree or not. It might be worthwhile to talk with him. I have his address and phone number if you're interested."

By the time he hung up, Bill had made up his mind to fly to New York and see Rachael before going to Mississippi. He made the reservations and left instructions with the intern where he could be reached.

When he was out of sight, Megan picked up the phone and made a call to her master.

Fullmore was in his garage creating a software program when the cell phone rang.

"Mr. Fullmore," said a voice on the other line. "This is Dr. Weston from Charleston University. John Elesbaan has been in contact with me about the project you're working on."

"Who's this?"

"Bill Weston."

"Who told you to call me?"

"John Elesbaan said he was on a committee. You applied for a grant."

"They turned me down."

"I know. John told me. Nevertheless, he said he was very impressed with your knowledge. Are you still there?"

"Yes, what do you want?"

"I'd like to discuss your project."

"Which one?"

"The one to perfect a computer software program that would decode ancient languages.

"What did you say you wanted?"

"I'd like to fly out there to meet with you."

"We don't have an airport here."

"What's the closest one to you?"

"That would be at Jackson."

"I could fly in there."

"I'll be home. What time are you going to get here?"

"Let me call you back after I've had a chance to check the plane schedule."

"I'll be right here."

When he hung up, Bill said under his breath, "How could John have been impressed with this guy?"

Ronald Fullmore didn't get visitors often. He was an introvert by nature. This trait was magnified by his obsession with ancient civilizations. Over time, he had lost contact with the few friends he had in his youth. He lived on a farm inherited from his parents, leasing out the cleared land and selling timber from the woods for income while he pursued his interests. Like his high school classmates, no college degree hung on his wall. It simply wasn't in his cultural background to pursue formal education beyond the twelfth grade. Now, at fifty, the lack of a degree served as a roadblock in obtaining funds for the thing he loved most, expanding the use of computers into the area of ancient civilizations.

***

Rachael was sitting up in the hospital bed reading her father's manuscript when she heard someone enter the room. She looked up and was surprised to see the professor standing in the doorway.

"What are you doing here?"

"I heard you had a little too much to drink," he said.

Rachael's face turned red, and he knew the attempt at humor had only embarrassed her. He felt a sick churning in his stomach from the comment that appeared so uncaring.

"I'm sorry. That just didn't come out right. I was worried about you, so I took the first flight out."

She was surprised he dropped everything to fly to New York. *Could it be he had begun to notice her at last?*

Rachael was going to Mississippi despite the professor's concern for her health. Although out of the hospital, she had not completely recovered. She still felt weak and had recurring nightmares. At the Jackson Airport, they would meet with John, who had decided to take time away from his busy schedule and join them. The plan was to rent a vehicle at the airport and travel north to the Delta region where Fullmore's farm was located.

This warm August day, the traffic was light as the three traveled through the Mississippi countryside. The fields were filled with cotton bolls waiting to burst forth and turn the fields into a sea of white. Passing through Leesburg, they followed Fullmore's directions to his farm. It was off the main highway down a dirt road that came to a dead end in front of an old house. The knock on the front door brought no response, so they walked down to a barn a short distance away. Just before they reached it, a small African- American man exited.

"You must be the ones what is been calling," he said.

After they introduced themselves, he invited them into the barn, which he had converted into a workshop. It was spacious inside with one whole wall of shelving filled with histories of the ancient world and their treasures.

"Have you ever traveled Mr. Fullmore?" Bill asked.

"In my mind, I've traveled the world."

While they sat at a table, Bill explained about the staff and how they were stumped in their attempts to decipher it.

Everyone could see the excitement in Fullmore's eyes as he listened.

"The history of Enoch is fascinating," Fullmore said.

Then he began to tell of legends he had read. When he finished, Fullmore brought them up to date on the computer software he was designing to decipher ancient text.

The three of them sat back in amazement at the man's knowledge and intellect. Bill understood now why John had been impressed with the man. It only went to show that accent and lack of a college education could be deceiving.

"Let me show you some sketches we've made of markings from the staff," Bill said.

Without blinking an eye Fullmore said, "Resembles some ancient writing from Sheba."

They went from being impressed to stun by his knowledge.

Then the man said, "I'd be glad to work on the inscriptions for you."

"That was the answer we were hoping for," Rachael said.

"I can authorize you fifty thousand dollars from our expedition fund," Bill said, wondering if this expenditure would cut him too short on funds.

"That would be helpful. Then I could devote full time to the project. You mentioned an expedition. Tell me about it."

When Bill finished, Fullmore said, "I sure would like to come see ya'll there."

"If you can help us on the staff, I promise to fly you over to look at the dig."

"I've never flown before, but guess I can get up the nerve."

When they were leaving, Rachael said with sincerity, "It was a real pleasure meeting you, Mr. Fullmore. I hope you get to come visit us in Iran."

8

As his last official act before shutting down the business, Henley reviewed the accountant's report on the expedition. The withdrawal of fifty thousand dollars for a Ronald Fullmore caught his attention. Packing this information into his briefcase, he left the store and drove to the airport. This operational site was close. It was the assassin's responsibility to clean up any loose ends.

Henley knew he was in trouble with The Society. A police investigation was something they could ill afford. Who would have thought the placing of the drug in Rachael's drink in a plot to bring her under his physical control would not only fail but also disrupt the organization's business. Of course, the usefulness of the corporation had almost run its course anyway. He knew that was the only reason he was not going to feel the wrath of the council.

***

Thomas O'Conner had followed the events of Rachael's illness and reviewed the blood test. It gave him reason to believe a criminal act had been involved since the lab report indicated the presence of *Rohypnol*, a *benzodiazepine*. It was a potent tranquilizer. And combined with alcohol, it could put a person in a semi-comatose state. When they woke, they frequently couldn't remember what had occurred. Many people after such an occurrence had recurring nightmares. Unfortunately, for the villain, she was on a medication for an infection. The two combined to cause a negative reaction, which made her deathly ill. Following up on this report, he tried to interview the two men she was with to ascertain if they had any knowledge of who might have spiked her drink. One, Irad Lamech, was back in Israel, and a phone call to the other, a Walter Henley, got a message from the company's answering device stating he was out of town. Thomas didn't see a connection yet between this act and the murder. There probably wasn't one, but he would follow it closely to be sure Bill's assistant wasn't in danger.

John received a call from the detective. It seemed that, after attending the seminar given in New York, he had decided to run DNA tests on a victim in a murder investigation. The lab, which used a new testing system, came up with some interesting results. It showed the deceased had a bloodline unknown even to scientists who specialized in this area. The lab's explanation was simply that the new test hadn't been perfected.

"This may sound strange to you, Detective, but it's becoming increasingly evident to some people that there could possibly be an extraordinary gene mixed in with what is normally called the human gene. However, at this point the scientific community doesn't accept such a theory. As testing gets more accurate, it may provide us with an answer."

John referred him to Dr. Samuel Rison, an expert on the *Nephilim*, and to Dr. Henry Weston, the author of several books on Middle Eastern mythology. The next day Thomas was knocking on the door of Dr. Risen's modest apartment.

"Thank you for seeing me on such short notice."

"It's always good to see anyone who is interested in the *giants* of the ancient world. Come, let's go into the den. You will have to excuse the noise. Some carpenters are renovating my study."

"Did you get my fax on the lab report?"

"Yes, I did."

"What do you think?"

"What I think it might be would get me committed and you fired," he said laughing.

"Is there any recent history on this sort of thing?"

"Not with the sophisticated tests conducted on your murder victim. However, there was a case in France in the 1970's, which, at the time, used a more primitive and less-reliable test. A scientist claimed he had examined a murder victim whose blood contained genes not of this world."

"What happened?"

"All kinds of UFO nuts came out of the woodwork. Later, after the body was stolen, the scientist was discredited."

"Did they ever find out who stole the body?"

"Not that I recall, but it's been a long time. Wait here just a moment. I save those kinds of articles in binders. Let me go see if I can locate them."

Dr Rison disappeared into another room for a few minutes. While he was gone, Thomas browsed around the den. There were pictures of Dr. Rison on an archaeological site in the desert.

Rison returned with a copy of a news article in his hand.

"I'll make a copy at the station and return it to you."

"Oh, don't bother. My days of chasing down legends are over, so I won't need this anymore."

He noticed the detective looking at a photo of him on the wall.

"That was taken in Yemen. I was one of the first to suggest that the Romans and Jewish writers had it all wrong. The Queen of Sheba was from Yemen. That's me at an archaeological site looking for the remains of a tribe of *Nephilim*. The storytellers in the region claim the giants inhabited those hills shown in the background. Unfortunately, we never found any bones to substantiate those legends."

It had been a week since his discussion with Rison, and now Thomas was sitting in Henry Weston's two-story antebellum home in Greenville having tea with his wife, Pamela, while he waited for her husband to get home.

"I'm sorry Henry is running late. He must have been held up in traffic. Could I get you some more hot tea?"

"Yes, thank you."

She poured him another cup from the silver tea pitcher.

"So you met our Bill while investigating a murder? How interesting. Did you catch the killer?"

"The matter is still active."

"Bill said you met in Charleston. It's such a beautiful city."

"Yes, it certainly is that, and he was good enough to give me a tour of the Citadel. Told me his father graduated from there."

"While you're waiting, let me show you some pictures of Billy. That's what his dad and I call him."

There were numerous photographs on the piano in the corner of the room. One picture was an old black and white showing a beautiful young woman holding a small child dressed in long trousers and a sport shirt.

"This is him with his mother, the day he started the first grade."

She saw the look in his eyes even before he blurted out, "Mother?"

"Oh, please excuse me. I should have told you. I'm Billy's stepmother. That's a picture of my sister, who was Henry's first wife. She died of cancer when Billy was ten. He took it very hard. His father and I married shortly after her death. Probably, we were insensitive to his feelings, but we were young, and Henry reached out to me in his grief. I've always loved Henry, and my sister, Mary, knew it. She would have wanted us together. But like I said, it was hard on Billy, and he became a very rebellious child. After the Panamanian campaign, he and his dad reconciled."

Thomas saw the resemblance between her and the woman in the photograph–both beautiful.

The front door opened, and Henry Weston came bouncing into the house, full of excuses for being late. He was a tall man with a full head of silver hair that gave him a distinguished look. He insisted that Thomas stay for dinner. While the housekeeper was preparing it, Pamela excused herself and went upstairs.

Henry invited Thomas into his study.

"Would you care for a cigar?"

"No, I don't smoke anymore."

"I don't generally smoke either. However, these are a birthday gift from my housekeeper. She obtained them from her cousin, who's in the export business. They're from Cuba. I swear to you there is nothing like them. I allow myself three smokes a week."

Thomas reached out and took one. A moment later, he had to agree it was heavenly.

"Now that we're relaxed, Thomas, let me read something about the mythology you're interested in."

"God saw that man was lonely so he put him into a deep-sleep, then took from him a rib and made a different type of creature that he called woman to act as a companion. Now Adam and Eve were without sin, not knowing good from evil. He planned in time to give them this knowledge when they reached the proper point of development.

One day while Eve was alone, a beautiful creature came to her. It had the form of a man and was over nine feet tall. She was naked but did not know it in her innocence. She was a virgin with no knowledge of sex. He placed his hands upon her body and it gave her pleasure. She felt no sin because the concept had not been given to her. All Eve understood was that it felt good, as any animal would understand it. He laid her upon the carpet of grass that covered the ground in that part of the garden. When Eve saw Adam that evening, she instructed him in what she had learned from the creature. God saw what happened and drove them from the garden. In a few months, a child was born. This child was not of Adam's seed but of the creature. The child born was a giant."

"Was this where the *Nephilim* came from?"

"If you believe the story, it would be a good place to start. Now, from this myth have come rumors of giants and legends of secret societies. I wouldn't put a lot of stock in them. That's why I didn't call when Bill mentioned you were interested in such things for your investigation. There's never been any solid evidence to add credence to these stories. However, I do have some books to loan you on the subject. They make for some interesting reading."

The men heard the dinner bell ring in the background.

"Come. Let's go to the dining room. I have the best housekeeper in the world. Zillah comes from, of all places, Yemen. You don't know how lucky I was to get her."

***

The Leader put down the telephone. The *Lonsho*, Henley, was safe in Iran. From there he could monitor the progress of the expedition. The Leader was aware that Henley placed the remaining balance of the three hundred thousand dollars in the professor's account.

It was the last act of the corporation before Henley left town. Things had begun to unravel a bit, but the assassin would take care of that problem. At this very moment, all known connections with the corporation, with the exception of those belonging to The Society, were being eliminated, starting with the board of directors.

It was getting harder to operate. His predecessors didn't have as difficult a task, the Leader thought. In earlier days, one only worried about local law enforcement, and there was no fingerprint system. Now, Interpol, international communication and the dangerous DNA testing were creating problems. Despite this, the group had managed to keep its secrets. Yes, keep its existence quiet while pursuing the organization's goals. These varied with changing times. Right now, it was important to closely monitor the dig and obtain any useful information, while at the same time making sure the rest of the world remained ignorant of the group's existence. Of course, The Society never lost sight of two important goals: The destruction of the *Children of the Lord* and the possession of their most venerated religious objects. Over time, they had their successes, such as the control of the bones of Noah and the body of the Prophet Daniel. But they had failed to obtain the two most precious things they sought: the staff of their ancestor, Cain, and the Ark of the Covenant.

The secretary brought in two dispatches. One concerned an investigation he ordered, and the other was a dispatch from Yemen on the search for the Ark. The first he opened was a response to his request for information on a Dr. John Elesbaan. The report was thin.

Elesbaan had obtained his undergraduate degree at the university in Addis Ababa and his graduate degrees at Oxford. His area of expertise was Arabia although he had extensive background on the history of the Ark. Information on his life before he attended school at Addis Ababa was non-existent. His application on file at the school listed his home address in Axum, but the *Noba*, an investigating arm of The Society, had been unable to find anyone there who ever heard of him.

Strange, the Leader thought. Who was this person who appeared out of thin air? He would have the *Noba* continue its investigation. He lit one of his favorite Cuban cigars and poured a glass of brandy before opening the other dispatch.

9

Rachael was in Jerusalem staying at her father's home on the outskirts of the Holy City. It was a spacious house built on a knoll centuries ago. Dr. Rabon had made substantial renovations since he purchased it. The courtyard was enlarged and a pool added. Rachael's bedroom opened onto the courtyard, which was shaded by several trees. This past week she had taken advantage of the good weather by exercising in the pool and lying out afterwards for hours soaking in the warm rays of the sun. This activity brought her health back to normal and gave her so deep a tan, her father commented that she could pass for an Arab. Irad came over to the house several times. They had become close since her return to Israel. She knew he was still upset that someone had spiked her drink. He told her so many times, as they lay by the pool. Strange, she felt no romantic attraction to him. A few kisses were the extent of their physical intimacy, though his actions indicated he wanted more. One day at the pool, the wet bathing suit he was wearing was quite revealing. Romantic attraction or not, she was aroused. It must be true. Once a woman experienced physical intimacy, she could never go back to a virginal state of mind.

In two days, the professor's arrival would mean the end of this relaxing interlude. It would be a busy time making last minute preparation for the trip. Then she and the professor would take a flight to Tehran.

***

Bill received a strange correspondence from Henley stating that he authorized the deposit of the remaining three-hundred-thousand dollars into the expedition account, and that he was involved in a business deal, which would make him incommunicado for some time. He didn't understand the workings of the shady people who dealt in the treasures of the past, but at least he had the money to go forward with the expedition regardless of what Henley might be up to in his other business dealings. Bill still questioned if Henley was involved in what had happened to Rachael. He would call the detective before leaving for Israel and inquire if he had any new information.

When Thomas received the call there had been no developments in Rachael's case, but he listened carefully when the Bill divulged the contents of Henley's letter. He was cautious not to comment. As soon as the Bill hung up the phone, Thomas called the district attorney's office and spoke to his contact there. By the end of the day, with a search warrant in hand, Thomas was at Henley's place of business. Finding the store locked, he had the uniform police officer assigned to him for the execution of the warrant break the door open. The front of the store was empty except for some furniture. In the back room, they found a conference table, three empty filing cabinets, and the aroma of a cigar that Thomas recognized. The kind he had smoked in Henry Weston's study one afternoon.

Two days after the search of Henley's store, Thomas' secretary walked into his office late in the afternoon and handed him the Imnah file.

"I added new material that came in an hour ago," she said.

"Thanks Betty, I'll take it home with me. The way things have been popping the last few days, I wouldn't get a chance to read it if I stayed here."

When he arrived at his apartment in the suburbs, Thomas switched on the air conditioner and got a cold beer out of the refrigerator. Sitting down at the kitchen table, he opened the file.

FAX

From the Department of Vital Statistics to Thomas O'Conner, Detective, Homicide Division, Fourth Precinct, City of New York Police Department.

Dear Sir,

There is no person listed as Walter Henley in our records. This agency is in the process of investigating the issuance of a driver license to the person using the above name and who provided the Driver's License Bureau with a false social security number.

So there is no Walter Henley. That was just great. He'd hit a dead end, and the chief was already demanding that he spend more time on other cases. He'd made it perfectly clear to me yesterday that there would be no more money spent traveling on what he considered nothing more than a wild goose chase. If something didn't break soon, the pressure would be on to put this case aside and work homicides that were more recent.

He pulled out another new piece of information that Betty had placed in the file. It was a fax from the National Clearing House for Serial Killers in the Department of Justice at Arlington, Virginia. He had requested they keep him posted on any murders involving the symbol of a serpent. A list of five names scattered across the country appeared.

Walter Jones	Realtor	Chicago, IL.
Ronald Moses	Banker	SanFrancisco, CA.
Samuel Mendel	Financial Advisor	NewYork,N.Y.
Robert Osborne	Antique Dealer	New Orleans, LA.
Lee Johnson	Attorney	NewYork, N.Y.

He would personally look into the two murders that occurred in his city.

That evening, Thomas decided to read the books Henry Weston loaned him. He meant to review them earlier, but his schedule had been too hectic. Then the last two weekends he had his son for visitation. Tammy was unwilling to switch days regardless of his work schedule. Of course, it didn't surprise him. She hadn't been that understanding when they were married, and this was one of the things that led to their divorce. He got another beer, lay down on the sofa and began to read.

"For thousands of years, so long ago no one knows where the stories originated, there have been tales of a group that claimed to descend from a creature of darkness. A figure mentioned in the mythology of many civilizations under a variety of different names. Sometimes the group is given

such names as the Evil Ones, the Sons of Darkness, the Children of the Devil, the Sons of Cain or the People of the Serpent. Regardless of the name used, the mythological stories are all similar. They claim descent from either a super race or a being from another world. Believers in recent years have been those who feel there are UFO's visiting the earth.

Historically, the Serpent played a central role in most of these mythological groups. One fable used the story of Adam and Eve in the Garden of Eden as a reference point. In the interpretation of that particular legend, the term Serpent was symbolic for the male phallus."

Thomas laid down the book. It was getting late, and he had a full schedule the next day. In the morning, he would meet with Richard Howard, the detective who was working on the murder of the attorney and the financial advisor.

The former partners met at Mingos, the restaurant they frequented ten years ago while assigned to the third precinct. When Thomas' assignment changed to the fourth, the pair had gone in different directions. Even though they rarely saw one another socially, they had remained friends.

"Good morning," Richard said as Thomas approached the booth in the back. "So what's up with you these days?"

"Same old crap. Overworked and underpaid," Thomas said. "Did you bring the two files with you?"

"Right here, partner." Richard picked up the Johnson and Mendel files lying on the seat beside him and handed them to Thomas, now seated across from him in the booth.

"That was an interesting story you were telling me on the phone last night about your murder investigation. I don't know if anything in those files will help."

While Thomas reviewed them, Richard finished the breakfast he had ordered.

"The only thing in here that may connect the murders is the imprint of a serpent," Thomas said.

"That sounds like a pretty good connection to me."

"But Richard, why are these killings taking place, and what is the connection between your two people and Imnah?"

"I'm going over to the lawyer's office this morning. Do you have time to join me?"

The office was nearby on the first floor of a business complex. A sole practitioner engaged in the general practice of law, Mr. Johnson had only one secretary, a Miss Marilyn Jubal. She was a tall, thin, blonde-haired woman, about thirty years of age, who couldn't stop crying long enough to get a full sentence out.

"Did he have any Middle East clients?" Thomas asked.

"I'm not sure. Perhaps he did," said the woman who appeared nervous. "How would I know if they were?"

"What about a corporation called Henley Antiques?"

"I could look in his files if you would be so kind as to give me a few minutes."

She went in his office and retrieved a file.

"I guess it's all right to give it to you. I'll be closing his office as soon as I notify all his clients."

Thanking her, they left and went back to the car.

What fools, Marilyn thought, after the detectives departed.

"Poor thing," Richard said, "She doesn't have a clue what happens when a lawyer dies."

"What do you mean?"

"As soon as the court is aware of the death, they'll appoint an attorney as trustee over the files in his office. We may get a call in a few days to return the file, but by that time, we will have gleaned any relevant evidence we need."

Back at Mingos, the two men went through the material. The articles filed with the Secretary of State showed the names of the incorporators. Another document listed the names of the board of directors after the incorporation. The two lists were the same.

"I guess you have the connection now," Richard said.

"The victims were all involved in business together."

"And look here. The lawyer not only incorporated them but served as registered agent," Thomas said.

"That's not all. Look at this copy of the lawyer's billing. Apparently, he also served as the corporation's tax attorney. No wonder he was killed if this Henley fellow was involved."

"He may be involved or perhaps his body just hasn't been discovered yet," Thomas said. "I need to go back and talk to the lawyer's secretary. Now that we have this information, perhaps I could ask the right questions and get some leads.

"I wish I could go with you, but I have a meeting at noon with the chief. Just keep me informed."

The door was locked when Thomas arrived at the law office. A note stated it was closed by court order. It gave the name of the trustee appointed and a statement requesting that clients of the deceased call the number listed on the note. Thomas would call the trustee later, but right now, he wanted to speak with the lawyer's secretary. He called his office.

"Betty, I need you to find an address of a woman named Marilyn Jubal. She may have some information on the Imnah case."

"How fast do you need it?"

"I want to talk to her before I come back to the office."

"I'll get right back to you."

Five minutes later she called with the address: Apartment 321 at 5907 Plymouth Street in the Kirsten Building.

The apartment was in an upscale neighborhood. Thomas was surprised that a legal secretary could afford such a place. Maybe her husband had a high-paying job. Then he remembered that the lady hadn't been wearing a ring. He parked in front. A doorman quickly came out.

"You can't park here."

Thomas flashed his badge and stepped into the lobby. The staff watched him with curiosity as he ascended the stairs. When he got to her apartment, the door was slightly ajar. He knocked. No one responded. He pushed the door slightly, and it opened. He called out again, then entered the apartment. There was no one home. Reaching into his jacket, he removed his cell phone and called the third precinct.

"What's going on?"

Thomas told Richard what had transpired since they separated.

"I'll leave now and come over."

While waiting, Thomas looked around. Something wasn't kosher here. A minimum of clothing remained in the closet. Nothing else of a personal nature was present anywhere. And there was no trash. Everyone had trash.

With a blue light flashing, Richard pulled up behind Thomas's car. Getting out, he ignored the doorman's questions and went straight up to the apartment.

"So, Thomas, what do you think happened?"

"I don't know. Maybe nothing. I didn't go into any of the drawers. I was waiting until you got here. Otherwise it would just be my word against hers if something was missing."

"I'm glad to see something from the Police Academy stuck in your brain," said Richard laughing. "Well, let's check them now."

There was nothing other than a few items of clothing. No phone numbers, bills, addresses or writings.

"Strange to say in the least," Richard said. "She may be a material witness so I'll put a uniformed police officer on surveillance for the next forty-eight hours and see if she turns up. If she doesn't, we can assume she's the victim of foul play and put out a missing persons report."

"This may all just be a false alarm," Thomas said.

"Yes, I've been there more times than I'd like to remember."

10

After Bill enjoyed Labor Day in Greenville, he caught the red-eye flight to Jerusalem. On the plane, he reached a decision to let Rachael know how he felt. He would approach the matter slowly, and if she indicated no interest, he would accept just a professional relationship. He never thought he would put himself in this position again. He had loved his wife, and her rejection of him still hurt.

The plane landed in Jerusalem that afternoon. Although the invitation to dinner wasn't until later that evening, Bill took a taxi from the airport directly to Dr. Rabon's home. No one answered the doorbell. Leaving his bags at the front door, Bill walked around the side where a wrought-iron gate led into a courtyard. When he reached the gate, he saw Rachael. She was embracing Irad on a blanket laid out under the shade of a palm tree a few feet from a large swimming pool. He stepped back out of sight and then retraced his steps. After a few minutes, he once again walked toward the gate. This time he called out in a voice loud enough for everyone to hear. When he arrived back at the entrance, they were standing up and Rachael was walking toward the gate to greet him.

"I thought you were arriving later."

"I managed to get an earlier flight."

"Let me change and then I'll make us all a drink."

When she walked away, he was so distraught that he didn't even notice the skimpy French bikini she was wearing.

Rachael was glad to see him. Thank goodness, he hadn't seen her on the blanket with Irad. It would have spoiled everything. She was tired of denying to herself the attraction she felt toward this man, geek though he was, interested only in dusty old books and biblical history. The difference in their ages didn't matter to her anymore. She was going to find the right moment and let him know how she felt. She also needed to make Irad aware of her feelings toward the professor.

Over drinks, Rachael insisted the professor stay at her father's home while he was in Jerusalem. There was an extra bedroom next to hers, which opened onto the courtyard. She explained that in the evening after a busy day, they could both relax in the pool. The professor was resistant to the idea, saying he already had hotel reservations and getting ready for the expedition would require him to work late at night. He was acting so professional, so aloof. She was upset. Didn't he realize what she was offering? Maybe he just wasn't interested.

That night after dinner, Rachael invited the professor to join her and Irad for a night of dancing at some of the clubs in the city. He declined saying he had a long day tomorrow. Yet when she returned at one o'clock in the morning, he was in the study with her father in an intense discussion on the biblical history of the Ark. She was furious. After giving him a polite but cool goodnight, she marched off to her bedroom. *Why was she so angry with him, and why did this anger make her desire him even more?* She tossed in bed until the sun came up the next morning.

When Bill checked into his hotel room, it was two a.m. Unable to sleep, he opened a book Dr. Rabon gave him on the Ark of the Covenant and read about an ancient text found near the Dead Sea.

"And the Almighty One said to Moses, I want the people of the Lord to make a temple where I can have a home in their midst. The Ark is to be made of Acacia wood, a material that will never decay. It shall be two cubits and a half in breadth and length and a cubit and a half in height, overlaid inside and outside in pure gold. It should have two poles made from the same wood as the Ark, so that the

Ark can be carried without the hands of man touching it, for the Ark shall contain a spirit sent from me. The two tablets containing the law written by my finger shall be place inside the Ark.

There shall be a mercy seat built of the sacred wood, covered in gold and placed as a lid upon the top of the Ark and on the lid shall be placed the figures of two angels made of gold, each facing the other and both looking down upon my seat of mercy. A table shall be built for the Ark to sit upon. Constructed of sacred wood, and covered with gold. A piece of the special bread, Manna, sent from the heaven by me shall always be kept upon it."

The ringing of the phone startled him. Looking at the clock, he saw that it was four a.m.. Who could be calling at this hour? When he picked up the receiver, Detective Thomas O'Conner was on the other line.

"Is this a good time to talk? Hope I'm not interrupting anything."

"No, you aren't, but do you know what time it is?"

"Oh, I apologize. I completely forgot about the time zones. I'll call back later."

"No, that's ok, I was reading."

"Just wanted to bring you up to date on Rachael's case. The man you've been dealing with, Walter Henley, has disappeared."

The detective then informed him of developments since they last talked.

"Henley's disappearance is strange, especially in light of his action in depositing the remaining three hundred thousand dollar commitment into my expedition account. I'm not a detective, but it seems to me that whoever is behind this probably killed Henley."

"You may be right, but the chief has clipped my wings on traveling. So whatever I do from this point forward will be limited."

By the time the conversation was over, Bill was wide awake. He put on a pot of coffee and then began reading more of Dr. Rabon's book.

"And the Almighty said to the people, you must build a tent to house my Ark to protect it from the climate. It must be made from ten sheets of linen, which shall be dyed purple and have figures of angels embedded in it. The roof shall be made of the hair of goats from the best of your flocks and it shall be placed upon a framework made of the sacred wood."

***

"The chief wants to see you right away," Betty said.

"Let me sign a few more letters; then I'll go downstairs and see what he wants."

"Thomas, I think when he said right now, that's what he meant. Something is up."

Down the stairs he went, not nervous but curious what might have the boss' dander up today. When he entered the reception area, he could feel tension in the air. In a moment, he was shown into the spacious office of the man responsible for the safety of the city: a fellow Irishman named Timothy McCrae.

"Good morning, Chief," Thomas said as he entered. He was surprised to find three others, whose faces he did not recognize, in the office.

"Thomas," said McCrae, rising from his padded swivel chair. "This is Harry Beacham, attorney with the United States Department of Justice, agent Kinsey Riley in charge of the New York Terrorist Command Center and agent Douglas Abrams with the Customs Service."

"We're interested in your murder investigation of a man know as Imnah," Harry Beacham said. Your inquiries to the National Clearing House for Serial Killers and the Department of Vital Statistics brought the case to our attention.

"We think terrorism could be involved," Kinsey Riley said.

Douglas Abrams said, "The removal and sale of treasures of antiquity have been used in recent years to fund all types of illegal and prejudicial political actions against the United States."

"And I thought this was a simple murder case," McCrae said. "Isn't that right, Thomas? I've been on his back about spending too much time on it. Should have known better. He's one of my finest detectives, and it will be the department's pleasure to grant your request to put him on temporary assignment with the terrorist unit."

Thomas was almost lost for words. "Chief, what are you talking about?"

"We promised to provide the terrorism unit with some help when it was organized last year. In light of their interest in your case, I decided you'd be a perfect candidate."

"We've done a background check on you, Thomas, and have already told McCrae you're acceptable," Beacham said. "The assignment will be for twelve months. That's, of course, if you're willing to accept."

"How long do I have to decide?"

"Tomorrow will be soon enough."

He handed Thomas his card.

"I'm staying at the Hotel Acropolis. Meet me at the bar tomorrow evening. Should we say six o'clock?"

"That's fine."

"Then I'll see you tomorrow."

"Okay," Beacham said, looking at Kinsey and Douglas, "I think we need to get out of McCrae's hair so he can get back to work."

***

"Hello, Richard, what's up?" Thomas asked.

"I'm going over to Samuel Mendel's house to speak to his widow this afternoon and wondered if you wanted to ride along.

"Sure. She might know something about her husband's dealings with Henley's corporation."

On the way over, Thomas told Richard about the opportunity to be on special assignment with the terrorist unit.

"I think you ought to do it. It'll look good on your record when promotion time comes around."

"More importantly, maybe I can pursue the Imnah matter without having my hands tied by the provincial attitude of the New York City Police Department."

The Mendel home was located on the north side of the city in a gated community. When they arrived at the security entrance, the guard checked his clipboard.

"Yes, detectives, I see it right here. Mrs. Mendel is expecting you." The guard then rambled on, telling the detectives about his experience on the Washington Police Department before retirement, until he saw the detectives were getting impatient.

"Well, you guys have a good evening and let me know if I can ever be of any help."

The road wound for more than a mile past large two-story homes. They passed a sign pointing to the pool and tennis courts, and then later a sign giving directions to a golf course and clubhouse.

"Quite a layout," Richard said.

"Yeah, the financial advisor must have been doing quite well to afford a place in here."

They took a right on a side road, which came to a dead-end in front of a mansion that lay near the back end of the golf course. A maid answered when they rang the ornate doorbell encasement on the side of a massive double door.

"We have an appointment with Mrs. Mendel," Richard said.

"Yes, she just called," the maid responded in English, but with a heavy foreign accent. "She's running late and wanted me to put you in the study until she gets home."

They followed her down a hallway whose walls were covered with paintings that smelled of money. The study itself was not particularly large, but it was expensively furnished. The maid went over to a bar located beneath a bookshelf lined with historical writings on ancient civilizations and made them drinks. A few minutes later, they were sitting on the leather sofa enjoying the taste of expensive whiskey.

The sound of tennis shoes entered the front door and came down the hallway toward them. An attractive woman in her late thirties, with long brown hair and a beautiful set of green eyes, stuck her head in the door. "Detectives, sorry I'm late, but my tennis match went over. I see Milcah has taken good care of you. Let me go freshen up. I'll be right back. Have another drink if you want. There are some Cuban cigars in a box on the desk. Smoke if you like. I don't mind."

Before either of them could respond, she was gone from the doorway. A moment later, they heard the sound of her feet going up the winding staircase at the end of the hallway.

"You care to take her up on the offer?" Richard asked.

"Not for another drink, but I might on the cigar."

"Sounds nice, but I quit years ago," Richard said.

"I thought I had, but this case has me smoking cigars again," he said with a laugh.

Thomas got up and walked over to the desk. He recognized the cigars as the same brand he had first seen at Henry Weston's home and then later smelled their aroma in Henley's place of business. This couldn't be a coincidence. He picked one out of the box and placed it in his coat pocket.

"You're not going to light it?" Richard asked.

"No, I think I'll save it for later."

When Linda Mendel entered the room, it was obvious from her wet curly hair that she had showered before putting on a pair of tight jeans and a loose-fitting blouse that revealed she was bless by nature or cosmetic surgery. She sat in the matching leather chair positioned directly across from the sofa.

"Thank you for seeing us, Mrs. Mendel," Richard said.

"Oh please, just call me Linda. Now, detectives, what can I do for you?"

Richard led with the first questions.

"I know from the file that another officer has already interviewed you, but perhaps now that we have more evidence, our questions could be more specific."

"Do you know who murdered Sammy?" she asked.

"No, not yet, but we do have some leads to follow. Detective Thomas O'Conner is working on another murder case that may be connected."

"I'll help in any way I can." Linda crossed her legs and looked up at the ceiling in an emotionally detached manner.

"Let me show you a list of your husband's business associates. Do you recognize any of them?"

She looked at the list containing the names of the corporate board.

"No, I don't. But let me explain something. My husband and I never discussed business."

"Have you ever heard of a Walter Henley or The Antiquity Store?"

"Only to the extent that Mr. Henley was a business associate who sent him a box of cigars every Christmas. But I don't know anything about that relationship."

"Did your husband seem to be all right financially?"

"As far as I know, he was doing well. He seemed to be involved in numerous business dealings, but didn't talk about it. Frankly, I wasn't at all interested in his business affairs."

"Do you know of any safety deposit boxes other than the one listed in his will?"

"If I did, you certainly could have that information. But the answer is no."

"Did you ever hear anything about a serpent?" Thomas asked.

"Now that sounds like something out of a movie, Detective O'Conner. Of course not."

"Do you know of anyone who might want to kill your husband?"

"I didn't have a lot of social contact with his friends. We were somewhat—well we lived our own lives. I know that sounds awful, but that's the way our marriage worked.

Before they left, each gave Linda a business card and asked her to call if she thought of anything that might be useful.

The afternoon spent interviewing Linda appeared to have been a waste of time. No new leads uncovered and now Richard was leaving on a two-week vacation, temporarily drying up that source for Thomas. Perhaps the resources of the terrorism unit would be helpful in breaking the logjam in this unusual case.

Richard dropped Thomas off at the apartment in time for him to shower before his meeting with Harry Beacham, the attorney with the justice department. Thomas didn't know Beacham's drinking habits, but he intended to take this opportunity to indulge. And that was a good reason to travel by taxi tonight.

After the cab left Thomas in front of the hotel, a doorman gave him direction to the bar. He took the elevator up to the top floor. Getting out, he saw why this was the nightspot for the elite of the city. All four sides were surrounded by glass in a circular shape giving the occupants a view of all the things that made New York the cultural and financial center of America. On the right side of the room, a small band was playing music to a dance floor filled with beautiful people. He spied Beacham at the bar chatting with a woman. The back of the bar was solid oak from which hung a huge mirror. On either side of it was arranged a large selection of expensive whiskey.

When Harry Beacham saw Thomas, he left the bar and came over to greet him. "Glad you could make it. Come. I reserved a place for us." Leading the way, Beacham went to a table more secluded than the others.

A waiter appeared immediately out of nowhere.

"Good evening," he said with a familiarity that made Thomas aware that his companion was a regular patron.

"Get me a scotch and bring this gentleman whatever he wants. Put it on my tab."

"Thanks Harry. I'll have a Jack Daniel on the rocks." His choice of alcohol showed his roots as a Southerner from North Carolina whose protestant ancestors had come to America from Northern Ireland centuries ago.

"It looks like you're well known here."

"Yes, this city is my home. I plan to return as soon as I can get a transfer from the Washington office. Who knows, perhaps I'll run for office some day. However, that's in the future. Let's talk about something that's more current. Have you made a decision?"

"Yes, I'm going to accept the assignment."

"Good. I'm flying back to the Washington office tomorrow. I'll let my superiors know that you're on board."

"There's just one thing."

"What's that?"

"I want to continue to be in charge of the Imnah investigation."

"That's fine with me as long as it doesn't interfere with the objectives of the unit."

The waiter brought their drinks. The first Bourbon went down so smoothly, Thomas ordered another. He intentionally didn't drink often, having seen too many careers go down the tubes from alcohol. Nevertheless, on occasion, he would allow himself to indulge, and this was one of those nights.

Later in the evening after they had a third round, Beacham said, "I'm going to call it a night."

Standing up, he placed his hand on Thomas's shoulder.

"I know you'll enjoy working with the unit. I'll be flying in frequently to see how the office is doing. Any time you feel the need Thomas, give me a call. Have another drink. I'll tell the waiter on my way out to put it on my tab."

Thomas was having a fourth drink when he heard a soft voice from behind.

"Mind if I join you?"

He looked up into the same set of green eyes seen earlier that day.

"No, of course not."

Linda took a seat across from him. She was wearing a cocktail dress so flattering he suspected it was made specifically for her. It was the same deep green as her eyes, and had shoulder straps just low enough to tastefully reveal a hint of cleavage. The material was of a silky quality, giving the appearance of being loose but fitting snugly over the contours of her body.

"I've never seen you here before, Detective. Do you come often?"

"No. This is my first time. I met someone here on business."

"When I was dancing with a friend, I saw your acquaintance leave."

The band started to play.

"Would you like to dance?" she asked.

"I must warn you that I'm not that good."

Her feet guided him gracefully across the floor as the band played one of the few slow dances for the evening. Her perfume stirred a primeval desire, which had already begun to surge from the pressing of her flesh against his body. He knew she was the type of woman who was beyond his reach. She belonged to that group of beautiful people who never had to work and whose days were filled with social activities. When the dance was over, she said goodnight and rejoined her friends. He finished his drink and was soon out of the door.

When Thomas walked into his apartment, he noticed the light blinking on his answering machine. There was a meeting tomorrow morning of the New York Terrorists Task Force.

The alarm buzzer went off. Thomas struggled out of bed and put on the coffee. His head ached, the effects of a hangover from a body not accustomed to alcohol. When he picked up his shirt off the floor, he smelled Linda's perfume that had been absorbed into the material. He felt a stirring in his loins. It had been a long time.

The task force office was across town from the apartment. On the way, Thomas stopped at a diner for breakfast. The food eased the throbbing in his head. By the time he reached his destination, he felt better. The receptionist directed him to Kinsey Riley's office.

"Come in, Thomas. Glad you got my message. We'll be meeting in the conference room down the hall. But first, let's go see your office. It's on the next floor."

Thomas was surprised his new quarters had an outer office.

Seeing the look on Thomas' face, Kinsey said, "You know a secretary will be assigned to help you."

"No, I didn't."

"Just one of those perks that goes with the assignment.

If there is any administrative personnel from the police department that you particularly want, we could talk to your chief."

"Betty."

"What's that?"

"I'd like my administrative assistant, Betty Marlow."

"I'll see what I can do."

The meeting in the conference room started with Kinsey introducing Thomas. Then Thomas was asked to brief the group on the Imnah case. He did so but left out anything that might imply he put any stock in the mythology that had surfaced in the investigation.

When Thomas finished his presentation, Kinsey Riley said, "Some of the facts in this case may seem somewhat strange, but the bottom line is terrorists will use naïve people who believe in the occult to further their objectives. That's exactly what all this talk of a serpent is about. I'm glad to say we've taken some positive action this morning by freezing the expedition bank account of Professor Weston. Unfortunately, there was only a balance of one hundred thousand dollars left in it. I wish we had acted sooner."

Thomas' face turned red. When the meeting adjourned, Thomas followed Kinsey out into the hallway.

"I need to speak to you," he said.

"Come back to the office."

They passed Kinsey's secretary, who looked up with an inquisitive eye.

"Pull up a seat and take a load off your feet," Kinsey said, as he plopped into the chair behind his desk.

"I'm the new kid on the block, but Harry Beacham promised me control over the Imnah case. Seizing Professor Weston's expedition funds won't constitute a blow against terrorism and will certainly add nothing toward solving the murder case."

"Is William Weston a friend of yours?"

"Just an acquaintance. I met him during the murder investigation. But, I can tell you this: he is not involved in the murder, and I would stake my reputation that he's not a terrorist."

"Well, we both agree on that."

Kinsey saw the puzzled look on Thomas' face.

"The order came from Harry. I'm aware of the professor's academic background and the service he's performed for his country. He's a patriot, but Harry has his own political agenda. He plans to be the governor of New York one day and this job is going to be his springboard. The poop I put out this morning is simply what Harry expected me to say. Hope this doesn't poison our relationship."

Thomas left the office a lot calmer than when he entered. The attractive secretary in the outer office smiled at him as he walked by.

"Your things are ready to go," Betty said when Thomas entered.

As she spoke, her hands were busy pulling items out of her own desk.

"What are you doing?"

"Getting packed to move with you."

"Betty, I hope you don't mind. I was going to speak to you about it. Just asked them this morning if it would be possible to have you over there with me."

"The chief's office called an hour ago. Said I was going."

"You aren't upset, are you?"

"Hell no. It'll be fun. Besides, a year away from this hole in the wall will be a relief. Is it true that they have free coffee and donuts every morning?"

"I wouldn't be surprised."

The last thing Betty needed was donuts to add more weight to her small frame, which already had to support a few extra pounds with each passing year.

Thomas was tired from the stress of the day. When he reached his apartment that evening, he grabbed a cold beer and stretched out on the sofa. Before he could finish, the phone rang. The voice on the other end of the line was almost hysterical.

"Detective, this is Linda Mendel. I need to see you right away."

"I'll be glad to meet with you tomorrow."

"This can't wait."

"What's wrong?"

"I wasn't completely forthcoming when you interviewed me."

"In what way?"

"I've suspected for months that Sammy might be having an affair. Now I'm not so sure. The private detective I hired contacted me a month ago to say that Sammy's name, degrees and everything else about him are phony. I told the detective to continue his investigation and find out who Sammy really was."

"Can't this wait until tomorrow?"

"No, I'm afraid, Thomas. I hope it's all right if I call you Thomas."

"Sure."

"I went to see the private detective at the agency this afternoon. I haven't talked to him in days because of Sammy's murder. His secretary said he was killed. You can't imagine how shocked I was when she told me that. I think his death is connected to Sammy's murder. A car followed me when I left the agency. Whoever it was stopped, just before I reached the security gate. I told the guard about it. He said he would keep an eye out for anyone suspicious."

"I'll come over later tonight."

"Please come soon. I've a real creepy feeling about this whole thing."

After he hung up the phone, Thomas showered and shaved. He put on a fresh shirt and located a jacket.

On the way over, Thomas listened to his favorite song playing on the radio. Hard to believe it was on the oldies station. The song brought memories rushing back to his mind. Where had the time gone? It seemed like only yesterday that he was a young officer. Now he was forty-three, divorced and had been without a woman for two years. It was time for a change in his life.

When Thomas arrived at the gate, the guard recognized him. He got an ear full about how the guard was scrutinizing everyone closely since Mrs. Mendel said someone was following her.

Linda was the one who answered when Thomas rang the doorbell. The maid was nowhere in sight. From her demeanor, he would never know this was the same person who spoke almost hysterical on the phone earlier. She was wearing a simple black skirt and a white shell with the first three buttons unfastened. She greeted him in a soft calm voice and led him toward a room at the end of the hallway that opened up into the secluded back yard. It contained a bar and she made him a Jack Daniels on the rocks without even asking what he wanted. She placed the drink in his hands and then sat down on the sofa at the opposite end, turning her body in his direction so that every portion of it had his attention. She spoke slowly, seeming to choose every word carefully.

"I've searched this house from top to bottom to find anything that might give me a clue as to Sammy's real identity. The only thing I turned up was a key to a safety deposit box taped beneath a desk drawer. I should have told you about it the other day."

"What's in the box?"

"I don't know. The key has a Newark address on it. I planned to go there in a few days. It may be an important piece of the puzzle for the both of us. The question is can I trust you? You seem like a strong man, but I don't know much about you."

"There's not much to tell."

"You're divorced."

"How would you know that?"

"The loneliness in your eyes."

"Linda, why did you want me to come over here tonight?"

"Professionally or personally?"

"Professionally," he said, stuttering the word.

"I needed someone to talk to. I have friends. Well, more like acquaintances. They're only interested in having a good time. Nothing that would involve any heavy lifting. I can't be critical of them since, frankly, I'm the same way. But this thing with Sammy has shaken me. All of a sudden, my life has been turned upside down. Can you imagine the shock of finding out the person you've been married to for five years is not the man you thought? Financially, I'm not sure where I stand. My lawyer is trying to determine what assets are available."

"What about his business?"

"A corporation that was nothing but a shell. I think it was a front for some other activity. His marriage to me was simply what men do to appear successful. You know—a beautiful wife with social connections. That's what I brought to the relationship. It worked for me. When I married Sammy, I had all the right attributes and social skills to live the kind of life I wanted; but my financial assets were, should we say, so very limited."

She got up and freshened his glass of whiskey. When she returned, she sat close to him. As she continued to talk, she placed her hand on his leg in a manner that seemed perfectly natural.

"You asked me the other day about a serpent. I picked up the phone one afternoon when Sammy was on a conference call. Before I hung up, I heard someone mention the word *Serpent* and another person comment about, *The League of Seth*."

"League of Seth?"

"Yes, strange words for an investment banker to be using, don't you think? Thomas, have you ever heard of such an organization?"

"No I haven't," he said, not being completely honest with her.

He remembered reading something about it in one of the books Henry Weston had given him.

Linda put her face close to his as she continued to talk.

"I need you to go with me to New Jersey and make sure I'm protected. After today, I'm afraid to go alone. Someone might follow me. I also need help finding any assets my husband might have had. I don't have the money to hire another private detective to investigate this matter. You have the ability and resources.

You help me, and I'll keep you informed when I learn anything that might be useful to your investigation."

She removed her hand from his knee and put it on his shoulder, at the same time bringing her lips in close proximity to his. Her perfume was intoxicating–the same one worn the night they danced at the club.

"Thomas, there are other fringe benefits for helping me," she said, with a conviction in her voice that could make one think it would all be worthwhile.

There nothing she was asking that he couldn't do and still maintain the integrity of the operation. Besides, she would be providing useful information just like any informant.

Music played from some central location in the background. The song was one that had been a favorite of Thomas' in the past. The liquor, the atmosphere and the long time without intimacy were all too much for him to resist. She was skilled in how to please a man, and Thomas wanted to be pleased.

12

It took a full week to organize the trip to Tehran. At one time, it seemed the Iranian Government might deny Bill's visa because of his Marine Reserve status. Then, for some unexplained reason, they did an about face and approved it without explanation.

The travel plan called for Bill and Rachael to fly to Jordan and then take a connecting flight to Tehran, where arrangements were made for transportation to a base camp in the Zagros Mountains. A few weeks later, the rest of their party would join them to begin the excavation under the watchful eyes of the Iranian Ministry of Archaeology.

When she heard the taxi horn blow, Rachael was packed and more than ready to leave for the flight. The last few days had been uncomfortable. She had not spoken to Irad about her feelings toward the professor, deciding it would be foolish to do so in light of her employer's complete business-like attitude toward her. Despite that, it would be good to be once again working in the field, even if the man wasn't attracted to her. After all, that was the relationship which existed during the last two years. She was glad to be leaving for other reasons. In the short time at home, her family had started treating her like a child again. She wondered sometimes if they would ever accept that she was a woman now. She had the opposite problem with Irad. It was best to get away from him for a while before she was tempted to say yes to his advances.

Bill was waiting at the airport when Rachael arrived. For a moment, the dam holding back his emotions broke when he saw her enter the front door of the facility. By the time she reached him, he had them firmly under control.

"It looks like a good day for flying," he said.

"Yes, I'm anxious to be back out in the field. It's tiring, but interesting work. I can't think of another vocation that would attract me."

And it was almost true. Rachael was drawn to the field of ancient civilizations, dead languages, and archaeology. Nevertheless, she thought, there is more to life than that—things more worthwhile. Maybe one day the professor will wake up and realize it.

The plane landed at dusk, and a hired guide was there to meet them. Much to their surprise, the deputy head of the archaeological ministry was also waiting.

"I am Dr. Cirus Sirhan," the man said, as he emerged from the back seat of a black limousine. "The government asked me to extend a welcome to you on behalf of Iran. It is my understanding that you have reservations at the Ratum Hotel. Come. We will ride in my vehicle."

Then turning to the guide, he barked some orders. The guide bowed and then headed to the baggage section.

"He will see that your things are delivered to the hotel."

The hotel was at the western end of the city. Bill chose it on the recommendation of a contact. It was the place where foreigners stayed. The location was ideal for departure to their destination the next morning because a main artery of the Iranian highway system passed by it, going in the direction of the Zagros Mountains.

"Your expedition has attracted interest," Cirus said, as they drove toward the hotel. "We are a very ancient culture and have always believed that civilization started in our land. The experts for a long time agreed, but, for the last hundred years, it has become popular to assign the cradle of civilization to Africa. Imagine what would happen to those theories if you were actually able to find the City of Enoch. It would turn the experts on their heads."

It was true, Bill thought. Iran had a great civilization long before the Egyptians. Now its historical heritage was buried beneath several waves of Muslim conquest. Islam was so embedded in its people's mores that the average Iranian felt little connection to the great people who were their ancestors or to the fact that these ancestors served as an important foundation in man's development.

The hotel built just before the fall of the Shah had remained the best maintained in Tehran. When the ministry's limousine pulled in front, the staff gave them the royal treatment.

After they signed the registry, Cirus said, "I hope you enjoy your time in my country. Someone from the ministry will be staying at the base camp to observe the dig. The paperwork has been cleared with internal security. You should have no problem on the road to the Zagros Mountains tomorrow."

After he left, the guide brought their luggage into the lobby.

"I am Bahodore," the small-framed man said. "We did not get a chance to speak earlier because of that pompous ass from the ministry. As you can see, I speak English. I was educated in America before the revolution."

"You come highly recommended by my friends."

"That is good to hear. It is my livelihood now. Working on excavations in isolated places keeps me out of trouble with the authorities."

"Has everything arrived?" Bill asked.

"Your equipment came two days ago, and I had it delivered to our camp in the mountains. What time do you want to leave tomorrow?"

"What would you suggest?" Bill asked.

"We need to get an early start to arrive at our destination before night falls on the third day. I recommend we leave at sunrise."

When the guide departed, Bill suggested to Rachael they meet for dinner.

"I'm famished," she said. "Do you have an idea where we should dine? If not, we could ask the concierge at the desk."

"I think it's best if we eat at the hotel dining room. It's not safe traveling around Tehran."

Always the careful one, she thought. Hotel food, ugh. She had hoped to enjoy a nice dinner in one of the fashionable restaurants in the capital. Of course, he was right. With him an American and her a Jew, it probably was a wise choice, but she would have chosen otherwise.

Rachael decided to take a hot bath. While the water was running, she heard the professor in the shower next door. Surprising how thin the walls between the rooms were in such an expensive hotel. An image of him naked flashed through her mind. She felt the physical yearning return. *Why wouldn't the man give her more attention as a woman?* Then she remembered that Jerome once said he fell in love the moment he heard her sing.

Bill heard Rachael next door. He listened, infatuated by the sound of her voice. How little he knew about her. He'd never heard her so much as hum a tune before tonight. Too bad she was so interested in Irad.

When Bill entered the dining room downstairs, Rachael could tell from his demeanor there was a crisis even before he spoke. Sitting down at the table, he broke the bad news to her.

"We have a problem.

"What kind of problem?"

"The money for the expedition has been frozen by the justice department."

"Why?"

"It has something to do with Henley."

"I never trusted that man. Was the money stolen?"

"I don't think so. It concerns the war on terrorism. They think Henley might be involved. I guess the money was frozen because it came from his company."

"Can we go forward with the dig?"

"Yes. We have enough to get started. Nevertheless, there's no way we can finish the project without more funds. In fact, I always knew the five-hundred thousand dollars from Henley's group wouldn't be sufficient to finish the excavation. I assumed they would give us the additional funds when the time came."

"Is there anyone else who might help?"

"There is one possibility."

"Who's that?"

"Jimmy Jones. He's a billionaire from Texas. Over the last few months, he's written me several letters. Then a month ago, he called. Jones wants to find the Ark of the Covenant. I told him I wasn't interested in that project, but Jones said he was willing to spend whatever it took to locate the Ark."

"That's not what our research is about."

The waiter brought them the menu. The choices were the same as one could find in any fine restaurant in Europe. Wine came with the meal. The hotel was exempted from the strict Islamic laws of the Republic since their guests were primarily westerners. Afterwards, Rachael hoped they would spend time in the club next door, but the professor said they should call it an evening since the guide expected them to leave early the next day. She was disappointed. If Irad were here, he would have taken her dancing.

The next morning before leaving the hotel, Bill sent a message to Jimmy Jones suggesting that if funds were made available for the excavation of Enoch he would consider committing to a search for the Ark of the Covenant.

The lead vehicle was a jeep driven by the guide with the Bill sitting in front and Rachael in the rear. A truck carrying the luggage and other supplies for the camp followed. The first two days of the trip would be on a paved road, but the third would be dirt, as they got closer to the Zagros Mountains.

The first night they stayed at a hotel near the highway. It was one Bahodore suggested. The second evening they set up camp beside the roadway where Bahodore built a fire and cooked some Joojeh, a chicken Kebab, which he served with hot spicy tea and dried dates. When they arose the third day, they could see the mountains in the distance through the light fog that would soon evaporate from the heat of the sun. These mountains extended over a thousand miles from the Turkish-Armenian border and then along the border with Iraq down to the Straits of Hormuz.

"We will be turning off the main road soon," said Bahodore, who was hunched over the campfire having a second cup of coffee.

"How long before we reach our base camp?" Bill asked.

"We should be at the village of Noqdi by late this afternoon. We will then go on to the base camp in the mountains if it's not too dark when we reach the village."

After traveling for two hours that morning, they turned off the main artery onto a gravel road that quickly became one of red clay, a substance brought down from the mountains and used as building material. They had traveled only a mile when a military roadblock stopped them. Bahodore got out and conversed on the side of the road with the captain in charge.

"There have been attacks in the area by rebels," Bahodore said, upon his return. "The military is in the midst of an anti-insurgent action in this area. The captain said if we continue our trip, we may be in danger."

"We've come too far to turn back now," Bill said.

Bahodore gave a hand signal to the driver of the truck, indicating that the convoy was going forward.

As the day progressed, the landscape in the valley they passed through was covered with numerous large walled gardens filled with family orchards that contained a variety of fruit trees. Later the road conditions deteriorated so that, by the time they reached a hill overlooking the village Nogdi, it had become not much more than a sheep trail.

Their plans to push on to the base camp before dark were change when a detachment of soldiers stopped them on the village outskirts.

"It seems that there is a government bureaucrat who wants to meet with you," Bahodore said, after conversing with them. "We must set up camp here for the night. The officer is sending one of his men into the village to let the official know we have arrived."

"Is there any place I could get a bath?" Rachael asked. "I'm filthy from eating dust on the road all day."

"Perhaps we could arrange for you to take one in town. I will see what I can do after we get the tents up and a meal prepared."

The local administrator, Arsham, was at the Mayor's house in Nogdi, sipping from a cup of spicy hot tea when he received the message. It was his job to keep an eye on them during the dig. Although his educational background was as an archaeologist, he had been a member of the Iranian intelligence service since the revolution. Someone high in the government had for some unexplained reason granted this American permission to conduct an archaeological dig near a secret nuclear project, which lay to the west of the proposed excavation. Was this about archaeology, or was there a more sinister motive? It was Arsham's intent to find out.

13

Thomas informed the unit of information Linda had disclosed and received permission to escort her to New Jersey. With a court order obtained by her attorney, they gained access to the safety deposit box. Inside was fifty thousand dollars and beneath it several correspondences written in a language that neither recognized. When they returned to New York, Linda turned the money over to her lawyer to put in the bank account for the estate. Thomas had the unit send the materials to their foreign language division for translation. The response was immediate. No known language corresponded with the material sent. Thomas forwarded it to the code-deciphering unit. A week later, Thomas received a report stating it wasn't written in a known code.

A few days after returning from New Jersey, Thomas arrived home one evening to find a message from Linda inviting him to dinner and stating with excitement that she had discovered something interesting.

What a difference Linda had made in his life. Even Betty commented on how he seemed more relaxed. If he were rich, he could keep Linda. But he wasn't, and that meant when he had served her purpose, she would shut him out. He had never been under any illusion it would be otherwise.

***

The assassin had no problem getting by the guard at the gate. He flashed a phony FBI badge and then listened for twenty minutes to the man's story about how he was a retired police officer. Unfortunately, for the guard, the assassin knew the retired officer would retain a visual recollection of him.

On the pleasant drive to the Mendel home, the assassin reminded himself that this assignment involved more than a murder. The Society wanted information. They now believed Samuel Mendel was more than just an interested investor in Henley's corporation. He might have also been a member of the League. If only the council had suspected it earlier, he could have tortured the man to obtain information before killing him.

When the assassin pulled into the driveway there was no car in sight. Perhaps no one was home. But as he approached the door, he could feel the eyes of someone watching. He pushed the doorbell. A few minutes went by as he waited impatiently. Finally, the door was opened by a small-framed woman whose clothes immediately told him she was the maid.

"Can I help you?"

"I'm here to see Mrs. Mendel."

"She's not home right now."

"When do you expect her?"

"She went shopping two hours ago. She shouldn't be long."

The assassin opened the inside portion of his jacket so a badge pinned inside could partially be seen.

"I'm with the FBI. May I come in and wait for her?"

That statement having been made, his hand pressed against the door, and the maid backed away.

"I'm sure it will be all right," she said, as he was stepping through the door. "Perhaps you should wait in the study."

"That would be fine."

"Please follow me," she said, then turned and walked down the hallway until she reached a room with double doors. When they entered the room, the maid walked over to a well-stocked bar.

"Could I fix you a drink while you wait?"

"Scotch."

As the maid handed him the drink, she noticed the ring on his finger with the symbol of a serpent.

"Please excuse me. I have some cleaning to finish."

She flipped a switch beside the door as she left, and soft music began to play from a speaker located somewhere in the ceiling.

As he sipped the expensive Scotch, the assassin strolled over to the window and gazed across the backyard to a river flowing in the distance. On days like this, he enjoyed his work. It was getting time, however, to move up to the next level. His pedigree was sufficient and his record unblemished. He knew at the next meeting a friend would put his name in nomination for the council. Suddenly, a reflection in the glass caught his attention. He instinctively sensed danger and turned. At the same time he pulled a pistol from his inside holster. The maid's stab, initially aimed at his back, caught him in the front shoulder instead. She grabbed the hand that held the pistol, but his strength was more than she could handle. He forced the barrel of the pistol to her chest and pulled the trigger. Her body quivered for a moment, then collapsed on the floor.

Blood gushed from the assassin's shoulder. He located a bathroom off the hallway that had a cabinet with a wide assortment of bandages. Removing his shirt, he cleaned his shoulder. Although bleeding profusely, it was only a flesh wound. The thick materials in his coat had prevented any serious damage. In a closet, he located a dress shirt and a fresh tie. When he looked presentable again, he went back into the study to inspect the body. The woman was around thirty years of age with middle-eastern physical characteristics. Why had the maid attacked him?

The assassin did a thorough examination of her body even to the point of removing her clothing. He found it. The symbol was small and almost hidden by the pubic hair. She was definitely a member of the League. He moved the body behind the sofa out of sight, but there was little that he could do to hide the blood on the rug. He cleaned it up as much as possible and rearranged the furniture to cover it.

The assassin was looking out the front window when the Mercedes pulled into the driveway. He knew from a picture in his possession it was Linda. He watched as she removed shopping bags from the car and then walked toward the door. He took a seat in the hallway. When she entered, he rose from the chair.

"I'm with the FBI. Your maid said it would be all right if I waited here.

He watched her relax.

"What can I do for you?" She placed the shopping bags down.

He walked nonchalantly toward her so as not to alarm.

"Just some questions concerning your husband's death," he said as he drew closer.

"I didn't know the FBI was involved."

Now he was only six feet away. "Let me show you some identification," he said reaching into his coat.

She noticed the bloodstain seeping through the front shoulder of her husband's favorite shirt. Even before she saw the pistol, Linda knew her maid was dead.

Linda wanted desperately to live. Offering him her body, she used every skill in her arsenal. If she could only delay him long enough, Thomas would come and rescue her.

She pleased him like no woman before ever had. Her sexual prowess surprised even him, a direct descendant of the *Serpent*, but, in the end, he knew she had to die. He was no fool. Everything the woman did was because she was terrified. As she lay exhausted on the floor, he tied her hands to a piece of heavy furniture in the corner of the study and went to his car to get the instruments. He returned and proceeded to torture her, trying to discover information she might have concerning the *League*. When it was over, he had obtained nothing but the pleasure of inflicting extreme physical pain. Linda had given him no information. He was confident it was because she had none to give. She had been like most of his victims. In the beginning, she had desperately wanted to live, but in the end, like the rest, she just begged him to kill her.

The phone rang in the study. The answering machine took the message. It was the detective, calling to say he was on the way over. The assassin knew the apartment location and assumed the detective called as he was leaving it. That meant he had approximately forty-five minutes to search the house for anything of interest and remove any incriminating evidence. That didn't allow much time. He collected his bloody shirt and wiped up the bloodstains in the house caused by his wound. Locating the maid's quarters, he ransacked it but found nothing useful. Returning to the study, he lit the gas fire logs. When they were sufficiently hot, he pulled from his tool packet a small branding iron with the symbol of a serpent upon a staff.

On the way over, Thomas was concerned. It wasn't like Linda not to answer her phone or return his messages. Where was the maid? It wasn't her day off. Then to make matters worse, it began to rain, which delayed him longer. Finally, he reached the exit lane and shortly thereafter saw the security gate in the distance. A familiar face appeared when he approached.

"Good evening, detective. Is Mrs. Mendel in trouble?"

"What do you mean?"

"An FBI agent came in here some time ago. Said he needed to talk to her. I gave him directions. He hasn't come out yet."

"Thanks for the information."

Why was the agent questioning Linda? Thomas put his foot down hard on the accelerator. Rounding a curve in the road, he was blinded for a moment by the bright lights of an oncoming car.

The guard saw the FBI agent's vehicle coming toward him. It stopped in front. Seeing the agent motioning for him to come to the car, the retired officer grabbed an umbrella and stepped from the protection of the guardhouse. When he reached the vehicle, the man put down the window. Suddenly a pistol was stuck in his face. Paralyzed with fear, his body didn't move until the first bullet passed through his brain.

The assassin opened his door and picked up the umbrella the guard dropped as he fell backward. Using it to shield himself from the rain, he walked over to the guardhouse and retrieved the clipboard that contained the list of vehicle license tags that entered the gate during the guard's shift. In case there was something else of importance in the guardhouse, he placed an incendiary device inside with a timer.

As Thomas stepped out of his car in the driveway, he heard the explosion and turned just in time to see the flash of light that followed. The incident with the car on the road ran through his mind. In a panic, he raced to the door and entered screaming Linda's name. When he reached the study, the door was ajar. The first thing he saw was Linda's body tied up in the corner of the room. Even from a distance, he knew she was dead. Moments later behind the sofa, he found the body of the maid. After calling the police, he went out into the backyard and vomited until there was nothing but a dry heave coming up.

The first person to arrive on the scene was Richard. He found Thomas in the backyard. "I happened to be on the interstate when the call came across my police radio. From the location and description given, I knew it was Linda."

"It's awful, Richard, just awful. The maid is dead, too. She was the lucky one, died instantly. Linda was tortured. Both have the symbol of a serpent branded on their bodies."

The sound of squealing tires told them that other police units were arriving.

"We'd better go inside. Are you up to giving the police a statement, Thomas?"

"Richard, I don't want this investigation turned over to some rookie."

"This is in my precinct. I'll make sure the investigation is assigned to me."

14

Rachael sat on the side of the slope overlooking the village of Noqdi. One building that stood out in the cluster of structures that lay in the small valley below was a two-story building with an Iranian flag flying overhead. She looked around and watched Bahodore and his servant finish erecting the tents, after which they proceeded to build a cooking fire. She looked back toward the village. Two vehicles were slowly winding their way up the mountain in their direction.

Pieces of goat were roasting over an open fire, and the rice and vegetables were almost ready when the vehicles arrived at the campsite. Bill left Bahodore and his servant at the fire and walked toward the expected guest.

The Iranian, stepping out of the jeep, had a certain air about him. A muscular man in his late fifties, one could tell by the way he carried himself that this was a person confident in his ability to carry out the will of the government.

"I am Arsham," he announced in English with a tone of arrogance in his voice.

Back at the fire, Bahodore eyed the official with suspicion. He knew the man had fallen out of favor with the leadership in Tehran and had been transferred to a position in this remote area. Bahodore had a personal reason to dislike him. The man had personally signed the order imprisoning his father after the Shah's regime was overthrown, and then he had seized the family's assets. Shortly thereafter, his mother died of heartbreak when his sister committed suicide following her rape by revolutionary guards. Overnight, Bahodore's world collapsed around him. His future bleak, he managed to become a guide for expeditions by foreigners to ancient sites in Iran. His work traveling around the country made him especially useful to his most important employer, American military intelligence. Recently, the pay had been particularly good as the intelligence community scrambled to monitor Iran's nuclear development.

The two men approached the fire.

"Bahodore, this is Minister Arsham. He is the local administrator for this area and will be responsible for observing the excavation for the government. Bahodore bowed in a subservient manner to the man and continued rubbing the sauce on the goat meat.

"Come, Mr. Minister, and join us for dinner," Bill said, then waved to get Rachael's attention. He motioned for her to come down and join them.

Arsham watched Rachael walking down the slopes toward the fire. He felt the lust beginning to rise within him. Three wives back in the village should have been enough. But it wasn't. His debauchery in the Tehran had kept him in trouble with the mullahs and led to his current assignment in his tribal area.

When Rachael was introduced to Arsham, she got the same feeling as when she first met Henley. It could be the way he leered at her. But she felt it was something deeper. Something she couldn't quite define with words.

The three sat at the table for a meal of young tender goat, subtly seasoned with turmeric that lay on a bed of Patna rice surrounded by vegetables. After the meal was finished, they indulged in a local brew Arsham brought from the village. In this region, the people ignored the prohibition against alcohol and continued to brew their local beverage made from fermented grain as they had for thousands of years.

"You know I was an archaeologist before the Revolution," Arsham said.

"Did you ever have an opportunity to research your people?" Bill asked.

"My tribe settled in this area of the mountains so long ago that their origin has been lost in time. However, I do know a great deal about the lore of the region because I grew up here. As a young man, my head was filled with village legends, none of which you will find in a textbook at the university. They say that Adam himself was created from the red clay of these hills. Even the experts agree man's first attempt at agriculture and domestication of animals began here. There is even a theory that the great flood stopped at the base of these very mountains."

Two hours later the home-brewed alcohol was consumed.

"I need to return to the village. Rachael, you should go with me. There's no point spending the night in a tent when you could sleep in a soft bed. I'm sure you feel the need to bathe after riding on that dusty road all day. My three wives will take good care of you. And if you are interested, I can show you an artifact that has been in my family for generations."

Rachael had some reservations, but she was tired, dirty and the alcohol had clouded her judgment. The promise of a bath and sleeping under clean sheets was too much of a temptation to turn down.

"How will I get back tomorrow?"

"The professor can pick you up on his way through town."

"Then I'll accept your offer."

Arsham stood up and motioned to the soldiers, sharing the campfire with Bahodore, that it was time to go.

In the village they were met at Arsham's front door by the house servant, a man so old he had lost all of his teeth. He immediately alerted the wives their husband was home and had brought a female guest.

This house had started as a simple structure but was added onto by each generation so that it now contained twelve rooms. Arsham had put his own mark on the home by constructing a large room on the front so that it now had a grand entrance. It was the most impressive private structure in the village. To furnish it, Arsham used funds he obtained from victims he tortured during the chaotic days of the revolt before the new regime restored order.

Arsham missed those days of looting and rape in Tehran. What he didn't miss was being an impoverished student at the university. In the end, he had his revenge on the teachers who had snubbed him. One of their granddaughters was now his wife. The old man had been only too willing to sacrifice her to save his own life.

Arsham introduced Rachael to his wives. Then barking orders to them like they were soldiers under his command, he sent them scurrying toward the rear of the house to prepare a bath for her. He motioned for Rachael to have a seat on one of the pillows in the room that surrounded a table. Once seated, the servant brought them tea and then disappeared. In a few minutes, he returned with a small golden box. He held it out for Arsham, who opened the lid, removed a stone figurine, and handed it to Rachael. It had the carvings of two serpents on a staff facing in opposite directions with their tails joined at the bottom.

"This is the item I was telling you about earlier," Arsham said. "This symbol of the serpent coiled on a staff was popular in the earliest cultures that developed in this part of the mountain chain. It probably adds credence to the theory that we are east of the Garden of Eden and that somewhere close to us is the Land of Nod and City of Enoch. Unfortunately, although this figurine has been in my family for a long time, we don't have a story that goes with it. I'm sure there was at one time, but it has been lost. Similar figures appeared in Mesopotamia over five thousand years ago. It could be argued that civilization actually started here and then descended down into the valley."

"Substantiating the theory that the Garden of Eden was destroyed by the flood, and the Land of Nod survived," Rachael interjected.

"I think that theory might be validated when the excavation begins," Arsham said.

One of the wives returned and announced the bath was ready. Rachael excused herself and followed the woman down the hallway and out of a side door to a crudely constructed building. Inside, a blazing fireplace served the dual purpose of providing warmth from the cold desert air, and at the same time for heating water. Once Rachael was in the tub, the woman disappeared. The hot water felt good. She scrubbed away the dirt and grime. Finished, she stepped out and walked over to the corner to get a towel that was hanging from a nail protruding from the wall. She felt the presence of someone watching her. She looked out of a small window but saw no one. A knock on the door startled her. It was the wife, who had brought her to the bath.

"Are you ready to go to the bedroom?" she asked.

Rachael was surprised she spoke English.

Seeing the look on Rachael's face, the woman said, "I am from Tehran. My grandfather was a professor at the university before the revolution. My birth name was Rebecca, but my husband has changed it to Ameneh."

Rachael started to speak, but the woman put a finger to her lips indicating that someone was listening. So she said nothing.

When they were back in the house, Rebecca led her to the bedroom. It was a large room with photographs of a family on vacation at a beach.

"Those are my parents with my brother and me on vacation on one of the islands near Athens. They were all killed during the revolution."

Looking closer, Rachael could see that it had been taken many years ago. Rebecca appeared to be about three years old at the time.

"Is this your room?"

"Yes, but I will sleep with one of the other wives tonight."

"Why don't you stay? I can sleep on that sofa in the corner."

"No, Arsham would be mad. He wants you to have the bedroom to yourself."

Then she leaned over and whispered in Rachael's ear, "If you don't want a visitor tonight, you had best find a way to secure the door."

She pointed to a chair in the corner of the room. "I only wish I had your options." Then, raising her voice, she said, "I will come and wake you tomorrow morning for breakfast."

Before leaving, Rebecca gave her a smile that contained within it a worried look.

Rachael checked to see if there was a lock on the door. Finding none, she took the wooden chair from the corner of the room and lodged it firmly under the doorknob. Checking the two windows in the room, she found them secured. She lay down and drifted off as soon as she closed her eyes.

In the middle of the night, someone trying to push open the door awakened Rachael. She jumped to her feet but there was no danger. The chair was made of solid wood just like the door. No one was going to gain admittance from the outside. Whoever it was finally gave up. She could hear a pair of heavy boots walking away. The faint odor of cheap alcohol drifted through the door. It smelled like the homemade brew that they drank earlier at the camp. A short time later, feeling secure, Rachael went back to sleep.

Rachael was awakened the next morning by a knock on the door. She was relieved to hear the sweet voice of Rebecca on the other side.

"We are having breakfast in the courtyard. Arsham has already left the house. There was an attack by insurgents on a military outpost near here early this morning, and he has taken soldiers to investigate."

Rachael was glad he was gone. What was it with men anyway? For the rest of the expedition she intended to wear baggy work clothes so no one would even notice she was a woman.

15

Thomas opened the letter from Bill. The expedition had arrived in the Zagros Mountains, and for the foreseeable future, mail would be the only way to communicate since there was no phone service at the base camp and no cell towers, or electricity.

Betty stuck her head in the door. "The lab just called. Said they found something interesting during the autopsy. I told them you'd be over right away."

On the way to the lab, Thomas called Richard.

"I'll meet you there," his former partner said.

Richard knew his friend needed him for support. It was going to be traumatic just being in the same area where Linda's beautiful body had just been dissected like a piece of beef. Luckily, they didn't actually have to go into the forensic pathology/autopsy room to speak with the medical examiner. The man was in his office on a lunch break when they arrived.

"Detectives, come in and have a seat. If you don't mind, we can talk while I finish lunch. Hate to do this, but we are running three weeks behind in performing autopsies."

"We're here on the Linda Mendel case," Richard said.

"That's right. I had my office call you. Just one moment please."

Turning his swivel chair around to the filing cabinet, he retrieved Linda's file.

"Let's see. Yes, we removed this from her stomach." He held up a small key. "She must have swallowed it before the torture began."

He handed the key to Richard and pushed the folder toward them.

"If one of you will just sign a receipt on the inside of this folder that will be sufficient."

While Richard was executing the receipt, Thomas asked about the DNA results.

"There was skin under her fingernails and semen in every entrance to her body. It's not often we have such a quantity for a test. Of course, any amount is sufficient."

He looked at a stack of mail on his desk.

"I see the report on the results came in. Haven't had a chance to read it yet."

Tearing the seal on the envelope, he looked at the contents inside.

"Very interesting. Yes, this is very interesting indeed. This lab used the newest testing procedure–much more informative than the usual test. But, this report doesn't make sense. I guess that's why I'm not a detective, and you boys are."

"What doesn't make sense?" Thomas asked.

"The report on the blood of the suspect found at the crime scene. It says the blood contained material not from any known species. Well, that's not exactly what it says. Some of the genetic material cannot be traced to any specific group."

"What does that mean in laymen terms?"

"I'm not exactly sure. It's not my field of expertise."

When they left, the two detectives went to Mingos. Thomas hardly touched his food.

"You know Linda had more in her core being than I would have given her credit for," Thomas said. "She obviously collected skin from his back in such a manner that he never realized it."

"She wanted us to catch that son of a bitch," Richard said. She wanted it real bad. In the end, she had a lot of guts."

"Yes, and even with the torture, she never gave up the key, determined that she was going to beat him at his own game."

Taking the key out of the envelope, Richard examined it carefully.

"It's to a safety deposit box."

***

The Leader was not pleased with The Society's top assassin. He gathered no new evidence in the Mendel matter and left a trail in the process. By monitoring police radios calls, he knew about the lab report. It probably would lead the police to a dead end. But The Society didn't want to stir public curiosity, remembering what happened in France when the body of one of their own ended up in a murder investigation. They were able to cover themselves, but the next time they might not be so lucky.

The assassin had let the tart outwit him by swallowing the key. That item might have led to useful information about the League. Maybe the woman's use of sex had clouded the assassin's judgment. The medication the members used didn't always reduce their sex drive to a normal level. This abnormal drive was a trait passed down in their genes from their common ancestry. Sometimes it was a blessing and at other times a curse. But that was how it had been since the beginning.

Things were changing and the pressure of being leader grew more stressful every year. Police techniques were getting sophisticated, and their cooperation across national boundaries meant The Society had to strive harder to preserve its secrets. It was time to stop placing the seal of the serpent upon their victims. In today's world, it was helping the police connect the dots. The Leader had placed the issue on the agenda for the next meeting. There would be opposition from the traditionalists in the group, but that was always the case when change was suggested. Over the years, the members had dropped other customs. They discontinued the practice of having the symbol placed upon their forehead after the catastrophe at Enoch, when their members were hunted down and killed like animals by the descendants of Seth. Cain's tribe had since started placing the symbol on their chest and in recent times in less conspicuous places. At least the present practice of tattooing in the world meant it drew less attention.

The Leader was looking forward to this evening. He was meeting Marilyn in the park. It wasn't often that he went out in public. His seven-foot frame drew too much attention. That's why he took his meals indoors and only dealt with members of The Society and their underlings.

The Leader's position was not hereditary. The Council of Twelve elected from their group a leader for life. He guided its everyday activities, and the council met on occasion to review his actions. The organization operated this way since its inception eons ago. On rare occasions, a leader who fell out of favor had been eliminated. The Leader never lost sight of the fact that ultimately power lay with the council.

***

Thomas and Richard studied the contents of the box. It contained a passport and driver's license from Yemen for a Saba Aden. The photographs on these items were of Sam Mendel. There were several other pieces of material: a map of an unknown place with writing on it in a foreign language, and a small booklet, which contained writing of an unknown origin. Embedded on the front of the booklet was a strange symbol, which appeared to be a garden with a flaming sword in front. Thomas knew the terrorism unit would be particularly interested in these documents in light of the fact that they involved Yemen, a training ground for terrorists.

After they parted, Thomas drove to unit headquarters. It was important to have their experts review this material. It should give him a lead on Samuel Mendel's identity and the reason for the entire charade. As he passed a park, he saw Marilyn walking into it from a side street. She was in the company of an unusually large man. He circled the block with the blue light flashing on his car. There were no parking spaces available, and he couldn't leave his car in the middle of the narrow street. Finally, he was able to find a spot three blocks away. When he reached the park, Marilyn and the man were gone. He spent considerable time checking the side streets and shops but to no avail.

The surveillance on Marilyn's place had been discontinued, and the few items from her apartment were in police storage. Both Richard and he had wrongfully assumed the woman was dead. He called Richard who offered to have officers canvass the neighborhood with a sketch of her.

The Leader saw the blue light and took the precaution of disappearing from the park onto a side street where Marilyn's new apartment was located. There was no reason to suspect the person in the police vehicle had any particular interest in them. But just in case, he would have the police communication from this precinct monitored.

When the couple arrived back at the apartment, Marilyn warmed up a snack in the microwave oven, then went to take a shower. He knew from experience it would take some time. While waiting, he opened his brief case and withdrew a sealed envelope received just as he was leaving to meet Marilyn. It was from Henley. He was in Nodqi posing as a rug merchant and monitoring the professor. The correspondence reminded him there needed to be action on the Fullmore matter. From his sources, he knew this man was in the process of trying to decipher the inscription on the staff. He had to be stopped.

The recovered staff was now in a vault at the university in Jerusalem. It had been within The Society's grasp earlier, but events intervened, and Irad let the opportunity slip out of his hands. Now the Jewish girl had it in a safe place. Recovery of the Staff of Cain had been on the priority list of the organization since its disappearance after the calamity at Enoch. Once they had it, they would be able to focus more attention on the Ark of the Covenant. The Leader knew the clues to the Ark's whereabouts were getting stronger each day. Once it was in their possession, certainly the *Serpent* would return to claim his own. Though the members prayed for his return for thousands of years, there had been no sighting of him since the destruction of Enoch. Surely, he would be pleased if they had the Ark, which held a spirit of God. Perhaps it would entice him to make his presence known to the faithful.

Marilyn came into the room. The succulent fruit could be seen through the thin material of her negligee. She walked over to him. He reached up with one hand and touched her. The sound of a pleasant moan came from her lips causing his animal instinct to rise. She reached down and took his other hand, pressing it against the softness that lay between her thighs. Passion rose within him like a torrent of water flowing with an unspeakable force. He rose from his chair.

"It is time," he said.

They went to a small room in the back of the apartment that had been turned into a chapel. Getting on their knees before the large stone statute with the heads of serpents facing in opposite directions, they began to recite their prayer to the Serpent.

"Almighty One, who came to the Garden of Eden and planted thy seed within the womb of God's creature, thereby multiplying the fruit of thy loins and spreading thy descendents across the face of the earth, hear our prayer and return to us, those who have followed thy course of evil, oh root from whence we sprang."

16

Fullmore was in hiding. He didn't know where to go or whom to trust. It had been several days since his narrow escape from death. The stranger appeared at his place early one morning just as the sun was beginning to rise. Fullmore saw him through the cracks of the loft in the barn where he spent the night, as he frequently did when he was involved with a project. The man stepped out of his Mercedes and went straight to the front door of the house. When no one responded to his knock, he pulled a gun from his coat and forcibly entered. Fullmore had seen too many Godfather movies not to realize this was a contract killer.

Scrambling down the ladder, Fulmore quickly put several disks into a backpack. Then he deleted the information from his computer before smashing it with an axe. As a last precaution, he placed a bale of hay on top of the computer and set it on fire before he slipped through the back door of the barn and fled into the woods nearby.

Fullmore knew killing the stranger would be his only hope. He would have to put his skills to good use if he were to survive the man who was stalking him. He was a born hunter. Since childhood, a firearm and skinning knife had been his constant companion. Unfortunately, the firearm was in the house, but he had the knife. Now for the first time in his life, he had become the prey instead of the predator.

The man followed the footprints in the mud from the barn into the woods until they disappeared in the overgrown brush. After that, he pursued his prey by the sounds that always seemed to be just a few yards ahead of him. As he did, he went deeper into the swamp. He felt out of his element. He was city born and bred. The only experiences he had in the woods were those that lay within the boundaries of a park. The assassin had told him this would be an easy kill–a black man living on a farm in a rural area. His orders were to kill him and secure any information that existed on the staff. Seizing the computer would have been logical. Now a fire had destroyed it.

Fullmore watched from a distance. When the man stepped close to a thicket where he was hiding, one quick movement through the brush and the knife in his hand felt the softness of the man's belly. As quickly as it entered, the knife was withdrawn. The man looked down in shock at the blood gushing from his wound. Recovering from the surprise attack, he unloaded his automatic into the thicket from where the knife had appeared. It was too late. Fullmore was already yards from the thicket on his way to pick up the backpack he had hidden. The man managed to retain consciousness until he got to his car. He called his contact before passing out on the front seat.

The Noba sent an agent. Once he ascertained the man in the car was dead, he went down to the barn. The computer had been destroyed, but a sprinkler system had put the fire out before it damaged the structure. An inspection of the premises failed to turn up anything of interest. He called his superior who sent help to dispose of the body.

When the Greyhound bus stopped beside the road, Fullmore had just enough money in his pocket to purchase a ticket to the next town where his friend, Rufus Shackle, lived. They shared the same interest. Both were computer freaks. Fullmore's friend would provide a safe haven until he could decide his next step. Somehow he must get in touch with the professor.

Henry Weston heard his wife call from downstairs. He could tell by the sound of her voice that she was in distress. When he got to the front door, a black man was standing there.

"He says it is important that he speak to you. Wouldn't give me his name nor say what it's about." She seemed exasperated by the situation.

"It's all right, honey. Why don't you go back into the kitchen and see what Zillah is preparing for supper. Tell her to bring ice tea to the study."

"What did you say your name was?

'I didn't say."

When they were seated in the study Fullmore started to speak but stopped when the housekeeper came in. She seemed a little slow in leaving the room.

"That will be all, Zillah," Henry finally said.

When the door closed, the man turned to Henry. "I need to get in touch with your son."

"That's impossible. He's in the mountains of Iran, and there's no telephone communication with him at the base camp."

A moment of silence seemed to last forever. Then Henry spoke. "Sir, if I am going to be of any help, you must give me your name, and disclose why it's so urgent that you get in touch with my son."

For a moment, the man looked at Henry without saying a word. It was obvious he was trying to decide what to do. Finally, he spoke.

"I'm Ronald Fullmore."

"You're the one decoding the inscription on the staff."

The man looked relieved.

"I'm glad to hear you know about that. Now I feel comfortable telling you what has happened."

He told him of his flight. Henry sat enthralled by the story. Then Henry's eyes grew even wider when Fullmore said he had decoded the inscription on the staff.

"How?"

"The software I've been working on has been perfected."

"You mean you can now decode ancient language with a computer software program?"

"Yes."

"I know Billy will be excited to hear this."

Henry rented Fullmore a motel room on the edge of town and gave him cash to tide him over for a few days. The next obstacle to overcome was arranging for Fullmore to accompany him to Iran. Henry had long ago made reservations to fly to Jordan where Dr. Rabon would join him for their flight to Iran. Now he had to use his connections in the Pentagon to get Fullmore on that plane.

It took two meetings before Fullmore developed a level of trust in Henry sufficient to disclose what he had discovered about the staff. Henry sat back in amazement one day, when Fullmore put a disk into the notebook computer that Henry provided and let him peer over his shoulder as he translated the ancient language from the staff.

"Let all who see this Staff know that I am Cain, leader of the people of the Serpent and son of Eve and the Mighty One, who rules the world of darkness. I am the slayer of Abel and the builder of the great City of Enoch to which I have gathered the gold and precious stones of the world. My enemies, the Children of the Lord, fear me and run from my presence."

"Let me show you the enhanced picture of the map on the staff they sent me from the university in Jerusalem. The infrared equipment brought out the markings."

He put another disk in the computer. Henry listened with interest as Fullmore explained the map and its notations.

"If you look closely, you'll see that this is the Land of Nod. It lies in the Zagros Mountains."

"That's where Billy is now."

Henry was excited the map his son found in the basement of the library of Timbuktu was authentic.

"What we now call the Babylonian Plains is marked as the Land of the Children of the Lord."

"Yes, I see it," Henry said studying the map on the computer.

"Is that Yemen down on the end?"

"The notation calls it the Land of Frankincense and Myrrh."

"Very interesting that these three places are connected on this map. I wonder what this could mean?" Henry asked.

"Perhaps there was trade between the three."

"Or they were the three centers of civilization," Henry responded.

17

Irad had finally arrived yesterday. He told Bill that Arsham had detained him in Noqdi for several hours. Despite the minister of archaeology's promise that their excavation would be unfettered, Bill saw this as another example of interference by the government. Just two days ago, Arsham had placed four soldiers at the camp on a permanent basis. He said it was for their protection from the rebels, but Bill thought it was more likely they were there to spy on the expedition.

The morning after Irad arrival, Bill slipped from his cot and walked to the entrance of the tent. The sun was rising, and as the light spread across the valley, he could make out below the faint images of buildings in Noqdi and the orchards surrounding it. Shivering in the early morning air, he stepped over to a nearby fire where Bahodore was making coffee.

"The others will be stirring soon," Bahodore said as he handed Bill a cup. "I have received a report. We should leave tonight while the others are asleep. It may be our only opportunity to get the information you seek."

"Have all the arrangements been made?"

"Yes."

Irad, standing in front of his tent, saw Bill and Bahodore talking. He decided it was time to join them at the campfire.

"Good morning," Bill said when Irad approached.

"What time will we get started?"

"As soon as Rachael is ready. I don't think she's up yet."

Irad wasn't surprised. After the others had gone to bed, he and Rachael stayed up and killed a couple of bottles of wine. It is just a matter of time before she yielded, he thought. It was true that her resistance had been stronger than with the others, but, in the end, he would have her and not by resorting to drugs like Henley.

Bahodore left the two men and went over to where his assistant was preparing breakfast for the camp.

"How is the excavation going?" Irad asked.

"Our progress has been slow," Bill said. "We have ten laborers but they've been working only four hours a day. In that short time, they produce more material than Rachael and I could possibly examine. It's good that you're here to help. It should speed things up. Of course, when the others arrive at the end of the week, we will be able to move things even faster. With the plateau less than a mile wide, we'll find what we're looking for soon."

Laughter from behind interrupted their conversation.

"You aren't giving away any secrets, are you, Professor?"

They turned to see Rachael's smiling face. Bill was glad to hear her laugh. She seemed to be despondent around him lately. He assumed it was because she missed Irad. The smile on her face left him without any doubt his analysis was correct. He felt a sense of regret. Perhaps if only he had approached Rachael earlier.

"Let's see if breakfast is ready," she said. "I'm famished."

Even in the ugly work clothes she wore, Bill found her attractive. Was she sleeping with Irad yet? Of course, she would be. How foolish to hope otherwise.

After eating, the three climbed into the jeep and drove to the site. The entrance was just a hole in the ground eighteen feet deep and six feet wide. Inside, a timber framework had been built on the sides of the tunnel to prevent a cave-in. Taking flashlights, they climbed down a wooden ladder attached to one side of the framework.

"We haven't uncovered anything that's ancient, but we've noticed something interesting. At this depth, the soil changes to a layer of ash several inches thick. There's no way to know at this point whether it was produced by nature or by the hand of man."

"Professor, perhaps this substantiates those legends," Irad said.

"You mean the one about a catastrophe?" Rachael asked.

"Yes."

As they walked through the confined space, the elevation descended and the temperature began to drop. Near the end, the tunnel took a sharp right.

"We couldn't go in a straight line any farther," Bill said. "See this massive white stone? It blocked our way, so we changed directions to run the tunnel parallel to it.

When they emerged, the rays of the sun had already increased in intensity, and the workers with their tools and buckets were standing around the entrance waiting to start the day.

"Let's go to the pile of debris and start sifting," Bill said.

This was the most laborious part of the job for any archaeologist. In sifting through the dirt, they were looking for anything that would verify an ancient city had once been located here. So far, no artifacts had been discovered, but Bill wasn't discouraged. The dig was in the early stages.

A mile from their tents, up a long narrow path, a small waterfall flowed into a depression in the rocks before it ran down the mountain toward the village. It was the spot where Rachael bathed every day. The water was cool, and the basin was deep. The surrounding rocks and vegetation hid it from prying eyes. She discovered it one afternoon while exploring the area. When everyone else was bathing in the afternoon in the makeshift shower, she would slip off to her own private pond. Afterwards, she would lie out on a large flat rock and let the rays of the sun dry her deeply tanned body.

Rachael slipped out of the back flap of her tent and soon was on her way up the mountain to the basin unobserved, or so she thought. It was unusually hot and seemed to take forever to reach her destination. When she arrived, she stripped and dove into the pool of water.

The water level was dropping a few inches each day because of a local drought. Today one end of the pond was especially shallow. As Rachael swam there, her eye caught a glimpse of something not natural to the terrain. Reaching down she picked up the object. In her hand was a broken water jug. After she washed the mud off, a figure of a snake with an inscription beneath appeared on the surface of the pottery.

Hidden behind a boulder, Irad watched. He saw her come out of the water clutching something. He gave only a passing thought to what might be in her hand.

His eyes were riveted to the naked bronze body. Rachael looked in his direction. He froze, afraid to move. Apparently, she hadn't seen him because she climbed onto the flat rock and lay on her back as she continued to study the item she still held. As she dressed a few minutes later, Irad slipped away.

There was excitement when Rachael returned. Everyone gathered around the table where the broken vessel lay. No one recognized the language of the inscription until Bill retrieved from his bag a sketch of the writings on the staff. It was the same language. This had a tremendous impact on everyone. It seemed to confirm that Enoch lay close by.

"The basin of water where you discovered this item probably served as a water source for the city," Bill speculated.

The next morning the camp rose early. Even the common laborers were infected by the turn of events. Bill announced his plans for the day.

"As much as I'd like to visit the basin, the dig must have priority. Rachael, I want you and Irad to spend today up there and see what you can find. The camp cook will pack you a lunch so you don't waste time coming back to eat."

Rachael wondered if he noticed the disappointment on her face. She had hoped the two of them would go together and share in the joy of her find.

As the sun broke through the clouds, Rachael and Irad set off on their journey. They stopped for a few minutes to rest. When they started again, Irad took the lead and turned right on a path that led up the mountain toward the water. She expressed surprise that he knew the way.

"Look at the footprints," he said pointing to her boot marks from the day before. "I don't have a mysterious sense of direction. You left a clear trail that anyone could follow."

When they arrived, the two unpacked the items they had brought and placed them on the flat rock. Both had worn shorts since the initial search would be in the water. Rachael dove in while Irad was removing his shirt. In a minute, he joined her. They searched but didn't locate any man-made objects. Tired, they climbed up on the rock and stretched out to rest before having lunch.

Bill was suffering, and it wasn't just from the heat. Rachael and Irad alone at the basin bothered him more than he would admit. Every time the thought of her popped into his mind, he would push it out. There were other things that required his attention. Any private life he might desire would have to wait. Sacrifices had to be made for the greater public good. He learned that during the Panamanian campaign.

After lunch, Irad and Rachael searched again but they again came up empty handed. On the way back to the flat rock, Irad, without warning, pulled her to him. As their lips met, his body pressed hard against her. Wet clothing made it feel as if there was nothing between them.

Rachael realized her breathing was now coming in short breaths. He was whispering in her ear, saying all the things a woman wants to hear. She felt dizzy, as if she were losing control, something she had never felt with Jerome. She knew, if she let go, it would give her instant satisfaction but destroy the one thing she wanted most. And he was back in camp. At the last moment, she tore herself away.

"No," she said in a weak voice.

He approached again. This time her voice was stronger.

"I said no, Irad. I like you, but I'm in love with the professor."

Irad was dumbstruck for a moment. He had never suspected. Immediately he fell into role-playing, placing a mask over his true feelings. Irad said he had misread her desires. Inside, he had entirely different state of mind. He would have her and when he was finished—His thoughts were interrupted by a voice nearby.

"The professor needs you back at camp."

It was Bahodore.

"Someone has arrived from America," Bahodore said. "A man named Jimmy Jones."

18

A self-made billionaire from Texas, who made his wealth from oil, Jimmy Jones stood six feet and weighed three hundred pounds. Now, in the twilight of his life, Jimmy was devoting the same amount of energy to the occult that he had once used to make money. His interests varied from investing in quacks, who were trying to find the Fountain of Youth to seeking objects that might possess extraordinary power. His most recent quest was to find the Ark of the Covenant. He had become convinced the Ark existed and that Dr. William Weston was the man who could find it. Despite his offer of a large sum of money to finance the project, Professor Weston had shown no interest in his proposal until recently. The arrival of a correspondence three weeks ago indicated the man had a change of heart. Apparently, he was desperately short of funds to complete his excavation in the Zagros Mountains.

It was a simple matter for Jimmy Jones to arrange the trip to Iran. He found out long ago that money could open doors closed to the less fortunate in the world. A cash payment to a man who held a high position in the Iranian government was all it took to smooth the way for his trip.

When Rachael and Irad arrived at camp, they found Bill seated at a table talking to their recently arrived guest in a large newly erected tent that had all the conveniences of the modern world.

"Jimmy, I'd like you to meet two valuable members of the expedition. This is Rachael Goldstein, an expert in dead languages, and Irad Lamech, an aspiring archaeologist."

"This is the first time I've felt air-conditioning since our night in Tehran," Rachael said.

"I try to carry the comforts of home with me wherever I go. Actually, a company I own makes this. The tent comes with its own battery-powered generator and all the accessories you see here. Like a commercial once said, "don't leave home without it.""

The tent did indeed have everything–from a shower to a miniature battery operated stove. In addition,

Jimmy brought his chef. That evening he invited them to dine with him. They looked forward to it. Although they had been at the base camp only a short time, they missed the comforts of western civilization.

That evening dining on steak, shrimp and fine wine would have been perfect if Arsham had not made an unexpected appearance and invited himself to dinner.

"Would you tell me about the jug that your assistant found at the water basin?" Arsham asked. "I understand that it had writing on it in the same language as the staff."

Bill raised his eyebrows, surprised that Arsham knew this information.

Jimmy watched as Bill tried unsuccessfully to dodge this bureaucrat's questions. Perhaps I should have made arrangements to pay this man a bribe, Jimmy thought. But he was so far down on the food chain I didn't think it necessary.

"I see you have your sources of information," Bill responded. "What you've said is true. We can't decipher the writing, but it does add credence to my theory that this is the location of Enoch."

"When do you think you will decipher it? Certainly with your able assistant here, it is not an impossible task."

Arsham looked over at Rachael. She saw the expression in his eyes. He might actually be interested in the artifact she found, but at this moment his thoughts were on something of a more personal nature. Her skin crawl just knowing what that might be.

On the way back to the village, Arsham was filled with the same insecurities he felt as a child. The luxury of the tent, the rich American and the two trucks he had brought to supply his needs reminded Arsham of the discrimination he suffered until the revolution. Then he remembered what he had learned that morning. The man, Henley, had given him a reason to feel a source of pride. Disclosing to him for the first time that he came from an ancient bloodline. One older than Iran's ruling class or their religion. He was a descendant of Cain. Thoughts of this made the insecurities begin to dissipate.

After the others left the tent, Bill stayed behind to discuss his need for funds. The fact that his superior in Washington managed to lift the freeze on the remaining one hundred thousand dollars from Henley's group did not mean he had sufficient resources to complete the project without Jimmy's money.

The temperature dropped when the sun went down so Jimmy had a table placed beside the fire. The butane gas gave off a beautiful blue light and another tank nearby kept the insects away so the night could be enjoyed. Sitting there, Jimmy told Bill about his dream of finding the Ark.

"I'm Southern Baptist by background. After childhood, I quit going to church, thinking that religion was for weak people who needed a crutch to get them through life. I've accumulated wealth and enjoyed the pleasures of the flesh all over the world. I've been divorced three times. There isn't presently a Mrs. Jones, and with my prostate cancer, I don't think there will be another one. There aren't children to leave my wealth to. Now that I'm getting near to the end of the road, I need new challenges. I also want to get close to God. Find out the meaning of life. What can I say? I'm an old fool grabbing at straws."

Bill couldn't help but feel sorry for the man. He had spent his life collecting treasures on earth that he couldn't take to the afterlife. He was a typical American, making the accumulation of material things the center of his existence and leaving spiritual matters out until the very end. At least he realized it. Most people didn't until they were on their deathbed about to meet judgment.

"I had a real smart professor from the School of Divinity at Harvard working on this for me," Jimmy said. "He was hired because I was impressed with the book he wrote on the Ark. Perhaps you've heard of him. His name was Dr. Harvey Simons. He came from a long line of New England aristocracy. Didn't believe in God. Surprising too, him being a Doctor of Religion and all that. I once asked him about it. He said it was an academic thing for him, just loved the history of it."

"I recognize his name. Wasn't he murdered?"

"Yes. The day after he called and told me he had uncovered some interesting information. He didn't want to talk about it on the phone. I sent my private jet to pick him up that weekend. Of course, he was murdered before it arrived. I have his book in the tent. I'll get it for you before we retire for the night. I know this is an area in which you are well versed, but maybe there's some information in it that could be useful when you start to work for me."

Bill could see that Jimmy was a man that liked to control things and was used to getting his way.

"I haven't committed yet to take on the project you have in mind."

"Okay, let's talk about that now. What will it take? Name your price."

"You understand that I don't necessarily believe the Ark exists."

"Do you believe it ever existed?"

"I believe in a literal interpretation of the Bible."

"Then you must believe that a spirit of God dwelt in the Ark and actually spoke from it to Moses and a few chosen ones."

"Yes, that's certainly true. The scriptures clearly state that."

"That's all I need to know. If the ark once existed with a spirit of God within it, then it may still exist. If it does, with your help I intend to find it."

Back at his tent, Bill lit the kerosene lamp beside his cot. He put an extra pillow under his head so he would be comfortable reading the book Jimmy gave him. When it was published, the newspapers sung the praises of the author, emphasizing their belief that he brought new information to the mystery of the missing Ark. Bill remembered some of his colleagues laughing about the book at a seminar shortly after its publication. The word in academic circles was that it was nothing but a rehash of legends, which had been around for centuries. Professor Simons had initially only published it because Harvard had a rule with its department heads, publish or perish. Apparently, the author was surprised when it made the bestseller list. There was even talk about a movie. That ended with the man's death. The entity that purchased the rights to the book from the estate refused the plea for another printing or a release for a movie.

"The story of the Ark of the Covenant starts in the book of Exodus, which is recognized by both the Jewish and the Christian faiths as an accurate and divinely inspired text. Within the Ark, according to these scriptures, were the Ten Commandments, a golden bowl containing a sample of the Manna sent from heaven to feed the people of God during their march from Egypt, and the rod of Aaron.

A Spirit of God was present upon the lid of the Ark, and from it the spirit spoke to Moses and the Priests of Israel. As they moved toward their destination, the Ark was carried by the Levites, persons chosen to be caretakers of the temple. It was eventually placed in a permanent structure when Solomon built a great temple at Jerusalem. The Ark disappeared from the pages of history between the reign of King Solomon and the destruction of the great temple by the Babylonian Empire. The last biblical mention of Israel having physical possession of it is in Second Chronicles. It has been lost for over three thousand years. There are many theories on what happened. For the sake of the reader, the list below states a few of the theories that exist.

- *The Ark is taken by Menelik, to the kingdom of Ethiopia.*
- *A group of Jewish Priests, unhappy with the pagan worship of their king, secretly take the Ark to Elephantine Island in Egypt.*

- *The Ark is hidden in a tunnel beneath the rock where Solomon's temple once stood.*
- *The Ark is in Heaven according to Revelations.*
- *There is a secret brotherhood, composed of descendants of the high priest that hid the Ark. They will bring forth the Ark and return it to its rightful place when the temple is rebuilt."*

Working in the heat of the day had taken its toll. Bill's eyelids became heavy, and he drifted off to sleep. The next morning he was awakened by Rachael's hand on his shoulder shaking him.

"Are you going to sleep all morning?" She handed him a cup of steaming hot coffee.

He sat up in the cot. "What time is it?"

"Seven-thirty."

"Between working in the heat yesterday and the late-night drink with our rich guest, I overslept."

Through his sleepy eyes, he could see that she was smiling.

"You seem to be in good spirits today."

"Jimmy has been up since five. He's insistent that we take him to the basin. Irad has agreed to supervise the dig while we're gone."

He was surprised that she hadn't suggested that Irad be the one to join her and Jimmy for the excursion.

"I really do want to see where you discovered that artifact."

"Well, you better get moving. That old man is getting impatient."

Bill watched as she left the tent. That was the happiest he'd seen her in a long time.

The trip took longer than it should have because Jimmy frequently needed to stop and rest. The old man had with him two of his people who were equipped with shovels and a treasure detector. He said the detector would find any metal objects buried less than six feet deep.

When they reached the water basin, Jimmy and his crew disappeared from sight searching for treasure with their detector. Bill went behind some boulders and changed into a pair of long shorts. Meanwhile, Rachael dove into the water. She immediately realized it had dropped another eighteen inches since yesterday.

Looking up, Rachael saw the professor standing on the flat rock watching her. It was only a short distance from where she was standing in the water. She couldn't believe that he was wearing a tee shirt. And why was he wearing those long shorts? What a geek. At least he was solidly built. She waited for him to join her, but he kept staring at something in the water nearby.

"Over to your right about three yards. There's a shadow."

She saw something jutting out of the side of the bank just beneath the waterline.

Bill dove in. With a few strokes, he was by her side. Together they went to investigate. She reached down and, after tugging with both hands, dislodged a water jug smaller then the first one. He helped her clean it. Writing appeared beneath a symbol. The same type of writing that was on the other artifact. But they both realized immediately, the symbols were different. Taking it back to the rock, they examined it closely in the bright sunlight.

"What do you think it is?" Rachael asked.

"You see what's on the right and left side?"

"Trees, I think."

"Yes, and there's vegetation in between."

"It's a garden," Rachael said.

"I believe you're right. Perhaps it symbolizes the Garden of Eden, the Tree of Life, and the Tree of Knowledge."

"Do you really think so?"

"I have the right to speculate as much as anyone, don't I?" Bill said laughing.

The find had so excited them that the next two hours were spent in the water looking for additional artifacts, but their search was fruitless. Climbing back onto the rock, Rachael opened the knapsack that Bahodore packed. Not being a good Muslim, he had included a bottle of wine with the sandwiches. The wine was from the provisions that Jimmy brought.

When Bill and Rachael finished lunch, they stretched out so the rays of the sun could dry their wet clothes. They were only two feet apart. He felt the urge to reach over and kiss her. What would be her reaction if he did?

"Do you and Irad have any permanent plans for the future?"

Rachael startled by the question, asked, "What do you mean?"

"I hate to pry, but you seem to be hitting it off so well with Irad, I thought maybe there was a wedding for me to attend in the near future."

Exasperated, she sat up.

"You have misinterpreted everything. I've never been interested in him romantically. In fact, he got fresh with me yesterday. I made it clear that I wasn't interested in any type of intimate relationship, permanent or otherwise."

The words struck Bill like a thunderbolt.

"Hello," cried a voice from the other side of the basin.

It was Jimmy, holding something in his hand and waving wildly.

19

The camp stirred when the party returned with another jug and a coin Jimmy had found. Even the common laborers gathered around the table were excited to examine the items.

The coin was the size of an American fifty-cent piece. On the front was the image of a man, but what was more interesting was the backside, which had the identical symbol as the jug: two trees in a garden.

Jimmy had enjoyed his visit. Finding the coin was the icing on the cake. He wanted to stay longer, but his plane was scheduled to leave tomorrow. That evening when the two trucks pulled out, Bill and Rachael watched until they disappeared into the sunset.

"You know, I'm going to miss him," Rachael said.

"And his air-conditioned tent."

They laughed, then turned and went to join Irad for dinner.

Later that night, Bill was sitting on his cot reading when Rachael stuck her head through the open flap of the tent.

"Mind if I come in?"

"You couldn't sleep either?" Bill asked.

"No, I'm afraid that today's excitement has my adrenalin flowing."

"Mine, too. That's why I'm reading."

"What's that?"

"A book Jimmy gave me on the lost Ark."

"Did you agree to help him find it?"

"I'm afraid I did."

"On what terms?"

"That he fund the completion of this dig."

"Then you won't have to take any action on the Ark for months."

"No, that's not quite true. While the dig proceeds, I'll need to make some effort to locate it. So at times, I'll be gone. Our fathers are capable of taking charge of the excavation while I'm away."

"What about me?"

"I'll really need you to travel with me."

"I was hoping you'd say that."

"I think you'll find this pursuit challenging."

"Do you really believe we'll find it?"

A serious look spread across his face. "No," he responded.

"I don't understand. Why did you agree to it?"

"To fund this dig and make an old man happy. Our excavation here could reveal the beginnings of civilization. But it's more than that. It might even provide evidence of the origin of man."

"What will Jimmy say if you don't find the Ark?"

"He has prostate cancer. He expects to be dead within a year. It's sad, I really like the old man."

"I do too."

For the first time, he noticed she was holding something behind her back "What's that?"

"I just thought that if you were awake we could share this last bottle Jimmy left behind."

"Sure."

He opened his footlocker and removed two glasses wrapped in newspaper. "I think this will do the trick."

After pouring the wine, the two sat beside each other on the large cot. At that very moment, Bill saw Bahodore walk past the front flap of the tent. It was a signal. The guide was waiting for him on the outskirts of the camp. Bill hoped the meeting with the guide arranged by Bahodore would go smoothly. The mission tonight was a necessary one. National interest was at stake. He could not afford to fail. Decisions in

Washington would be influence by his report. And if the mission didn't go well, he might be dead by morning.

With her back to the entrance, Rachael didn't see the guide nor notice the serious expression that came over the professor's face. Her mind was too busy concentrating on other matters. It was time to let him know how she felt. If he rejected her, it would be better than never knowing how he felt. She was just going to take the first step and see what happened. Maybe nature would take over from there.

"Professor."

Bill looked up from his glass just as Rachael reached over, placed her right hand on the small of his neck, and pulled him toward her until their lips met. She felt his arms go around her, as his lips responded to hers with passion. She was aroused, pressing him backward on the cot until he was lying flat on his back, her flesh pressed against his. She had never wanted anyone so much, not even Jerome. Suddenly she felt him pushing her away.

"Rachael, I'm sorry. I want to explain, but I can't right now."

Stunned by his rejection, she fled the tent.

Bahodore was waiting with someone when Bill reached the road that led to Noqdi.

"This is DelAvar. He is with the insurgents," Bahodore said. "He will take us to the nuclear site."

"Come. We must hurry," the stranger said.

They got into a World War vintage-truck parked nearby and drove in the direction of the village.

Little conversation occurred as the truck passed through the village and a few miles later made a sharp right turn onto a narrow dirt road. When DelAvar cut the headlights off, Bill knew they were near their objective. Soon the road ended.

"We can't go any farther in the vehicle," DelAvar said.

Bill got out and placed a backpack over his shoulders. It contained one of the items Jimmy secretly left him—a special camera, the best that existed. Its ability to photograph images at a great distance was why military intelligence let Jimmy act as a special courier to get this equipment to Bill. The other item left was a device that operated off a military satellite in space. This would allow him to communicate directly with his superior in the Pentagon.

***

In his office at the Pentagon, Colonel Bonham sat behind his desk looking at his watch. He was worried about the mission. Iran was full of treacherous people. Many times agents in the region turned out to be double agents. It was hard to know who to trust over there anymore. The Revolution had been quite successful in eliminating the intelligence community sources.

Prior to the revolution, many of the military officers trained in the United States were graduates of the Citadel. Most had been executed. However, some survived because their family members belonged to the inner circle of the Revolutionary Council. Now Bahodore and a limited number of active military officers were the few effective ones left for the Americans. He had been kept in a low profile status, and military intelligence only used him when it was absolutely necessary. His survival had been enhanced by the fact that he was a "safe contained" spy. Only a few select people, like Colonel Bonham and Samuel Mann, the Secretary of Defense, knew of his existence in the network. This mission was so important that not only were they putting the agent's life on the line but also that of an American intelligence officer, Dr. William Weston, who in addition to being a well-known biblical scholar, was also a captain in the Marine Reserves. He had been assign to the intelligence department because of his ability to speak Arabic and his knowledge of the Middle East. The professor's expedition to the Zagros Mountains had not been planned with espionage in mind, but a ripple on the international scene made the Pentagon decide to use him. If caught, his country would have no choice but denial. Then after torture, the Iranian government would execute him.

A short distance from the truck, another man was waiting. It was Ghadir, the leader of the insurgents that Bill had met earlier in the week. He had arranged the trip that night to the nuclear site.

The last few yards to the facility, they crawled on their hands and knees. When they finally stopped, Bill understood why Washington could not rely on the space satellite photographs to obtain the necessary information. Half of the facility was inside a large opening in the mountain, a cavern enlarged by the Iranian government.

"It goes back a long way. Perhaps as much as a mile," Ghadir said. "Every day bulldozers bring out tons of rocks. They have been enlarging its depth for two years."

Bill started to take some pictures.

"Wait until we get closer," Ghadir said.

He saw the expression on Bill's face.

"My people have eliminated the guards in this section. We have a man on the inside who will guide us through the outer perimeter."

As they crawled the next few yards, they passed several bodies along the way with their throats cut. At last, they met the employee at the outer perimeter. He led them into the mountain. No one was on duty. Confident of the security of the cavern, the soldiers and workers were all fast asleep. For fifty uninterrupted minutes, Bill traveled inside taking pictures. Then the employee indicated it was time to go.

"There is a change of the guard soon," he said. "You'll need to be back at your camp in the mountains before that. This place will be crawling with troops once they find out their security has been compromised."

Leaving the employee, the men traveled at a fast pace until they reached the truck.

"I will leave you now," Ghadir said. "My men are moving our headquarters high into the mountains. Things are going to get hot here. You must get these photographs to your superiors, as soon as possible."

A moment later, he disappeared into the night before Bill could thank him.

On the way back, Bahodore got out at Noqdi saying he had some unfinished personal business there. Afterwards DelAvar continued his drive toward the base camp.

"Stop here for a few minutes," Bill said, a mile from their destination. Leaving the truck, he scrambled up a nearby hill and headed in the direction of the basin.

When Bill reached the basin, it took him only a few minutes to locate the device he hidden earlier. He removed the special film from the camera and placed it in the device, then turned the rotating knob on the instrument to the appropriate coordinates. When everything was ready, he pushed a button. A moment later, a small beeping noise went off. The photographs had been relayed to the intelligence satellite. They were probably already being viewed in the Pentagon, he thought. The task completed, he pulled a cord and the device self-destructed, burning from within. Since the camera had no such system, Bill crushed it with a rock and threw the fragments into the water at its deepest point.

Rebecca had carried out her part of the plan. It was easy to entice Arsham to the bedroom. He frequently came anyway and imposed himself on her. She had been a virgin when the forced marriage had taken place. She had no choice. Arsham would have killed her grandparents if she hadn't complied with his wishes. Moreover, she had to please him. He had been brutal from the first night, and it hadn't helped that she was just a child of eleven at the time. She dared not do anything about her circumstances while her grandparents were still alive. Then one day, word reached her from Tehran that they were dead. This freed her to enact her revenge. Like a dog that had been abused, she was ready to turn on her master.

Bahodore opened the back door. He made his way quietly to the bedroom where he knew Arshan would be asleep from the powder Rebecca put in his drink. When he opened the door, he saw the look of apprehension on her face.

"Thank goodness it is you. I was afraid the devil would wake."

"There was no danger of that. The powder I gave you yesterday was strong enough to keep him sedated until I arrived."

He wanted to stab Arsham in the heart, and be done with it, but his niece would have none of that. She insisted that they tie and gag him. The man was so sedated, he didn't open his eyes until the gag was placed in his mouth. He tried to scream for help but couldn't. Then he tried to get up, but he was bound too tight to the king-sized bed. He lay there in a perfect state of nature, the same as when he went to sleep, naked from head to toe. Rebecca leaned over and whispered something in his ear. Bahodore watched as a look of terror came over Arsham's face. In a moment, Bahodore understood why. With a single sweep of a hand, she grabbed his phallus and with the knife in her other hand, severed it from his body.

Looking at Bahodore she said, "Now you can kill him."

When Bahodore arrived back at camp, he slipped through the back of his tent to avoid detection. Changing his clothes, he was careful when he walked out the front of the tent to drop his dirty ones in a large barrel of soapy water placed there for that very purpose. Destruction of any evidence that could tie them to the nuclear facility was important. He stopped at the cook's table, poured himself coffee, and was joined by Bill, who approached from the opposite direction. They were careful to be sure the soldiers saw them. It would provide them with an alibi.

"Did you get the photographs transmitted?" Bahodore asked.

"Yes," Bill said. "Do you think the Army or Revolutionary Guards will visit us today?"

"I believe they will be here before noon. That's why I'm telling you that Arsham was killed."

"That wasn't part of the plan."

"It was a personal matter. He killed my parents and caused the death of my sister. Then he took my eleven-year-old niece as his bride. The pig had to die."

Bahodore took a ring off his finger and showed it to Bill.

"I will hide this beneath the main support pole of my tent. If anything happens to me, be sure my son, who lives in America, gets it. Colonel Bonham knows his address."

Bill looked at the ring. The inscription inside read "Jeremiah Bahodore." It was from the Citadel and contained the Latin phrase Animis Opibusque Parati–Prepared in Mind and Resources. Bill was surprised he hadn't seen the ring before. Perhaps Bahodore put it on for the mission. Citadel men were a strange bunch. He should know. After all, his father was one.

20

Rachael's concern about her personal relationship with the professor was pushed to the back of her mind that morning when the army jeep pulled into camp followed by a truck loaded with soldiers.

The officer in charge had his men scurrying through the camp rounding up everyone. Soon they were all huddled in a group near Bill's tent.

"We are here to interrogate you," the major in charge of the military attachment announced.

Bill stepped forward.

"What's going on?" he asked.

"I am Major Hami," the man said in English. "Who are you?"

"Dr. Weston. I'm in charge of this excavation, and these people work for me."

"Then I will start questioning you first and use this tent for our interrogation." He pointed at the tent behind him. "If you don't have your papers with you, go get them now," he said to the group huddled in front. "I warn you that no one will be allowed to leave this camp until I have finished here."

"My passport is in my tent," Bill said. "It's the one that you commandeered for your interrogation."

"Get it."

While he was retrieving the paperwork out of the footlocker, the officer entered followed by a sergeant.

Turning to the noncommissioned officer, the Major Hami said, "Get some men in here. I want that table in the corner placed in the middle. When you get it set up, we will bring them in one at a time. Post two men as guards at the entrance. I also want you to remain with me during the questioning."

The sergeant saluted and left. Bill and the officer were now alone.

"I will speak quickly while there are no listening ears. You must cooperate. We will get through as quickly as possible and I will file a report that this is nothing more than an archaeological dig. However, I warn you that the Revolutionary Guards are about. I will do what I can to protect you. In urban areas they control, but in an isolated area like this, the Army was still dominant. My temporary headquarter is in Noqdi. If you run into trouble, send me a message, but be careful what you write. It may be read by someone not within our circle of friends."

At that moment, the sergeant entered, followed by two of his men.

"Dr. Weston, I don't believe you had any involvement in the attack. I am going to ask you to remain to interpret. My English is not quite as good as it needs to be to question the members of your staff."

Irad was brought into the tent. He appeared confident to the point of being cocky. This was in contrast to Rachael's subdued demeanor. She kept glancing at Bill when telling the officer where she had been the night before. She tiptoed around the time spent in the tent with him. When she finished and left, the Major Hami announced he was taking a break.

"Sergeant, take the men and go get us some food. I saw someone cooking when we entered the camp."

When the men left, the major said, "You need to talk to your assistant. If anyone, other than I had questioned her, they would have immediately sensed she was holding something back."

"To be perfectly honest, a sensitive personal encounter happened between us last night."

"Sensitive or not, you two need to get your stories straight."

"I'll speak to her about it."

With the interrogation over, life returned to normal in the camp. At the dig the next day, Bill and Rachael went down to inspect the tunnel. Once they were out of earshot of others, he whispered, "We need to get our stories straight about what happened last night in case there is further questioning."

"What do you mean?"

"Your answers seemed somewhat evasive."

"Evasive?"

"Yes. We should decide what to say if the question concerning that time is asked again."

Before she could stop them, a gush of words flowed from her lips.

"It's a simple story. I made a physical advance toward you, but you weren't interested."

"That's not true Rachael. One day I'll explain, but this isn't the time or the place."

"Why?"

"Because it could put your life in danger. There are things about me you don't know."

"What are you saying?" she asked, looking up at him in the dim light of the tunnel, now more confused than ever about his feelings toward her.

At that moment, two laborers came toward them carrying fresh buckets of debris they had just removed from the end of the tunnel.

"One day you'll understand. Let's discuss this later when there aren't other ears listening."

***

Colonel Bonham received information from the spy satellite just in time for a presentation to the National Security Council meeting at *Camp David*.

"These are photographs of what we have long suspected was the heart of Iran's secret plant for the production of nuclear bombs," the colonel said. "They were obtained from a highly classified source deep in the Zagros Mountains where there is presently a rising insurgency against the mullahs in Tehran. If you will closely examine the photographs on the screen, I think it will be clear to everyone that Iran is going at full steam in their attempt to develop weapons of mass destruction. Dr. Gayle Smith is here to answer any technical questions you might have."

"Dr. Smith, how can you be so sure the summary Colonel Bonham has given us is true?" Chairman Rouse asked.

"In the short time between the receipt of these photographs and this meeting, we brought to Washington eleven experts who are highly regarded in the field of nuclear production to supplement our meager staff. Mr. Chairman, it's not often that you get a consensus from such a group. I can tell you there was not a dissenting voice. They agree this facility represents the final phase for the production of nuclear warheads."

"Colonel," said another member of the committee seated near the end of the table. "I see, from the written summary provided, military intelligence believes Iran already has a delivery system."

"Yes. This system can reach anywhere in the Middle East. With their continued advancement, it's my belief that within five years, they'll have a system capable of reaching the United States."

"Colonel, how long before they will actually have a nuclear bomb for this delivery system?" the chairman asked.

"I'll defer to Dr. Smith. She has at her disposal more expertise in that area than I do."

"Well, what about it, Dr. Smith?"

"It's hard to pinpoint an exact time. My panel of experts have differing opinions on when the first bomb will be produced. They range from two to four years. Of course, once the first one is ready, many others could follow. It's similar to the mass production of an automobile. It may take time for the first one to roll off the assembly line, but after that, a large number could be produced quickly."

On a closed-circuit television, President Macer watched with a serious look of concern. She said to the chief of staff, "Contact the secretary of defense. I want a meeting with him tomorrow. Time is beginning to run out for this country and our allies to prevent a major shift of power. After the fall of the Soviet Union, everyone wondered what great powers would rise to threaten the security of the western world and its commercial interest. At the time no one expected Iran would be on that list."

***

It happened early one morning. As he lay in the dark, Bill heard the sound of vehicles racing past his tent. Then loud voices brought him to his feet. He slipped on his clothes and stepped out just in time to see people forced from their beds by a straggly group of paramilitary men. He heard Rachael scream out from the darkness. Rushing toward the sound, he found her struggling with two men. A quick punch to the back of the head sent one spinning into a vehicle parked nearby. The other one looked up just in time to eat the knuckles of his right hand. Then something solid struck the back of his head. Everything went black.

Bahodore was on the way back from a meeting with members of the underground. He was only a few yards from the village when he saw a movement of trucks going in the direction of the archaeological site. Watching from behind a boulder, he realized it was the hated Revolutionary Guards.

Major Hami was annoyed to be awakened from a deep sleep by his guard.

"What is it?" he demanded.

"I'm sorry to disturb you, Sir. There's a man outside who insists it is urgent he speak to you."

"What is it about?" Major Hami snapped.

"He would not say, but he gave me a note."

"Let me see it." He lit the lamp beside his bed.

The note read–Animis Opibusque Parati.

Bill could hear Rachael's voice somewhere in the distance. He felt her hand upon his forehead. Was he dreaming? Slowly he began to regain consciousness. When he opened his eyes, the first thing he saw was her face leaning over him. He was back in his tent. What was happening? Then he remembered. He started to speak, but Rachael placed her finger to his lips and whispered.

"Be quiet. There's a guard right outside."

Rachael was so close to him that he could hear the pounding of her heart. Having been dragged out of bed, her clothing consisted of only a thin pullover. Her uncombed hair hung across her face. Even at this time of danger, when their lives might be hanging by a thread, his thoughts were diverted by a desire to have her. Strange how danger often acted as an aphrodisiac upon the human body.

Bill's moment of diversion from their present situation ended when several men entered.

"Get up," the one in charge said.

Rachael helped Bill struggle to his feet. The effects of the blow to his head made him unsteady. He was dizzy and collapsed into a chair beside a table.

"I am Captain BalAsh of the Revolutionary Guards. We have some questions for you and the woman who claims to be your assistant."

BalAsh was intent on finding the killer of Arsham who had been an original member of the Revolutionary Guard. Though he had moved on to a position with the government, Arsham was still considered one of their own. BalAsh had no reason to believe the American was involved. The killing had probably been nothing more than a personal matter involving a tribal feud, but it gave him an excuse to humiliate an

American. This was his first opportunity since the fall of the embassy.

Not satisfied with the American's initial response, BalAsh continued to hammer him with questions.

"So you were reading in your tent until late in the evening, and your assistant can verify it because she came by late that night."

"Yes."

"Why?"

"To discuss the dig."

BalAsh didn't like the response, so he slapped Bill hard across the face. Rachael started crying.

"Tell him the truth," she said. "We are lovers. I always go to his tent at night when everyone is asleep."

She knew these enforcers of the morality code believed the western world was morally corrupt and would be inclined to believe such a story because it fit with their perceived ideas.

"Is that true?"

Bill didn't respond. In BalAsh's mind, this only confirmed that this immoral American was screwing the Jewish slut.

"So it's true," he said with disgust in his voice.

The sound of a commotion outside interrupted them. A moment later, the major and several soldiers stormed into the tent.

"You have no authority here. I am Major Hami, and this district is under the jurisdiction of the Azarbod Brigade."

"I'm Captain BalAsh of the Revolutionary Guard. We are here to find the killer of one of our members."

"That's a matter for my men to investigate. Unless you have authorization from the government in Tehran, I want you out of here."

BalAsh wanted to continue, but the major was in no mood to listen.

Turning to his sergeant, he said, "Any Revolutionary Guard still in this camp ten minutes from now will be arrested and put in the stockade in Noqdi. And that includes their officers."

The sergeant saluted, then turned and barked orders to a group of soldiers gathered outside the tent.

"You will be hearing from Tehran," BalAsh said before leaving.

When the tent was empty, the major said to Bill, "Hopefully this will be the last time they will bother you, but I would not count on it."

As he spoke, he gestured with his hand. For the first time Bill noticed the Citadel ring on the officer's finger.

21

After all the excitement, matters settled down to the monotonous task of carefully going through every parcel of debris, looking in vain for anything that might be evidence of an ancient city located on the plateau. They would have become discouraged except for the pottery and coin found nearby.

During this period, Bill received a coded message from his father. Fullmore was coming with him to Iran under a false identification. Their plane would land in Jordan where Benjamin Rabon would join them for the remainder of the trip.

Using code was something Bill's father taught him. As a child, it had been simply a game. Later in life, it turned out to be quite useful. His father had been in military intelligence, and using code was natural when he wanted to communicate something in secret to his son.

Excitement stirred the camp the day a jeep entered carrying the three men. At last, help had arrived which would quicken the pace of the dig. Bill took Rachael into his confidence. Fullmore was using the alias name James King. No one should be told his true identity, not even her father. The charade had Fullmore coming as Henry Weston's cook. She didn't understand the need for such secrecy but agreed not to disclose the information.

The men arrived too late in the evening to go into the tunnel, so once they unpacked, everyone gathered for dinner. Bill had been worried about the cover Fullmore was using until he discovered that one of the man's hobbies was cooking.

The meal had some new dishes that night, and everyone appeared pleased. Afterwards, Irad excused himself saying he was going to the village. The rumors were he had a female friend there.

After Dr. Rabon retired for the night, Fullmore joined the others in Bill's tent.

"At last, we can speak freely," Henry Weston said. Then realizing how that must sound to Rachael he said, "No offense intended."

"And none taken," Rachael replied, although she did feel a tinge of disloyalty to her father.

Bill went over to his footlocker and retrieved a box his father had given him for safekeeping. From it, he removed a miniature device and laid it on the table in the tent.

"What's that?" Rachael asked.

"The newest thing in technology," Fullmore said. "Henry gave this to me before we left the States. It's wireless and has a battery life that lasts forever. It operates off a space satellite.

Sitting down at the table, he opened up the small computer that was no larger than a cigar box.

"Let me show you the translation of the inscription on the staff."

"You mean you've deciphered it?" Rachael asked.

Without commenting, Fullmore put in a miniature CD. A copy of the inscription appeared on the left side of the screen and a translation on the right. Bill and Rachael looked down at the screen in amazement. They squinted to read it on the small screen. Neither said a word until their minds had time to absorb the display.

"Fascinating," Bill said.

"Are you able to translate other inscriptions from dead languages?" Rachael asked.

Henry Weston spoke up.

"He has perfected a software program that's a major step in that direction."

"How?"

Henry continued, "It's always been the accepted concept of the academic community that our ancestors learned to speak gradually, and then over thousands of years acquired a written language, basically one word at a time. It appears we may have missed the mark. At least the descendants of the Tribe of Adam may have started with the ability to speak and write. When you think about it, why would God have given him a brain, a soul, and dominion over the animal kingdom and not have given Adam the ability to communicate verbally or to record information? There's not a lot of logic for God creating an illiterate man. You see we have failed to take into account the ebb and flow of civilizations. In some places on this earth where a highly civilized people once existed, their descendents are now illiterate peasants scratching out a living in or at the edge of a jungle or desert. Their ancestors too once had a written language, knew about the movement of the stars, and were well versed in mathematics. So it could also be true with the descendants of Adam. Regression is no stranger to history. All we have to do is look at the Mayans of Central America or the tribes of Yemen for examples."

"Henry is right," Fullmore said. "My studies in trying to perfect this software have led me to conclude that all the world's languages started from the same source based on recent excavations that have uncovered older text. In my analysis, I've used the ancient Sumerian writings along with the more recently discovered ones in Yemen. If we could go back one more step, we might find the actual root of the tree of written communication."

"Could you decipher the inscriptions on the articles we've uncovered?"

"From what you told me over dinner, the answer is yes."

"It will have to be done in secret," Bill said.

"I'll work on it while ya'll are at the dig tomorrow."

***

In Noqdi, Irad met with Henley. He tried to come to the village as often as possible. The story that he had a woman was a fabrication to divert attention from his real purpose.

"What is the latest news from the camp?"

Irad told him about the visitation from the Revolutionary Guard and the new arrivals.

"The Revolutionary Guard is a backward group of people but effective inhibiting Iran from having a decent government," Henley said.

"It's amazing how we've been able to manipulate them for our purposes," Irad said.

"Sometimes those who preach religion are our greatest allies in the war against good. As the Sacred Book of our ancestors said, 'You shall know them by the fruit they produce.'"

"When you look at it from that perspective, you're right. They've produced mayhem and murder. Maybe we should adopt them into our Society," said Irad, a smile emanating from his lips. "They meet all the requirements except the blood of our ancestor running through their veins."

"That may or may not be true. Our lineage records are not complete," Henley said. "Actually – "Henley suddenly stopped in mid-sentence as a small red truck drove by the side street where they were standing. He asked, "Isn't that John Elesbaan?"

Irad caught a glimpse of it before the vehicle disappeared from sight. He too recognized the man in the passenger seat.

"That's him. He was supposed to arrive here several days ago."

John Elesbaan saw the men out of the corner of his eye. The sighting only confirmed the information he had received. These two were involved in The Society and were in Iran carrying out its goals. He would keep this information close to his chest. At this point, he didn't know whom to trust in Iran. Maybe there was no one.

***

Rachael was in her tent waiting for Fullmore to come. It had been decided last night that while the rest were at the dig, her tent would be the safest place for Fullmore to decipher the items. Since she was the only woman at the camp, the tent had been placed some distance from the others in order to give her privacy. She stepped outside to see if Fullmore was nearby and ran into Irad standing at the front entrance.

"I just got back. Thought I would check on you. Someone said you weren't feeling well."

"It must be a virus. I decided to stay down this morning. I'll feel better tomorrow."

In fact, there was nothing wrong with Rachael. Bill had only spread that information, so remaining in the tent would not arouse attention. When Irad left for the dig, Rachael went back inside just as Fullmore was entering through the back entrance.

"You almost ran into Irad," she said.

"I saw him when I approached. I hid behind that rock at the back of your tent, until he left." Then added in his Mississippi accent, "The professor done told me he didn't trust that man. So I been keeping a sharp eye out when he's around."

Why didn't he trust him? she wondered. He had never told her that, so why would he tell a perfect stranger? Could it be Bill was just jealous? Then she smiled. Ever since he had come to her aid the morning those two Revolutionary Guards dragged her from the tent, she had known in her heart that he cared about her, even though Bill might not realize he loved her yet.

The first man John saw when he arrived was Bahodore, who had taken it upon himself to be responsible for the camp and leave the excavation to others. No sooner had John introduced himself then Bahodore had two men pull a tent out of the back of an old truck.

"We were expecting you to arrive a few days ago."

"I got delayed by some other pressing business."

Bahodore ordered the men to carry the tent for John to the edge of the encampment where he supervised its erection.

John knew the League was right to send him to this political hot spot of the world. It was a necessary, though a dangerous move. Their organization might not be as powerful as The Society, but they had been quite successful in blocking many of its evil schemes over the centuries. He knew from colleagues at the university that the evil ones were on his trail. They were asking questions. If he survived this assignment, the League would give him a new identity.

John had spent his formative years in Ethiopia, the ancestral home of his people. And he was a *Falasha* by birth. Unlike many of his fellow tribesmen, John's family line had converted to Christianity eons ago. Since the League recognized the Christian faith as a branch of Judaism, it allowed him and other Christian converts who carried the blood of Seth within their veins to belong to the ancient fellowship. He was initiated into its ritual at twelve, the biblical age of accountability. The coming weeks would test his dedication to the brotherhood.

***

The Leader was in his office reading the latest correspondence from Henley. The report informed him the expedition was moving slowly excavating the site. That pace had increased since the others arrived. The Leader had a dossier on two of them, Henry Weston and Benjamin Rabon. His agents were still having a problem on the background research of Dr. John Elesbaan. The more they failed to find information, the more it appeared this was not the man's true identity.

Sitting back in his specially built chair, the Leader lit a Cuban cigar. Their life span was why the Sons of Seth outnumbered them, he thought. It was the same with other groups in the world. Regardless of wealth or military power, history proved breeding and a long life are what ultimately decided who controlled. The Sons of Cain were cursed in ancient times with a shorter span than their enemies. The physical size of Cain's descendants was the root of the problem. Giants simply did not live as long as other humans.

The secretary brought in checks for the Leader to sign.

The cost of operating the organization continued to rise, and The Society had now resorted to gem theft from Sierra Leone and the drug trade in Columbia to finance its causes.

One thing that brought great satisfaction in recent years to The Society was their infiltration of the terrorist organizations. It allowed them to wreak havoc on the empires of the world. Every step brought them closer to the disintegration of civilization. Evil was slowly gaining ground, and The Society was secretly in the forefront. Times were better than when the members sat on the inner circle of Hitler's Third Reich or assisted Stalin in his reign of terror. The present wave of evil had the advantage of being a worldwide phenomenon.

The secretary interrupted again to leave some invoices on the expenses in Iran.

The Leader remembered when the council had first discussed the issue of secretly providing funds for the expedition. They preferred the dig not go forward but realized if they did nothing, the professor would eventually find someone to finance the project. It was better to be involved behind the scene than not at all. The stakes were high. The Leader knew from the oral history passed down that Enoch was the capital of Cain's empire and the original headquarters of evil in the world. When Cain died, his descendents continued to rule, using his staff as the symbol of their authority. Strangely, it was not embedded with gems, as one might think, nor covered with gold as might befit a sovereign. Instead, it was of wood, unadorned, except for a golden knob. The simplicity was deceiving, for the staff was made of Acacia wood from a tree that had once grown in the Garden of Eden. Adam had secretly taken a seedling with him when forced to leave the garden. The wood was indestructible. Before Cain fled to the Land of Nod, he cut a limb from the tree to take with him. Later in history, the Ark of God was constructed with Acacia wood from the last tree that existed. The tree had grown from a seedling that Isaac had taken to Egypt when he went there to live out his remaining days with Joseph.

22

The Leader was standing at the window enjoying the view of the Hudson River in the distance when the courier left the package. Inside was a coded message from Henley. He would not be able to return to New York as planned. With Arsham dead, Irad needed him to remain to help with the project in Iran.

The message also confirmed the staff in the vault at the university in Jerusalem was authentic. Irad uncovered a copy of the decoded message on the staff in Rachael's tent. It was the same interpretation as contained in *The Sacred Book*. Now that the staff had been authenticated, the Leader would have members of The Society retrieve it.

The end of time was at hand or at least a little closer, thought the Leader. Verses in *The Sacred Book* said the recovery of the staff would be a sign. Another would be the possession of the Ark of the Covenant. The Society did not have a complete copy of the book, only bits and pieces composed long ago from memories of the dam catastrophe survivors. The search for an original text had been futile. The complete text had last been seen in Yemen before the great dam at Marib burst, destroying everything before it. This loss was not the only catastrophe The Society suffered. They also lost many other relics, the most important being the bones of Noah and the body of Daniel.

The clock on the wall striking five reminded the Leader it was time to meet Marilyn at a hotel room for their weekend tryst. As a precaution, he had stopped visiting her apartment when he saw the blue light that day near the park. On his way out of the door, he picked up the latest transcript of radio communication from the third precinct. He used the opportunity on the way over to peruse it while the taxi drove him to the hotel.

Marilyn put the finishing touches on her makeup. The Leader would be arriving soon. This was a special weekend. He would learn she was carrying his seed within her womb. The two methods that the

Leader required to prevent this circumstance had been thwarted. She quit taking her pills and punched holes in the condoms. Now, he would be confronted with an accomplished fact. The test results had come yesterday. He might initially be upset, but she knew that she was not just another plaything to her lover.

Like the Pope, no Leader in recent history had married. Nevertheless, Marilyn knew in ancient times the chosen one had been like the other heirs of Cain, taking numerous wives and producing many offspring. There were those among the membership who desired a return to the ancient rule, and she was one of them. She often fantasized about being the Leader's wife and standing at his side as the First Lady of The Society.

The Leader finished reading the disturbing information in the transcript. The police were scouring the neighborhood with a sketch of Marilyn. He knew it was only a matter of time before someone recognized her. A decision had to be made immediately. There was no way she would be allowed to return to her apartment. The Noba would remove any items there that might provide the police with leads. He reached in his coat pocket, removed a cell phone, and punched in a number to the Noba. A look of regret came over his face. Marilyn had become a liability. He would personally take care of the problem, something he hadn't done since becoming the Leader. Normally the council's approval was necessary because she was a *Cai'sh*. Nevertheless, in exigent circumstances one could act and get approval later. What a shame it had come to this. He had even fantasized about getting the council's consent to marry her. In reality, they would never have approved. The requirement that the Leader never wed had been established many years ago after one tried to establish a hereditary chain of succession.

The Leader woke. For a few moments, he looked at Marilyn as she lay there in a deep sleep. Every muscle clearly showed the exercise she put it through each day at the gym. Earlier Marilyn had disclosed to him the secret she had been keeping; within her womb was the product of his seed. Looking now at her nakedness, he could see the beginning of a small pouch. The child forming within her had started to push outward. Slipping out of bed, he looked for something to use. Locating it, he quietly straddled her and looped the electric cord around her throat.

Marilyn stirred. Too late, she realized what was happening. She struggled, her hands instinctively grabbing at the cord that cut off her air passages. She tried to get up. Her body was strong and powerful. Despite the lack of oxygen, she managed to rise on her hands and knees. She became like a horse, with the heavy-framed

Leader's body a rider upon her back. In a desperate surge, she threw her body off the bed.

He couldn't believe her strength. On the floor, he continued to hold the cord tight. In the fall from the bed, a heavy desk lamp was knocked from a table. It lay on the floor beside them. Still clutching the cord tightly with one hand, he reached and grasped the lamp. Blood splattered everywhere as he struck her with a terrific blow.

**

When the specialist could not decode the strange language from the safety deposit box, Thomas decided to seek permission to fly to France and Iran to get the investigation off dead center. He needed Kinsey Riley's approval.

When Thomas entered, the attractive young secretary greeted him. Her accent placed her origin south of the Mason-Dixon. Before he could engage her in conversation, Kinsey stuck his head out his door and motioned for Thomas to come into his office.

A few minutes later, the secretary entered and brought Kinsey a cup of coffee. Her red hair brushed her shoulders as she walked across the room in her tight-fitting long shirt. When she leaned over the desk and placed the coffee in front of Kinsey, the unbuttoned top of her blouse revealed a glimpse of petite breasts supported by a push-up bra. She turned to Thomas and gave him an appraising look. He felt his face turn a crimson red.

"Can I get you something, Detective?" she asked.

"No thanks. I've already had too much caffeine this morning. Another cup and I'd be bouncing off the wall."

"Her name is Melinda Lessene," Kinsey said, after she left the room. "If you're interested, she's from Charleston and the daughter of a friend of mine. She just went through a nasty divorce and needed to get away. I was able to accommodate an old classmate of mine from the Citadel and give her a job."

"Thanks, but I'm sure she has better prospects in the pipeline." Thomas said.

"You'll have to make our discussion short. I'm leaving for Washington in a few minutes. I assume it has something to do with the Imnah case. That file has interesting issues. Based on your memo, it appears you've hit a stone wall in your investigation."

"That's why I'm here."

"You want to investigate that strange case in France and then fly to the Zagros Mountains to see the professor."

"You must have read my mind."

"No, but I've been reading your reports. I'll fill out the necessary paper work recommending the trip and take it to Washington. I should have the approval when I return."

When he got up to leave, Kinsey stopped him.

"I've just received some information that I'd like to share with you. The money in Professor Weston's account has been unfrozen."

"Why?"

"I don't know why, but I understand that Harry Beacham is in hot water for his involvement in freezing that account. Seems it interfered with some military intelligence operation. That's all the information I have at this point. Another matter that I need to speak with you about involves Ronald Fullmore. You remember him. He was the man who received fifty thousand from the professor's account. Well it seems that Fullmore wasn't home when the FBI went to question him. But a trail of blood led from the driveway in front of his house to a swamp. They're puzzled by what occurred out there. I hope to have a report in the coming days. When I receive it, I'll burn you a copy."

"I'd appreciate that."

"When you get to Iran, find out if Professor Weston knows anything. After all, he did pay Fullmore the money."

Two weeks after his conference with Kinsey, Thomas was packed and ready to catch the flight to Paris, when Richard called. Someone recognized the sketch of Marilyn and knew the whereabouts of her apartment. After the conversation, Thomas contacted the airport and changed his reservation until a later date.

When Thomas arrived at the apartment, a uniformed officer was standing outside. He directed Thomas to the third floor where Richard was waiting for him in Apartment 3A.

"It's like the other apartment she lived in," Richard said. "I tell you, it's downright spooky. Everyone has mail, bills, and credit card receipts but not this woman. If it wasn't for the fact that we questioned her, I'd say she was a phantom."

"She's real all right," Thomas said. "And Marilyn wasn't the confused person she appeared to be the day we did the interview."

"There's no doubt she's up to her eyeballs in these murders. We have the fingerprint expert on the way over. Hopefully, he'll be able to lift some prints."

"I wouldn't count on it. I hope you have better luck than the last time. I still find it amazing there were no prints at her last apartment. I've never seen a criminal so successfully clean a room."

"Yes, whoever heard of an apartment not having the tenant's own prints? Like I said, this is a weird case."

"Did you find anything out of the ordinary?" Thomas asked.

"Yes," said Richard with a smile on his face. "And it may be something we can trace. Come let me show you."

Thomas followed Richard back to the bathroom.

"Look at these," Richard said, as he removed two boxes of condoms from the bathroom shelf.

"What the hell?"

"That's not all. Here, read what's on the box."

"These are specially made for men who have an extra-large penis," Thomas said reading the information.

"Oh, to be so lucky," Richard said with a chuckle.

"We should be able to contact the company and find out who ordered these."

"Yes. It's the best lead we've had so far."

The agent from the Noba was standing in the doorway of a restaurant across the street from Marilyn's apartment observing the activity and trying to remain inconspicuous. He came directly after receiving the call from the Leader, but it was too late to remove any incriminating evidence because the police were there. While the agent watched, his cell phone rang. The agent explained the situation. His superior understood, but now there were more pressing matters at the hotel.

The Leader had already taken a shower at the hotel to clean the blood from his body when the Noba arrived. Moreover, he called his place of residence to have his manservant bring over a change of clothing. There was blood caked on the floor around Marilyn's head and splattered on the wall beside the bed. At least the room was rented for the weekend. That would give the Noba time to clean it and dispose of the body.

A retired police officer working security at a hotel saw several men leave a room carrying an old wooden trunk, which they loaded into a vehicle. Suspicion aroused, he wrote down the license number and then obtained the key from the desk clerk. A homicide detective before retirement, he immediately noticed upon entering the room that the carpet had been shampooed recently. He called Richard.

Finally a break in the case, Richard thought. The desk clerk recognized the sketch of Marilyn. Then an instrument that was the newest device for ascertaining the presence of blood confirmed the caller's suspicion when the chemical spray reacted with the surface of the carpet.

23

It was Thomas's first trip to Paris. Because of the flight delay, it was midnight by the time he arrived at the hotel. He went straight to bed hoping for a good night's rest, but he couldn't relax. After tossing beneath the covers, he switched on the lamp and retrieved a book Henry Weston loaned him. He flipped to the chapter on the League.

"The League of Seth was believed by many of the Jewish faith to be an organization formed to combat the descendants of Cain. In mythology, it became more than a simple feud between two warring families. It grew to encompass the gigantic struggle between good and evil. The Society of the Serpent represented the forces of darkness, and the League of Seth represented the forces of light. These

mammoth powers went head to head, each determined to wipe out the seed of the other. In the modern era, very few people, except those who made the occult their life's work, have ever heard of these groups. It is generally thought the legends hold no grain of truth."

***

The French officer studied the file. It had been gathering dust for some time in a warehouse where old records were kept. No one had bothered to look at it for years. When the inspector opened the box where it was stored, the dust nearly brought on an asthma attack. The American detective would be arriving at the station soon, and Adrien wanted to review it before he got there. Flipping through the materials brought back memories about the incident and the scientist, Alain Feagin.

Adrien Legare had just joined the force when this case was plastered across the front pages of the newspapers. At first, the press treated it as a possible great scientific discovery, but, within a few weeks, they were describing it as a hoax. The officer took the file back to his office. An hour later, when the secretary informed him the detective had arrived, Adrien was sipping a cup of gourmet coffee and eating one of a dozen beignets that lay on a silver tray next to his desk.

***

"Thank you for seeing me," Thomas said.

"Detective, I am curious to know what brought you all the way to Paris to review a file from our archives."

"I believe it may have relevance to several murder cases that I'm working on."

The Frenchman held the file in his hand, but instead of surrendering control of it to Thomas, he placed it on the desk in front of him.

"Are you at liberty to disclose any facts?" Adrien asked. "Of course, anything you tell me in this room will be held in the strictest confidence."

"It may take some time to brief you on the circumstances."

Adrien picked up the plate of beignets and placed them in front of Thomas. "I'll have my secretary bring you a cup of coffee. It is excellent, imported from Costa Rica."

Between sipping coffee and eating three beignets, he told the Frenchman the facts of his investigation, placing special emphasis on the occult.

"That is most interesting," Adrien said, handing him the file. "As to the blood test, you will find what you're looking for in there. It was a most bizarre set of facts. Before he disappeared, the scientist, a man by the name of Alain Feagin, issued an opinion that the blood samples were not of this world."

"Disappeared?"

"Yes. It's all in the file. Despite an intensive search, no trace of him was ever found. Finally, we closed the case. If you like, I will have my secretary make a copy of the file for you. Normally, this wouldn't be allowed. In this matter, however, no one will care since the identity of the body, on which the DNA tests were performed, was never ascertained. It's as if he appeared out of thin air. This, of course, added initial credibility to the scientist's statement."

"Where's the body?"

"I don't know. It was stolen right after the publicity started."

"This trip may turn out to be a waste of time, but I remain hopeful that somewhere in your case file a lead for my investigation will turn up."

"Do you have any friends in Paris?"

"I'm afraid not."

"Then perhaps I could be of service. Why don't you review the materials and then join me for dinner tonight. We could discuss this strange case then."

In the hotel room, Thomas studied the copied file. It reflected that Adrien Legare, then only a young police officer, assisted in the investigation of the case.

There was a *curriculum vitae* on the scientist in the file. The man certainly was no slouch, having graduated with honors from every school attended. Not involved in the case initially, he was called upon to review the blood test results when the physician at the lab was having difficulty interpreting it. He immediately ordered new tests saying the first ones were faulty. They came back the same. He demanded a third test and directed that a different lab conduct them. This time he was personally present through every step of the process to be sure procedures were followed to maintain the integrity of the sample. Still the results were the same. When this last result arrived, he had the body removed to the institute where he was employed.

The directions given by the inspector were very detailed, and Thomas had no problem finding the quaint little restaurant located on a side street. When he entered, he knew right away it was a place where the locals dined. Everyone was speaking French, and there wasn't an American tourist in sight. The maitre d' motioned him to follow as he led the way to a private room in the back of the restaurant. There the inspector was sitting with an old man. A large half-empty bottle of wine on the table told Thomas the two men had been there for some time.

"I want you to meet Antoine Feagin," the inspector said.

The last name sounded familiar. Then Thomas remembered. The missing scientist. Adrien saw the look on Thomas's face.

"You are wondering if they are related. They are brothers. I first met Antoine during the investigation, and later we became friends."

A waiter brought Thomas a wine glass and remained hovering.

"Thomas, I would recommend the *boeuf bourguignon*," the inspector said. "It's the specialty of the house."

"Since I can't read the menu, the suggestion sounds good to me."

While they were waiting for their entree, Adrien said, "It was just the usual mundane matter at first. A large body, without any identification, washed up on the bank of the Seine River. When the blood test came back, it aroused some curiosity in the office, but everyone thought there would soon be a plausible explanation. Then the press became interested and started asking questions. There was a lot of hype at the time. The scientist, unskilled in public relations, made the mistake of thinking aloud in their presence. That was his downfall. Soon the man was portrayed by the press as a mad scientist. Even his colleagues began to shun him. The police department felt the scientist went off the deep end when he dissected the body."

"There's nothing about that in the file."

"That's true. With so much publicity, we felt it best to put nothing in the file, hoping the press would not find out. Our office leaked like a sieve back then. In fact, it still does. The department at that point just wanted the case to go away so we could focus on more pressing matters. Then the scientist disappeared, and the press was once again on our necks until we put out false rumors that he had gone to the seashore and drowned himself. After that, the press lost interest. They moved on, and so did we. That is to say, the department moved on, but I remained interested in the matter, investigating the case on my own time. That's how I met Antoine. The two of us over the years have pursued a logical explanation for what happened. I wish I could tell you that we found some answers, but the fact is, we haven't ascertained any reasonable explanation."

"Thomas, let me show you something I think you will find intriguing," Antoine said, pulling from the inner pocket of his coat a sketch and laying it on the table.

"Have you ever seen this type of marking before?"

In front of Thomas's eyes lay a sketch of the same symbol he had seen on Imnah and Linda.

"I told the inspector about such a symbol earlier today."

"That's when I knew you two needed to meet," Adrien said.

"Where did you get this?"

"My brother's notes," Antoine replied. "Most of his comments and drawings read as if a lunatic had written them. This drawing shows a symbol that was on the body."

"What did you learn from the notes?"

"They spoke about the body not being from this world and also describe the organs as abnormal."

"Abnormal?"

"Yes. Larger than found in humans."

"I'd like to see those notes."

"Unfortunately, I don't have them. I came home one evening to find my apartment ransacked. Strange, the only thing missing were those notes."

"That is so very interesting," Thomas said. "I wish there were more time for me to spend in Paris and conduct a more intensive investigation. But I have to leave on a flight to Tehran tomorrow."

24

Thomas received a call from Richard just before he left on the flight to Tehran. An interesting fingerprint at Marilyn's apartment had been discovered on the doorframe. It was most unusual—twice the size of a normal thumbprint. So far, they hadn't been able to trace it. That didn't surprise Thomas. He felt sure it would be another dead-end. There was also a possible lead from what appeared to be a murder at a hotel. A woman fitting Marilyn's description had checked into a room but never checked out. Blood on the carpet in sufficient amounts indicated a crime had been committed. A body had yet to be recovered.

***

Henley received word from the Leader that the Staff of Cain was in the vault at the university in Jerusalem. It would be Irad's responsibility to retrieve this most sacred object. In the meantime, Henley would remain in Iran and keep a close eye on the dig.

Irad needed an excuse for visiting Jerusalem, so he told Bill he was obliged to meet friends vacationing there. A grain of truth existed to his story. In fact, he was meeting some people in Jerusalem, but they were members who were to assist him in stealing the staff.

***

When Thomas landed at the airport in Tehran, he was surprised to see Irad there waiting for a flight.

"What are you doing in Iran?" Irad asked.

"I came to see Bill. I hope he'll answer some questions on the occult. Questions that involves a criminal investigation. What's the progress on the excavation?"

"The removal of debris is slow. It might be necessary to hire extra laborers. If we don't find something soon, the morale at the camp will suffer."

"I have some good news. Jimmy Jones called and asked me to deliver a message to Bill. A check was deposited two days ago to the expedition fund."

Their conversation was interrupted by an announcement that Irad's flight to Jerusalem was boarding.

***

Bill was glad Irad was gone. There were things he wanted to discuss with the others that he didn't feel comfortable doing in the man's presence. Some of his suspicions were gut instinct, but most were based on information Bahodore gave him from an informant. The day Irad arrived, Arsham had not detained him as he had told Bill. Instead, the two had held a meeting with a third person for most of the afternoon. Bill wasn't sure what the meeting was about, but he felt it wasn't a positive thing for the excavation or America's interest in the region.

John Elesbaan was apprehensive about Irad's visit to Jerusalem. He needed an excuse to go into the village to meet with his local contact so word could be forwarded that Irad was coming.

Over lunch, Rachael said she was going to town for some personal supplies. John and Bahodore volunteered to join her. Each had his own agenda besides providing some semblance of protection for her.

Arriving at the village, Rachael was nervous. She had a vivid memory of her first visit. A lot had occurred since then. Arsham was dead. The man's wife, who warned her to keep the bedroom door locked, had disappeared into the hills and was rumored to be working for the insurgents.

Rachael was concerned she wouldn't be able to find the personal feminine products she needed. She certainly didn't want to buy them in front of John or Bahodore. She told the men to go and take care of their errand; she would be all right alone. A few moments later, she saw a young woman dressed in a western-style outfit. After apologizing for interrupting the woman's shopping, she asked the necessary questions in the local dialect.

Making her way down the street, Rachael located the building. She was glad to see the shopkeeper's wife working behind the counter. The woman went in the back of the shop and returned with the items in a plain brown paper bag.

As Rachael stepped outside the shop, a jeep came by the store. She couldn't believe her eyes. The Revolutionary Guard officer that had interrogated Bill drove by in a jeep, and Henley was with him. They were engaged in a conversation and didn't notice her. When they were out of sight, she hurried away to look for her companions.

Bill listened in silence as Rachael explained what had occurred.

"Rachael, I don't want you to go there again."

What she didn't know was that he was aware of Henley's presence in the area. Bahodore had informed him. Henley's purpose for being in the village wasn't clear. Did it concern the intelligence operation or the excavation?

***

Henry Weston laid down the manuscript he was writing. He hadn't planned to publish another book, but recent developments were giving him second thoughts on his theories about the origins of civilization. Unfortunately, these were in conflict with what he had expounded on in his previous books.

Fullmore's deciphering of the artifacts found in the water basin and the coin discovered by Jimmy Jones were enlightened moments in Henry's professional life. He examined the two pieces of pottery. One had the symbol of a serpent coiled around a staff and below the following inscription, "*Oh great is Cain, Son of the Chosen One.*" The other had the imprint of a garden with two trees prominent in its design. The inscription below it read, "*The Children of the Lord.*" Henry reached and picked up a sketch of the coin from his table. On one side was the identical garden scene that appeared on the water jug. On the other side of the coin was the portrait of a man. Below it was inscribed the word, "*Seth.*" Even if the stories of The Society and the League of Seth were myths, he knew they contained some grain of historical truth.

25

Thomas' appearance at the camp was unexpected. Bill was at the dig when he received word. Although he had invited Thomas to come to Iran in their last conversation, he never expected him to accept. Leaving the workers behind, Bill climbed out of the tunnel and drove the short distance to the camp.

"I can't believe you're here."

"Neither can I. We can thank the terrorism unit."

"Come in my tent and tell me what you've learned in your investigation."

"Very interesting," Bill said, when the detective finished giving him a summary. "I suggest you take the rest of our group into your confidence. If we put our heads together, perhaps we can come up with some theory that will connect the dots behind these murders."

"Who's in your group?"

"You've already met most of them. There's Rachael, Benjamin Rabon, John Elesbaan and, of course, my dad. The next name I need you to keep in confidence."

"Who's that?"

"A man named Ronald Fullmore."

"Fullmore is here?"

"It's a long story," Bill said.

That evening over dinner, the group listened as Thomas told about the murder investigation and the information the police had uncovered.

"Of course, I'm a detective dealing in facts and evidence. The occult is not logical to me. In my career when this sort of thing appeared, it was just in the defendant's mind. Total nonsense, though the accused may have actually believed it."

"This may be a little different," Henry said.

"What do you mean?"

"The symbol of the serpent could belong to a cult whose roots stretch back to ancient time."

"But I read the book you gave me. You said not only were these stories about a society that used the serpent a myth, but there wasn't even a grain of truth to them."

A smile crept across Henry's face. "I think I was wrong in my assumptions there was no foundation to support the myth. You see, myths generally arise from facts that are distorted over time. In the past, I never found any evidence on which the stories of The Society were based. But that's changed since we now have items with ancient writing which clearly establish a foundation for what we're still calling a fable."

Henry explained to Thomas the translations on the staff, coin, and jugs.

"So are you saying The Society exists?"

"No, I'm not saying there is such a group today, but at one time it may have existed."

Bill and Rachael looked at one another across the table. They were surprised by Henry's change of opinion on the subject.

"You know the symbol of the serpent at the beginning of time was used synonymously with the male phallus," Fullmore said.

"That true," John said. "The earliest civilizations were deep into fertility rites, and the phallus was worshipped."

"What about the female anatomy?" Rachael asked, whose blush for such a question was hidden by the darkness of the evening.

"The female genitals were seen simply as a receptacle for the sacred phallus," Bill said. "Later, religions developed the belief that when a man had intercourse, he only opened the vagina so God could enter and plant the seed of life."

"How could anyone ever believe such nonsense?" Thomas asked.

"You are Scotch-Irish by background, aren't you Thomas?" Henry asked.

"Yes."

"Presbyterian?"

"What does that have to do with it?"

"How was Christ born?"

"Of the Virgin Mary conceived by the Holy Ghost."

"And who was his biological father?"

"God."

"Do you still believe it's foolishness?"

"I get your point, Henry."

"That's why I don't find it too far-fetched to believe there is some basis for the myth that the Devil impregnated Eve with her first child, Cain," Henry said.

"The term *Serpent* in the Garden of Eden could simply mean Lucifer's phallus," John said. "You see the use of the term *Serpent* to mean snake is of recent origin and is based on a poor translation of the original language."

"That's a very interesting theory," Bill said. "Although I personally believe it's a myth, it does spring from some actual facts."

"The stories could actually be true," Henry said.

Everyone looked at Henry surprised by his statement.

"How else do you think evil came into the world?"

In the light provided by a fire blazing nearby, Rachael noticed something strange. John and Fullmore were sitting beside one another, and although both had black skin, John's had a reddish tint. She was curious but didn't know how to broach the subject. She was glad when her father asked John about his ancestry.

"Since you're from Ethiopia, you must know a lot about its history concerning the origins of Ethiopians. Do you think the stories that they came from India are true, and that's why they referred to themselves as the Reds?"

"It is undisputed that the earliest Ethiopian civilization did in fact refer to themselves as the Reds. This distinguished them from the surrounding tribes. Skin texture and the fact there was trade between India and Ethiopia gave rise to the theory."

"I'm in the process of developing another theory based on my research into the Garden of Eden and the Land of Nod," Bill said.

"What's that?" John asked.

"That the first Ethiopian civilization was built by people from the Zagros Mountains."

"Why would you say that?" John asked.

"Because the first civilizations created were by two tribes, Seth and Cain. At least an argument could be made that originally Seth and his descendants had a reddish complexion."

"Professor, where do you get a basis for the red complexion?" Rachael asked.

"Because in old Hebrew, Genesis says God created Adam from red clay. Haven't you noticed in the heat of the day, the earth on the side of these mountains has a reddish tint to it?"

"I find this conversation very stimulating, but Thomas came a long way to seek our help," Henry said. "So Thomas, how can we be of assistance? Feel free to ask this group any question you like."

"Let me say that I've already heard things here that shed light on some of my questions. Henry, you said it's possible there was at one time a society that used the symbol that keeps popping up in my investigation. Now, assuming just for the sake of argument that such a society exists today, what would be its objective?"

"I can only tell you what the numerous legends that have floated around for centuries have said. The Society's members believed they were the direct descendants of Cain, who was born of a sexual liaison between Eve and the Devil or a fallen angel, or some other evil personage, depending on whom you choose to believe.

This group worshiped the Creature and believed that it was the opposite of God, endowed with evil. Unlike Christians and other branches of Judaism, they looked forward to the coming of the *Antichrist*. The legends don't speak in terms of specific goals, other than it is their duty to do whatever is necessary to bring in the age of the *Antichrist* and eventually the return of the Creature to Earth.

"This group is probably some satanic cult that has no connection to ancient times but simply bought into one of those legends," Thomas said.

"Well, as bad as that might be, it certainly is a whole sight better than if it was the real thing."

"I'm only going to be here a few days," Thomas said. "Is there a possibility we could decipher the items I told you about earlier? The ones I obtained from the safety deposit boxes."

"You'd have to ask Fullmore about that," Bill said.

"I'll start to work on it right away," Fullmore said.

Noticing the puzzled look on Benjamin Rabon's face, Bill knew it was time to disclose Fullmore's true identity.

Later that evening Thomas gave Fullmore the items with the strange language that none of the terrorist experts could decipher. Then he questioned him about what happened in Mississippi. When Fullmore finished telling his story, Thomas said, "We are testing the blood found at your place. The lab should have the results by the time I return to New York."

26

When Bill entered his tent that evening, he would have liked nothing better than to sleep. But Jimmy had deposited five hundred thousand dollars into his account. So he reached for the book on the Ark written by Dr. Simmons. It lay on top of the old wooden crate next to his cot.

"After the death of Solomon, the Kingdom of Israel was torn apart. The Assyrians conquered the Northern Kingdom. The Kingdom of Judah, whose capitol was at Jerusalem, survived as an independent state for a time thereafter. Their kings began to worship the gods of neighboring nations. The Ark was replaced with materials glorifying other deities, though there were times under certain kings when the people returned to the worship of Yahweh. It

was during one such period that possession of the Ark by the Jews is mentioned in the Bible for the last time. This occurred during the reign of King Josiah, who restored the Ark to its proper place of worship in the temple at Jerusalem.

One of the oldest legends of Israel losing possession of the Ark is an Ethiopian story. There are many different versions but the central theme is that Menelik, the child of Solomon and the Queen of Sheba, spent time in Jerusalem with his father. When it was time to return to his homeland, the king directed the first-born male of each family to accompany him. The son of the high priest, Zadok, was furious about the order. So in revenge, he and several others, who were being forcibly exiled, stole the Ark and hid it among the baggage on the caravan that was going to the Kingdom of Sheba. A long line of emperors claimed direct lineage to Menelik to propagate this legend as a basis to justify their divine right to rule.

Another Ethiopian story places the Ark at Elephantir. This legend has the high priest of the temple, who was loyal to the worship of Yahweh, secretly removing the Ark from Jerusalem during the reign of Manasseh who had converted the temple into a place of pagan worship. It was taken from the country for safekeeping. The high priest chose Elephantir, an island off the coast of Egypt, and the

Ark remained there for several hundred years. The remains of a Jewish temple are still visible today. According to this story, the Ark was taken later to the city of Axum in Ethiopia where many believe it is still present today.

A third story about the disappearance of the Ark is that it occurred when Nebuchadnezzar conquered Jerusalem. Many scholars think it was taken as war booty to Babylon. However, the scribes in his court were excellent record keepers, and the Ark is not listed among the items taken from the temple.

***

Rachael's clothes were torn from her body. She tried to stop Irad, but he was too strong. Henley was in the corner of the room watching. A grin on his face revealed the gold fillings in his teeth. She struggled but it was no use. Suddenly Henley was on top of her. Then she woke, sweat pouring off her forehead and running into her eyes. It was only a nightmare. Seeing Henley in the village must have triggered it. She rose from her cot and walked over the entrance of her tent where a breeze dried the sweat on her face.

John watched Rachael through the flap of his tent. He wished he could talk to her. Hell, he wished he could talk to anyone about what his life was really like.

The modern world was so ignorant of the true nature of things. So involved in the everyday mundane matters, they weren't aware their world was on a collision path with powers they couldn't even comprehend. The forces of evil were gaining strength, and the day of reckoning was coming. The days of the *Serpent* were near.

Thomas joined Bill at the excavation. Matters of the occult weren't something that attracted him before these murder cases. He always thought it was foolishness. But his mindset was beginning to change.

The tunnel was lit by kerosene lamps placed at strategic points along the way. The two heavy-duty flashlights they carried as they walked deeper into the bowels of the earth added additional illumination.

"See that massive boulder up ahead," Bill said. "It blocked us from continuing in the direction planned, so we dug parallel, hoping eventually we would reach the end and then make a turn toward our original path."

Thomas looked at the huge rock. It was flat, and the surface was perfectly smooth.

"It looks like the side of a building."

Bill put his finger to his lips.

"Thomas, the walls have ears. We speak of it in front of the laborers as just an obstruction. There are spies among them."

Thomas placed his hand against the surface and let it run along the smooth stone for a few feet. He felt strange inside. His instincts told him this was the outside wall of a temple. Suppose there had once been an ancient city here. One that was built by Cain.

Rachael promised to show Thomas the water basin. She was glad he would be with her. She had been a little nervous the last time she swam there alone. She had felt the presence of someone watching her.

They followed the stony path through the mountain range until they reached the pool of water, now shrunk substantially in size because of the drought. Rachael went behind some rocks and changed into a bikini she brought in a backpack. It was the first time she had worn it in Iran, fearful some Muslims might be offended. But today, with Thomas, she felt safe and decided to throw caution to the wind.

Thomas turned his gaze from the water in time to see her approaching. He couldn't help but notice her trim, tan, and neatly packaged body. He had been a detective a long time and in those years became a good judge of body language. She was flirting with him.

"It's your turn to change. I'll be in the water when you get back." She climbed onto the rock, and after taking a few stretches that flexed every muscle, she dove into the water.

The cold water splashing Thomas in the face did little to cool the heat rising in his body. He stepped behind some rocks and changed into a swimsuit he brought in case he decided to go swimming. And Thomas decided most definitely that he was going swimming.

27

As Thomas and Rachael entered the camp that evening, they heard Fullmore call out.

"I've some good news."

When they entered Rachael's tent, a table had papers strewn over it.

"I've deciphered the items from the safety deposit boxes."

Fullmore sat in front of the computer and opened his software program. They peered over his shoulder in excited anticipation as the translation came up on the screen.

"Actually, this wasn't that hard to decipher. The basic language was the same as on the staff. I think they both originate from the same root language. The only differences were minor modifications that occurred over a period of time when people began to add words to their vocabulary. The map you gave me is of recent origin. We know this because, although it is in an ancient language, current names are used."

"There's the village of Noqdi," Rachael said.

"That's right, and as you can see the place where we are on the plateau is noted as the City of Enoch."

"How did a person get this information?" Rachael asked. "I thought we had the only map in existence."

"Apparently not. Let's look at the other materials. Here are the three brief correspondences. I have numbered them as a, b, and c on the computer. The letters are addressed to a Saba Aden, the same person using the alias Samuel Mendel. They are from a person who calls himself Enosh."

Looking over Fullmore's shoulder, they read the translation.

The Society is involved in locating the City of Enoch. You are to establish contact with a man who uses the alias Walter Henley and become part of his investment group. Funds will be deposited in your bank account for this purpose.

Thomas and Rachael continued to the next letter on the screen.

We believe The Society has obtained information on the location of the missing Ark of the Covenant from

Dr. Harvey Simons who they murdered. Henley may be involved.

The third letter read showed how dangerous the situation had gotten.

Be careful! The Society has reached the stage of their operation where it might be in their interest to eliminate the investors. We will provide you with a new alias and send you to Yemen to cover the Ark project.

"What about the small booklet I gave you with the strange symbol on top?" Thomas asked. "Have you deciphered it?"

"No. It's a codebook. It uses symbols rather than language. My software wasn't appropriate. I'll have to develop a program for it."

Just then Bill entered the tent.

"You won't believe what we just found out," Thomas said. "The Society really exists."

***

Irad met with his co-conspirators in the new King Solomon Hotel suite. The four men mapped out their strategy to remove the Staff of Cain from the vault at the university. One of the four, Adah was a custodian of the building. He was not connected to The Society, but he was simply paid a substantial sum for his assistance in providing access to the campus buildings. He was even able to secure from the president's office keys to the room where the vault was located. His usefulness over, Irad gave the signal, and the other men grabbed the unsuspecting custodian. They held him while Irad stuck a needle into his arm. The shot would heavily sedate him. After pouring whiskey down his throat, they picked up his limp body and placed him in a bathtub filled with chlorine water. Irad shoved the man's head under. After dark, the body was taken to a motel and dumped into a swimming pool.

It was midnight in Jerusalem when the van pulled up outside the university. Irad and the two men left the vehicle and walked quickly across the street onto the campus grounds. Crossing the tree-shaded area, they went directly to the large structure located at the far end of the Quad. Here they used a key that gave them access to the floor below where the vault was located. Its large steel structure encased in the wall wasn't an obstacle. They had the combination. It was easy to obtain once the custodian stole a document with the names of persons who knew its secret.

Irad had chosen from the list a middle-aged divorcee with two teenage daughters. When the mother came home from work, he was waiting. The twin girls were tied up in the bedroom. All it took to get the information was a knife at the girls' throats. He knew they couldn't be left alive. But he didn't kill them immediately. Instead, he took his time, assaulting the girls while their mother watched in horror as she struggled helplessly against the ropes, which secured her to a chair. When he had finished, he slit the distraught mother's throat and then walked over to the bed and strangled her children. Irad knew the *Serpent* would approve.

Many artifacts of antiquity were inside the vault. Irad would have loved to browse through them, but time was of the essence. The men knew they had only thirty minutes before the next security patrol. The staff was attached to the wall on the right side of the room. Irad held it in his hands for a moment. Then focusing his thoughts back on the mission, he placed the staff in a flexible container. They arrived back at their vehicle without incident.

***

Thomas stretched out his legs and relaxed. The airline stewards came by and poured him a Bourbon. It was nice flying first class back to New York. The government only paid for coach, but the flight attendant saw his profession on the passenger log and escorted him to the front where there were empty seats. Since the

9-11 terrorist attack, the airlines had shown respect to police officers traveling on their planes.

The first Bourbon went down so smooth that Thomas ordered another. While waiting for the stewards to bring it, his mind drifted to the afternoon spent with Rachael. He became physically restless thinking about it. After they swam, loneliness caused him to use poor judgment. In the water that day, he slipped his arm around Rachael and pulled her close to him. She didn't resist so he kissed her. Then his hand moved from her waist and cupped one of her small breasts that was barely contained by the skimpy, flimsy material covering it. A groan of pleasure had escaped her lips, then she pushed him away. "I can't do this," she had said in a trembling voice. As he released her, Rachael began to cry, and then said she was sorry if she misled him. On the journey back to the camp, they hardly spoke a word, but when they arrived and for the rest of his stay, she acted as if nothing had happened. He remembered his analysis of Rachael the first time he saw her at the lecture in New York. He believed it had been a correct one. She acted cool, aloof, and in control in public, but she lacked confidence in herself.

***

"Dad," Bill said as they were sitting around the campfire. "I remember when I was growing up you were always strong in your belief that worshiping saints or religious artifacts was only a step away from paganism. So how do you feel about the importance of the Ark of the Covenant?"

"The Ark is a little different because a Spirit of the Lord once spoke directly to man from the mercy seat which sat on the lid of the Ark."

"But what relevance does it have today? Didn't the coming of Christ make it irrelevant?"

"It will always be relevant in a historical sense. The Ark was actually a carbon copy of one that existed in heaven. The Acacia wood from which it was made came from a tree in the Garden of Eden. This tree was brought from heaven, and planted in the garden by the angels. Pieces of this sacred wood were in the possession of Moses who used it to build the Ark. In fact, the staff of Moses was made from this very same wood. Legends say that even the rod of Aaron kept inside the Ark was made of Acacia wood."

Dad hadn't changed, Bill thought. It was hard to pinpoint him on an issue without first listening to a lot of information.

At that moment, Rachael joined them.

"Hope I'm not interrupting a private conversation, gentlemen." She sat beside Henry.

"No, we were just discussing the importance of the Ark," Bill said.

"It's still relevant to many people of faith," Henry said. "And to certain segments of the Jewish community it's important in more than a historical sense."

"In what way?" Rachael asked.

Henry said, "Some believe that before the end of time, the temple will be rebuilt in Jerusalem. The Ark is to remain hidden until it can take its rightful place in the temple."

"Some of the signs for those who believe in that theology are coming true," Bill said.

"What signs?" Rachael asked.

"The reestablishment of the *State of Israel*, which, of course, has occurred. Another sign is the return of the eleven tribes of Israel. As you're aware, that's in the process now. The *Falasha*, descendants of the *Tribe of David*, have recently returned. The lost groups in India and Southern Africa that DNA has shown are originally from *Canaan* are also migrating to Israel."

"You said eleven, but there were twelve tribes of Israel," Rachael said.

"The Tribe of Dan is omitted."

"Why?"

"Because several passages in the Bible point out the Tribe of Dan will produce the *Antichrist*."

28

"Is Kinsey in this morning?" Thomas asked.

"He's with someone now."

While he waited, Melinda left her desk and strolled over to a filing cabinet. She leaned over and pulled open the bottom drawer. The skirt she was wearing moved up a few inches exposing a pair of attractive legs. Removing a file from the drawer, Melinda took her time walking back to the desk. As he watched, Thomas thought maybe he should take Kinsey up on his suggestion and ask her out. Then remembering what happened with Rachael, he knew his ego wouldn't take another rejection so soon.

"Are you going to the party tomorrow night?" Melinda asked in her soft Carolina low-country brogue.

"What party? I just got back in town last night and haven't checked my e-mail."

"The one at Saline's. I hope you can come."

She said it in such a way that it sounded like she actually wanted him there.

Just then, Kinsey came out of his office with Harry Beacham.

"It's good to see you again," Beacham said when he saw Thomas. "I've got a busy schedule on this trip to the city, but next time I'm in town perhaps we can get together."

"I'd like that."

Before he left, Beacham stepped over to Melinda's desk.

"I'll see you at Saline's tomorrow."

"I'm looking forward to it," Melinda said, her face turning a crimson red.

She's trolling for a bigger fish than I am, Thomas thought.

After Beacham left, Kinsey invited Thomas into his office.

"I've been looking forward to an update on those weird cases of yours," he said.

***

Sam Rison had been up since daybreak. He looked forward to the detective's visit. He was a lonely man in retirement. So when the detective called and said he wanted to talk about the *Giants* again, Sam was delighted.

"Good morning, Thomas," he said, opening the front door of his apartment for his guest. "Come back to my study. We can talk there about those matters in which you expressed an interest. I spent a few hours at the university library updating my information. You know, most people don't realize how quickly our knowledge of the ancient world is expanding in this age of information."

The room was exactly what one would have expected an archaeologist's study to look like. It contained numerous pictures of expeditions and a bookshelf with writings on the ancient world, some authored by Sam. The beautiful mahogany desk in the center of the room with the solid wooden chair behind it gave one a sense this was a man of authority in his field. Beside the desk was a small table holding a silver-plated pot full of freshly brewed coffee from Ethiopia, the land of the original coffee-bean tree.

"I appreciate an audience on such short notice."

"Oh, it's my pleasure. I'm glad to share any information that might help on your cases."

"I was in Paris investigating the story you told me about."

"What did you find out?"

"Apparently, the scientist was a brilliant man who was much maligned by the press, as well as the scientific community. He disappeared and hasn't been seen since. Everyone assumes he is dead. My trip raised some interesting issues, but as to any new leads on the killer, it was a dead end. Afterwards I flew to Iran and spent a few days at the excavation site near Noqdi. I had a discussion with Henry Weston about a group called The Society."

"What did he say?"

"He's in the process of reevaluating his thoughts on the matter. Seems to think there may be some basis for the myths that developed."

"So, Henry still thinks it's a myth. I respect him, but over the years, we have disagreed when it comes to events in the Garden of Eden and the question of the *Nephilim*."

"That's why I came. I'd like to know what you think."

"During my entire career, I've chosen my words carefully on this subject. People can be so close-minded. Surprisingly, the worst offenders are the academic community. What occurred in Paris was an example of what can happen to a person's career. It showed the scientific community was also close-minded. For the rest of your life you simply lose all credibility with your colleagues."

"I know the feeling. It's the same in my profession."

"Well, my career is over, but like most people, I'm still concerned about damaging my reputation. I'd like to die with it intact."

Sam paused a moment and then continued.

"The story of The Society has come down through the ages in bits and pieces. A legend here, a myth there, brief mention in an inscription found during an excavation or the recovery of an ancient artifact. It seems there's never enough to get a clear picture. But archaeologists and persons interested in the occult continue to make progress in accumulating materials on the subject. I became interested in this area when, as a young man, I did my thesis on the *Nephilim* for my doctorate. That's how I was first exposed to stories about The Society. Over the years, I became a true believer. That is to say, I am one who has come to the conclusion that *Nephilim* once roamed the lands of the ancient world and that there existed an organization of their descendants called The Society, who truly believe they were the descendants of a sexual union between Lucifer and Eve."

"Do you believe that it exists today?"

"Now this is where I may be on thin ice."

"But what do you think?"

"They do."

"Really?"

"And I will tell you why."

Thomas sat back in his chair and listened.

"What I'm going to tell you is a mixture of fact and fiction. Over the centuries, they have merged until sometimes it's hard to separate one from the other."

"After Cain fled to the Land of Nod, he took a wife. Scholars have often debated the origin of this woman. The Bible mentions children who were born of this union. Meanwhile living somewhere nearby were Adam and Eve who had a child named Seth. His descendents called themselves the *Children of the Lord*."

"In the early portions of the Bible, there were *Nephilim,* who were *giants*. There is confusion on their origin. Some theologians believe they sprang from Cain's bloodline. In those early days of human existence, a constant war waged between the two groups. The *Nephilim* were ultimately defeated and disappeared from the pages of history. But that's not quite true because it's now becoming apparent they simply went underground."

"What's the function of their organization if it still exists?"

"It's all laid out in The Sacred Book."

"The what?"

"Sacred Book."

"Where can I get a copy?"

"I'm afraid that it too has disappeared over time. We do, however, have stories of its contents."

"Could you tell me about that?"

"It told the history of how the remnants of the *Nephilim*, after their last great battle with the *Children of the Lord*, fled to Sheba where present-day Yemen is located. There in the hills, they regrouped and created a new civilization on the backs of the primitive indigenous inhabitants whom they made slaves. They never lost sight of their objective to spread evil throughout the world."

"So that was the goal?"

"There are several subplots to their desire of world domination. One of them seems to be the accumulation of relics that are held sacred by the *Children of the Lord*. We know from stories over the centuries they have had their successes. They obtained the bones of Noah, which tradition says were buried near his boat upon his death centuries after the flood. Later they obtained the body of Daniel from its crypt. It's said by some that even after hundreds of years it had not decayed. Now, some people believe it was because he was a holy man. But it may be simply a case of embalming. All of the many relics collected were kept in Yemen; what we today would call a museum.

The Society has long wanted to acquire the Staff of Cain, which they apparently lost during the last great battle with the *Children of the Lord*. But the centerpiece of their desire is the possession of the Ark of the Covenant. Since it contains a spirit of God, the Society's possession would mean evil would actually have control of a part of the Supreme Being."

"Why do they want to acquire those things?"

"They believe that each of these items contains a source of power."

"That seems like foolishness to me. How could any intelligent person think the old bones of famous people or ancient artifacts could have power?"

"Are you Catholic?"

"No, I'm Protestant."

"Many in my faith believe that touching the bones of a saint will cure an illness.

When Thomas left Sam's apartment, he felt the man had given him an understanding of The Society. But he would have to keep these thoughts to himself. No one would believe Sam's story about a mysterious group who were the descendants of the devil. Even Thomas found it hard to admit he believed it, but he did.

29

The club was rented for the evening from money donated by agents. It was an opportunity for the employees to bond on a social level. By tradition, it only happened once a year at a time chosen by Director Charles Cagle, whose headquarters was in Washington. This party was the only time many of them had the opportunity to meet him on a personal level. While not mandatory, it was expected that everyone working at the agency would be present. Betty, who heard all the scuttlebutt, let Thomas know it was vital they go to be seen as part of the team.

When Thomas entered the club, he spotted Melinda talking to Beacham near a side entrance away from the crowd. He watched as Beacham placed his hand on her waist. Melinda took a step back dislodging it in a move that would not embarrass but at the same time send a message. Maybe I misjudged her, Thomas thought. When Beacham walked away in apparent frustration, Thomas made a beeline to her.

"Hello."

"Detective, I'm glad to see you made it."

Her expression seemed genuine.

"Would you like me to freshen that drink?"

"Why thanks."

He wondered if she would disappear while he was gone. He had that trick pulled on him before.

When Thomas returned, she was engaged in a conversation with Kinsey.

"I was just telling Melinda that my wife was to meet me here, but I just received a call. It seems she's not feeling well, so I have to leave. She's eight months into her first pregnancy."

"I'm sure she'll be all right," Thomas said.

"Melinda rode here with me. Would you give her a ride home?"

"That's okay. I can catch a cab."

"No, I'll be glad to take you. That's if you don't mind."

"Of course, I wouldn't, mind, and it is awfully sweet of you to offer."

"Then it's settled," Thomas said.

They were separated during most of the evening. He was busy networking, and she was constantly on the dance floor accommodating men whose wives weren't present. At ten o'clock, he heard a voice from behind.

"Hope I'm not interrupting anything important, but the detective promised me a dance."

He turned around to see Melinda standing there.

"Excuse me gentlemen, but a pleasant duty calls."

"You can hold me a little closer," she said, on the dance floor.

Thomas had intentionally held her at a distance. He had watched her through the corner of his eye all night as men tried to pull her tightly against them and noticed how she constantly pushed them away.

"Detective, do you like working at the Unit?"

"Just call me Thomas."

"All right, Thomas."

"It's interesting, although most of my time has been spent working on cases I brought with me from the precinct. What about you?"

"It was good of Kinsey to give me the job. I'm working hard to improve myself and correct my deficiencies, but I know what people think."

"What's that?"

"Oh, I'm sure you heard the scuttlebutt. That I only have this position because I'm sleeping with him. Of course, that's not true. He's deeply in love with his wife. I only hope to find a man one day that will love me as much as Kinsey loves her."

"I believe you. He tried to get me to ask you out."

"He did?"

"Yes."

"And you didn't?"

"Thought you'd turn me down."

"You shouldn't jump to conclusions, Detective–I mean Thomas. Do you mind taking me home now?"

"I hope I haven't said anything to offend you."

"No, of course not. It's getting late, and I have a flight to Charleston tomorrow. I'm going to spend the weekend with my family. If you want to stay longer, I could catch a cab."

"Are you kidding? Without your presence, I wouldn't want to be here."

That's a good line, Thomas thought. Nevertheless, he really did feel that way.

Melinda lived on Gillard Street, which was only three blocks long and lined with trees. The large homes on the street, built in the eighteenth century, had long ago been turned into apartments. Stairs built onto the side of the house accessed Melinda's apartment. Because of light traffic, the drive from the party to the apartment took less than twenty minutes. Thomas pulled under a large tree in front and parked.

"Do you want to come up for coffee?" she asked.

When they entered the apartment, he was surprised it was so spacious. In New York, most were small unless you were rich enough to purchase one of the old warehouses that yuppies were turning into residences. They went back to the kitchen, which was down the hallway past a bedroom. Thomas looked through the open door and saw an antique queen-sized bed covered with a traditional spread.

While Thomas stood watching near the kitchen door, Melinda switched on music and started the coffee. He noticed she was talking at a rapid pace about her trip to Charleston. Had Melinda consumed too much wine, or was she just nervous about his being there? She walked by him to get the cups out of a cabinet. The smell of her perfume excited him. He felt the urge to reach out and take her into his arms.

Melinda didn't wait for Thomas to act. She placed her arms around his neck and pressed her lips to his. Her body moved forward, clinging to him in such a manner that her small breasts were crushed against his chest.

"How bad do you want that coffee?" she asked.

They kissed again. It was long, filled with emotion and passion. She led him toward the bedroom. She ripped the spread off the bed and pushed him toward it. Then she paused. Breathing heavily she said, "I'll be back in a minute."

Melinda fumbled though the bathroom drawer. Finally, she found the diaphragm her older sister had insisted she purchase before she left for New York. She remembered resisting, saying it wasn't necessary. She would never want a man again. Devastated when Charles had left her, she hadn't slept with a man since.

Thomas waited in the bed with a thin sheet pulled over his naked body feeling somewhat foolish and wondering what was taking her so long.

Uncomfortable letting Thomas see her naked, Melinda reached out the bathroom door and switched off the light. A moment later, she slipped beneath the sheet.

***

"I saw you speaking to Director Cagle at the party," Betty said, when she brought in some new files the unit wanted Thomas to work on.

"Just touching base with him so he would know I was there. Seems he's keeping up with our investigation."

"Someone," Betty said, "told me Director Cagle was into the occult."

"He apparently cut his teeth early in his career investigating a murder involving a group of devil worshipers. He invited me to drop by if I came to Washington."

"Are you going?"

"Hell, no. I don't have time for office politics. Besides we'll be back at the precinct soon."

Richard was sitting at the booth in Mingos when Thomas entered.

"We've got a lot to discuss," Richard said.

"And I have a bucket full of information to give you on the occult. I won't even ask you to believe it."

"We got a break on Marilyn's case."

"What?"

"She was murdered."

Richard gave the details of what the investigation had uncovered and how they were certain that the person killed in the hotel was Marilyn.

"The license number a witness gave us was from a stolen vehicle," Richard said. "But thank God we found the abandoned vehicle. Based on the pools of blood in it, I believe she was dissected. You spurred my interest the last time we talked about this Society thing. After I received the report on Marilyn, I checked to see who the best person in the field was on blood analysis.

Turns out, the expert is right here in New York. I had an appointment with her last week. Told her our story about the DNA tests in all our cases, and about the body in Paris. It turns out her father was an archaeologist. She spent most of her early life trekking around the world living in tents while her father conducted excavation."

"With her background it sounds like she'll have an interest in our endeavor from a historical view, as well as a scientific one," Thomas said.

"She wanted to see the reports on the tests. I had my secretary send her a copy. She called this morning. Wants to see me at two-thirty today. Can you come?"

"You're damn right, I can. Now let me add to your confusion."

Thomas told Richard what occurred in Paris and at Noqdi.

***

Doctor Geneva Peterson, it turned out, didn't practice medicine, but taught at the medical university. Her expertise was in the composition of blood and in the developing genetic code of the human body. Her students, if asked, would tell you she was the most serious person they had ever met, never smiling and always on task. Forty and single, she had devoted her life to the medical profession. She was a woman who had never felt the loving arms of a man around her, except for, of course, her father's–whom she adored. He had been dead for five years. There still wasn't a day that went by that she didn't think of him. He had been her only family. Her mother died in childbirth, giving Geneva life while losing her own, a guilt she carried.

The doctor's office had the look and smell of a hospital room. She was seated behind a gray metal desk when they entered.

"Dr. Peterson, I'd like you to meet Thomas O'Conner," said Richard "He's also a detective with the city but temporally on duty with the national terrorist unit."

She reached over and shook Thomas' hand. She had a grip like a man.

"Have you had a chance to review those reports?" Richard asked.

"Yes, I did. They were most interesting. I'll take the easy ones first. On Linda Mendel, nothing unusual. The blood of her husband and his maid, Milcah, were similar. Both had ancestors who came from the land of *Canaan*, the old biblical term for Israel. Now, Marilyn's blood and the blood found at the Fullmore farm in Mississippi have the same basic genetic matter. They contained some materials not currently in our database of humans. But it does have some genetic material that is in our data bank from the Middle East. The third, Imnah, is the most perplexing. We have no information in our data bank. It's as if he was not in the human chain."

"Not of this world?" Thomas asked.

"Now, I wouldn't go so far as to say that, Detective. I'd like to get samples of the blood and run my own test, if that's possible."

"What's the cost involved? I'm not sure I can get the department to approve it," Richard said.

"I'll do it for free. This could have such ramifications. The very idea that there might be another chain of descent would shock the scientific and academic community. You can't imagine what a stir it would cause. But I'm getting ahead of myself. First, get the samples and let me see what I can uncover.

When the detectives left, they had obtained a few answers but accumulated a complete new set of questions.

30

The Leader pushed the hidden button behind some books and the bookshelf opened into a secret chamber. Walking in, he paused and admired the Staff of Cain enclosed in a glass case attached to the wall on the far end of the room. He visited the secret room often to admire it. The council was ecstatic about the recovery. It heralded another milestone in the road toward revenge on the *Seed of Seth*. They directed the Leader to focus his energies now on finding the Ark.

It was good the organization had at its disposal the Noba, one of the most sophisticated intelligence operations in the world. This group was augmented by assassins whose skill at eliminating enemies was unparalleled in history. Because these two organizations coordinated their activities, The Society knew when Dr. Harvey Simmons obtained and translated an ancient document uncovered in a cave by an illiterate shepherd boy in an area near the Dead Sea. Under torture, the doctor disclosed the secret place in his study where he had hidden the script. With a little more encouragement, he translated the writing on the parchment. The document dispelled many rumors that circulated for centuries about the Ark.

The Leader returned to his desk after closing the bookshelf to the secret room. He put a disk into his computer and made a copy of the translated script.

Irad opened the sealed envelope delivered that morning. Inside was a disk. Hands shaking with excitement, he put it in the computer.

"I, Zadab, of the Tribe of Levi, knowing that my days are numbered upon this earth, and believing a history on the disappearance of the Ark of the Covenant should be recorded, so that it will not be lost in the passage of time, set forth this story handed down in my family for generations and maintained in secrecy by an oath sworn to Yahweh within the Holy of Holies.

"I am the last of my family line. All the others are dead by war or pestilence. Alone in this cave on my deathbed, I was visited by the Spirit of the Almighty and have been

directed, as the last direct descendant of the High Priest, Nadab, to inscribe upon this document the secret.

In the days of our great King Solomon there was a son conceived of his sexual union with the beautiful Queen of Sheba. She returned to her own country. Many years later, the son born of this relationship was sent by the queen to visit his father in Jerusalem. He carried with him the ring that the great king had given the queen when she left the holy city.

When the son, Menelik, arrived at Solomon's court, he sent the ring to Solomon, along with a message that he was his son. The king immediately recognized the ring and ordered the young man brought before him. He was accepted into the royal circle and was recognized as one of the princes of the realm. In Jerusalem, he studied Hebrew and learned about the worship of Yahweh.

After five years, he informed his father that he must return to Sheba as he had promised his mother. His father begged him not to go, but when he saw that the young man was determined, he relented. He wanted his son to enjoy the rank and power that he was entitled to have had he chosen to remain in Israel. So he required that the first-born of the leaders of each tribe and of the palace hierarchy accompany him back to Sheba. And to further establish Menelik as a true heir, he directed that a replica of the Ark be carried back with him as a symbol of his power.

After Menelik departed, there arose a rumor that Menelik had stolen the Ark, so the priests had to carry the true Ark through the streets of the capitol to quell the rumor.

Shortly thereafter Solomon died, and the Kingdom split. Ten tribes rebelled and refused to recognize Rehoboam, the son of Solomon, as their ruler Instead, they established the kingdom of Israel and elected Jeroboam their king. In the south, Rehoboam ruled in Jerusalem with the support of the remaining two tribes.

The kings in Jerusalem turned away from the worship of Yahweh. They installed pagan idols in the temple itself. The high priest was horrified. In the middle of the night, he stole the Ark and sent it with his two sons to Sheba for safekeeping. To protect himself from the wrath of the king, the high priest had a copy of the Ark built and placed in the temple. This copy of the Ark was later taken to Elephantine, when it appeared Jerusalem would fall to a foreign invader. The true Ark of the Covenant, when it arrived in--- ."

That was the end of the document. The rest of the script had disintegrated with the passage of time.

***

The twenty new laborers made a tremendous difference in the earth removed each day. This shifted the burden on Bill and the other professionals. No longer could the group work half days. Gone was the opportunity to refresh one's self at the water basin or relax in a hammock during the heat of the day. It was exhausting dirty work from daylight to dawn. Everyone collapsed into their cots at night as soon the evening meal was over. To add to their burden, the Iranian government sent an official from Tehran to live in the camp and watch their every move. His name was Khandan. Although, as it turned out, he wasn't such a bad chap after all. Though he didn't have formal training as an archaeologist, he did have a keen interest in it. And this frequently placed him in the way inside the narrow tunnel that was beginning to snake along at a rapid pace.

Every day the work was the same, shifting dirt and ash for hours looking for signs of a civilization. Images of the glory of working at an excavation site soon disappeared. That was why Khandan's announcement, that the following week was a national holiday and excavation must stop to celebrate was greeted with a sigh of relief. Rachael noticed even Bill seemed happy for the mandatory work stoppages.

"Tomorrow the workers will be going to their homes for the holiday," Khandan announced. "We should take this opportunity to visit Noah's grave."

"And where do you think that was?" Rachael asked.

"A day's journey from here."

"But wasn't he supposed to be buried near the Ark that floated upon the water during the great flood?" Rachael asked.

"That's true," Henry said.

"Well, that's *Mt. Ararat*."

"Our legends have it here in the Zagros Mountains," Khandan said.

"Those stories may be true," Rachael's father said. "You see, as we learn more about the early history of man, it's becoming apparent the genealogy we know puts Noah somewhere close to this part of the world."

"The people in this region have an old tradition that Noah's Ark rested at *Judi Dagh* in these very mountains," Bill said.

"But doesn't that conflict with the Bible, which names Mt. Ararat as the boat's resting place?" Rachael asked.

"It's all a matter of interpretation and translation of the original text from the root language that was used," Bill said. "Some experts believe the proper translation would be the *Mountains of Ararat* and not *Mount Ararat*. Now that makes a big difference. For in ancient times that mountain range extended to our present location, and in fact, is today known as the Zagros Mountains."

"If that's true, then Noah's boat would still be at Judi Dagh," Rachael said.

"Probably not," her father said. "Over the years the locals and some famous personages, such as *Sennacherib*, have taken pieces of it for souvenirs. If the boat was ever there, it's totally dismantled by now. But I'm still intrigued about Noah's grave."

***

Irad sent the professor a message from New York stating his return to the excavation was delayed because his father was ill. Actually, one of the reasons was because of his assignment to the Ark project. But that was a long-range endeavor. What required his presence in the city immediately was a short-range assignment, Dr. Geneva Peterson.

Conceiving the plan was the easy part, it was the execution that would be difficult. But Irad was confident in his abilities to seduce women. First, he read the extensive file on Dr. Peterson's background and activities, which the Noba had put together. Next, he followed the woman to establish her routine. Then he visited the bars, where he met some of her students. Over drinks, he found out her interests and her pet peeves. When he had a complete picture firmly in his mind, he waited for an opportunity. It came quickly in the form of a sudden rainstorm one morning when the doctor finished having her usual breakfast of coffee and a bagel with cream cheese at a small café located a few blocks from her apartment. The sky opened up just as she was paying the bill.

Irad saw his opportunity. He approached her at the counter.

"Doctor Peterson, it looks like a bad downpour. Could I walk you somewhere?"

Geneva saw he had a large umbrella in his hand. She had an early class that morning. She believed in being punctual and was hard on any student who was late. Now there wouldn't be time to dry her hair if it got wet, unless she was willing to be late. And that she wasn't willing to do.

"Yes, thank you. I live a few blocks away."

On the way, the driving rain forced them to be physically close, the closest she had been to a man since her father died. And what was that cologne he was wearing? It seemed to bring out an animal instinct deep within.

"How do you know who I am?" she asked.

"I think everyone knows a person as famous as you, Dr. Peterson. I've read your book on, *Blood and the Genetic Code*."

"Are you a student here at the medical university?"

"No, I am studying dead languages at graduate school in Jerusalem, but I'd like to transfer to the States."

"Any place in particular?"

"I haven't made a decision yet. I guess it depends on where I can obtain financial aid, and what field of study I pursue. I'm torn between the medical field or becoming an archaeologist. Early in life I developed an interest in the ancient world because I traveled with my father."

"What type of business was he in?"

"Archaeological. He's deceased now."

"What about your mother?"

"Died in childbirth."

"Your birth?"

"Yes. I've always carried a lot of guilt because of it."

They reached the door to her apartment.

"If you decide on the medical field, give me a call. Perhaps I can be of some help."

She handed him one of the cards she always carried. As he walked away, she had an unusual feeling inside. She hoped he would call. Then Geneva remembered, she hadn't even asked his name.

31

Rising early, Rachael looked forward to the trip. She was sorry John Elesbaan wasn't with them. He left for New York to attend to some personal matters. He would be missed. His knowledge of antiquity always enlivened the group's conversation.

They packed for a three-day excursion. Once they reached the farthest point a vehicle could transport them, it would take several hours to reach the plateau opposite the mountain slope where the bones of Noah lay buried. They would not move the second day, until the morning fog was burned off by the heat of the day.

Bill was getting nervous. He had received a message from military intelligence to make contact with the insurgents. The White House had directed the Pentagon to conduct a clandestine operation. The military would furnish the rebels with the materials necessary to sabotage the nuclear facility.

Bahodore thought the trip to Noah's grave was an ideal cover for the contact, but Bill didn't like putting the other members of the group at risk. Bahodore and he were professionals. The others were mere innocent by-standers. Bahodore, however, had already put things in motion by sending word of the trip to Ghadir. There was no turning back now.

Khandan was delighted when the three laborers packed his items in the back of the truck. He was going to see the grave of Noah, *The Mighty One of God*. He often dreamed of visiting it. His lack of a formal education in archaeology didn't reflect his true depth of learning in the field. He was an avid reader. That is how he obtained his position with the government. That, and a letter from his nephew, a religious leader, who was also an advisor to the *Ayatollah*.

Khandan was a good bureaucrat, actually enjoying the paperwork that was involved in government employment. His present assignment was to record anything of interest that the expedition uncovered.

The weather was hot, a dry heat. This part of Iran was in its third year of drought. Bill and Bahodore rode in the front of a jeep with Rachael in the back. The vehicle kicked up a stream of dust into the truck following it. Ben Rabon, Khandan and Henry Weston shared the cab with the truck driver. Although the large cab was cramped, the three laborers had it worse riding in the bed of the vehicle as it bounced along the rough dirt road. They were eating sand for hours until they finally crossed the *Turkish* border.

When the vehicles reached their destination, the party unloaded the baggage and placed it upon the back of three donkeys Bahodore arranged to have available for the trip to their campsite. Bahodore and Bill led the way up the trail.

Rachael watched with a tinge of jealousy. She hoped this trip would give her an opportunity to spend more time with her boss. But from the get-go, he seemed to have attached himself to Bahodore. In fact, for the last few days she had seen them together frequently. Why was it he preferred this man's company to hers?

The path, which started wide with a gradual elevation, became narrow with a steep incline by the afternoon. Everyone was glad when it finally opened up onto a small plateau. While the men were putting up a large tent, Rachael took a path up the mountain. She could hear running water in the distance. Turning the corner of a bend in the pathway, she saw a small stream gushing from the side of the mountain and crashing into the valley below. She took the opportunity to strip her clothing off and let the stream of water rinse the dust from her body. A short distance away, the piercing eyes of two men observed her beauty from behind a set of boulders.

"We will wait until it is dark," the man with the black turban said to the other.

"Rachael, we were getting worried about you," Henry said when she came down the path toward the tent.

"I didn't mean to be gone quite so long, but I located a waterfall and took the opportunity to shower. Afterwards, I sat on a boulder overlooking the valley."

"Looking for Noah's tomb?" her father asked with a smile.

"Yes," said Rachael, laughing "but the fog gathering in the valley made it difficult to see."

"In another hour it will be thick as pea soup here," said Bill, who had just walked over from a blazing fire several feet away. "That's why I had the dinner table set up inside the tent."

Cots were placed in the tent for everyone, except Bahodore and the laborers, who would sleep in the truck. Around the table that evening, the group was enjoying their food and looking forward to their journey the next day when Bill surprised everyone.

"When we get back, I'm going to Texas for a few days. I promised Jimmy Jones I'd go see him."

Why hadn't he said anything to her earlier, Rachael wondered.

Bill had received word Colonel Bonham wanted him in Washington as soon as the sabotage was complete. The trip to Texas was a cover for returning to the States.

"You better finish reading the book he gave you," Henry said.

"How is the book on the Ark?" Fullmore asked.

"I've just finished the chapter discussing its powers."

"What powers?" Rachael asked.

"It was thought by the Israelites to be a powerful instrument. They carried it into battle believing it would make their armies invincible."

"Did it?"

"Not always. In one instance, the Philistines captured it."

"What happened to it then?"

"The Philistines took it to their city and placed it into the temple of their local god, Dargon. The next morning, when they went into the temple, the statue of their God had fallen on its face before the Ark. Then the people in the city were afflicted with tumors. Because of the afflictions, they sent the Ark back to Israel where some of the locals in an Israeli village made the mistake of opening it. They were all struck dead."

"Radiation," Fullmore said.

"What?" the startled group around the table asked.

"I believe God is energy, and the spirit in the Ark was of a nuclear variety."

"While that might sound plausible, it doesn't explain the parting of the water in the Jordan River mentioned in the *Book of Joshua*," Bill said. "Besides, there are many other references about the Ark's power. Having learned them by heart in Sunday school, I can recite them in detail. First, there was the –." He stopped in mid-sentence. Everyone turned to see what he was staring at. Several armed men were standing at the entrance to the tent. The one in command spoke English.

"Stand up and place your hands in the air. I am Captain Ghadir of the People's Liberation Army."

One of the men came over to where they were standing to make sure there weren't any weapons.

"Everyone outside," the commander ordered.

The group lined up in front of the tent. Nearby Bahodore and the laborers were standing against the truck. Their hands were tied behind their backs.

"You are in forbidden territory," Ghadir said. "When I point to you, step forward, and tell me your name and what you are doing here. The last person to step forward was Khandan, his body shaking like a leaf in a storm as he gave the requested information.

"Government dog," Captain Ghadir screamed out. "You will die now. Bring him over here."

Two of his men grabbed Khandan by the arms and dragged him to the captain.

"Down on your knees, swine."

Khandan was on his knees, now looking up at the officer, who withdrew a pistol from his holster and put it to the bureaucrat's head. Khandan looked down at the ground, expecting to feel the impact of the bullet entering his brain at any moment. Then suddenly Bill was there. He had his face only a few inches from the commander, giving him a blistering lecture, comparing his actions to those of the Revolutionary Guards, and the Turkish Army. The officer seemed to hesitate, than he placed his pistol back in its holster. He turned and walked away, barking orders for his men to follow. They simply walked out of the camp and into the darkness, leaving everyone standing in a daze.

"What in the hell was that all about?" Henry asked, breaking the silence.

"In the shifting political sands here, who knows what their intentions were?" Bill said.

Khandan, who was still on his knees, grabbed Bill's hand and kissed it profusely as he expressed his gratitude.

Because of what occurred, a decision was made to make the trip to Noah's grave the next day and then get back to their camp at the excavation site in Iran with as much haste as possible. It took a while for things to settle down after the insurgents left, but finally everyone turned in for the night.

Rachael couldn't sleep, so she went outside. She removed from her clothing a cigarette borrowed from Bahodore. Leaning against one of the big tires on the truck, she lit it. She felt foolish, afraid to smoke in front of father at her age. But she just couldn't do something in front of him when she knew he would disapprove. She saw Bill come out of the tent. He looked at his watch and then up at the sky. Her heart began to beat fast as her hormones kicked in. How brave he had been tonight. She called out his name. He looked up and appeared startled to see her, then walked over to the truck.

"What are you doing up, Rachael?"

"Just couldn't sleep."

"I didn't know you smoked."

It was then Rachael realized she was still holding the cigarette.

"I don't. Just thought I would try one. They say it calms one's nerves."

She dropped the cigarette on the ground.

"I want to tell you how brave you were, risking your life to keep that insane man from shooting Khandan."

Bill seemed at a loss for words.

Rachael stepped forward and put her arms around his neck.

"Rachael." He tried to say more, but her lips were against his, and the warmth of her flesh pressed tightly against his body. Her hand slipped beneath the back of his shirt and ran across his naked flesh. He wanted her. The scarring left by his wife dissolved for a moment, as his hands slipped beneath her blouse.

She groaned at the touch of his hands and then whispered, "After what happened tonight, I can't deny how I feel." In the light of the moon, she could see an odd expression on his face. What was it? Had she said something that hurt or offended him? Her mind raced back over the words spoken, even as he began to utter something to her.

"Rachael, I care for you. One day I'll explain everything. Then you'll understand."

Releasing her, he walked off into the darkness. She just stood there not knowing what to think. Love, rejection and frustration fueled her emotions. But not anger. He almost lost his life today for someone he barely knew. No, she couldn't be angry with him, at least not tonight.

In the darkness with only the light of the moon to guide him, Bill took the trail past the waterfall where Rachael showered earlier that day. Soon thereafter, he heard Bahodore's voice call out to him from a clump of bushes. Going through them, he entered the mouth of a cave lit by oil lamps. In the flickering light, he saw the figure of Ghadir in his black turban and Bahodore, standing with a group of men in a semicircle.

"I was wondering if something happened to you," Bahodore said.

"I was delayed."

And I bet it was the fault of the young woman under the waterfall, Ghadir thought. The image of the naked bronze body he had seen earlier that day flashed before him. Bahodore had told him the woman had a terrible crush on the professor.

"It is good to see you again, Ghadir. I'm glad that neither the Revolutionary Guards nor the Turkish Army has captured you yet."

"It is good to see you again, my friend," Ghadir said. "Did the ruse with that bureaucrat have the desired effect?"

"I believe it did. Khandan thinks he owes me his life, and that could make a difference if we run into a problem."

"What news do you bring us from the Pentagon?"

"They want you to sabotage the nuclear facility."

"There is no way we can destroy it."

"Washington knows that. They want to delay the development of an operational weapon. They needs time to weigh their options."

"Very well, my friend. We'll do as you ask."

"The munitions drop will be at these coordinates," Bill said, as he drew them in the sand, along with the expected drop time. After Ghadir read it, his foot slid across the sand, erasing the information.

When Bill stepped quietly into the tent at the campsite, he was glad to see everyone asleep. As he passed Rachael's cot, he paused and looked at her lying there. He felt a pang of regret. Her eyes looked swollen. Was it possible she had been crying? *I did the right thing*, he told himself. *I couldn't take her love under false pretenses only to have her find out later the attempt on Khandan's life was all staged.*

32

The League's agent was waiting to meet John Elesbaan when he landed in Amman, Jordan, for a connecting flight to New York.

"We circumvented The Society," the agent said. "We effectuated the removal of the staff and replaced it with an exact copy the night before they broke into the vault. There is now a debate within the League on whether to destroy the staff or keep it as a trophy. Until a decision is reached, it remains secure in an Ethiopian monastery."

Henley received word about John Elesbaan's trip. The Noba would be waiting for him in New York. At last, the man would be within their grasp. With a little persuasion, the missing details of his life would be revealed.

***

The group in the Zagros Mountains was anxious. The fog was delaying their descent from the plateau into the valley and up the slope of *Judi Dagh*. Their thoughts that morning were on the Great Flood and its aftermath.

"You know," Khandan said, "the Gilgamesh Epic, recovered from the ruins of the Assyrian capitol at Nineveh, was about a flood similar to the one in Genesis."

"That shouldn't surprise anyone," Dr. Rabon said. "The story comes from the Sumerians. That civilization had a very close connection to this mountain chain. As we learn more about the origins of civilization, it is becoming clear the Bible is correct in the limited history it gives of man. For instance, it states in Genesis that after the flood, Noah and his family traveled to a plain in Shiner. We now know this was the Babylonian Plains. The Bible also declares the whole earth had one speech and one language at that time. Some scholars now interpret the word, *language*, to mean a written one."

"There is folklore in this region that a city was established by the survivors of the flood," Khandan said.

"The name of one of the nearby cities has recently been translated to mean *City of Noah*."

"There are so many gaps in the historical narrative of the Bible. It may have been a century before the migrations to the Babylonian Plains took place," Bill said. "The establishment of a city in this region would not necessarily be inconsistent with the Biblical story since Noah lived several hundred years."

"There has been a recent find," Rachael said, at last glad that she could add something to the conversation. "A tablet discovered in Syria has an epic of the great flood. Even more interesting was the fact that it's in a language whose roots are from this mountain chain and, strangely enough, is on a recently discovered tablet in Yemen."

"That's fascinating," Fullmore said. "I've read that the majority of domesticated animals have been traced to this region."

"And the residue of the first wine," Henry said. "In fact, the first cultivation of wheat is thought to have originated in this region. There's even a school of thought that the Neolithic revolution began in the Zagros Mountains."

"The what?" Fullmore asked.

"I mean the invention of agriculture."

At last, the fog lifted and the group began their journey. It was a rugged landscape. Only with great difficulty was the group able to transverse the slope to the valley below without injury. They stopped briefly to consume the food in their backpacks. When they finished, the group began their climb of *Judi Dagh*. Bahodore led the way; the rest struggled to keep up with him. They didn't complain because they understood the reason for his haste. He was concerned it would be difficult to get back to their encampment before dark unless they made good time scaling the slope.

At four o'clock in the evening the group saw Bahodore turn and wave with excitement. "I can see the tomb!"

When they reached him, they stood in awe for a moment at the site before them. On the plateau lay ruins, and there was a tomb carved into the side of the mountain. The group collapsed on the ground from exhaustion in the high altitude, but only for a few minutes. The adrenalin flowing through their bodies soon made them forget their fatigue.

Some form of primitive cement had sealed the entrance to the tomb once, but it had long since deteriorated. The large stone that once blocked the entrance, lay shattered as if by a giant hammer. Bahodore lit a small kerosene lamp. Its light illuminated the inside of the tomb. Because it was small, they took turns going inside. Any body laid there had been removed. There were no artifacts within its walls, except for a small stone in the corner. Bill picked it up. It had the symbol of a *serpent* upon it.

Outside, the group huddled around the stone; each took turns holding it. For a time they were silent, each contemplating what this could mean. Then Bill spoke.

"This is identical to the symbol on the jug found at the water basin back at the excavation."

"What's it doing in the tomb?" Fullmore asked.

"I'd speculate that whoever took Noah's remains left it as a calling card," Bill said. "Similar to what a serial killer does today. Sort of a boast, to let the world know they have it."

"It could be the ancient group known as The Society, if they ever existed," Henry said. "And I'm beginning to believe they did."

The group examined the ruins around the area of the tomb.

"These are the remains of structures built by the Nestorians," Khandan said. "For centuries, people from the surrounding countryside made pilgrimages to pay their respect to Noah, whom they considered the father of all mankind. Later, when Islam conquered the region, they converted it into a Muslim holy place."

"That doesn't surprise me," Dr. Rabon said. "Islam recognizes this mountain as the place where the Ark landed and as the location of Noah's tomb."

A shot rang out. A bullet hit a rock nearby.

"On the ground," Bahodore screamed.

They found cover behind the remnants of the structures.

"Who's firing, Bahodore?" asked Bill, who was lying on the ground beside him.

"I don't think it is the resistance. The shot sounded like it came from an old bolt-action rifle. It's probably a group of Kurdish tribesmen. They have lived in this area for eons and consider this their homeland. They don't like intruders.

Bahodore yelled out something in Kurdish. The firing stopped.

"Let's go," he said to Bill.

After they traversed a few yards, a group of men dressed in traditional garb appeared from the vegetation growing out of the side of the mountain.

Bill understood *Kurdish*, so he was able to follow the conversation.

Bahodore explained to the Kurds why strangers had invaded their territory.

When Bahodore finished the explanation, Bill spoke a few words in *Kurdish*, displaying his knowledge of their history and dropping the names of ancient Kurdish heroes. The leader of the group seemed impressed, giving him a broad toothless grin. Bill reached up, and removed the binoculars from around his neck and handed them to the leader as a sign of friendship. The man looked pleased.

"You are accepted as friends by my people. We will provide you with safe passage back to your camp."

Bill understood. The intruders would be escorted out of the area. But it wasn't to be a time of their choosing. They were to leave immediately. Bahodore remained with the Kurds while Bill went back to inform the others.

"We have to leave now. Khandan, it would be best if you don't speak. They would kill you if they realized you are a government official."

Henry reached in his backpack and pulled out a hat.

"Here, put this on and pull it down over your forehead. Fullmore handed Khandan an American shirt from his backpack to slip into, and Rachael contributed by walking toward the group of Kurds holding the man's hand as if he were her husband. It worked. They took no special notice of Khandan, who felt eternally grateful. In his mind, this was the second time his life had been spared.

"Praise be to Allah," he said under his breath.

Although the trip back was much shorter because the Kurds knew a quicker route, it was still dark when they arrived at their encampment. The Kurds disappeared into the night without lingering, afraid of being spotted by units of the *Turkish* Army, who were in the area searching for insurgents in rebellion against the government in *Istanbul*.

***

Back at the excavation site in Iran, the group had time to unwind while the laborers were away. Khandan departed for Noqdi where the government was sponsoring a celebration honoring the Revolution.

One evening, after everyone else turned in for the night, Bill sat outside on the hood of the jeep drinking some fermented local brew Khandan insisted he take as a gift. His thoughts were on the operation against the nuclear plant. Tomorrow night, a special transmitter would be dropped along with explosives. Only he knew the code that would enable it to function. Once the mission was accomplished, he would communicate with one of America's spy satellites when it passed over the area. The Pentagon wanted to know immediately of the raid's success. That was priority for him. To get that information to them.

"Professor," a voice said from the darkness. Bill recognized the Mississippi accent.

"Thought it best if I waited until everyone was asleep, before I talked to you about the codebook."

"How's that going?"

"I broke the code before we went on the trek to the tomb. But there wasn't a time I could catch you alone. I wasn't sure who you wanted to know about it."

"You did the right thing. Sometimes it's best not to say too much about this type of information."

"Let's go closer to the fire where there's light, and I can show you."

Fullmore explained the way to decipher the code. He had reduced the secret to one sheet of paper. When Fullmore left him, Bill threw the paper into the fire along with the codebook. With his photographic mind, Bill would not need to look at it again. In the future, he could translate any document written in this strange code. Back in the tent, Fullmore erased all the information about the code from the computer as Bill directed.

The next day everyone was relaxing. Rachael went up to the water basin early that morning, while her father wrote some long-overdue letters to his colleagues back at the university. Henry Weston worked on a new book, *The Myths of the Ancient World*, second edition. Bill finished reading the book on the Ark. Bahodore left camp, telling everyone he was going to see a relative that lived nearby. Bill knew the truth. Bahodore was heading into the hills to meet with the insurgents about the drop tonight. As for Fullmore, the man was down in the tunnel with a shovel doing what he had always dreamed about–digging at an archaeological site of the ancient world.

At noon, everyone stopped their activities when they heard a vehicle approach with someone hollering at the top of his lungs. It was Fullmore driving toward them. The jeep came to an abrupt stop in front of the encampment. He jumped out waiving both hands in excitement.

"I found it," he said.

33

It had been a week since Dr. Peterson met the man who offered to walk her home in the rain. Normally she would not have noticed nor cared that he hadn't responded to her offer to assist. But she did care, although she would never admit it. She should have asked for his name, she thought, and then pushed such a thought out of her mind. She went a little earlier and stayed later at the café where she had met him, her eyes always scanning the room to see if he was there. She was a classic example of a person in self-denial. Then one morning he came through the door and took a seat at a booth near the cash register. She watched and thought how attractive he was but quickly dismissed such nonsense, replacing it with thoughts of how she would like to guide him on which course of graduate work he should pursue. Yes, she was strictly concerned with his education, or so she told herself.

Irad noticed Dr. Peterson the moment he came through the door. Since their meeting, he had followed her on several occasions and knew her routine had changed. The first step had been successful. Now it was time for the next. Perhaps this woman would succumb to his charm soon. And that was important because time was of the essence.

When she approached the cash register, he pretended to be reading a newspaper.

Perhaps she should go over and speak to him after she paid her bill. After all, he had been nice enough to go out of his way to be helpful.

Irad saw her turn and approach his booth. She had taken the bait.

"I want to thank you for your assistance last week."

"Oh, Dr. Peterson," he said, acting as if her appearance surprised him. "Please, have a seat."

She wanted to accept the offer. Before she had time to reflect, she heard herself say, "I can't. It would make me late for class."

The words that flowed from her lips came from habit. And as soon as they were out, she regretted them.

"I'll walk over to the university with you. I have a meeting with the financial officer to see if there's a way I can afford the medical school here."

"So you've made your decision?"

"Tentatively. I've registered. Now it's a matter of money for tuition."

Geneva generally went back to her apartment after breakfast and then drove to the campus where she had a reserved spot. But it is a beautiful day. Why not walk for a change? They left the café together and strolled in the direction of the campus.

"Do you have another card? I wanted to call, but somehow I lost your number in the rain."

She reached into her suit jacket and removed another business card.

"I never got your name."

"It's Irad Lamech."

He removed a pen from his pocket, scratched his name and cell number on the back of a breakfast receipt.

After class that day, she went back to her office and made a call to the director of financial aid.

"Roger, this is Dr. Peterson."

In his five years at financial aid, this was the first time Roger Crane had ever received a call from her, though he had met the woman at numerous faculty functions.

"I would like you to help a student who wants to attend our medical school. He seems bright but apparently doesn't have the funds."

Faculty members frequently pressured him to assist students. Sometimes a family member was involved, and at other times, it was because of an ongoing affair. But Peterson had never made a request, and he knew it had to be based on her belief the applicant was outstanding graduate material. After a brief discussion, he agreed to honor her request.

"Is there a place for him in your department for a work study scholarship?" he asked.

"There's a project I'm working on where help is needed."

She couldn't believe she had committed to that. She never liked student assistants. She was a person who always worked alone.

Three days later Irad came by the office to thank her. While there, he talked about his days as a young man and the trauma he went through when his father died. She could relate to that. Before Geneva knew it, she was telling the man about her own father and the times spent as a child around excavations in the Middle East. Soon the discussion turned to ancient artifacts. She had many of them at her apartment. When he left the office an hour later, Geneva couldn't believe she had extended an invitation for him to come over that evening and look at those artifacts. She had never invited anyone to her apartment before. She was an introvert. What possessed her to invite him, she wondered. Geneva had difficulty dealing with anything involving human emotions so she put it out of her mind and focused on work.

The Society had accumulated knowledge over the centuries. Dr. Geneva Peterson was a challenge who would require its use. Irad selected a cologne, the one he'd worn the morning they met. Produced from an ancient formula by The Society's chemist, it worked most times. On occasion, it failed to stimulate an attraction. It certainly hadn't worked with Rachael. He removed a wine bottle from his collection whose ingredients were known by the ancients. Its effects rarely failed. Of course, atmosphere was important, and that had Irad worried. He didn't know what the apartment was like.

The apartment was located in an ideal neighborhood not far from the university. Geneva had been delighted that it was available when she accepted her present position. It contained four rooms, all painted white. The floor plan provided an entrance from the street into a small hallway, which led to the den. The open kitchen was to the left. Straight through the den was a short hallway leading to the two bedrooms, the smaller of which had been converted into a study. It had the look of a sanitized office.

The bedroom was large with a window that looked out over the street. In its center stood a canopy bed that had been in her family for three generations. The covering was a quilt of pure cotton made by the slave of an ancestor, who had owned a plantation in Virginia. On the right-hand side was a door that opened into a small bathroom decorated in a nineteen-twenties décor. The apartment met her needs, though others might think it could use more color.

It was almost time for Irad. Geneva was dressed in what she usually wore to class, a drab long skirt and white blouse. It had crossed her mind to get something more feminine, but she quickly dismissed such a thought. She had never had an interest in a man and never would, she keep telling herself that afternoon.

The doorbell rang. She knew it had to be him.

"Good evening," Irad said stepping through the door.

Was that a bottle he was carrying?

"I brought some wine."

"I don't drink," she said in a voice that was close to being sarcastic.

"I'm sorry, I didn't realize. It was a gift from a relative before he died. I just thought since you had been so nice to me, I'd like to share this bottle with you."

She regretted her abruptness. Hearing the story behind it simply made her feel worse.

"I'd love to share the bottle with you, but I don't have any wine glasses."

"We can improvise," he said. "Two juice glasses will do just fine."

While she went to the kitchen, he removed the cork from the bottle with his Swiss knife. When she returned, he poured them each a glass.

"What a beautiful place you have here," he said, lying through his teeth. If atmosphere was that important, Irad knew he was in trouble.

"Let me show you the artifacts," she said.

They started in the den. This place could have been a museum, he thought, as she explained each item. After Irad got the first glass down her, the second one disappeared quickly. She was so absorbed in explaining the artifacts that she never noticed he was still sipping his first glass. By the time she was through the second glass, she had finished with the artifacts.

"I'd like to see the rest of your apartment."

She heard the words, *follow me this way*, come from her lips. She led him down the hallway to the study. The smell of his cologne was beginning to excite her.

She had a flashback to the day they met. It was the same scent. When they reached the room, he expressed an interest in her new computer.

"It's voice activated," she said. "This model just came out this year."

Sitting in front of the computer, she opened it simply by speaking the password. Now that information would be useful later, he thought. He purposely leaned over her shoulder bringing the side of his face close to hers as he pretended to observe the screen.

The closeness of a man normally would have been offensive, but the wine had started to remove her inhibitions, layer by layer. On the way out of the room, he said, "That must be your bedroom."

Then, without seeking permission, he walked into it.

"What a beautiful view," he said, crossing the room to look out at the street below. Strangely, she did not object to his presence but joined him there.

"I enjoyed the tour of your place."

He looked into her eyes and knew she didn't want him to leave. Moreover, he had no intention of doing so. He reached over as if he was going to give her a goodbye peck on the cheek. His hands moved to her shoulders; his lips brushed her cheek and then moved to her mouth. She offered no resistance. Although he could feel her body shake, she made no attempt to remove herself from his embrace. The aphrodisiac was working.

Earlier that evening Irad had memorized every obstacle on her clothing. And now his hands worked quickly on his objective. The skirt fell to the floor from its own weight; the blouse followed. His hand unsnapped a clasp, and her breasts found their freedom.

Geneva had never known a man before. Not only that, she had never in any way been intimate. Her personality said *no*; something deep within screamed *yes*.

He moved her slowly toward the bed. Along the way, the rest of her clothing fell to the floor. As they reached the bed, he pushed her gently until her back was flat upon it; her long legs dangled to the floor. She felt a sharp pain, quickly replaced by immense pleasure; her loneliness evaporated. What a fool she'd been all these years, she thought. Then it was over, and she felt a sense of shame. But he wasn't finished. He placed her entire body on the bed. His lips and hands began to explore it. She felt the desire return and the shame disappear. She lost control of her body, climbed to a new height, screamed out in pleasure and then collapsed in his embrace.

34

The group returned with Fullmore to the tunnel. They struggled down its narrow pathways and reached the object of his excitement. While he held the kerosene lamp, they viewed the inscription carved in large letters. It was in the same language as that inscribed on the Staff of Cain. He read it to the group, who listened in awe.

Behold the temple of the Serpent built by his son, Cain. All glory is to him and to his seed forever. Let no one enter this gate without tribute to honor them."

"It's the wall of a temple, and the entrance must be nearby," Bill said.

"Probably only a few feet," Ben Rabon said.

Leaving Rachael to hold the lantern, Fullmore went outside and secured several shovels and a wheelbarrow. When he returned, everyone pitched in, lengthening the tunnel until they came to what had been an entrance. It was filled with a mound of debris that once supported an arch. They worked removing it until an opening appeared. Bill shined his flashlight into the darkness.

The room had a high ceiling and a width of eighteen feet. It was full of an accumulation of loose materials, but somehow a portion of the timbers supporting the roof remained intact and prevented it from caving into the space.

"We need to be careful," Bill said. "The ceiling could give way at anytime."

When they entered the room, the air was stale and the group able to breathe only with great difficulty.

The light from Rachael's lantern revealed a skeleton in the center of the room. The body lay where it had apparently fallen, undisturbed for thousands of years. It was over seven feet long.

The insufficient oxygen in the room soon caused the group to withdraw.

"In a few hours the air in the tunnel will have time to circulate," Bill said.

Back at camp, they discussed the find. When enough time had expired for the air to be pure, they returned to the excavation site. They were disappointed entering the room to discover that it contained no artifacts. Whatever this temple once contained had been removed. Their disappointment soon evaporated when the light from their flashlights revealed inscriptions on the wall and several large-scale drawings of a beautiful man of large stature. The group went to work recording each inscription in their notebooks. Then they examined the skeleton. Dr. Rabon pointed out that the skull had a sharp gash in it.

"Probably caused by an ax," he said. "And look at the right arm. It's broken in three places."

When they were through, the group gathered their equipment and exited the room. Bill turned and scanned the room for one last look. Something caught his attention.

"Wait a second," he yelled to the group, some of whom were already a few yards down the tunnel.

"My flashlight has picked up a small opening in the center of the wall."

He went back inside to explore it.

"The crack is too small to see what's on the other side. We need to make it larger. But let's be careful. We don't know the stability of the structure, and too many vibrations could cause it to cave in."

Bill chiseled away until it was large enough to get a crowbar wedged into it. When he applied pressure, a brick gave way, creating enough space to shine his light through. The first thing he saw was a skeleton sitting upright against one of the walls of this inner chamber.

"The wall was not part of the original room so the structure on each end of it should prevent a collapse," Fullmore said.

Bill gradually made the space bigger while the others provided light and removed the debris. It was a slow process, but after an hour, it was large enough to allow them into the chamber. After they squeezed through, everyone just stood there for a moment taking in their surroundings.

"Be careful not to disturb anything," Henry said.

"It'd be so easy to accidentally damage something with so many people in this confined area," Fullmore said.

The room was eight by ten with a twelve-foot ceiling. The skeleton sitting upright had a clay tablet on his lap. The remains of a small leather pouch lay two feet from the skeleton, its contents of precious stones, gold and jewelry now spread in a small circle on the floor. Bill reached down and collected them. He held them in front of a light for all to see. What stood out most was a ring. It had two *serpents* facing opposite directions and a strange inscription on it.

Fulmore studied the ring. "It must be someone's name. In translation the letters are *Springca*."

"Who was she was." Rachael asked.

"Obviously, someone of great importance," Bill said.

"Fullmore, can you translate the writing on the tablet?" Rachael's father asked.

"*The end has come. I viewed the killing of the High Priest Mehujael, by the hand of The Children of the Lord. I was able to observe this through a crack in the wall. The priest had been among the people in the streets waving the Staff of Cain exhorting them to drive the enemy back through the gate breached yesterday. He returned despondent, saying it was only a matter of time before the inner wall around the temple would also fall to the enemy. Knowing the time was near, we built a wall across the entranceway to the Holy Place. I remained inside. We left one brick out so that the priest could pass the Staff through if he saw the temple was about to be invaded. We said our farewell and he departed to make one last display of the Staff from the steps of the Temple before passing it through the wall to me. A few minutes later, he returned with several attackers pursuing him. In fear, I put the missing brick in its place. Through a crack, I saw them crush his skull with an ax and remove from his hands the sacred staff before setting the temple on fire. It was this fire that kept the men from discovering my hiding place. The smoke is now thick and the heat unbearable. I am going into the other world where my master, the Serpent, awaits me.*"

"There's something not legible scrawled at the end," Dr. Rabon said.

"Probably because he was overcome by the smoke," Bill said.

Other clay tablets arranged in a semicircle near the right wall, apparently, in some type of order because there were gaps between them.

"We need to record everything," Rachael said. "These tablets can never be moved without destroying them. They've become part of the floor. The intense heat preserved them but also made it impossible to remove them."

While Fullmore remained to study the tablets, the rest of the group climbed out of the cramped chamber and went back to the surface. Later, Bill and Rachael returned and brought Fullmore's computer and software. It would make the translation go faster. Within the hour, Fullmore had the information from two sets of clay tablets typed into the computer. They took this information back to the camp where the other members of the group anxiously waited.

"The arrangements of the tablets into three divisions served a purpose," Fullmore said. "The first group of tablets was similar to a last will and testament by the High Priest Mehujael."

The software did the translation with ease.

"*The end of the City of Enoch is near. The forces of the Children of the Lord have drawn closer every year. Now they are within sight of the walls of the city. I have sent the other priests away to the land where frankincense and myrrh can be found in abundance. They have secretly taken to our new colony nine of the twelve writings that are the record of our history. I have kept the staff and the remaining tablets because they are always on display in the temple. If the people were to see them missing, they would lose heart in our struggle against the descendants of Seth. But I have made plans with Tubal, my trusted aide, that if the walls of the city are breached, the tablets and staff will be hidden in the sacred inner chamber where no one but the priests are allowed. I will wall up the room with him inside, so he shall be hidden from our enemies. When the Children of the Lord have departed, he shall take the tablets to our colony and deliver them to the priest at the new temple. Praise to the Serpent from whence we came.*"

The group listened intently as Fullmore read the translation of the first tablet.

"That's a lot of information," Bill said. "It confirms the Biblical story of *Enoch*."

"Read the next set of tablets," Rachael said.

"This story doesn't name an author, but it could be Cain."

No one stirred as Fullmore read the second translation.

"I arrived in this valley surrounded by high mountains. Game was in abundance. There were also creatures similar to me, except they were short in stature, measuring no more than four feet. They had neither written nor oral language. These creatures lived in groups varying in size from six to thirteen. They communicated by means of grunts similar to some of the animals in the region. When I came upon them, they fled in fear, never having seen an animal walking on its hind legs, who towered over eight feet high. Their weapons were very primitive and their hunting skills elementary. I made my home in a large cave in the side of a mountain, the entrance of which faced a plateau.

On occasion, my father, the Serpent, in the form of a man, would visit in the evening as I sat at the fire, eating an animal I killed. He declared to me that my heirs would one day rule the world.

"But I have no mate," I said.

"Is the land not filled with animals that walk on their hind legs?" the Serpent replied. "Are they not creatures like you, except without a soul? Take the female species and mate with them. The children will have a soul as you do, because you were born of Eve. And Eve had a soul because she was made from Adam. And Adam was the first being with a soul. For as it is written, the Creator breathed into

Adam, and he became a living soul." Then the Serpent said, "For the offspring of anyone with a soul shall also have a soul."

One day I came across a female, who was alone by a spring. I seized her and took the thing to my cave. I kept her tied until she understood I was to be her master. I taught her how to make fire and pottery. She was made to understand some language. I named her Sprinca because she was captured beside a spring. She mated as an animal would and in the spring had a child that I named Enoch. Afterwards, I captured many more of the female species and taught them elementary things. Eventually I captured some of the young males and made them my slaves.

After the first hundred years, the hills and valleys were filled with my descendants. We built a city, which I named Enoch after my first child. The Serpent visited me on the mountain that looked down upon the city and was pleased."

Having reached the end of the second set of tablets, the three returned to the tunnel, and put the script from the remaining clay tablets on the computer for translation after dinner. When they arrived back at the camp, the others had warmed up the goat stew and eggplant left over from the day before and cooked some new rice in the black iron pot that hung from a steel contraption over the fire. They fixed their plates and poured some hot tea from a container warmed by a butane burner outside Bill's tent.

The excitement in the air was so high that the group seated at the table didn't wait until they finished eating to discuss the implication of the stories from the tablets.

"You know that last tablet Fullmore translated could explain what happened to the *Neanderthals* and other groups that reached a certain level of development and then disappeared without a trace," Henry said.

"What do you mean?" Rachael asked.

"Interbreeding with Cain and his descendents or perhaps extermination could have destroyed their line," Henry said.

"We must understand just because it's in writing doesn't mean it's true," said Rachael's father. "We have fables that are thousands of years old, but no one believes them to be anything but what they are, fiction."

"What about the division of the human race between those with souls and those without?" Henry asked.

"It's possible that a higher form of the animal kingdom existed, and God chose only a particular one to breathe a living soul into, leaving others of the same species to continue as originally created," Bill said.

"All this talk reminds me of the movie, *Planet of the Apes*," Fullmore said.

When dinner was over, Fullmore read from the computer the translation of the last set of clay tablets.

"*Glory be to the Serpent and blessed be his son, Cain, the father of our people. I, Lamech, High Priest of the Temple of the Serpent, have been requested by the Council of Twelve to write the history of our people since the founding of our capital at Enoch.*

The great Cain lies buried beside the temple, his body placed there upon his death at the age of two-hundred-four years. Our ancestor left behind a thriving empire and a stable social order. The empire is governed by the Council of Twelve. Each member a leader of one of the tribes and, therefore, a direct descendant of the union of Cain with Sprinca, the mother of our race. Beneath the twelve tribes are the Cai'sh, the double soul ones, a result of sexual union between the descendants of Cain and women captured from the tribe of Seth. The third level of the hierarchy is the Lonsho, who are the descendants of the Sons of Cain and slaves. On the bottom of the social order are the Drones in whose veins run neither the blood of Cain nor his half brother, Seth. They are without souls. They are like the other animals, except they resemble beings, and the largeness of their brains allows them the ability to imitate those with souls."

"This obviously was just the beginning of the story," Fullmore said. "Unfortunately that's the last tablet in the chamber."

35

John Elesbaan was hungry. It had been days since he had been kidnapped, while leaving the airport in New York. Although not interrogated yet, he knew the attempts to break him had already begun. Tied tightly to a chair, unable to move with a blindfold over his eyes, his body reeked of urine. He waited for the torture to begin. Yet he remained calm.

Members of the League underwent training to deal with pain if captured. He had spent two years in a Tibetan Himalayan monastery learning how to withdraw into his own mind and use it as a weapon against tormentors.

The assassin looked forward to his first meeting with John. It would be a great challenge to test his professional skills against those of a league member. The joy of this forthcoming challenge almost made him forget his anger toward the Leader who had blocked his admittance onto the council to fill a seat left vacant by the natural death of one of its members. The Leader used the assassin's less-than-stellar performance in the torture of Linda Mendel as ammunition against him so he could promote the candidacy of his nephew for the vacancy.

***

Because of time spent on new files assigned to him, Thomas had been diverted from the murder cases. That ended the day Melinda had called to say Kinsey wanted to meet him for lunch.

"I am glad you were available," Kinsey said, as he entered Mingos.

"Why did you need to see me?"

"I received a call from Director Cagle this morning. He reminded me that I hadn't sent him a report lately on those weird cases of yours. I told him you hit a dead end and were now occupied on other files. Cagle made it clear; he wants your energies devoted to the weird ones.

"Richard, I'm glad you had time to meet," Thomas said. "I'm getting a lot of pressure from my superiors on these murder cases."

"I was just about to call you anyway. We've had a break in Marilyn's case. The corporation in Singapore that sold the condoms sent us the information requested. The company ordering them proved phony, but the address where they were delivered to was a residence. We're starting a stakeout this afternoon. That's the good news. The bad news is that I'm the first one on the roster to watch the place."

"Would you like some company?"

"Sure, it'd be like old times."

That afternoon the two men parked in a shady spot beneath a tree. From this position, they could see the apartment. Like a typical stakeout, hours went by with nothing happening, so they killed the time with conversation.

"How's it going with Melinda? Seems like you are together a good bit."

"We're getting close. She wants me to take a few days off and spend time with her family in Charleston."

"You should do it. Looks to me like she's serious."

"I'm so busy now between work and visitation with my son two weekends a month that I don't have the time."

"Has your son Jay met Melinda yet?"

"No, I guess I don't want his mother to find out I'm involved with a woman."

"Why? Tammy's practically engaged to that guy she's been sleeping with."

"I know, but I'm afraid she might still try to use it to harass me."

"How?"

Just then, a man left the sidewalk and rang the doorbell on at the residence.

"It looks like our suspect has a visitor," Richard said.

"I can't believe it."

"Believe what?"

"I know him. That's Irad Lamech. He's with Professor Weston's expedition."

"It looks like you might have been wrong about the professor."

"Yes, I might have been suckered."

"We'll follow the man when he leaves and see what he's up to." Thirty minutes later, Irad exited the building.

Tailing Irad took them to a warehouse district now comprised of abandoned buildings. He parked his vehicle in front of an old packing plant. Although the place looked deserted, they watched as Irad exited his car and went in a side door.

"Should we follow him in?" Richard asked.

"No. Let's wait and tail him when he leaves. We can always come back later and explore this building to see what's in there."

***

Irad observed John for a moment without speaking. He looked awful. But that was to be expected with no food or water for three days. He walked over and removed the gag and blindfold.

"You are going to tell us about the League sooner or later. You might as well save us the trouble of torturing you."

John remained mute.

"What's the matter? You can't speak? Before we are finished, that tongue of yours won't stop moving," he said. Irad was tempted to do some preliminary work on his own, but knew if he touched the subject, the assassin would be upset.

When Irad left the building, they followed him across town to Raven Street where he went into a hotel, leaving the key to his vehicle with the valet outside.

"Looks like he's staying there," Thomas said.

"With the amount of manpower this case is requiring, I think it's best to end our surveillance and return to the warehouse," Richard said.

John sat in the dark remembering the things that were important to him. Images of family and friends passed before his eyes. He hoped his resolve not to give information would be strong against the torture and that the ability to control his thoughts would stand up against the truth serum they would inject. He heard the door open in the distance and the sound of people approaching. The time had come. He offered a prayer to *Yahweh* and *Jesus*.

"Dr. Elesbaan!" exclaimed Thomas, who was surprised to see him. Removing the gag, he said, "What in the hell is going on here?"

"I was kidnapped."

"Who did this to you?"

"I don't know. They never said anything other than, 'Get in the van,' after a pistol was stuck in my ribs."

At the police station after John had eaten, he showered in the officer's locker room. Richard scrounged around and found some clean clothing. Then the two detectives questioned him in the interview room.

"I don't know who did this or why I was kidnapped."

"We want every detail from the time you were accosted until we rescued you," Thomas said.

"After arriving at the airport, I rented a vehicle. I was looking for the spot where it was parked when a van pulled up, and two men jumped out. One of them stuck a gun into my ribs and made me get in the van. They literally threw me in the back of it, jumped in and pushed my face down. Then they tied my hands behind my back, placed a gag in my mouth and blindfolded me. Later they took me out of the van and tied me in a chair.

"What was said during this time?" Thomas asked.

"Nothing, absolutely not a word. I'd hear people come and go, but they never uttered a single word."

"Can you describe the two men and the van?" Richard asked.

"No, it happened all too fast. I do remember the van was white, but that's all."

"Why would anyone want to kidnap you?" Richard asked.

"I haven't the foggiest idea."

"Where do you stay when you're in the city?" Thomas asked.

"I'll be at the Hotel Acropolis, if you need to get in touch with me."

We'll stay in contact, and please let us know when you leave the hotel so the department can provide surveillance," Richard said. "Whoever was behind this may try again."

After John left, the two detectives remained in the interview room with puzzled looks on their faces.

"What do you think?" Richard asked.

"He knows more then he's telling us."

"I agree. Do you think the terrorist unit could place surveillance on him and get a phone tap?"

"I'll see to it. The tap on his room probably will be a waste of time. I'll see what can be done to monitor his cell phone."

"Well, at least we know one person that's involved," Richard said.

"You're dammed right. I never trusted that son of a bitch. I'll be sure Irad's followed by the terrorism unit day and night until we see who his contacts are in this city."

"This is all tied into the cases we've been working on," Richard said.

"Yes, and I get the feeling we are about to find out what really happened."

John checked into his hotel room, made one phone call on his cell, and then exited the building through a side entrance. A few hours later, he had all the necessary documents for a new identity and was on a flight out of the country.

***

It was the weekend. The Leader sat in the apartment with a worried look on his face. He had just received word that the police had rescued John Elesbaan. How had they found him? He rolled the Cuban cigar around in his mouth while he contemplated what happened and delayed looking at the dispatch that had arrived from Iran that morning. The new housekeeper came in and brought him lunch.

Serving as the Leader's housekeeper was a new assignment for Megan; her usefulness as an intern in the Professor William Weston's office had recently ended. With that source of information dried up, The Society was lucky to have a drone, working in Henry Weston's home. She kept them apprised of what the man was telling his wife. And he told her everything.

"Megan, just leave it on the table, and I'll eat in a few minutes."

As she was leaving the room, he felt desire rise within his loins for her but quickly suppressed it. After all, she was a *drone*, a descendant of those with no soul. He could easily have her, if the law of the council had not prohibited it for the last two thousand years. Of course, that had not always been the case. Cain and the members of the *Tribe of Twelve* bred with them originally. However, as time went by, their number had been reduced to the point that it became important for The Society to preserve the remaining ones. They made good foot soldiers for the forces spreading evil across the land. They were neither good nor evil. The Society constantly monitored them because the drones would adopt the mores of any group they were around for any length of time, even regurgitating ideas as if they were their own independent thoughts.

The Leader read the correspondence Henley sent from Iran. The alliance with the forces of terrorism were about to bear fruit. The creation of nuclear weapons was in sight. It would bring about *Armageddon*, which the council had waited for these many years. A period mentioned in the *Holy Bible* of Seth's descendants, the *Sacred Book* of Cain and the *Mayan* Calendar. There had been a few false starts, like Hitler and Stalin. These men had failed to bring about the death, disease and pestilence hoped for by The Society. The more recent prospect had been Iraq's dictator. He had been so close on three different occasions. But events overcame him before the nuclear and biological weapons he sought had been obtained, thus denying the Society what it sought: the unleashing of Three Horsemen of the Apocalypse: *War, Famine and Death*.

All was not loss. The current alliance with terrorists was serving a useful purpose for the followers of the Serpent. Their tentacles reached deep into the hierarchy of every country. This enabled them to help the terrorists' movement. Their new allies never understood whom they were dealing with, attacking Satan in speeches without realizing they were carrying out his will.

36

Dr. Geneva Peterson received samples of the DNA from the police department and immediately began working to solve the puzzle. It required extra hours each day after class. She didn't object. Irad was there in the lab assisting her.

The day Geneva's research concluded, it confirmed the existence of a group with some genes not recognized in the human chain of descent. She told Irad this astonishing discovery would be acceptable to the scientific community because the test results were so conclusive. However, the other finding that some samples showed a group not human would be met with much skepticism. Perhaps, she thought, they were *Homo Floresiensis* that had somehow survived. But how had it been possible to escape detection in the modern world?

Geneva excited about her discovery told Irad she would present a written report to the detectives the next week. He knew the report would never get delivered. In a way, he would miss spending the evenings with her. The woman had such an appetite for sex, it left even him frequently exhausted.

***

Friday afternoon Thomas received the surveillance report on Irad. He immediately picked up the phone and called Richard.

"You won't believe this," he said. "Irad has been seen in the company of Dr. Peterson. And it gets even worse. The agent assigned to the stakeout did some further checking and found out he was working as an intern on the DNA project."

"I can't imagine she was knowingly involved," Richard said.

"We can't assume anything."

"What do you propose we do?"

"Put a tap on her phones. Then I'll call and tell Peterson what we know and see if she calls Irad. If she does, we'll have the benefit of their conversation."

"That's a good plan, Thomas."

"In the meantime, the terrorism unit will provide surveillance on her apartment this weekend," Thomas said.

It was Saturday morning and Geneva had just finished typing the report on her notebook computer. The material was printing when the phone rang.

"Dr. Peterson?"

"Yes."

"This is Detective O'Conner."

"I'm glad you called. I've finished the report on the DNA. I'd like to meet with you and Richard Monday morning."

"What time?"

"Nine o'clock."

"We'll be there. Now, there's something that I need to bring to your attention. There's a man named Irad Lamech who is part of a group called The Society that's involved in terrorist activities. He's in New York and may be interested in the DNA cases you're working on. I just wanted to warn you to be on alert for him. We'll talk more about this when we meet."

There was a long silence. Then she spoke; her voice was cold and distant.

"I'll see you Monday."

When Geneva hung up, she was in a state of shock. She sat in the chair in front of her computer screen.

There was complete silence, except for the sound of the printer, as the final pages of her report emerged.

Geneva had known such happiness these last few weeks. She had changed the type of clothing she wore and made the apartment brighter. There were fresh flowers in the den and an interior decorator was coming Tuesday to suggest new paint colors for the walls. Now her new world had completely collapsed. A return to her old life was unacceptable. She got up from the chair and went to the bathroom where she took a shower. Afterwards, she put on the type of drab outfit she had always worn before meeting Irad. Looking around the apartment, she located something that would serve her purpose. In the bathroom, there was a crossbeam.

Irad pushed the buzzer to the apartment and waited. When no one answered, he tried several more times. She must have stepped out for a few minutes, he thought. Reaching into his pocket, he withdrew the key she had given him and entered. He took this opportunity to check the computer room. Seeing the report, he read it. Then he reached into his jacket, removed a nylon rope and went to the bedroom where he slipped it under the bed. Later that evening, he planned to strangle her.

Irad decided, while Geneva was away, to wipe down every room to remove any fingerprints he might have left on previous visits. When he entered the bathroom, there was Geneva hanging from a crossbeam. He was puzzled. Why would she take her own life? For a moment, he stood and gazed, then focused on the task at hand. After cleaning the rooms to remove fingerprints, he picked up her computer and the printed report. He then went straight to his hotel room where he deposited the items before going to the university to destroy the research materials.

The phone rang. Thomas reached over Melinda in the bed and answered it. It was the officer on stakeout at Peterson's apartment.

"I hate to bother you on Saturday morning," he said, "but I just observed the subject, Irad, leave the doctor's residence with a notebook computer and some materials."

"How long was he in the apartment?"

"About thirty minutes."

"What about Peterson?"

"She hasn't left the apartment today."

"Call me if you see anything else suspicious."

"Who was that?" Melinda asked.

"Someone on stakeout. I'm afraid we won't to be able to spend the day together. I'll call you later."

"Okay, honey. I understand. Let's try to have dinner at my place tonight."

"Sure, I'll be free by then."

Before getting into the shower, he called Richard. They agreed to meet at Peterson's apartment.

When the detectives arrived, the door was unlocked. It wasn't long before they discovered her body.

"I'll call and obtain warrants from a federal judge. I think its imperative we get to his hotel before evidence can be destroyed."

By the time the detectives reached the hotel, agents were on their way with the warrants.

Irad was returning to the hotel when he saw Thomas and another man exit a vehicle and go into the lobby. He hit the accelerator. They must have found Geneva's body, he thought. Strange how the computer left in the hotel room would tie him to a death where he hadn't murdered the victim. He would call the Leader and then go into hiding until a new identity was obtained.

That afternoon Thomas called Jimmy Jones to find out when Bill was returning to the States. After the conversation, he reached into his desk drawer, pulled out the form to request a warrant under the Patriot Act. The name he filled in was Professor William Weston.

It was Saturday evening and the Leader sat in his chair looking out the window at the river in the distance. It had been a hectic weekend. Now at least, Irad was on his way to Yemen, a place of safety for the seed of Cain. He reflected on the fact that Irad's bloodlines, although not unique, were unusual. Not only did he carry the blood of Cain and Springca but also that of The Tribe of Dan. It was prophesied by the sacred writing of the children of Seth that this tribe would produce the *Antichrist*. This theology was never accepted by the seed of Cain who believed they would provide the *Antichrist*. Interestingly, Irad bloodlines would fit both prophecies.

Tuesday morning Kinsey walked into Thomas' office with a disturbed look on his face.

"I just received a personal phone call from Director Cagle. He told me to stop the process you started to obtain a warrant for Professor Weston. And he wants me to put you on an agency plane for Washington by noon."

"What's this about?"

"I don't know. When I tried to question him, he was tightlipped. Said it was top secret. All I know is that you've stirred up a hornet's nest in Washington by requesting that warrant."

"I don't understand."

"Neither do I. But remember when Beacham got into trouble for freezing the professor's expedition account?"

"Yes, I thought that was odd at the time."
"So did I."

The twin engine left the ground at noon. The pilot's flight plan called for a landing in Washington, but after they were airborne, he received a radio transmission instructing him to change course. His passenger was going to *Camp David*.

37

Bill tossed all night, torn between a competing set of agendas: national security, and his drive as a biblical archaeologist to substantiate the scripture's story on the origin of the species. He made a decision. The expedition must be abandon. To take any other course would compromise national security and put his group in imminent danger.

Rachael was waiting with the others for Bill at the camp table that morning.

"Father, if the translation is true, what would be the difference between creatures with souls versus those without them?"

"The biblical story of creation is unambiguous. As Genesis clearly says, the human race started when the Lord breathed into man's nostrils the breath of life, and he became a living soul. So the divine breath of God was what created the human soul. The soul of man, though unseen, is just as real as the body. Moreover, the soul is the fusion of matter and spirit. So they are not independent elements that are joined, but rather their union forms a single nature."

"It's similar to the Christian conception of Jesus," Henry said. "We believe *He* was both divine and human at the same time."

"What happens to the soul when a person dies?" Rachael asked.

"While the soul after death will continue to exist, it is incomplete until reunited with the body," Rachael's father said. "The resurrection of the body will come at the end of time when it is reunited with the soul."

"Ben, what you're saying sounds an awful lot like Christian doctrine," Henry said.

"Christians frequently forget that the prophet Jesus was Jewish. We just don't accept he was the Messiah. We still view Christianity as a branch of Judaism."

"If the translation is correct, what will happen to those without a soul?" Rachael asked.

"They are not dammed when they die. For them there is no Heaven or Hell, simply the grave just like any other animal," her father said.

"The end of the world will happen in the year 2014," said Fullmore, whose interest was stirred by the discussion about judgment day.

"What?" asked everyone.

"The ancient calendar of the *Mayan* civilization has been deciphered by a codex that was discovered. They were a very advanced culture and predicted when the world would end. At one time the experts thought the end was in 2012 but that was a mistake in the translation.

Before Fullmore could elaborate to his audience, he was interrupted by Bill's arrival.

"Sorry if I kept you waiting. But Bahodore came back this morning, and I needed to discuss some matters with him."

"Are we going back to the temple today?" Rachael asked.

"Yes, but before we go, I need to speak with everyone concerning the excavation. Bahodore informed me this area will soon explode in civil war. Our presence here will become untenable. As much as I hate to do it, the expedition must be abandoned."

"What about our discovery?" Rachael asked.

"We need to keep our find secret. This is my plan of action. Bahodore has some low-grade explosives. We will use them to bury the portion of the tunnel that goes to the temple. When Khandan and the laborers return, we'll dig the tunnel in a different direction away from the temple. That will mislead anyone who may decide to pursue the dig after we leave."

"When would we depart?" Fullmore asked.

"In three days. I'll tell Khandan we are going to our respective homes for a few weeks to take care of personal matters. It'd be a good idea if we all talked negatively about the prospects of finding anything here. If the rumor spreads the expedition was a failure, it will discourage the locals from bothering this site after we've gone."

What Bill told them was the truth mixed with fiction. He left out the most important reason for leaving. The attack on the nuclear facility would be occurring in a few days; and when it did, this area would be crawling with troops. No American or Jewish citizen would be safe. He needed to get them out of the country before the attack.

***

The president's chief of staff entered the room and informed her that the detective had landed. After the man left, she leaned back in the swivel chair behind the desk at the presidential cottage and focused on the coming crisis.

This was the president's second year in office, and events had sidetracked the domestic agenda that was to have been the hallmark of her presidency. International events had begun to take their toll. She was facing this crisis with a military that had grown so lean, that if the truth were known, it was incapable of defending the country's borders without using nuclear weapons. A bill to impose a limited draft had gone down in defeat after an important element of her party opposed it. Attempts to convince the antimilitary segment of her party that the United Nations was a weak reed on which to rely for their country's security had fallen on deaf ears.

When Thomas stood at the door and saw the president sitting behind the desk, he wondered if eventually he would wake up from a dream.

"Detective O'Conner, please come in."

The chief of staff remained standing by the door as Thomas sat in a chair across from the president.

"It's rare that an individual finds himself in the position you occupy today," she said. "This is a time your country needs you. Ultimately, the safety of future generations of Americans may depend upon it. When you leave here, a car will take you to a meeting with members of the National Security Council. I want you to listen carefully to them and give your full cooperation.

"I will, Madam President."

"Thank you for coming. I expect you to keep this meeting in the strictest confidence."

As he rose from the chair, she reached out and shook his hand with a grip that sent a message. This was a person of great inner strength. He felt that whatever the country was facing, this president was up to the task.

Colonel Bonham and Chairman Rouse of the National Security Council were standing in the corner of the large conference room when the military policeman escorted Thomas through the door. They stopped their conversation and turned toward him. Each gave him a long piercing look. Finally, Bonham addressed him.

"You must be Detective Thomas O'Conner. I'm James Bonham, and this is Thomas Rouse, Chairman of the NSC."

"Let's go to my office," Rouse said. "It's right down the hall."

As soon as they were seated, an aide brought them coffee.

"I guess you're wondering why you're here," Bonham said.

"That would be an understatement."

"It seems you have yourself entangled in a national security matter."

Bonham reached into his pocket and withdrew a card.

"This gives you a security clearance so we can disclose information that's necessary for this conversation."

"Do you have any idea why you're here?" Rouse asked.

"It must have something to do with my request for a warrant on William Weston."

"That's right," Bonham said. "Now, of course, what I'm about to disclose to you is top secret. We expect you to keep it confidential. Is that understood?"

"You have my word."

"Professor Weston is working for military intelligence. He's not in any way involved in the murders you're investigating."

"What about Irad?" Thomas asked.

"I can give you only limited information because, frankly, we don't know a lot. He's a member of a terrorist organization called The Society."

"So the devil worshipers do exist," Thomas said.

"We're not sure about their theology. Maybe this serpent thing is just a front they use. Frankly, we just don't know enough about the organization to analyze them. In fact, the source of most of our knowledge comes from Professor Weston."

And some of what he knows came from me, Thomas thought.

"You need to stay with us at *Camp David* for a few days," Rouse said.

"Am I in custody?"

"Let's just say you're our guest," Bonham said.

"We'll have Director Cagle inform the New York office that you'll be staying in Washington for a few days. No one needs to know where you are, and any messages will be forwarded here. Now, Colonel Bonham and I have some other matters to discuss. There's an MP outside to take you to your cottage. I hope you enjoy your stay."

Before he left, Bonham handed him a slip of paper.

"Here's my cell number. If you need anything, just give me a call. The MP will give you a schedule of meals in the cafeteria."

Thomas complained to the MP when they reached the cottage that he didn't have a change of clothing. The soldier returned later with army fatigues.

"There's a PX next door to the dining hall if you want to buy civilian clothes tomorrow," he said before leaving. And that was just what Thomas planned to do. He would never feel comfortable in the doggie outfit. After all, he had been in the Navy for four years assigned to the shore patrol.

Strange how all the different branches referred to one another. To the Army, he was a squid and to the Navy men, the Army was doggies. The Marines were jarheads, and for the life of him, Thomas couldn't remember what they called the Air Force personnel.

38

The earth above muffled the sound of the explosion. The tunnel that led to the temple were buried. Afterwards, Bill drew up a diagram of the route the new tunnel would take once the laborers returned the next day. Later that evening Rachael and he made their way to the water basin. They carried in a leather pouch the items found beside the skeleton in the inner chamber. Once there, he removed a large stone from the bank, then swam to where the water was deep and placed the leather pouch beneath it. Rachael watched from the flat rock. When he returned, they sat upon it and consumed the lunch they brought in their backpacks.

"How long will you be able to stay when we get to Jerusalem?" Rachael asked.

"I've decided to remain behind for a few days. Then I'll stop in Jerusalem before I travel to Texas."

"You're not leaving with the group?"

"No."

"But why not?"

"I need to supervise the digging of a new tunnel for a few days. Then, of course, the men will have to be paid. We must be sure the authorities don't become suspicious. My activities will set up a smoke screen. By the time the Iranians discover everything isn't kosher, you and the others will be beyond their reach."

"But what about you?"

"Don't worry. I'll get out in time."

After they finished lunch, the two sat on the edge of the rock and let their legs dangle into the water below.

Rachael worried that something might happen to Bill. The reasons he gave for not leaving seemed rather flimsy to her. She assumed, from the moment he announced they were leaving, the two of them would go together to Jerusalem. She had envisioned spending time relaxing with him beside the pool in her father's courtyard. She yearned to be intimate with the man. The desire was so strong, she had even started dreaming about it.

"Rachael, we may never be allowed to return here. There will be skeptics, when the time comes to make our findings public. I've decided to take something physical back with us as evidence that the expedition located Enoch."

"What are we taking back?" Rachael asked.

"The ring with the word *Springca* engraved on it."

He removed it from his pocket and placed it on her finger.

"Its such a simple design, no one will ever question you about it. You know if it placed you in any danger, Rachael, I wouldn't ask you to do it. I care too much for you to do that."

The way he said those last words had such tenderness. She looked up into his eyes, and it was as if they were a window to his soul, allowing her to catch a fleeting glimpse of his inner emotions. She knew that moment, without the words being spoken, he loved her.

The spell was broken by the voice of Khandan shouting as he came down the path toward the water.

"When I get to Jerusalem, there're other things we need to discuss," Bill said.

Khandan had returned a day early. He missed the group and their stimulating conversations about the ancient days. Besides there was only so much of the revolution's rhetoric that he could stand. And it had been especially feverish during this holiday. There was something in the air. Khandan could feel it. It was both a mixture of optimism and pessimism. His nephew told him, in a telephone conversation, the government believed there was going to be a confrontation with the hated United States soon.

Khandan viewed the damage to the tunnel. Bill said there had been a collapse of the timbers supporting the roof. He wondered how that was possible. He inspected them before he left, and they seemed sturdy enough at the time. But then, what would a paper shuffler like him really know about such things? Since Bill had saved his life, the weekly report to the government would confirm the man's story.

It was an emotional moment when the group packed their bags in the back of the truck. Bill embraced them. Seeing the worried look on his father's face and the tears that kept escaping from Rachael were almost more than he could bear. There was a strong possibility he would never see them again. As soon as they were out of sight, he borrowed Khandan's jeep, saying a trip to the village was necessary to get supplies. On the outskirts of the camp, he stopped beside the road and waited until Bahodore appeared. The two drove toward town, then exited on a dirt road and went in the direction of another valley.

Ghadir waited nervously. He didn't like being in the valley. It was much safer in the mountains where you could see the enemy coming for hours before they arrived. There one would have ample time to decide whether to fight or melt into the surrounding terrain. Down here in the valley, the army could swoop down and block any escape.

Bill and Bahodore parked in front of the mud hut that sat isolated out in an open field. There were no signs of life around the hut, nor in the waist-high grass that surrounded it.

"Are you sure we have the right place?" Bill asked.

"Yes. Ghadir and I grew up in the area. That house belonged to his grandfather."

They approached the hut cautiously and peered inside.

"Something must have happened. It is too dangerous for us to wait," Bahodore said.

As the men turned to leave, they saw Ghadir and several of his men emerging from the tall grass.

"Hearing a vehicle, we thought it best to stay concealed until we were sure who was coming down the road," Ghadir said. "Come, let's go inside. My men will keep watch while we take care of business."

Inside, Ghadir rolled out a map on the table next to the window.

"This operation will require the largest concentration of men since the insurgency started in this region six years ago," Ghadir said. "It will be hard to get my men to the area of operations without being seen from the air. I've decided on two methods. Two-hundred recruits from the local population have already started infiltrating the area near the nuclear facility. The remaining ones will come with me out of the mountains. We'll travel only at night, keeping away from the villages. The attack must be swift and the withdrawal quick. We are only lightly armed and no match for the Iranian army. However, God has smiled on this operation. The regular units have been withdrawn to participate in military exercises near Tabriz. They have been replaced by units of the Revolutionary Guard that are not as well trained nor heavily armed as the Army."

"What are your chances of success?" Bill asked.

"No better than fifty percent. But my men understand the importance of this mission."

"Have the supplies been dropped?"

"Yes, and my men also have the equipment the Pentagon sent for you. It's hidden outside in the grass."

Bahodore interjected himself into the conversation. "I hope part of that equipment was the special camera I will need to photograph the damage."

"It came along with the mechanism to transmit photographs to the spy satellite," Ghadir said.

The men stepped outside into the bright sunlight. Ghadir barked an order, and a man ran a few yards into the grass and retrieved a sack containing the items.

"Bahodore, after the attack we will meet here as planned," Ghadir said, and then the two men embraced.

Later, as they drove away from the hut toward Nodqi, Bill said, "He's a brave man."

"He comes from a race of warriors. His family has been in these mountains for thousands of years. Some say he can trace his ancestors all the way back to Seth."

On the way back, Bill stopped in Noqdi and bought supplies. When he came out of the store, he saw a military jeep parked down the street with two men in it. One was in military fatigues, and the other was in civilian clothes.

"I believe we're being watched, Bahodore," Bill said.

As they left, Bill noticed through the rear-view mirror that they were being followed. The men were some distance behind, so when they were out of sight, he made a sharp right onto a dirt road and parked behind a boulder. Soon the jeep came by their hiding place.

"I know those men," Bill said. "It's Captain BalAsh of the Revolutionary Guards. The civilian calls himself Walter Henley."

"It seems that evil attracts evil," Bahodore said.

39

Bill buried himself in a burst of energy on the new direction of the tunnel. No one watching would guess that in twenty-four hours he would be on a flight out of Iran. This afternoon was the last day of work at the excavation. He explained to Khandan that since there would be no one to supervise them while the archaeologists were away, it was necessary to pay the laborers their wages and release them. Khandan offered to supervise the dig in the interim, but he turned him down knowing the promise to return was nothing more than a smokescreen. On his hand, Bill was wearing the Citadel ring given to him by Bahodore, who instructed him to deliver it to his son in America.

Colonel BalAsh was enjoying his position as the temporary commander of the facility. One of his first acts was to raid the lockers of the scientists. As expected, the men's lockers were full of photographs of scantily clothed women. Then he observed female scientists not properly dressed. They didn't even have on a veil. He threatened to have them whipped, and would have, if someone hadn't made a secret call to Tehran. The minister of defense personally phoned him and ordered there be no interference with the scientists. BalAsh hated bureaucrats.

Henley was at his residence in Noqdi filling out a report for the Leader. He had been at the nuclear facility yesterday after receiving an invitation from Colonel BalAsh to visit. He was pleased with what he had seen there. The Iranians were in the final stage of their nuclear weapons production. He was present when some items of pornography were seized. Strange how things worked–alliances formed. The Society used its power and connection to inundate the world with smut for the last fifty years. This was one of the many factors causing the moral disintegration of the West. It even compromised the churches. Whenever they spoke out against it, the churches were accused of being narrow-minded and intolerant, until they had at last been cowered into submission. Now the trash had even begun to pollute their sanctuary.

***

In three hours, it would be light. Ghadir's runners had just returned with word that the men were in position. The attack would commence soon. He looked over at Bahodore, who was focusing on the terrain that lay ahead. Then Ghadir's thoughts turned to his wife, Mehri, the sister of Bahodore. She was safe at the mountain redoubt. If anything happened, the tribe would send her into hiding with a clan in a different region of the country.

Ghadir looked at his watch. It was time. He gave the signal to move forward. Ghadir moved his men out of their caves and down the paths in the darkness so the eyes of the enemy couldn't see their advance. They were armed with M-16 rifles, fifty-caliber machine guns, mortars, grenades, and high explosives.

Awakened by the first blast, Colonel BalAsh jumped out the bed, dumping the whore onto the floor. He rushed out the door and ran toward the explosion. He covered only a few yards when a concussion from several other explosions shook the ground beneath his feet causing him to lose balance. When he got up, he hailed a passing jeep driven by a revolutionary guard.

"What's happening?"

"The facility is under attack," the driver responded.

"Take me to the entrance."

The initial phase of the attack surprised the guards on the outer perimeter, and the insurgents quickly overran their positions. The Revolutionary Guards, assigned to the second layer of defense, fled. Now Ghadir and his men were closing in on the last line of organized defenses at the entrance into the mountain. There were two concrete bunkers with fifty-caliber machine guns protruding out of them. In addition, a hundred guardsmen assumed positions around vehicles parked nearby. Once word spread that it was insurgents and not the American military attacking, the guards found courage. But it was courage born of fear. They knew the attacker would show no mercy to any survivors. Too many of the tribesmen were kin to those whom the guards had tortured or worse. The insurgents would take no prisoners.

"Bring up the mortars," Ghadir ordered.

In a moment, the bunkers and vehicles were in flames.

"Forward men," Ghadir screamed as he charged through the flames with men trailing behind him.

Bahodore followed with the second wave of men through the opening. He was in command of a ten-man unit, who were to plant the explosives. Bahodore had a diagram from military intelligence where to place them for the maximum effect. Several days ago, he had made sure every man on the team had memorized the diagram.

Once the last line of defense was broken, Ghadir's men fanned out to destroy the few pockets of resistance remaining.

BalAsh arrived just as the mortars started landing on the last line of defense at the entrance. He knew that the attackers would soon overwhelm it.

"Turn this jeep around and go to headquarters," he yelled to the driver.

The driver looked up in surprise.

"I said turn this jeep around, now."

As they passed guardsmen scattered around the facility, BalAsh screamed at them to go to headquarters and form a defense there. When the jeep reached it, BalAsh said to the driver, "Go inside and have the radio dispatcher call the military authorities. I'll round up the rest of the men and bring them here." Taking control of the jeep, he spun it around and drove off at a high rate of speed. The guardsmen stared in bewilderment as he drove toward the back of the complex.

BalAsh knew any attempt to contact the outside by phone was a waste of time. The attacker had certainly taken the basic step of cutting the lines. He doubted a message would have gotten out anyway since the regulars who operated the equipment were on military maneuvers, and BalAsh's men weren't trained in its use. Even without communication, he knew the sound of the explosion and gunfire would arouse the authorities. It was only a question of time before army units arrived. He just need to stay alive. He'd hide in the building where he slept last night. By the time they suppressed the resistance the troops would be there.

BalAsh arrived in his area and parked the jeep in front of a building several yards away. When he entered his room, the whore he had slept with last night was still there. She was so frightened she was in hysterics. He slapped her across the face several times.

"Get out," he said.

When she refused to leave, he struck her again in the face with his fist until she was bleeding profusely. Then he grabbed her by the hair and dragged her bodily out of the door onto the gravel that was spread in front.

Now that the explosives were in place and the timers set, Bahodore and his men joined the others in the last firefight at the Iranian command headquarters. A dozen guards had converted it into a defensive position. A few smoke grenades were tossed into an open window, and the fighting was over. The men came out with their hands in the air. They were immediately lined up and shot. Bahodore's stomach turned over several times as he stood by and watched.

"Bahodore," called Ghadir, who was standing a few yards away with several of his lieutenants, "take your men to the far end of this complex. Search every building on the way. We'll cover this point to the entrance."

Bahodore and the tribesmen fanned out, knowing there could be snipers anywhere along their route. They reached their destination without incident. One of the men searching a car found a woman, with a bloody face hiding in its back seat.

"It's all right," Bahodore said, as he opened the car door. "No one is going to hurt you." He gave the woman a drink from his canteen. Turning to one of his men he said, "Take this woman and find some medical personnel to help her."

"Thank you," the woman said through a swollen lip. Blood gushed from an empty space in her mouth that once held two front teeth. "Before I leave, there is something I can do for you."

She led them to a building that stood near the vehicle where she was hiding. Pointing her finger, she said, "There's a colonel from the Revolutionary Guard in there." Bahodore and his men approached with caution. Entering, they saw no one at first.

BalAsh was afraid when he saw the feet of the men from his hiding place under the bed. He became more terrified after noticing the trail of blood left by his fist, which had been injured when he had pounded the whore. A few moments later, they dragged him, screaming and kicking, outside. When they dropped him on the ground, he crawled up on his knees in front of Bahodore and begged for his life. Even if he wanted to have mercy, Bahodore doubted the men would listen to him. Then he recognized the person kneeling before him. This man could identify both the professor and him. Bahodore, who had never killed a man before, removed the pistol from its holster, placed the barrel to the man's forehead and pulled the trigger. The explosion splattered the man's brains over his trousers. He turned to walk away. As he did, the woman tore loose from the person holding her, ran over and kicked the bloody corpse. It was all too much for Bahodore who could feel the vomit rising in his throat. A moment later, it gushed out of his mouth onto the ground.

Time was running out, and Ghadir knew it. They had to begin their retreat immediately. The Air Force would be there soon, and the ground troops would not be far behind. He had already released the lower civilian personnel and ordered them to leave the complex. All that remained were the scientists and their assistants. When Bahodore returned, Ghadir had them rounded up in a group.

"You need to leave now," Bahodore said.

He took one look into the commander's eyes and read his thoughts.

"The Americans instructed us not to intentionally kill any civilians," Bahodore said.

"They have their rules, and we have ours. The Americans will say they are appalled, but in their hearts, they will be silently pleased. The explosions will only damage equipment. The knowledge of these scientists will be much harder to replace."

"You've got only fifteen minutes before this complex is going to blow," Bahodore said. "I'll hide in the brush outside the complex until after the explosion, then return and take the pictures. I'll catch up with you on the trail."

"Good luck, my friend. May Allah go with you."

"And with you," Bahodore said.

As soon as he was out of sight, the sound of automatic gunfire told him the cream of Iranian scientists was no more.

Bahodore heard the first Iranian military aircraft fly over an hour after the explosives he planted destroyed their intended targets. His men were now walking at a fast pace. Their only hope was to reach their mountain redoubt. Everyone was praying darkness would come quickly and hide their movements. Then in the distance, they heard the hum of planes followed by the sound of several rapid explosions. "They have spotted Ghadir and his men," said a young rebel close to Bahodore. The men picked up their pace.

40

Bill was standing outside the tent watching the sunrise when he heard the crackle of twigs in the underbrush behind him.

"Professor," a voice said. He turned around. At first, he couldn't see because fog blanketed the area. Then a lone figure appeared. It was DelAvar, the man who had driven the truck the night Arsham was killed.

"I have come from Bahodore. He asked me to deliver this camera to you."

"Why didn't he come?"

"He couldn't. After the attack, the Iranian air force caught our men just before dark. Their planes strafed and bombed us. Many were killed or injured. The last time I saw Bahodore, he was staying behind with Ghadir, who was seriously wounded."

"Where were they?"

"In a mud hut halfway between the nuclear facility and the mountain redoubt. I must go now while the fog is still thick."

"Where are you going?"

"To our headquarters in the mountains."

"God go with you. And tell Bahodore my country owes him a debt of gratitude."

After DelAvar disappeared into the fog, Bill retrieved a flashlight out of the tent and made his way up the path toward the water basin where a barren hill would provide an unobstructed view of the sky. This location would enable Bill to transmit the photographs to the spy satellite when it passed over. Along the way, he left the path for a few minutes and secured the transmitter hidden under a pile of small rocks.

***

Thomas had been at *Camp David* for several days. He had watched all the television he could stand. The only message forwarded to him was from Melinda. It was brief. Her grandmother in Charleston was ill, and she took the week off from work to fly home. There were no words of endearment. It was so professional.

So cold. He wondered what happened to change their relationship in his absence.

Thomas picked up a box lunch. He would eat in the park nearby. Sitting alone in the cafeteria was boring. He was ready to get back to the city. He had called Colonel Bonham earlier that morning and was told he could leave in a couple of days.

The park was deserted. Thomas chose a table on a knoll overlooking a man-made lake teeming with wildlife. He watched a group of ducks take off from the lake, disappear and then return. He finished his lunch and was about to leave when he saw the president coming up the sidewalk that ran around one side of the lake. There were security men with her. She left the sidewalk and went over to a bench near the edge of the water. The security men spread out into the surrounding area, giving her some privacy. She seemed to have the weight of the world on her shoulders.

The president enjoyed nature. It generally relaxed her, but not today. Her mind was on the operation. She received word just before she left on her walk that photographs of the attack had been received. A meeting of the security council was scheduled this afternoon. The story of the attack had not yet been released by the Iranian government. But the news would certainly be broadcast within twenty-four hours. She would be called upon to respond whether America was involved. There was a chance, when all was said and done, her political career would be on the ash heap of history by the end of the week. Not only might she not be re-elected, but she could even face defeat in her own party's primary. If the attack had been a success, it was worth the price. If not, she had just thrown away what she worked her whole life to obtain.

All members of the security council were present for this important briefing. The president was there, seated at the far end of the table, so she had a good view of any visual projections that might be displayed on the opposite wall.

Colonel Bonham was in charge of the presentation.

"Madam President, members of the security council, the attack on the nuclear plant in Iran has been carried out by the insurgents. We've received photographs that I'm now going to put up on the screen."

He motioned to his aide who switched the lights off so the group would have a clear view of the images. They showed extensive damage to the facilities.

When the presentation was concluded, Bonham said, "Dr. Gayle Smith will answer any questions that you might have on the effectiveness of the attack."

All eyes turned to the president.

"Dr. Smith, how long will this delay Iran from obtaining nuclear weapons?" she asked.

"It's hard to be exact, but we had the best minds of our country exam the photographs, and they concluded the physical destruction will delay the Iranian government at least an additional two years. If we're lucky, perhaps three."

***

Thomas was watching a movie on television when the headlights of a vehicle in the driveway interrupted his evening.

"Sorry to disturb you, Sir," said the MP standing in the doorway. "We received word that Director Cagle just arrived. He wants to see you."

They met in a room at a small facility near the landing strip that serviced the airport. When he walked in, he was surprised to see Bonham seated at the table with Cagle.

"Come in, Thomas," Bonham said. "I told you it wouldn't be long before you could leave our accommodations."

Director Cagle studied the detective, who sat across the table. Would he make a good agent for the unit? His resume indicated that he would. It certainly would guaranteed his public silence on The Society. And it needed to be kept quiet. The world was simply not ready to absorb that kind of information any more than they could believe in intelligent life beyond the earth's atmosphere. The man must be convinced to join the unit. It would solve the problem of him being outside the intelligence service.

"Thomas," Cagle said. "I'm here on behalf of the unit and with the consent of the security council. We want you to come to work with us permanently."

"Permanently?"

"Yes. And if you do, I'll place you in charge of a new section being organized to work exclusively on The Society. Of course, it will involve a substantial increase in salary. You could even transfer your city retirement time to our agency."

"How long do I have to make a decision?"

"Right now. When I leave, the offer will be off the table."

This guy played hardball, Thomas thought. He wanted a change in his life. Maybe this was what he needed.

"Only on one condition."

"What's that?"

"That my assistant, Betty Marlow, comes with me."

"It's a done deal." Cagle reached across the table and shook Thomas' hand.

"Welcome aboard."

"Now that you've accepted Director Cagle's offer, let me give you a security clearance card," Bonham said.

"You've already given me one."

"This is different. It gives you a higher clearance. Now you're entitled to know why we kept you here for the last few days. Professor Weston was not only an archaeologist but also an officer in Marine Intelligence. He was involved in an attack on Iran's nuclear facility by insurgents, under the guidance of our intelligence service, with the direct approval of the president. We couldn't afford to take the chance of this leaking out."

Colonel Bonham was right, Thomas thought. Bureaucracy always leaks like a sieve, and law enforcement is no exception.

Thomas was glad when he felt the wheels of the agency's plane touch the ground on the runway of La Guardia airport. Richard was meeting him. It was going to be hard not telling him what occurred. However, his security clearance prohibited disclosing anything, except the fact that he was working with the terrorism unit on a permanent basis.

Richard was waiting in the airport lounge watching television when breaking news flashed across the screen.

Moments ago, Iran announced to the world there has been an attack on their nuclear plant. The United States has been accused of orchestrating the destruction. We're waiting for a response from the president. This is Reed Jones from the grounds of the White House.
Now back to you, Sheila, in Atlanta.

On the way from the airport, Richard said, "Tell me about your trip."

"I wish I could, but it's classified."

"Sounds like cloak-and-dagger stuff to me."

"Believe me, it's exactly that. Richard, I've accepted a permanent position with the Terrorism Unit."

A smile on Richard face hide the mixed emotions he felt about losing his friend to a federal agency. "That's a good move. More resources and better retirement."

"And don't forget, different types of cases. Maybe I'll find the passion I once had when we were partners."

"Dr. Peterson's report has been transcribed from the computer we found in Irad's hotel room. It makes for some interesting reading."

"I'd like to get a copy of it as soon as possible."

"I'm a step ahead of you on that. Look on the back seat, and you'll find it inside that folder."

***

The Leader was disturbed by the news of the American attack on Iran. The Society had been instrumental in helping the Iranians obtain the necessary materials to make their country a nuclear power. If that had occurred, the possibilities seemed unlimited. The economy of the United States would collapse without oil from the Middle East. America would then be hard pressed to continue sending the billions in foreign aid necessary to keep the State of Israel afloat. The shortage would bring all the powers of the earth to *Armageddon* on the hills of *Megiddo* to confront one another. The destruction by conventional weapons would be enormous. Ultimately, Iran would succumb to the pressure to fire its nuclear arsenal. Even if the United States did not respond, Israel would launch their small nuclear arsenal upon the capitols of the surrounding countries. The escalation would bring the *Three Horsemen of the Apocalypse* and right behind them the return of the *Serpent*. Now these hopes, if not dashed, were at least delayed.

***

Rachael was excited. Bill had e-mailed her from Iran. He was landing in Jerusalem the next afternoon. She went to her father's study to deliver the good news. Benjamin Rabon was sitting behind the desk with his nose in a book.

"What are you reading?"

"Just a scholarly work on the Jewish temple," he said. "I thought it would be wise to brush up on it before Bill arrives. He should be here in a few days."

"He'll be here tomorrow."

Her excitement was in excess of what one should feel for an employer. He long suspected she was attracted to Bill and that the attraction was mutual. The man was too old for his daughter. Even if Bill were younger, he would be opposed to a mixed marriage. That's the way his people, the Jews, had maintained their identity for thousands of years. Of course, Bill could convert, but that was unlikely. He appeared too well grounded in his Christian faith.

"Rachael, you seem so excited. Do you have a romantic interest in Bill Weston?"

Rachael's face felt flushed. She loved her father, but he was old and set in his ways. She knew he would never approve. Her mind raced to find an answer that he would accept. But there was only one answer that the passageway of her brain would deliver to her mouth.

"Yes. I'm in love with him."

There. The words were out, and Bill was not the first one to hear them. She braced for her father's reply.

"You're too young for him."

"I'll grow older."

"Yes, and he will just grow old."

She was hurt by his reply, and left the room in tears. Dr. Benjamin Rabon went back to his book and tried to push the conversation out of his mind.

***

On the trip to Tabriz, where he would board a twin-engine plane to the Tehran airport, Bill passed numerous convoys filled with troops going in the direction of Noqdi. The sky was filled with the activities of the Iranian Air Force. Occasionally in the distance, he could hear the faint sounds of explosions. He hoped to arrive in Tabriz before the military had time to react and start checking vehicles. If stopped, he would be detained because of his American passport.

A sense of relief came over Bill when the twin-engine plane lifted off the runway, circled the airport one time, and then flew in the direction of Tehran. It was a clear day, and he had a good view of the airport below. His eyes focused on activity at the flight zone. Several military vehicles were driving onto the strip. They were shutting it down. Perspiration popped out on his brow. This did not bode well for the landing in Tehran.

Bill knew he was in danger minutes after the twin-engine plane landed in Tehran. When the pilot parked in an area reserved for small planes, he looked out of the window and saw several members of the dreaded Iranian Security Police. He stepped down the ramp knowing that trouble was waiting at the end of it.

"Dr. Weston," said a small man in a suit two sizes too large for him, "you must come with us."

They placed him in the back seat of an old black SUV and left the airport. The two men with him spoke not a word. The way they puffed on cigarettes, Bill felt like he was sitting between two smoke stacks. He started to get nauseated. He didn't know whether it was from the smoke with the windows closed or anticipation of events to come. Maybe it was just fear. They soon arrived at a structure in the center of Tehran. The vehicle entered through a back gate that had guards posted at its entrance. Now, out of sight of civilians, the secret police dragged him from the car. One of them landed several blows to his mid-section while two others held him. They were interrupted by the man in the oversized suit who appeared out of nowhere and barked orders. The beating stopped, and they took him into a back door of the building, down a long corridor, and then descended several layers beneath the earth until they reached a row of cells. He heard the old iron key turn in the lock. He realized where he was. The famous Evin Prison, a well-known place of torture during the days of the Shah, now converted into a secret police headquarters for the new regime.

Bill thought the police careless. They hadn't even bothered to search him. Perhaps they didn't really believe at this point that he had anything to do with the attack on the facility. They were just taking this opportunity to brutalize an American. He needed to get out before they discovered the truth. He looked around the cell. There was no way to escape without help. Then he thought, how stupid of me. He had forgotten about the miniature device in his pocket. He removed the direction beeper that intelligence had given him, and placed it under some filthy debris in the corner. It was as small as a button but emitted a powerful signal. Unfortunately, the satellite couldn't pick up the signal three floors down through thick masonry walls. His only hope was to place it somewhere the signal could be heard. Until that time came, he needed to keep the beeper hidden and hope the authorities wouldn't find it.

The cell had a single low-wattage light bulb in the center of the ceiling. It gave off only a faint light. Bill knew its failure to illuminate the room was a blessing in disguise. It meant he couldn't see the filth or vermin. There were no toilet facilities in the room, and the stench was almost overpowering. Nevertheless, he did manage to fall asleep in the early hours of the morning.

The sound of a key turning the old rusty lock woke Bill. Three men entered the cell. Two grabbed him while the other proceeded to land a few punches. He gasped for breath, then vomited on the floor of the cell. "Take the American swine to *Mohaymen*," said the man who had assaulted him. He was dragged up three flights of stairs and then deposited in a small room with a table and two chairs. Moments later, the man wearing the oversized suit entered the room. The man put his hand over his nose. "Get this prisoner out of here. Go give him a shower."

"Yes, *Mohaymen*," one of the guards said.

They took him down the hall to a room with several showers where they removed his clothing. While he was washing the stench from his body, Bill observed them going through his clothing, removing his personal items. They then threw the clothes into the shower with him. After he put on the wet clothing, they led him outside to a small courtyard. There he stood for an hour. His two guards sat in chairs observing. When he returned to the interrogation room, his clothes were dry from the heat of the sun. The man called *Mohaymen* was waiting. He questioned Bill in *Farsi*.

"I'm sorry," Bill said in English, "but I don't speak your language."

Rachael and he in their work frequently pretended they didn't speak a language. Then people around them spoke freely in their presence, thinking the American and Jew didn't understand a word. It was an effective tool. He was banking that these incompetents didn't have access to his resume.

"All right Dr. Weston, I will question you in English. What were you doing in Noqdi?"

Much to Bill's surprise, the interrogator spoke English with a British accent. He thought, this man must have received his education at a British institution.

"I was there on an archaeological dig with the permission of your government."

"What do you know about the attack?

"What attack?"

"The one on our nuclear plant near Noqdi."

"I didn't even know there was an attack. I left Noqdi early yesterday morning."

The interrogation continued for the next two hours. It was obvious the man called Mohaymen already knew the answers before he asked the questions. It was also clear that the Iranian government didn't really believe he was involved, though they might hold him under some trumped-up charges. Even the blows to the midsection instead of the face where the bruises would show led Bill to believe this security officer thought his country might release him once the crisis subsided. Unfortunately, if he was detained long enough, they would find out the truth through torturing him or from leaks within the insurgents' camp. The thought of torture gave him flashbacks of Panama. The physical scars were not nearly as deep as the psychological ones.

After the prisoner left the interrogation room, Mohaymen called his superiors. There was more to this than simply an archaeologist on an excavation. The ring on his finger from the Citadel, a military college in the States, was one reason to be suspicious. As a young man, he had seen that ring many times on the hand of military officers. During the Shah's regime, the school graduated a large number of Iranians who were members of the ruling elite. Most remained loyal to the old order and were executed when the revolution toppled the government. Another reason for suspicion were the scars on the American's body the guards reported seeing. Their description of the disfigurement would lead one to believe that they were from acts of brutality. Not something you would expect on an American professor.

***

Khandan was roughed up when the troops arrived at the camp. They demanded to know where the Americans and Jews were hiding. He told them all he knew before being transported to a stockade in Noqdi. He was only there a few hours when a mullah with the religious police came by. Khandan called out the name of his nephew, FarAj, several times until the mullah recognized it. Curious, he approached the enclosure. Khandan immediately identified himself and told the mullah how he came to be in Noqdi. The mullah might have moved on if the man had not claimed to be the uncle of FarAj, the chief advisor to the *Ayatollah*. If Khandan was telling the truth and the mullah helped him, then one of the most powerful men in the country would owe him a favor. He took a chance and got access to the army communication room from where he placed the call. Khandan's release came quickly. The next morning Khandan left Noqdi for Tehran.

41

John Elesbaan was at the airport in Paris waiting for a flight that, after several connections, would get him to his destination in Yemen. When the news flashed on the screen in the airport lounge, he felt a moment of joy. The Society's efforts had been stymied again. Then he thought about the expedition. His contacts had kept him informed. He knew everyone, except Bill, was out of there. Where was Bill now, he wondered. Hopefully in Jerusalem or the States.

***

Henry was watching the breaking news when the phone rang. It was an old friend, Colonel Bonham, who worked at the Pentagon in military intelligence.

"I hate to be the one to make this call, but Bill has been arrested by the Iranian Internal Security Forces. I'm afraid there's not much we can do to help him. If I find out anything further, I'll give you a call."

***

FarjAd was agitated about the Army's action. At first, he thought Khandan's arrest might have been intentional. Despite the many purges of the officers' corps over the years, there were still elements that did not approve of the Revolution. But in talking to his father's brother by phone, he realized it had simply been a roundup of civilians by an Army afraid the attack would be used by the religious authorities as an excuse for another purge. Now FarjAd's concerns shifted to the possibility his enemies would use the contact between his uncle and the American to sow suspicion against him. On the inner circle of the religious elite, he had seen the effect of what mere rumor could do to a person in such a sensitive position as the one he held. Individuals had not only lost their status, but their very lives, on nothing more than rumors and innuendos.

Khandan waited in the outer office to see his nephew. FarjAd had done well. Their tribe was an obscure one that had never before risen to great prominence. But unlike many others, they had been in Iran since the formation of the Persian Empire, serving whoever held the reins of power, always involved in civil service, even if it was in some servile positions. But now, for the first time, one of their own had gained access to power.

FarjAd was a Machiavellian. His priorities were Allah, his clan and the nation. But his first priority was to himself.

"Uncle, so good to see you," he said, kissing the man on both cheeks. "I'm sorry about your misfortune in Noqdi. You said it was urgent we meet."

"Yes. I didn't want to discuss this matter over the phone. The head of the expedition I monitored was a man named Dr. William Weston. He had a flight booked out of Iran before the attack. I want to know if he left before they shut down the airports. If not, I want to find out if he's still in our country."

"Why such an interest in this American?"

"Because he saved my life from the insurgents."

Khandan explained what occurred and then told about the archaeological dig.

"Too bad they didn't discover what they were looking for in the excavation. Our leadership has no interest in the ancient days. Their attraction to the history of our country starts when Islam was brought here by conquest. Now as to the whereabouts of the American, I can already provide the information that you are seeking. We have received a report that he has been detained."

"Can you help him?"

"Let me see what I can do. In the meantime let us go to my home. My father is expecting you to join us for dinner."

While his father and uncle reminisced in another room, FarjAd sent for two men from his village that he could trust. They were underlings who had taken care of such things before. FarjAd could not afford any scandal that would involve his family and ultimately himself. Elimination was the answer. First the American, and if it became necessary, his uncle.

***

Rachael and her father heard the news followed by an announcement that the Israeli military was placed on a high state of alert. It frightened Rachael, who was already concerned, because Bill failed to arrive on his scheduled flight. She had been so excited yesterday waiting at the airport. But he wasn't on the plane when it landed nor on a later flight that day. She came home thinking he would certainly arrive tomorrow. Now in light of the news, she was afraid he would be delayed longer or even worse. She pushed the even-worse scenario out of her mind. She couldn't handle it.

Two days later, Rachael couldn't endure the wait any longer. She called Bill's father in Greenville. She could tell by the inflection in Henry's voice that he was worried about his son. She believed he knew more than he indicated over the phone. When Rachael hung up, she walked into her father's study and announced, "I'm going to fly to the States." The next day she was on her way to visit Henry Weston.

***

Bill heard the key turn in the lock of the cell door. He looked toward it expecting the security officers to take him again to the interrogation room, this time for more serious questioning. Perhaps they had learned of his involvement in the operation. Instead, he saw two civilians in the traditional clothing worn in rural Iran.

"Come, we must go," the larger one said in *Farsi*,
Bill gave them a puzzled look.
"We have been sent to help you escape."
"I only speak English," Bill said.
Then the man repeated the message in broken English, adding, "Put these clothes on for disguise." It was

a garb similar to what they were wearing. He changed over the spot where the beeper was hidden and concealed it on his person without the men noticing. As they stepped outside the cell, Bill saw a guard lying on the floor with his throat cut. Ascending the three levels, they were soon outside. It was night, and the only illumination in the area came from the stars. The back gate was unlocked and he could see, even in the dim light, another guard's body in some shrubbery nearby. They went through the gate and down the narrow street outside. A few moments later, an old covered truck came down the road and stopped.

"Get in," said the large man, standing beside him. The three climbed into the back of the truck, which then sped down the street toward the desert.

As they drove through the countryside, the men opened a large cooler. It contained food and water. Bill reached in and helped himself. It was the first nourishment his body had since he'd been taken into custody at the airport. The two men joined him in consuming the contents. He tried to question them in English, but they didn't respond. Finally, the small man turned to the other and said in *Farsi*, "This fool thinks he is on the way to freedom. How much farther before we cut the throat of this American dog?"

"Another hour, and we will kill him and dump his body out of the truck."

"Then FarjAd may have another job for us?" the small man asked.

"Perhaps."

Bill tried not to look stunned by what he heard. Instead, he continued to smile. He didn't want the men to suspect he understood their language. Meanwhile, his mind worked overtime on a plan of escape.

Bill knew time was running out. Finally he saw his opportunity when, around midnight, the large man went to the back of the truck and looked out at the empty street of a village they were passing. As the man let go of the wooden rail and turned, Bill lunged forward. His right shoulder caught the large man in his mid-section with such force that the Iranian's feet were lifted off the truck bed. He tumbled out of the back and hit the asphalt headfirst. The forward motion of Bill's body nearly took him out of the truck. At the last moment, he managed to grab the wooden rail. He immediately turned and charged the other man, whose hand was already pulling a dagger from its case. One quick punch to the face stunned him. Two more swift punches and the man went down. He was on the man in a split second. One knee went into the small of his back while his two hands grabbed the man's neck and pulled until he felt it crack. Standing up he looked at the lifeless form before him, then reached down and removed the dagger. It was just in time because the driver, hearing the commotion, pulled off the road. Since the man might be armed, Bill jumped out and raced toward the driver's side of the cab. He reached it just as the man was stepping off the running board. In the darkness, he drove the dagger through the man's heart. The driver never had a chance to use the pistol in his hand. Afterwards, Bill dragged the bodies off into the underbrush where he hoped they wouldn't be found for days.

In the cab of the truck, Bill was relieved to see the tank was full. That meant he could put some distance between Tehran and him before the sun came up. He switched on the beeper and hoped a satellite would pick up its signal. He read the road signs to get a sense of direction, then he made a turn on a narrow road that would take him through the desert toward the Iraqi border.

42

Rachael sat in a lounge at the airport in New York waiting for a connecting flight to Greenville and wondered if she was doing the right thing. Her father opposed the trip, and she hadn't even let Henry know she was flying to visit him. She felt the need to be with the Bill's family at this moment of crisis. There was no question the man she loved hadn't been allowed to leave Iran. It could only mean he was in danger or something worse.

The lounge suddenly got silent as an announcement came across the television screen that hung midway between the bar counter and the ceiling. The President of the United States was about to address the American people. Rachael turned in her chair to get a better view as the bartender reached up and adjusted the volume.

Twenty-four hours ago the government of Iran requested that the United Nations Security Council schedule an emergency meeting to consider allegations that the United States was behind the destruction of their nuclear facility. I received word a few hours ago they would honor the request. A meeting of the Security Council has been called for tomorrow. That is why I felt it necessary to address you, my fellow citizens, as well as the nations of the world. Iranian production of nuclear weapons would have upset the balance of power in the region, threatened our oil supplies and put the security of Israel in imminent danger. Ultimately, Iran would have had a delivery system capable of reaching our shores. None of those dangers was acceptable. After carefully considering the matter, I believed that under the Bush Doctrine of Preemptive Strike action was necessary. I, therefore, directed the various intelligence services to provide the insurgents in Iran the support necessary to destroy the nuclear plant. I have instructed our country's ambassador to the United Nations to present our position to the Security Council. I take sole responsibility for the action taken. Thank you for your attention. And may God Bless America.

✷✷✷

Bill was in a desert region when the gas gauge hit empty. He needed somewhere to ditch the vehicle. He came across a gorge, an ideal place to hide the truck. After removing the beeping device, truck canvas, water, and food, he sent the truck over a cliff. A moment later, he heard the impact below. Putting his training to good use, he dug a hole in the sand and covered it with the canvas he had staked in the ground. It provided protection from the sun during the day and the cold winds that blew during the night. He hoped the beeper would alert military intelligence to his location. Even if they had this information, there was no guarantee they could act on it. He felt sure the Iranian borders were sealed and the airspace closely guarded after the nuclear plant incident.

Two days later, Bill had exhausted the food and water. Without rescue or an alternate plan, he would perish.

Colonel Bonham had kept up a hectic pace for several weeks. He planned to take a few days off to spend time with his grandchildren. A message received that morning, however, put an end to that idea. The satellite reported receiving signals from a coded beeper belonging to intelligence officer, Captain William Weston. It came from an area in Iran only twenty miles from the Iraqi border. An American drone aircraft on the Iraqi side was launched. Photographs taken showed a canvas over a hole dug in the desert floor. This was consistence with survival training taught to Special Forces. Bonham ordered a mission to parachute supplies and a special communication device.

When the special Marine unit attached to the anti-terrorist command in Washington received word of the situation involving an intelligence operative in Iran, a two-phased plan was adopted. The first would be implemented immediately. It involved the use of a Drone aircraft in a manner not used before. Although its ability to successfully complete the mission was questionable, the order to launch was given as soon as darkness fell.

The 872 measured only five feet long. This made it hard for radar to detect. It had been reprogrammed to locate the beeper signal and drop a small package on the site. No one knew if it would work or how close the package would land, even if it did locate the beeper.

Bill was under the canvas shivering from the cold desert air when, in the stillness of the night, he heard a buzzing sound. He peered outside. The sound got closer. He squinted, trying to locate the faint noise. Then the sound passed right over him. Suddenly, he saw something with a blinking light float down from the sky and land on the ground a few yards away. He walked in the direction where it fell. The blinking light stopped. With no flashlight, he was on his hands and knees trying to find the object. The moon and stars reflected enough light on the surface of the sand to show the outline of a small package. He took it back to his dugout where, in the dark, his hands found a compass, five bottles of water, a small flashlight and two vitamin bars. But the most important item was a small but powerful communication box. He was familiar with its type. After flipping the switch on, he pushed in his military intelligence password.

Bill heard cheering in the background when he made contact. The conversation was brief. There was always the danger if you spoke more than two minutes, the Iranians would pick up the transmission on their monitoring devices. The major wanted him to travel to a plateau located a few miles away, where they would attempt a rescue tomorrow night. When the conversation ended, he filled in the dugout, covered his trash and released the canvas to the desert where the wind would blow it to an unknown destination. This task completed, he pushed the buttons on the compass giving it the coordinates to his rescue site. By walking the rest of the night, he could be at the site before the sun came up.

The major leaned over the table in his tent and pointed out the location of the landing site to his men. The force would be a skeleton crew composed of a pilot, captain, sergeant and two corporals. If they encountered heavy weapons fire, they were to retreat. Otherwise, the team was to extract Captain William Weston as quickly as possible. The helicopter was the smallest in the fleet. It could fly close to the desert floor below the radar screen. The major hoped the rescue would go as planned, but knew the unexpected always seemed to happen in this type of mission.

***

Pamela Weston was surprised, when she answered the door, to see a stranger standing there.
"Can I help you?"
"Is Henry Weston home?"
"No my dear, he is still at the university. Is there something I can do?"
The woman at the door blurted out, "I'm Rachael Goldstein. I've flown from Jerusalem to see him. When do you expect him home?"
Before Pamela could answer, the woman burst out crying.
"Now, dear, just come in."

When she entered the room, Pamela put her arm around Rachael and led her to the parlor.

"Zillah, make some hot tea and bring it in the parlor." Pamela heard the housekeeper respond, and then she turned her full attention to the woman who was sitting in the wingback chair across from the sofa.

"I'm here about the Bill. He was supposed to be in Jerusalem a few days ago, and he never landed."

"I'm sure he's all right. Let me call Henry and see if he can come home early today."

Pamela excused herself and went into the other room to make the call.

Rachael wiped her eyes with tissue from her pocketbook. She was embarrassed about crying. She wasn't normally one to show such weakness, but the emotions had been building up for days, and she just hadn't had anyone to talk to at her father's home. It had all been too much, and now she had come all the way to Greenville and made a fool of herself in front of a stranger.

Pamela returned to the parlor, followed by the housekeeper carrying a silver platter with a tea pitcher and accessories. After the cups were poured, the housekeeper left the room.

"Henry will be home early, and I'm sure he'll be able to answer many of your questions. Now, how serious is this between you and Bill?"

Rachael's face turned red.

"Why, child, he doesn't even know how you feel, does he?"

"I don't even know how I feel."

"Why, you're in love with him, honey. It's written all over your face."

Rachael's face again turned red.

"Bill must be just like his father. Henry had no idea I loved him until I told him so after my sister died. These Weston men are so involved with whatever they're doing, they never notice the roses until they're pricked. And that's what you need to do when Bill gets back to the States. You may draw blood, but I've got a hunch you'll draw love instead."

43

"We're in the parlor," Pamela called out when she heard Henry come through the front door. The moment he stepped into the room, Pamela said, "Henry, she's worried sick about Billy. I hope you were able to find out something."

"As a matter of fact, I contacted a friend in Washington.

What did he say?" Rachael asked.

"I can't give you all the details, but he's safe, hiding in the desert near the Iraqi border and will be rescued by a special operations unit tonight."

Zillah, the housekeeper, was eavesdropping from the hallway. She went into the kitchen, retrieved the satellite phone from her pocketbook and placed a call to her superior. The information quickly made its way up the chain of command until it reached the Leader, who was pleased he had placed a drone in Henry Weston's home. He called Henley and relayed the information. The professor must not be allowed to leave Iran alive. When the Leader finished the conversation, he turned in the chair just in time to see a special news bulletin flash on the television screen.

This is Reed Jones reporting to you from the United Nations in New York where we have just learned that the Security Council has condemned the United States for its actions in Iran. The vote was close to unanimous. Only Britain supported the United States. We will bring you further details in the next hour.

Now back to you, Shelia, in Atlanta.

The Leader smiled. Another victory for chaos in the world. The United States had, in recent years, become the world's policeman, attempting to spread democracy and at the same time maintain stability on the global stage. If the United Nations effectively tied the Americans' hands, it would remove a roadblock to The Society's goal of establishing the dominance of evil in the world.

Henley acted fast upon the information received. He placed a call to a contact who held a high command position in the Revolutionary Guards. The general combined this new information with the other report received on the location of the bodies. Everything pointed to a region near the Iraqi border. There was only one possible way for the man to get over the border. The United States would send a rescue helicopter. If they could prevent the American's escape, shoot down, and capture American troops on Iranian soil, it would further escalate the situation in the United Nations, which had just condemned the United States. He picked up the phone and made two calls. One was to Army headquarters, and the other was to the commander of the Revolutionary Guards in the area.

Bill managed to reach the plateau several hundred feet above the desert floor. He was blessed to find a nearby ledge to crawl beneath, which protected him from the sun while he waited for the rescue.

The helicopter took off from the secret American base in the darkness. It hugged the landscape as it flew toward its destination. The plateau was easy to locate. The copter's device simply picked up the signal from the beeper within a five-mile radius and followed it to the rendezvous site.

Bill saw the blinking light in the sky approaching. When it touched down, he made a mad dash, knowing the longer the copter was in the area the more likely the Iranians would discover its presence. As the copter lifted off the ground, a voice from the back of the copter said, "I'm Captain Benson with military intelligence. Glad to have you aboard."

"Not nearly as happy as I am to be here."

No sooner were the words out of his mouth than the pilot yelled, "We've got company."

Bill looked out and saw an Iranian military helicopter bearing down on them. The American pilot took evasive action as he flew toward the Iraqi border, now less than ten miles away. He flew between mountains peaks and down a narrow cannon. The larger attack helicopter had difficulty following, cutting its speed to maneuver. But in a short time over the open desert floor, the small American helicopter was within range again.

"Hold on," a voice screamed from the cockpit as the small copter dropped to the floor of the desert leaving a cloud of dust behind that made visibility for the low flying Iranian craft impossible. They were within a mile of the Iraqi border and safety when small arms fire erupted from the ground. The copter took several hits. It started spinning out of control.

"We're going down," the pilot yelled from the cockpit.

The copter slammed into the desert floor. For a moment, everyone sat there stunned by the impact, but the sound of an explosion nearby quickly brought the men to their senses. When their feet hit the ground, there was no place to take cover. The copter had landed in a dry riverbed. An Iranian copter hovered above. They stood there, staring into the star-lit sky and made their peace with God.

Suddenly the Iranian craft exploded from an incoming missile. Bill's eyes followed the white trail to the place from where it was launched. Hovering there in the darkness was an American AH-1 W Super Helicopter. From its cockpit, a voice said over a loudspeaker, "Welcome to Iraq."

***

In the United States, Americans watched as tension mounted between the States and the United Nations. Another breaking news story flashed on the screen.

This is Reed Jones speaking to you from the steps of the United Nations in New York. There has been a report from the Iranian Air Defense Ministry that one of their helicopters was shot down by the United States. Our ambassador has admitted the incident occurred, but insisted it was over Iraqi territory when the attack happened. According to our sources in the Pentagon, the ambassador's statement was correct, and this action was taken under the mutual defense treaty signed between the Iraqi government and the United States when we withdrew our forces from that country several years ago.

Now back to you, Sheila, in Atlanta.

The telephone rang in Greenville as the three were watching the breaking news in the parlor.

"I'll get the phone," Henry said.

"I wonder if that incident has anything to do with Bill?" Rachael asked.

Before Pamela could respond, Henry entered the room smiling.

"That was my source at the Pentagon. Billy's safe. He's at a military base in Iraq and will be flying to the States within the next few days."

Rachael's heart leaped when she heard the news. A moment later, the three embraced. When Pamela and Rachael began to cry, Henry excused himself and left the room to make some calls. He wanted to let the women have some time alone in the parlor to talk. Besides, it made him uncomfortable to be around such a display of emotions. In the study behind closed doors, a tear trickled down his cheek.

***

Bill put down the phone in the officers' barracks. The call was from Colonel Bonham at the Pentagon. Arrangements were being made to have him flown directly to Washington. Bonham and the Chairman Rouse of the N S C wanted to meet with him. He was disappointed. He had made a promise to himself in the desert. If he got to safety, the first thing on the agenda was a flight to Jerusalem and Rachael. That would be delayed. He placed a call to Jerusalem.

Bill was surprised, when speaking with Dr. Rabon, to find out Rachael was in Greenville. He tried to call his father's home several times but had trouble getting through from Iraq. He would try again from Washington. A direct military flight was leaving in an hour.

***

Thomas was on the way to his office when he noticed the unit's employees crowded around the television set in the lounge. Curious, he stepped in to see what had garnered their attention. It was another special news bulletin on the Iranian crisis.

This is Reed Jones bringing you the latest in what has been a week of crisis for the president. As I reported earlier this morning, a Spanish judge issued a criminal warrant on behalf of The World Court against the president. It charges her with violation of international law based upon the finding of the Security Council issued several days ago. I discussed this matter with the well-known constitutional scholar, Dr. Webster Dickerson. And this was his response.

The station switched to a faculty office at Harvard.

The question has been asked about the authority of the Spanish judge to issue such a warrant," Dr. Dickerson said. "There is precedent to do so. It is similar to the action taken a few years ago when a warrant issued for the arrest of Pinochet, the former President of Chile while he was visiting London. Now, unlike Britain, the United States does not presently recognize the Court, but we are committed to complying with the resolutions of the United Nations and, of course, international law."

"Thank you, Dr. Dickerson. This station will have a full hour discussion with several experts at seven o'clock pm Eastern Standard Time.

Now back to you, Sheila.

"What does all this mean?" Thomas asked a lawyer from the unit standing nearby.

"It means the president is in a pickle. The chief justice of the court is from Syria. Of the other eight members, only three are from Western Europe. The rest are from third-world countries with totalitarian regimes."

***

One morning, Pamela brought in a large scrapbook and laid it on the coffee table in front of Rachael.

She pointed to a fat little child in the nude lying on a blanket. "Now, that's Billy, when he was a baby."

There were also pictures of him in high school.

"There he was in his football uniform, the best blocker on the team. It was a surprise to us when he left high school to join the Marines."

"Yes, those were dark days in our relationship," Henry said.

"Oh, he was just a little mixed up, Henry."

"All the same, I'm glad that period is over."

"Henry was also in the Marines," Pamela said. "He was a colonel and, after active duty, served in the reserves."

"Until Pamela made me quit."

"Yes, every time I turned around, you were being called up for active duty. And I was getting a little too old to have you gone so much. That's not all either. Since he was in military intelligence, he always drew dangerous assignments."

"The military was short of young men, and they still are."

"Anyway, here's a picture of Billy when he was an enlisted man. Here's another one when he came back from his imprisonment in Panama."

"Imprisonment?"

"Oh, he hasn't told you about that?" Pamela asked.

"He hasn't told me much about anything."

"Henry, tell Rachael but skip over the graphic details."

"Billy was part of a military intelligence team sent in to support an uprising. He was a sergeant at the time. During that period, we were still trying to avoid a full-scale invasion with American troops. It turned out to be a trap. As soon as the helicopter dropped them in an isolated area near the edge of the jungle, the men were surrounded. A brief firefight ensued. The two officers were killed immediately. Billy took command. Their radio was destroyed during the initial attack. They had no way to call for outside help. Soon they ran out of ammunition and had to surrender. Of the sixteen men involved in the mission, only he and two lance corporals were taken alive. They were tortured. Later, both corporals' brains were blown out, and their tissues were splattered in Billy's face."

"Henry, stop it. I said avoid the graphic details."

"I'm sorry, Pamela. Anyway, Bill managed to escape and fled into the jungle. Two weeks later American troops on a recognizance patrol came across him. The incident changed him both physically and spiritually."

"Physically?"

"Yes, he still has scars on his body from the experience."

So that's why he'd worn a shirt that day when swimming in the water basin, Rachael thought. And no wonder he rejected her invitation to stay at her father's house and lay out at the pool in the courtyard. He was embarrassed for her to see his scars. What a fool she's been that evening in Jerusalem.

44

Bill made a call to his father from the military aircraft.

"We were worried about you, and so was Rachael. In fact, she flew to Greenville and has been staying at the house."

"That's what I understand. I talked to her father."

"Are you Okay?"

"Sure. Lost a few pounds in the desert heat and tried to avoid people who wanted to kill me."

"Things have really been popping in the intelligence community while you were gone. We're on a collision course with the rest of the world."

"That's what I understand. You'll have to fill me in on the details when I get there. I'd like to speak to Rachael."

"She and Pamela went to town. I know both of them will be sorry they missed your call."

"I've tried to reach Rachael on her cell phone, but it's not working."

"Can you telephone later?"

"I'm not sure, but it probably won't be today. But if things go as planned, I'll be in Greenville by tomorrow night."

"You're breaking up, Bill."

"Give Pamela and Rachael my love."

The transmission went dead.

It was late in the evening when the jet landed in Washington. A government vehicle was waiting to take Bill to the scheduled meeting at the Pentagon.

"I'm glad to see you," Bonham said, when Bill entered the room. "Chairmen Rouse was to meet with us, but at the last minute the president called. They're having an emergency conference at *Camp David*. Just have a seat, Bill, and we'll talk. I'm not going to bore you with questions on the operation because, when we finish here, there will be a debriefing by others in a room down the hall."

"Before we get started, I'd like to ask if you have any information on Bahodore," Bill said.

"No, we hoped you'd be able to provide us with an update on his situation."

"His friend Ghadir was wounded during the retreat. Bahodore was last seen by his side. I have his Citadel ring. He wanted me to give it to his son. I'm sure he'll have questions about his father.

"If we find out anything, I'll certainly get that information to you.

"I assume you received the photographs I sent."

"Yes. The raid was a success. Unfortunately, we've received word the insurgents executed the scientists. This is only going to inflame the world and force the Court at the Hague to act against our president. That's what will be discussed at *Camp David*.

"Sounds like the president has her hands full."

"Yes, but she's fully capable of handling it. Now let's talk about the main reason for this meeting. Rouse needs you to go to Yemen. We have reports from our agent, Oreb, that the terrorists are producing anthrax there. The group called The Society might also be involved. We know you entered into an agreement with the Texan, Jimmy Jones, to locate the Ark of the Covenant. Since Yemen is believed to be the location of ancient Sheba, this would provide cover for your visit there."

"Are you asking me to volunteer?"

"Well, I'd rather appeal to your sense of patriotism than order you. There's been a new unit formed under the Terrorism Department. Its assignment is to determine the apparatus of The Society. We know they're heavily involved in numerous illegal activities, but we're most concerned with their assistance to terrorists. Their operations are funded by profits from the drug, diamond and porno business. So far we haven't been able to pierce its structure. It's surrounded by a devil-worship mythology that seems to act as a blanket to cover its activities. The person put in charge of this special unit is a former police detective named Thomas O'Conner. He specifically requested that we assign you to this operation. He seems to think that your background and knowledge qualifies you as the best man for the job."

"Can I have a few weeks off before I go?"

"Two weeks is all I can allow you. Everyone is pulling double duty with the present shortage of manpower."

"I understand, Sir. How long do you think I'll be in Yemen?"

"I'm not sure, but you certainly will be back in time for the fall semester at Charleston University. Hopefully this won't be our last meeting before you go to Yemen. I wish we had more time to talk today, but my flight's waiting to take me to *Camp David*. Give me a call anytime you feel the need."

***

Rachael was nervous waiting at the airport. A great deal had happened since she had last seen him. Her father and Bill's parents all knew she was in love with him. Yet, the last time Bill and she were together, their relationship was still on a professional level. She had really made herself vulnerable if he didn't feel the same way. Then there was the question of the torture he underwent while in Panama. Maybe the reason he hadn't pursued her sexually was that he physically couldn't. She wanted to speak with Henry about it, but didn't know how to approach the issue. It was not something you just came out and asked. But, if true, it explained his conduct toward her every time it appeared they were on the brink of intimacy. It might even explain why his first wife left him. And if they couldn't have a sexual relationship, where did that leave them? Would either of them still be interested in marriage? She loved him now more than ever, but she wanted children. Was she willing to forsake that dream? And what about her needs? Could she live the rest of her life without physical intimacy?

Bill felt the wheels of the plane touch the runway. Although excited to see Rachael, he would hold back his emotions until they were alone. And he was anxious to be alone with her. He also wanted her to accompany him to Texas to see Jimmy Jones. The man was expecting him in two days.

It was hard to find time to get Rachael alone. Pamela must have sensed something because she said the pantry was empty and insisted in the afternoon that Henry accompany her shopping. When their car pulled out of sight, Bill saw signs of relief spread across Rachael's face.

"Rachael, there's a park within walking distance. Would you be interested in taking a stroll through it."

"Yes. I could use the exercise."

It was a beautiful area, tastefully designed, with paths running through the surrounding trees and shrubbery. Reaching a small pond, they sat on a cement bench and watched the activities of the wildlife. Just as the sun was beginning to set, Bill put his arms around Rachael and drew her lips to him. The pent up passion of the two exploded for a moment in that simple kiss. Then Rachael pulled back. She didn't know whether this man had the ability to respond to her physical needs. A need she wanted only him to fill, if he was able. But was he? And how would she know without embarrassing him?

Bill felt the emotional withdrawal. He didn't understand. Did she want him? He didn't know what to say. So he said nothing.

On the way back, not a word was spoken between them.

***

The Leader had noticed from his window that for the past few weeks a car was parked across the street from his residence. Suspicion aroused, he ordered the Noba to monitor the radio transmissions of the third precinct again. The typed translation made for interesting reading. So far, it hadn't turned up any relevant information except that Thomas O'Conner was now working for the Federal Terrorism Unit.

The police surveillance had produced nothing. The suspect, on occasion, came out of his apartment and took a walk. It was easy to follow him because his physical size made him stand out. The man was accompanied by a young woman who resided in the apartment. Initially they thought she was the man's daughter but decided later that she was the housekeeper. Now they suspected she must be his mistress, the way his hands recently were seen roaming over her body during their strolls.

Richard was at Mingos waiting on his friend. He was happy Thomas had taken the new position. It looked like his professional career was on the rise. Unfortunately, his personal life had taken a nosedive. Melinda decided to remain in Charleston and reconcile with her ex-husband. It had left Thomas in a slump.

The lunch was brief because Richard had a meeting with his chief that afternoon. Before leaving, he promised

Thomas he would obtain a search warrant for the residence under surveillance.

The translation of a radio communication was placed on the Leader's desk. There was a conversation in the transcript about executing a search warrant on his residence Wednesday. That was only twenty hours away. Prompt action was necessary. An urgent call went to the council.

A message received from the council ordered the Leader to leave immediately for Yemen and establish a new center of operation there. Yemen, the land of frankincense and myrrh that became the haven for the seed of Cain after they were driven out of Enoch. The place where the Sacred Book and the bones of Noah, along with the body of Daniel, were lost when the great dam at Marib broke, covering everything under tons of debris. It wouldn't take long to leave. He had so little to pack. The most valuable item, the Staff of Cain, was placed in a special container. At midnight, he and the drone, Megan, departed through a secret back entrance. The Noba would take care of everything at his residence.

Thomas and Richard were to meet that morning and execute the search warrant. So when the phone rang and Richard was on the other line, Thomas thought at first he had overslept, until he noticed the clock said four a.m.

"There's a fire at the suspect's place," Richard said. "Our man on surveillance called the fire department. They've already concluded it was arson."

"Any bodies found?"

"No, but there's something you might find interesting."

"What's that?"

"I'll show you when you get here. Stop and get me a cup of coffee on the way. I'm not used to moving around this early without my caffeine."

When Thomas arrived on the scene, he saw that the outside structure was still intact. But when Richard and he went inside, everything was a smoldering ruin, except a strange room, one enclosed by brick.

"It looks like this was some type of secret room, which used a phony bookshelf to conceal its entrance," Richard said.

When they examined the room, it had ten undamaged wooden crates marked cigars from Cuba marked. Thomas forced open the lid of a crate, took out a cigar, put it to his nose and smelled the aroma of the rolled tobacco leaf.

"Same as at Henley's antiquity store and Henry Weston's home," Thomas said. "Henry said he got them from his housekeeper as a gift."

"I don't understand the connection."

"The housekeeper is from Yemen."

Richard looked a little confused.

"Am I missing something here?"

"Yemen was a hot bed of terrorism. And my nose tells me that somehow The Society was involved in this up to its eyeballs."

"What are you going to do?"

"Call the local police in Greenville and have them detain the housekeeper until I can get there with an original order for her arrest."

"Can the terrorism unit get one that fast?"

"That's the advantage of the Patriot Act. A federal judge is available twenty-four hours a day. And the unit will fax a copy of the warrant to the police department."

Henry and Pamela had just returned home from the airport when the doorbell rang. Pamela looked out the window.

"It's the city police," she said.

"What could they want?" Henry asked, as he walked to the front door.

"Dr. Weston?"

"Yes."

"We have a warrant for the arrest of your housekeeper."

When Thomas entered the Greenville Police Station, the first person he saw was Henry Weston.

"Thomas, they told me you'd be here today. Pamela was upset that you didn't show us the courtesy of calling about this matter before you had our housekeeper arrested."

"Let's go outside, Henry. There are too many ears that can hear our conversation in here."

Outside Thomas explained the situation.

"I understand perfectly now," Henry said. "I was in military intelligence for a long time. You did exactly what I'd have done under the same circumstances. I'll explain the situation to Pamela. Now that the air's been cleared on that matter, I want to invite you to dinner this evening."

"Will it be all right with Pamela?"

"Sure. The unexpected appearance of the police after we had just returned from taking Bill and Rachael to the airport was what had her upset. When I explain what happened, she'll be fine."

Thomas need not have made the trip to Greenville. By the time the police officer went to get Zillah, the housekeeper had hung herself in the cell.

***

Bill and Rachael were met at the Dallas airport by Jimmy Jones' driver in a limousine.

"There's been a change of plans since he talked to you," the driver said. "Instead of going to his ranch, I've been instructed to take you directly to the hospital."

"Is Jimmy ill?" Rachael asked.

"Yeah, he spends more time there now than he does at the ranch. I'm not sure he's going to leave the hospital this time. He's in pretty bad shape."

When they entered the wing of the hospital where Jimmy was located, they passed under a sign with gold lettering. It announced to the world, *The Jimmy Jones Wing*.

"I'm glad to see ya'll," Jimmy said, when they entered the room, his pale face breaking out in a smile.

"I would have been here sooner," Bill said, "but some of those malcontents in Iran delayed me."

"So I've heard." Seeing the puzzled look on his face, Jimmy added, "You don't think I know what's going on? I have my sources all the way to the president. It's called political contributions, and I've made my share of them over the years. Now I understand that your excavation in Iran has ended. So I'll expect you to keep your commitment on the Ark."

"I'm going to Yemen in two weeks to investigate a rumor that it may be hidden there."

Rachael couldn't conceal her surprise. He hadn't discussed this with her. Every time Rachael thought they were getting close, she found out she was out of the loop.

"I can see by the look on Rachael's face that you haven't shared this information with her yet."

"She won't be going. It's too dangerous there."

Rachael bit her lip to avoid saying anything. Dangerous, she thought. What about all the grunt work she'd done in dangerous places trying to find information on the Land of Nod? She felt hurt by Bill's statement. But she didn't want to make a scene.

"I think I'll go get a cup of coffee. Would you care for one, Jimmy?"

"No, thank you."

When she left the room, Jimmy said, "Let me tell you something, Professor. You might be good at archaeology, but you don't know dilly about love. That woman cares about you, but if you don't watch out, she going to move to greener pastures. You handled that all wrong, boy. I should know. I've had many wives over the years."

45

The twin-engine plane circled the ancient city of Sanaa three times before the pilot received permission to land on the runway. From the air, the Leader could see the white facades glittering in the morning rays of the sun and the many formless mounds that, at various times during the history of this area, had been the center of great civilizations, some were built by the Sons of Cain, while others were built by the descendants of Seth. Waiting to meet them at the airport was Irad, who received word from the council to prepare for the Leader's arrival.

"It is good to see you, *Oh Great One*," Irad said, as he bowed and kissed the large golden ring with embedded diamonds and the symbol of a serpent upon it.

"We have arranged for temporary quarters here in the city until you decide where you want to be located permanently."

Then, turning around, he barked orders to the two heavily armed drones standing by the black Mercedes. The men scurried to the aircraft and removed the few items the Leader and Megan brought and placed them in the trunk of the car.

Since the airport was a half mile from the city, it took only a short time to reach the new headquarters. The Leader was pleased to see it was a three-storied structure in the ancient part of the city. Irad commented that it was more than a thousand years old. Inside, it was decorated with plasterwork friezes and painted decorations. The lower story was built with large stones, which supported the upper part of the structure made of plastered mud brick. A stairway went up through the various rooms to the upper floor. Inside, each room was smoothly plastered, and there were painted scenes depicting the wealth of an earlier civilization that had existed when the building had been constructed. On the second floor was the *mafraj*. It was decorated with beautiful alabaster and had two stained-glass windows. The third floor was reserved for him, while the first floor would be used for the everyday operation of the organization and the second for large gatherings.

The Leader chose a bedroom with a balcony and assigned Megan the adjoining small room. She would supervise the numerous drone domestics working at this new center of operation.

Irad had been asked by the council to act as chief of staff for the Leader. He was seen as a good choice since he spoke Yemenis and was familiar with the country. Besides, he was a direct descendent of Cain through the blood of *Enoch*, an individual that would eventually be a member of the council and a possible contender for the position of Leader when there was a vacancy. And a vacancy might not be far off. There were those on the council who were dissatisfied with the present turn of events. The receipt of any more bad news and the council might not wait for the Leader's natural death to replace him.

Irad loved Yemen. It was a country where evil could feel at home among its seventeen million inhabitants and thirty million guns. It was a place where kidnapping, rape and murder were a daily occurrence. Yemen represented how a great civilization could crumble and a people return to a life not too far removed from what existed after the Serpent seduced Eve in the Garden of Eden, sending humanity into a downward spiral from which it had never recovered. The population was a polyglot ranging from the descendants of Cain and Seth to drones in such large numbers it was impossible to keep count. The daily life of its people was largely spent chewing Qat, a plant that contained in its leaves a narcotic drug that discouraged the population from being productive. The people had become so addicted to it that they pulled up the coffee tree groves that had been cultivated since the time of the Queen of Sheba to plant more Qat. The production of this plant required such a large amount of water the whole country was now facing a shortage. But this threat had not deterred the people of this land, who continued to turn more acres from other agricultural production to growing even more of it. The result was that at any time of the day at least fifty percent of the people were on a drug high with even the small children participating in this national pastime ritual. Irad knew the *Serpent* would be pleased. The inhabitants were very close to creating their own hell on earth.

John Elesbaan's spies brought news about the arrival of the Leader. He directed them to watch the new headquarters and keep him informed. This put a strain on the League's resources, already stretched thin in Yemen by their other responsibilities: The surveillance of Irad and keeping the Ark of the Covenant from The Society. John was chosen for this important task because he was one of the League's most capable agents and carried in his veins the blood of Solomon and the Queen of Sheba.

Dr. Benjamin Rabon had received a coded message from his cousin, Shelah, in Yemen. It was about the Ark. That same day he took a flight to Yemen. When he landed, the cousin arranged his transportation to Sanaa which lay near the ancient city of Marib, which had been the capitol of the flourishing kingdom of Sheba until its famous dam collapsed, turning twenty-five miles of productive earth into desert. But a disaster even greater than that occurred to both The Society and to the League of Seth. They had lost possession of items that had taken hundreds of years to accumulate and, after the catastrophe, centuries to try to recoup.

***

Rachael was in her motel room waiting for the taxi to take her to the Dallas airport. Yesterday afternoon had been terrible. After they left Jimmy' hospital room, she had been as cold as ice toward Bill. When he tried to make light conversation, she ignored him. He called later to see about dinner. She declined, saying she had a headache. In fact, she was so agitated with him that if there had been another flight available that evening, she would have changed her ticket so she wouldn't be sitting beside him on the way back to Greenville. Rachael intended, when she got there, to collect her things and catch a flight home. What was that noise outside her room? She realized it was the cab blowing its horn. Later, on the way to the airport, the cell phone rang. It was her older brother, Jacob.

"Rachael, have you heard from father?"

"No. Is something wrong?"

"He left for Yemen three days ago. He promised to call us when he got there, but we haven't heard from him. We're worried."

"Why would he go to Yemen?"

"We don't really know. He said it was some kind of emergency. You know how secretive he always is about everything."

"Have you tried to contact any of our relatives there?"

"I wouldn't know where to begin. Most of them fled the country the same time we did."

"Check with our relatives in Israel. See if any blood kin are still in Yemen. Then call me back."

"When will you be flying to Jerusalem?"

"Not anytime soon."

"Why?"

"Jacob, I'm going to Yemen to find Father."

"Don't do that, Rachael. It's too dangerous."

"Despite what you men may think, I can take care of myself."

Rachael's determination to remain cold and distant toward Bill began to melt away on the route to the airport. It was true that he should have taken time to discuss the fact that he was going to Yemen. But after all, he had been in the desert of Iran fighting for his life only days ago, hardly giving him the time to worry about her feelings. Remembering that, she began to feel a little foolish about her conduct toward him. He didn't want her to go to Yemen because it was too dangerous. Would she want a man who was flippant about her safety? She realized how immature she had acted. By the time she reached the airport, Rachael was anxious to see him again and to share the disturbing news about her father.

Bill was at the airport waiting when Rachael arrived. He was distraught. Rachael's coldness toward him hurt more than being pricked by a thorn on a rosebush. Whatever it took to make her happy, he was willing to do. He realized now that he couldn't return to a life without her. And surprisingly, it had taken him fewer than fifteen hours to come to that conclusion, the time since he had last seen her.

***

The last two days had been a whirlwind of activity. Bill spoke to Colonel Bonham by phone from Greenville. He explained his need to be in Yemen immediately because of Dr. Rabon's disappearance. Military intelligence pulled strings and spread money around what little bureaucratic organization existed in that country to get the channel cleared for what was in theory an archaeological investigation.

Bill and Rachael flew to London where they had an hour layover before the last leg of the trip to Aden. Rachael was impressed with how Bill handled things from the moment she told him her father was missing. He even traced down the address of her father's cousin, Shelah, once she received the name from her brother. She had immediately sent Shela a telegram informing him about the date of their arrival.

Rachael looked at Bill sound asleep in the seat next to her. He was exhausted. The time in the desert and the hectic activities of the last few days had taken a toll. Too nervous to sleep, she reached over and took the book off his lap. It was about the ancient land where they were going. She turned to the first page.

"Sheba was the biblical name of a region located at the bottom of the Arabian Peninsula called Saba in Arabic whose inhabitants were called Sabeans. According to ancient writing and legends, the Sabeans' ancestor was Sheba, a great-grandson of Shem, the son of Noah."

46

In the mouth of a cave, sealed by tons of sand deposited there from the flood caused by the collapse of the great dam, stood descendants of the *Tribe of Levi*. Time had arrived to remove the Ark from the place hidden by the act of the *Almighty*, who had brought calamity upon this land. It had lain concealed from the eyes of man for thousands of years, but now the forces of evil were close to discovering the location. From across the globe these six men had been chosen from the descendents of the High Priest of the Temple of Jerusalem to remove the Ark and carry it to a safe location where it could remain hidden until the temple in Jerusalem was restored. Then it would be brought to the Holy City of God and placed in its rightful position in the Holy of Holies. Laborers had worked all night to remove the sand that blocked the entrance to the cave. It was important to gain access and remove the Ark before the sun came up when the prying eyes of strangers might see it revealed. The laborers were from an ancient order of *Falasha*. They were descendants of the first born of Israel, who left Jerusalem with *Menelik* for Sheba and later helped him establish a kingdom in Ethiopia.

The sand blocking the mouth of the cave at last removed, the *Guardians of the Ark* entered the opening. A narrow corridor gained them access to a large cavern. Suddenly the lights from their kerosene lanterns reflected from an object in the cave. The group fell to their knees for they were in the presence of the Ark. The senior member of the *Tribe of Levi* uttered an ancient sacred prayer before the men arose and, with trepidation, approached this most holy of objects. It was in perfect condition, preserved by its airtight tomb. The acacia wood was as solid as the day it was cut from the tree. And the gold covering glistened in the light of the lamps. The poles made of acacia wood were already through the rings. That made it an easy task to carry the ark out of the cavern and place it in the covered bed of the truck.

Outside, the *Falasha* knelt before the senior *Levi* and kissed the ring on the right hand of the man, who pronounced God's blessing, then said, "Be careful, the evil ones are about."

"We will not stop until we cross the border into Saudi Arabia," said the *Falasha* in charge.

The men of the *Tribe of Levi* stood and watched the truck until the trail of dust it left disappeared into the horizon. Then the *Senior Levi,* Benjamin Rabon, took the precious ring from his hand and placed it in his clothing, so it wouldn't be noticed by those not of the brotherhood.

***

At mid-day the plane neared the airport at Aden, a city that once served as the capital under British rule before Yemen gained its independence. Rachael could see oil refineries left behind when the British withdrew from this deep-water port that had once been of such strategic value to the empire. It was the most modern city in the area, but this speck of civilization was eroding as the evil ones from the north tightened their hold on the region.

When the plane landed, Shelah was at the airport. He took them to his home in the city. After unpacking, they joined him in the courtyard for tea.

"Shelah, on the way from the airport you said that Dr. Rabon was in Sanaa. When can we go there?" Bill asked.

"I will see if I can get you a pilot. It may take a few days."

"Cousin," Rachael said, "certainly you could make arrangements quicker than that. We are most anxious to see him. It's unlike him not to call as promised."

"I share your concern. He has not been in touch with me since he flew to Sanaa. I contacted the hotel, but he hasn't been in his room for two days. I wasn't worried at first because he told me he was taking a trip to Marib. But now I think something has gone wrong. I left a message with the clerk at the hotel in Sanaa that you were coming. Rachael, there's nothing that can be accomplished today, so you and Bill need to rest after your trip. I promise to make arrangements first thing tomorrow for a plane. There is a new merchant in Sanaa I have been dealing with the last few months. He goes by the name of *Oreb*, though I suspect it's not his real name. He's in the rug business. You should make contact with him when you arrive in Sanaa. Mention my name. Perhaps he can be of help."

Shelah was true to his word. The next morning, when they joined him in the courtyard for a late breakfast, he announced that a pilot of a single engine plane would fly them to Sanaa the following day. Their breakfast was interrupted by the houseboy.

"Master, come quickly. There is a special news bulletin."

Shelah was one of the few individuals with a television. It received telecasts from the small station operated by the government.

My fellow Americans, I come to you today after much soul searching. This morning, I received a summons to appear before the World Court to answer charges that I have, in my capacity as your president, committed criminal offenses by violating certain resolutions passed by the General Assembly of the United Nations and by violating international law. I do not believe this country can ever submit its political or economic survival to a collection of countries or to an international tribunal. Let me say we were not signatories when the World Criminal Court was established and, in fact, at the time opposed its creation. Since our country does not recognize its jurisdiction, I would be remiss in my duties if I established a precedent by complying with the summons to appear. The Attorney General of the United States has been instructed to notify the World Court, in writing, that I have declined to appear and set forth my reasons. I have also instructed our ambassador to address the members of the General Assembly on this country's position.

Thank you. And May God Bless America."

The old battered single-engine plane and toothless, sunburned pilot had both seen better days. And if it hadn't been for Rachael's determination to leave that morning, Bill would have declined the ride until a better mode of travel was available. It was a bumpy ride, but the real fear was the engine, which seemed to sputter most of the way. The narrow runway normally would have bothered both Bill and Rachael, but after such a hair-raising flight, they could not have cared less about its condition. They just wanted the plane and their feet on the ground.

***

Although in Yemen only a short time, the Leader was already feeling frustrated. Since he didn't speak Yemenis, he had to communicate to everyone, except Megan, through Irad. Being isolated was a threat to his power. With Irad in charge of the daily operation, the Leader had hours of free time on his hands. He found himself spending it with Megan, who seemed to adore him. Unlike Irad, he missed New York and was anxious to get approval from the council to return there. So far, his inquiries on that point were met with a wall of silence.

Irad was receiving secret communications from the council almost daily. Because of the situation in Yemen, the Leader held power in name only. Now that he held the responsibility of power, Irad wanted the title that went with it. And he wasn't willing to wait for the Leader's natural death.

***

The president sat alone in her office at the White House. It was almost midnight, and decisions must be made before the sun rose. Her thoughts drifted to the dream she had for her presidency when she was elected: eradicate the remaining pockets of poverty and rebuild the infrastructure of the country that had deteriorated. This was not only her dream, but also the platform on which she was elected. That was all in shambles now because of events beyond her control. The chief of staff had brought her word that tomorrow the *World Court at The Hague* would issue an order for her to appear and face criminal charges concerning the incident near Noqdi. Strange how things change. She had been the leader in the attack on previous presidents for their refusal to recognize the authority of the World Court. At the time, all the seats were occupied by judges from Western countries. In her present position, at least she could be thankful that the United States wasn't a signatory to the international treaty creating the court. Although to the United Nations, that didn't make any difference. They passed a resolution long ago finding that the court's jurisdiction applied to all countries of the world whether they were signatory or not.

The president's political advisors were divided on whether she should appear, submit herself to the jurisdiction of the court and defend her actions, or ignore the summons to appear altogether. The National Security Council was unanimous in its position. In their opinion, it would be a disaster for the United States to take this first step toward submitting itself to the authority of a foreign body–particularly one whose members were from countries that sought its destruction. Of course, if she failed to appear, there would be serious repercussions, the least of which would be her inability to leave the country without the danger of arrest on a warrant issued by the court. On top of everything else, the political base within her own party was disintegrating. Their blind faith in the United Nations still amazed her as much as their opposition to the very idea of a strong American military. In the past, she had won the primary despite her position, and was determined not to be sidetracked by these shortsighted people now.

***

Irad was surprised the day he saw Dr. Rabon coming out of the hotel. Was it just a stroke of luck, or was the *Serpent* looking out for one of his own? He ordered two drones to follow the man. Last night they had lost him in the darkness out on a desert road some distance from the city. When Irad received their report, he was furious. He had them executed on the spot. Who knew what their incompetence might have cost The Society. Then he directed the drone who carried out the execution to pick three of his best and seize Dr. Rabon if he returned to the hotel. And Rabon had returned that very morning. They grabbed him in broad daylight on the front steps of the hotel. Irad wasn't worried about repercussions from the police. They didn't exist in the traditional western sense in this part of the world.

Benjamin Rabon sat in the darkness alone. The ropes around his wrist and ankles were so tight it caused them to swell, which added to his discomfort. He was worried about many things, one of which was his daughter. He had tried since arriving in Sanaa to contact his sons in Jerusalem, but the communication was so poor that he could never get through. Then the day before he was kidnapped, he received a telegraph that his daughter and Bill were coming to Yemen to find him. He was surprised at the time because he didn't consider himself lost. Nevertheless, before he left the hotel, he gave a message to the clerk. The note assured them he was all right and indicated when he planned to return to the hotel.

At the hotel, Bill introduced himself and Rachael.

"We are looking for her father, Dr. Benjamin Rabon."

"I haven't seen him for days. But he did leave a message."

The clerk handed it to Bill.

"Rachael, we'll read the message later. Right now I think we need to get rooms and wait for your father."

She started to protest but saw something, a certain look, on the Bill's face, so she didn't say a word.

In the lobby Bill knew there were eyes watching them.

"We'd like two rooms for the next few nights next to Dr. Rabon's."

"That will be no problem."

With the two keys in hand, they went up to the second floor.

Irad couldn't believe his luck. A drone brought a message that two foreigners were seen entering the hotel. From the descriptions given, there could be no question but that it was Rachael and Bill. Now he would deal with them in a manner that would please the Serpent.

Oreb entered the hotel lobby in a disguise he often wore. He was an Arab from an unusual family. For various reasons, his ancestors had been involved in espionage and always on the side of the colonial powers. His family had worked for British intelligence, but for the last thirty years they had been on the payroll of American intelligence agencies. Although it paid handsomely, Oreb still maintained a genuine business in the sale of antiquities. He knew Bill's family from years before when Henry had been one of his contacts. They had bonded. So when Oreb heard rumors about the Staff of Cain's location, he had passed that information to Bill, whom he knew was trying to substantiate the Genesis's story of creation.

47

Oreb avoided the drones he had seen across the street from the hotel by leaving through a back entrance. He had let Bill know in a private conversation on the balcony that he was the contact man for military intelligence in Sanaa.

As soon as Oreb returned to the shop, he assigned a local tribesman on his payroll to watch the hotel. He wanted to know the foreigner's whereabouts at all times. It would be so easy for them to disappear into the landscape, just like Dr. Rabon, swallowed up without a trace.

The hotel clerk gave Bill and Rachael directions to an establishment where they could purchase a meal. When they left the hotel, two drones followed them.

The restaurant had a few tables located beside windows that looked out onto the street. Most of the customers, however, sat on cushions placed on the floor. After the meal, the locals would spend the rest of the afternoon chewing Qat.

When Rachael entered, all the men turned and looked at her in amusement. She noticed that she was the only woman in the room. At first, she was a little apprehensive, but Bill told her that the men, knowing from her clothes that she was a westerner, would not object to her presence–something they would not tolerate from their own women.

By tradition, men and women outside the home did not spend time with members of the opposite sex.

"It's hard to believe," Rachael said, "that the women we saw in the street in this heat are completely covered from head to toe with only a narrow open slit for their eyes."

"You're raised in Israel, which is thoroughly westernized. Even your local Muslim women rarely wear a veil. But here, it's the traditional garb. A woman's face is not allowed to be seen by any man, except a family member."

"What a repressive society."

"It's what you expect if you're raised that way. But, with modern communication, the ways of the Western world are beginning to intrude into even such isolated spots on the earth as this."

"Father believes its fueling the fundamentalist uprisings around the world."

"Western culture is more than just an attack on their dress code. It's an attack on their basic institutions. Concepts of western civilization, such as a representative form of government, free press and independent judiciary, are foreign to their culture. Though many of the educated ones want these things. But if it happened, it would be as radical a change as when the French people threw out the old order during their revolution. Look around and describe what you see."

"Men with guns and knives, dressed in checkered head cloth and with long shirts to their ankles," Rachael said.

"The weapons are mostly *Kalashnikovs*," Bill said. "They are Russian-made assault rifles. The knives are called *jambiya*, and the long shirt that has the appearance of a skirt is called a *futah*. Now if you went back in history, the scene you described could be fifteenth century Europe, minus the *Kalashnikovs*."

"What are you saying, Bill? That it will be six hundred years before they catch up with us?"

"No. Because of mass communication, it will be much quicker. And that's the problem. It's not a slow cooker but a microwave effect. And that is causing a tearing of the fabric of societies in the third world countries."

A smiling waiter, who knew from experience westerners were better tippers than the locals, interrupted their conversation. A short time later, he returned with two cups of *Mattaris* coffee, sweetened with sugar and ginger. He also brought a platter with two large bowls of *Saltah*. The two westerners who were famished soon consumed the delicious chicken soup in the Madr bowl.

When Bill and Rachael left the restaurant, the sun was beginning to set. They didn't notice a van with four drones parked outside. It followed them as they strolled back toward the hotel. A few yards from the hotel entrance, the two drones following them on foot approached from behind just as the van pulled up along-side. Bill felt a sense of danger and turned, but it was too late. The butt of a rifle caught him in the forehead. While Rachael screamed, his body was thrown into the back of the van, and she was forced in behind him. The vehicle sped through the streets until it reached the countryside where Irad was waiting at an old castle abandoned eons ago. The driver did not notice a vehicle following him.

Rachael sat on the floor of the van and held Bill's bruised and bloodied head in her lap. He had been unconscious for some time. She was beginning to worry that he might never come to, when finally he began to stir.

"Rachael," he mumbled, "where are we?"

Tears flowed as she told him what had happened.

Bill and Rachael were taken down into the bowels of the earth beneath the castle where there was a dungeon whose purpose, when the castle had been built two thousand years ago, was the same as it was today—incarceration and torture.

It was pitch black. The only light available was that of a flashlight carried by one of their kidnappers. Bill was shoved into the first cell, and from the sound of footsteps and the clanging of a door, he knew that Rachael was in a cell somewhere in another area of the dungeon.

He watched through the small window of the door as the light came by and ascended the stairway. He felt a moment of fear, but it quickly subsided when thoughts of Rachael entered his mind. He had to get out, not to save himself, but to free Rachael. He blamed himself. Why hadn't he been more careful?

"Bill?" said a voice from the darkness.

Startled, Bill turned around and stared toward the back of the unilluminated cell.

"I'm over here in the corner."

As his eyes began to adjust to the dark, he could see the outline of a man.

"Dr. Rabon, is that you?"

"Yes. They left me tied up. Can you get me loose?"

Bill remembered the Swiss knife he always carried. Had the kidnappers searched him while he was unconscious? His hand went into the pocket of his trousers. No, it was still there. He started to reach for it, then paused. If he cut the ropes, the guards would certainly realize he had a knife. Instead, he reached down in the darkness and found the knot of the rope around Dr. Rabon's ankles, it was poorly tied.

The sound of feet upon the stairway was soon followed by a dim light shining through the small window of the cell. Three men entered. Without saying a word, they grabbed Dr. Rabon and took him from the cell. They made no mention that he was no longer tied. Perhaps they were different than the ones who put him there, or was it because they acted almost like androids?

Irad arrived at the castle the next morning. The first thing he did was send two drones to get Rachael. But he gave orders to be sure Rachael washed before she was brought to him. He sent with them a complete change of clothing. He knew how nasty the cells were in the dungeon below, and he wanted her clean before he touched her.

Somehow in the dark filthy cell, Rachael had dozed off to sleep sitting in a corner during the night. She was awakened by the loud noise from the opening of the old rusty cell door. Two men entered, grabbed her by the arms and practically dragged her up the stairs.

Bill heard Rachael scream out briefly in protest. Before he could react and call out to her, they were out of sight. Her scream made him even more desperate to escape.

They took Rachael to a room with running water from an aqueduct. There she was left alone, after the men told her to wash. One of them returned just as she started to disrobe and then disappeared again, after leaving her a box containing fresh clothing.

What was this all about, Rachael wondered. Why were they so concerned with her personal hygiene? After she had scrubbed herself and dressed, Rachael sat down in a chair and waited for the guards to return.

When the guards took Rachael into a room some distance down a corridor. Irad was waiting.

"You see, I knew the Serpent would deliver you into my hands."

"So you are involved in this?"

"From the day of my birth. And now I shall have you." He approached her.

"Over my dead body."

"Whatever it takes, I shall possess you, Rachael."

He reached out and put one arm around Rachael, pulling her toward him. She tried to resist, but it was futile for he was strong. As he held her tightly, Irad reached inside her blouse and slipped a hand over one of her petite breasts. She stood rigid and glared at him with disgust, so he shoved her away.

"You still think you are in love with the professor. When we are finished with him, he will be a *eunuch*. So you can forget him."

"You're an animal."

"Only partially." He turned to the drones. "Take her somewhere, but not back to the cell. I will be leaving later today, and she will be going with me. I don't want her to have the stink of the dungeon on her when she rides beside me. Rachael, prepare yourself. You shall be my queen for a night, and after that, I may let the drones have you. Then you'll know what it's like to have a real animal in your bed."

Bill knew he had to escape. Using his Swiss knife, he picked at the lock. His efforts paid off as the door swung open with a loud creak. In the darkness, he found the steps and carefully made his way up toward the ground level of the castle. When he reached the ground floor, he heard voices coming down the corridor. He ducked into a room nearby and listened as two men passed where he was hiding. They were engaged in conversation about the woman they had with them. Bill followed them at a respectful distance. They went up three flights of stairs before entering a room. Slipping onto that level, Bill entered the room next door. It had a balcony, as did the room where Rachael was being held. But the distance between them was too great to attempt an entrance from that direction.

Both men were armed with *Kalashnikovs,* and Bill had only a knife. The longest of its blades was sharp, but short. Too short to reach the heart. He had to act quickly. It wouldn't be long before they discovered him missing from the dungeon. He had a plan. One born of desperation. Taking off his shoes, he went into the corridor and down the stairway for a short distance so his voice wouldn't appear to be too close. "The American is escaping with the truck," he screamed out in the local dialect.

He gambled that the guards would rush to the balcony to see which direction the truck was going. With lightning speed he raced to the room, the socks on his shoeless feet muffling the sound of his movement. The gamble paid off. Both guards were leaning over the balcony trying to spot the escaping American. Rachael watched in shock as Bill raced past her with his eyes focused on the men with their backs turned to him. In a flash, his hands grabbed the ankles of one man and propelled him over the railing headfirst. As the second guard turned, the blade of the knife went into the softness of his throat. Instantly, he dropped his weapon, as both of his hands reached up to remove the foreign object. It was all the time Bill needed. He grabbed the short man's legs and lifted his body over the railing. A moment later, his body hit the rocks below with a heavy thud. Picking up the *Kalashnikov*, Bill entered the room. He found Rachael standing there, dazed by what she had just witnessed.

"Rachael, we've got to get out of here."

They started down the stairway, but it was too late. The bodies falling from the sky had alerted the drones below. The first two were cut down by bullets from Bill's weapon.

"Here, we may need these," Bill said, as he handed Rachael the two weapons he had recovered from the dead drones.

He then removed from their bodies additional clips of ammunition. By the time they reached the next floor, Bill saw that it was no use trying to escape that way. There were at least six drones ascending the steps in their direction, and Bill knew there would be others not far behind.

"Let's go to the roof."

The drones had not seen them yet. While the enemy searched all floors, they had time to reach the top of the castle. The last stage involved a narrow stairway that opened onto a small enclosed outside area where one could see for miles around. Once there, Bill was glad to find it contained a system to catch water from the scattered rains. At least they wouldn't go thirsty.

"Rachael, you stay here. I need to go back into the stairwell."

He saw the look of terror on her face.

"Don't worry. Nothing is going to happen to us as long as the ammunition holds out."

Grabbing one of the three *Kalashnikovs* and some extra rounds, Bill went back and posted himself out of sight just behind a sharp turn. He didn't have to wait long. The sound of feet upon the steps below announced the drones were on the way up. Silently he waited, knowing he had a temporary strategic advantage. The drones didn't know for sure where he and Rachael were in the castle. He needed to conserve his ammunition so he withheld his fire until the men were upon him. When he swung around to confront them, the lead man was fewer than three feet from the end of his barrel. He cut loose with a quick burst of gunfire, killing four and wounding two others, who beat a hasty retreat. He scampered down and relieved the dead men of their ammo. A few minutes later, he heard shoes crush grains of sand beneath them. He raised his weapon and waited. As soon as a head appeared, he fired. He heard the man drop. A moment later, his ears picked up the sound of his companions removing the bodies. He stayed until darkness fell, but the drones made no further attempt to ascend the stairs.

Bill rigged several trip wires from material he found on the dead men. It wouldn't cause an explosion, but it would make a lot of noise. Once that was completed, he slipped back to the enclosure on the roof.

"Rachael, we need to move to a position where the steps come out onto the roof. That way I can hear if they attempt to come up during the night."

"Do you think they will?"

"No. I'm sure they will wait until morning, but I can't stake our lives on it."

"What will happen tomorrow?"

"I expect them to hit us from the air, or maybe they'll get grenades and force me from the stairwell."

"What are our chances?"

He looked at her face in the light provided by the stars. He could have lied and told her everything was going to be all right. But she was entitled to the truth.

"Rachael, unless someone comes to our aid, we can't hold them off forever."

"Then tomorrow may be it?"

"I'm afraid so."

For a long time after they assumed their new position, neither said a word. Thoughts of God, family and friends went through their minds. Finally, Bill turned to Rachael.

"I love you."

"I know," she replied. "I love you, too."

"I wasn't sure the way you seemed to pull back from me the last time."

"Pulled back?"

"Physically."

"I knew you had a problem–sexually because of what they did to you in Panama."

"I don't have a problem."

"That's not why your first wife left you?"

"No."

"Then why did you always pull back from intimacy with me?"

What would it matter now if he told her everything? They were going to die come morning. He emptied his heart out about everything. When he finished, she curled up in his arms and cried.

Irad was furious at the drones. They could take orders well. They could copy others, but they just didn't have the ability to think for themselves. Irad took the initiative and sent for grenades. They would be there by morning. But the most important weapon would be attack helicopters from the Yemenis Air Force. It had taken the promise of a substantial bribe and a call to the Yemenis government from Tehran, who reminded them where they were getting their military supplies these days. Irad needed to get to Sanaa, so he left the smartest drone in charge with orders to kill Bill and save Rachael—then bring her to Sanaa where her father was being held.

Rachael kept watch most of the night, so Bill could sleep. As the sun came up, she heard the sound of someone brushing against the loose metal objects strung across the stairway with strips of cloth.

"The trip wire!" she screamed, waking Bill up from his slumber.

There was an explosion from a grenade that went off in the stairwell, followed by the sound of feet moving toward the roof. Bill knew, if he had been down there, he would be dead now. He raised his weapon and hoped for a lucky shot. God blessed him with one. As a hand reached out to throw a grenade with the pin removed, Bill severed it with a burst of fire. The detached hand dropped down the stairwell still clutching the grenade until it exploded.

"Lucky shot," Bill said.

For the next hour, there was silence, then came the sound of helicopters. Looking across the desert that stretched for miles, they saw two coming their way.

"What do you think this means?" Rachael asked.

"It's not good for us. Get behind the water reservoir."

"What about you?"

Bill never replied, but instead just reached out and took her by the hand. He led her over to where she would find some protection from the firepower that was fast approaching. For a brief moment, he pressed his lips against hers, then left to assume a position where he could keep an eye on both the stairwell and the approaching helicopters. When they got closer, he could see the marking of Yemen's military. He knew they hadn't come to rescue them.

48

Henry and Pamela were at home watching television in their bedroom that evening when a special news bulletin appeared on the screen concerning the escalating tension between the American Government and the United Nations.

This is Reed Jones reporting to you from the steps of the United Nations in New York City. The General Assembly, in yet another special session, passed a resolution calling upon the American Government to comply with an arrest warrant issued by the World Court. This was after our president failed to comply with a summons to appear to face criminal charges arising from an attack on an Iranian nuclear facility and the death of many civilians, which included most of the country's top scientists.

In a side story, some members of Congress from our president's own party today filed a petition with the United States Supreme Court. They asked that it assume original jurisdiction and rule in favor of the World Court. They cited the fact that previous presidents had signed treaties recognizing the United Nations' authority and by inference the authority of the Court sitting in The Hague. The petition also requested that the Supreme Court require our president surrender herself to the custody of the authorities at The Hague until trial.

Now back to you, Sheila, in Atlanta.

Henry exploded when he heard the news, but before he could finish letting off steam to Pamela, the phone rang. He could barely hear the person on the other end of the line and the transmission kept breaking up before it went completely dead. Nevertheless, he got the essence of what was said by his friend, Oreb. Bill and Rachael had been kidnapped by The Society in Yemen.

When Thomas answered, the voice on the other end belonged to Henry Weston. He wanted him to break protocol and contact the Director Cagle in Washington about Bill and Rachael's situation. By the time Thomas hung up, he had decided to violate the chain of command.

The carrier in the *Gulf of Aden* was there as a show of force to deter Iran from interfering with oil transported through the shipping lanes. In the last forty-eight hours, the Yemenis Air Force had been intimidating oil tankers in the Gulf and had even buzzed the admiral's flagship. He wanted to respond to this flagrant challenge, but with tensions in the area running high, Washington had turned him down cold. Now off the coast of *Oatar*, the Admiral of the American fleet had just received a direct communication from military command in Washington to attempt the rescue of an American intelligence officer and his female companion in Yemen. The communication gave the exact location where they were being held by terrorists, with the support of elements of the Yemenis Government. The order would involve violation of the territorial air space of a foreign country, something not taken lightly.

Two military helicopters assigned to the rescue mission were standing by on the admiral's flagship waiting for an anti-terrorist civilian officer to arrive. Once he was on board, they would depart, accompanied by fighter escort. Discretion on the use of firepower was vested in the commander of the mission.

***

The helicopters were coming in fast now. Bill could see they were in an attack mode even before their machine guns started barking. He hugged the low wall of the enclosure during the first burst of fire. Then he opened up on the closest helicopter, firing two Kalashnikovs at the same time. The fire from his weapons was so intense it took the copter pilot by surprise. The pilot beat a hasty retreat while the second copter stayed in a holding pattern outside the range of the Kalashnikovs. During this interval, Bill raced for the cover offered by the entrance to the stairway. When he got there, he could hear movement up the stairs toward him. Before he had time to react, a grenade came through the air in his direction. He stumbled outside again as it exploded on the very spot he had been standing only a moment earlier. He immediately fired a burst of bullets in the direction of the entrance to let them know the grenade had failed to kill him. Perhaps it would delay them for a short time. Looking up in the sky, he saw one of the helicopters making a wide circle, which would soon place him between the two of them. He checked his ammo. Only four clips left. It was over. He mumbled a final prayer. *"Almighty God into thy hands I commit my soul."*

Then waited for the helicopter's final assault.

From a mile away, the commander of the military rescue force had a clear view on his screen of the firefight taking place on the roof of the old castle. There, a man dressed in western clothes was returning fire against two helicopters hovering nearby. A woman behind a water reservoir was trying to find protection from the incoming rain of bullets.

"There's our man," he said over the mike to the pilot in the accompanying helicopter. "I'm going to give the Yemenis an opportunity to withdraw."

With that, he sped toward them, speaking in Yemenis on an open channel that he knew they would receive.

"This is Captain Elroth of the United States Naval Task Force. Please disengage. The person you are firing on is an American citizen. I repeat, disengage immediately."

He knew they had received the message because both stopped firing at the civilian and turned in his direction.

"Incoming," his copilot said.

The captain swerved his Super Cobra at the same time he fired a decoy. The missile picked up the decoy and followed it into the ground below. The resulting explosion rocked the captain's copter for a moment.

"You son of a bitch," the captain screamed, as he brought his machine back under control. "Fire at will," he said to the other American helicopter.

The poorly trained Yemen pilot were no match. Their flying machines exploded, and for a brief moment, flaming debris filled the air. But the fight was not over yet. The Americans were taking small-arms fire from the ground. Their triple firing 20-mm machine guns quickly disposed of the enemy combatants in the area outside the castle. Once this was achieved, a transport helicopter landed nearby to let a special unit of the Delta Brigade disembark while American fighter planes provided protection overhead.

The fight inside the castle was over quickly. The drones were no match for the Special Forces. But they were not cowards. They fought to the last. And when it was over, they all lay dead.

The first person to pop out of the stairwell onto the roof was the head of a special division of the Terrorism Unit.

Bill and Rachael stood there for a moment speechless until Thomas said, "Isn't anyone glad to see me?"

Bill and Rachael huddled together in the crowded helicopter on the flight back to the carrier. Thomas watched them with a twinge of envy, for it was obvious the two were deeply in love. Until now, his position with the terrorism task force had diverted his attention from his loneliness.

"How did you know where to find us, Thomas?" asked Bill who was sitting across from him.

"Colonel Bonham at the Pentagon cut through the chain of command and had his people connect with an agent you know as Oreb. His people were watching when they grabbed you off the street. They followed your kidnappers to the castle. His report was still on an underling's desk. If it hadn't been for Director Cagle's intervention, it wouldn't have reached Bonham at the Pentagon for weeks. Then we found out the League was also following what was happening on the ground."

"The League?" Rachael asked.

"Yes, an underground organization that we don't know much about, yet."

"Does anyone know anything about my father's whereabouts?"

"If they do, I'm not privy to that information."

Back in the Gulf, the admiral anxiously awaited the return of the rescue force to the carrier. He breathed a sigh of relief when he saw them on the horizon. The mission was a complete success. But the return had not been without incident. Several of Yemen's fighters had attempted to intercept the rescue team on their way back to the carrier. They were shot down over the Gulf of Aden by fighter jets from the fleet, who took this opportunity to inflict maximum damage on a force that had been harassing them for days in the Gulf.

***

John was in Mecca near the site of King Solomon's mines at *Mahd adh Dhahab* that lay between Mecca and Medina on the *Wadi al Jarir*, mines that the world's history buffs and archaeologists had tried for centuries to find without success. There he received word from his agents in Yemen on the location of the *Senior Levi* and later gained the approval of the League to provide information to the Americans on The Society's apparatus in exchange for a rescue. John then called Henry Weston, knowing he had the necessary contacts.

The Americans were not concerned with rescuing Benjamin Rabon until Henry Weston informed Colonel Bonham that he had a friend with valuable information for the N S C. A friend who was willing to exchange it for Dr. Rabon's safe return.

When the helicopter landed on the deck of the carrier, there was a message waiting for Bill from Bonham to call him from the carrier's communication center. Once Bill confirmed from the communication room the reliability of John Elesbaan, Colonel Bonham made the necessary call to the Chairman of the N S C who then requested an immediate meeting with the president. After the meeting, President Macer made a call to the Israeli President.

***

The assassin had landed in Yemen after the council called him from his duties in the Sudan. The interrogation of Dr. Benjamin Rabon was to be given top priority. The council believed he could provide them with information that would lead to the Ark. On the road to Sanaa, the assassin had reached over and stroked his tools of torture. It gave him comfort just to touch them. This could be the highlight of his career. He was excited about the prospect and couldn't wait to get to Sanaa, the Yemenis Capital.

When the assassin arrived at The Society's headquarters, the drones were busy packing. Word had reached Irad about the attack on the castle. A few minutes later even more bad news arrived. The old airport hanger, where Dr. Rabon was held had been attacked by an Israeli commando team. If that wasn't enough bad news, The Society's contact within the American National Security Council sent a coded message–The Society's structural organization was compromised.

The council made a decision to disperse to safe havens in Iran, North Korea and the Sudan. Before dispersing, they made one last decision. The Leader had failed the organization. His elimination was ordered. Irad was given temporary command of the entire Middle East region until things calmed down enough for the council to meet and elect another Leader.

Irad met with the assassin and gave him a summary of events. Then showed the assassin the coded communication received from the council.

"A sedative was put in his morning tea," Irad said. "It should not be a problem subduing him. Make his death as painless as possible. After all, he is a member of the inner circle."

"Leave two drones," the assassin said. "He is such a giant, I might need them despite his sedation."

"Consider it done."

I'm leaving for the airport now and taking the staff with me. When you finish your business here, meet me in Khartoum and bring the diamond-studded ring that is on the Leader's finger."

He bade the assassin goodbye.

"May the *Serpent* go with you."

"And with you, Brother," the assassin replied.

As soon as Irad's vehicle was out of sight, he and the two drones went up to the third floor. Despite instructions to the contrary, the assassin didn't make it easy on the Leader. He still held a grudge against him for blocking his admission to the council. Once the Leader had been secured with heavy ropes, he took out his tools of torture. When it was over, he left the dismembered body in the room.

The assassin's car drove away from the building only minutes before three American Tomahawks slammed into it. In the pile of rubble lay the body of the drone, Megan. The fetus in her womb died with her, denying the Leader the immortality he sought by leaving a bloodline.

***

The information from John Elesbaan given in exchange for Dr. Benjamin Rabon's life provided military intelligence with a list of thirty of The Society's members and their locations across the globe. Just as important was the disclosure of a biological lab on the outskirts of Sanaa, which was producing the *anthrax virus*. When the Special Forces arrived in protective chemical clothing to secure the facility, a hundred barrels of the deadly virus awaited delivery to an unknown location.

***

This is Reed Jones bringing you the latest in what has been a flurry of activity at the United Nations. The delegates to the General Assembly only minutes ago in a close vote expelled the United States from its membership, the first time this has occurred since the expulsion of South Africa. The move was made after the call on the United States Government to surrender its president went unheeded.

The situation was aggravated by the series of attacks upon numerous targets in Yemen this week.

In a side story directly related to this crisis, the United States Supreme Court in a six to three decision, issued this morning, ruled the Constitution of the United Stated remains the supreme document governing our country. The body of the opinion states that no organization, international or otherwise, supersedes our constitution, despite presidential or congressional actions in the past approving treaties or international resolutions to the contrary.

Now back to you, Sheila, in Atlanta.

EPILOGUE

Spring came early to Charleston. Flowers were in full bloom on the historic Citadel campus, as the school observed graduation. In the crowd stood Jeremiah Bahodore II, watching his namesake march by while Scottish bagpipes played.

Most of the parents in attendance did not know Jeremiah Bahodore personally. However, they all understood the significant of the monument to his grandfather that stood at the end of the parade ground.

Jamie stood with his fellow graduates and felt the perspiration trickle down his arm beneath his uniform. Some of the beads of sweat came to rest against the edge of his grandfather's ring, which was a gift from his father to commemorate this important day.

Thomas' special unit investigating The Society set up headquarters in New York. From there he made frequent trips to Charleston to see Melinda, whose attempts to reconcile with her former husband had failed.

Kinsey Riley moved to Washington after the death of Director Cagle, and he assumed command of the national Terrorism Unit.

Irad assisted the Sudan government with its genocide program. He planned to return to Yemen soon and act on information concerning the location of the Sacred Book.

The assassin learned from torturing a member of the League that Cain's staff in The Society's possession was only a copy of the original one.

The United Nations' action in expelling America from that body brought about a political realignment. The world split into three powerful blocks.

The president faced a tough battle in her party's primary from discontent caused by an ideological split.

Rachael flew to Texas from Jerusalem to attend Jimmy Jones's funeral. Afterwards, she began research on a biblical project at Charleston University, which was funded by a trust established by Jimmy.

The Jimmy Jones Trust employed Fullmore to track down artifacts that would authenticate the accuracy of events portrayed in the Bible.

Professor William Weston returned to his duties as Department Head of Archaeology at Charleston University. Shortly thereafter, he received secret orders to excavate John's tomb where it was rumored the original text of Revelation was hidden.

The Serpent's Seed is the first book in a Trilogy that includes The Mullahs and Megiddo. Visit the author's website at www.dmaring.com to read about these books and his other novels.

Made in the USA
Lexington, KY
26 August 2013